# TIN CAN TOMMIES

# DARKEST HOUR

## MARK C. JONES

Tin Can Tommies: Darkest Hour is published by Source Point Press, a division of Ox Eye Media, Inc.

# www.SourcePointPress.com

Printed in the United States of America
**First Printing Edition, 2022**
ISBN: 9781954412545

Follow the @tincantommies Facebook page now and be first to receive news, exclusive content, merchandise and updates on all future books!

## COMING SOON
## TIN CAN TOMMIES: RETRIBUTION

# Contents

**Dear Reader...**

This book is a work of pulp fiction. It is set in an alternate historical universe using real and fictional characters, situations and events, and no attempt has been made to maintain the timelines of actual occurrences, which in many cases have been changed to enhance the story.

The best and worst parts of writing an action/adventure series set during World War Two are that eighty years fall away as I emerse myself in one of the ugliest conflicts in history, yet amongst the bravery and the bad guys, the courage and the carnage that feature in the Tommies' adventures, I hope to imbue the spirit of that era in these stories, and pay homage to a generation of heroes whose sacrifices saved our world.

**Mark C. Jones**

TIN CAN TOMMIES: DARKEST HOUR

# PROLOGUE

## *The Somme, July 1, 1916…*

**THE BOY IN THE CRATER** shivered.

Death crouched in waiting nearby.

Cowering in a pool of blood and filth, the boy gripped his rifle with trembling hands.

Fear gripped him tighter.

Lowering his Lee-Enfield, the boy looked nervously about the mist, his breath pluming in the chill twilight air. A second boy, younger, his head wrapped in bandages, hunkered in the dirt beside him, shaking fearfully. They were a far cry, thought the boy, from the king's men exemplified so splendidly on conscription posters back home in Blighty.

A year prior, the boy had been a baker's apprentice with a bright future and the prettiest girl in the village on his arm—now he was here, trapped in this hellhole waiting to die.

An executioner's whistle had sent them over the top but their charge, cut short by the enemies' guns, had been in vain. The boys' unit was massacred in seconds; the remains of their friends now scattered about the battlefield—glistening piles of meat that hours earlier had smoked and played cards, joked and sang songs, and—

Shouts through the mist.

*German.*

Faint at first, then louder as the enemy closed in.

It was just a matter of time now.

The boys had long since given up hope of being rescued. They were the only living proof that men had been there at all—twin survivors being slowly consumed by the battlefield's nightmare gloom. Stranded on the front-line they were alone, unwilling participants in a war as grotesque as the horrors in the mud around them.

More shouts—louder now—they'd been flanked!

Shrinking into the mire, the boys fought the urge to cry out. Their lungs clamoring for air as terror constricted their chests.

The Germans were taunting them, of course, trying to flush them into the open and the crosshairs of their guns, so eager to spit death.

Unable to contain his fear, the bandaged boy cried out involuntarily then wide-eyed, clamped both hands over his mouth.

Abruptly, the shouting ceased.

Silence swept over No Man's Land.

Silence…

Something whistled through the air. It bounced down nearby sloshing into a puddle—a canister. Hissing irritably, it rolled from side to side releasing a plume of yellow smoke that crawled inexorably toward the boys.

*Gas!*

The boys snatched gas bags from their belts, pulling them over their heads as the toxin swirled about them, obscuring their vision. Sulphur mustard—the name derived from the odor it produced—was a poison that at worst caused horrific injuries, at best a swift death.

The canister whistled dry and a breeze curled wisps of the smoke across No-Man's Land, dissipating the poison.

Dusk bled into night as the yellow haze diminished.

Thunder rumbled overhead.

It started to rain.

"Was haben wir hier?"

Startled, the boys looked up to see raindrops spatter against the spiked Pickelhaube helmet of a German infantryman. Clad in muddy boots and a trench coat, their enemy stared at them through the misty lenses of a gas mask, his dripping rifle poised.

Resigned, the boys dropped their guns and raised their hands.

The German jabbed his Mauser carbine, its bayonet scything the air.

"*Ratten*, uh?" he sneered, the shouts of his comrades echoed around them.

Thunder rumbled again, louder now.

The shower became a deluge.

"Ich spreche ihnen, junge! Wo kommen Sie her?"

While the boys shook their heads in ignorance, the man's intention was clear.

"Gehörlose, als auch die toten!" the German growled. He raised his Mauser, took aim and slowly squeezed the trigger.

The ground began to quake.

The German paused, looked nervously about.

Something was pounding toward them.

*Something big!*

The tremble beneath their feet became quick, rhythmic thuds like the feel of an oncoming train. The boy looked down to see the puddles around him display concentric ripples as the first beat was joined by a second, then a third and fourth. It sounded, he thought, like the Indian war drums he'd heard in picture house westerns back home.

"Was ist das?" whispered the German. Peering into the haze he took a cautious step back. "Hier drüben!" he shouted to his comrades.

Seizing his chance the boy grabbed a rifle, swinging it to bear on his aggressor. He tried to shout but his voice wavered and his hands trembled visibly. Glancing back, he strained to see through the mist toward the drumbeats steaming toward them.

The German parried the boy's rifle from his hands with the Mauser's bayonet, then aimed his carbine and pulled the trigger—

A blurred colossus exploded through the mist!

The shot went wide, ricocheting off its shell with a spark.

"*Gott im himmel!*"

Vaulting powerfully over the boys' crater, the juggernaut slammed into the German like a freight train, carrying him on into the mist.

An empty jackboot slumped in the mud.

Awe-struck, open-mouthed, the boys heard the German cry out, then flinched as his body reappeared, crashing into the dirt before them, his neck and rifle twisted.

A shout went up from his comrades followed by gun fire and screams as three more titans whooshed overhead, vanishing into the mist.

Gunfire lit up the night—

The bandaged boy scrabbled frantically from the crater, grabbed his pal's tunic and tried to haul him out. Transfixed by the fireworks, the older boy remained rigid, hypnotized by the beings his senses so vehemently denied. The bandaged boy released him, retreating into the darkness toward the refuge of the Allied line.

Alone now, the boy stood captivated, listening to the melee beyond his vision. His eyes grew wide with disbelief as two burning blue headlights emerged slowly through the haze. Tilting sideways, they appeared to examine him curiously, blinking off and on as droplets of rain flecked onto them and hissed into steam.

While the boy didn't know what it was, he'd heard rumors.

Whispers at night in the trenches.

Whispers of *ghosts* in the mist.

Terrified, yet fascinated by his mysterious savior, the boy took a cautious step forward.

The giant regarded at the boy for a second, its features obscured in the darkness, then with a deliberate nod of reassurance, vanished into the night.

# 1

---

# IN AT THE SHARP END

*Dunkirk, May 27, 1940...*

THE ACRID STENCH OF CORDITE jarred Jack Stone from oblivion. Deep in his subconscious he heard voices—echoes from his past rising through a haze of confusion.

"*You're a sloppy excuse for a soldier!*"

"*You'll swing for this, Stone!*"

"*Your life won't be worth living!*"

*Living?* He wasn't dead yet? Jack certainly felt like he was.

The boy in his mind's eye watched him through the flames, then opened his mouth to scream—

Jack's eyelids snapped open!

His eyes stung instantly in the smoke from the truck's inferno. He was still in the vehicle's interior—it was ruined but he was alive. Which made him luckier than the other poor sods he'd been with; men now scattered around him like broken dolls. Staring into their eyes Jack swore an oath. He wasn't going to die. Not here. Not like this.

But that meant his left hand had to go.

This was *really* going to hurt.

Jack coughed, spitting blood, the pain coursing through his body now testament to the fact that he *was* alive: a miraculous truth in a place where death had become a daily fact of life.

Unconsciousness beckoned.

Jack tried to focus. The truck he was in had been hammered—blown through the air by a mortar—and had landed on its roof. The irony, reflected Jack, was that the shell had probably been left behind by the British Expeditionary Force during their harried retreat through France.

A support strut snapped as the heat in the wreck intensified. The vehicle lurched overhead and Jack flinched as the truck's boarded floor groaned closer. Shredded tarpaulin billowed in flaming tatters, the embers swirling around him like blazing autumn leaves.

Jack tugged at the manacles securing his left wrist to a bar above his head. No stranger to military restraints, he knew they wouldn't yield, but with the vehicle on its back he now hung helpless, like a rack of beef in a butcher's shop—one that would soon be a Sunday roast if he didn't gather his wits.

Jack had only two choices, neither of them good. As the handcuffs secured both his wrist and his fate to the burning wreck, he'd either have to shatter the bones in his left hand or cut it off completely.

Neither option appealed.

How the hell had he gotten here?

On his arrival in Europe the previous year, Jack had high hopes of victory—of repelling the Hun and returning to Blighty a hero. All too quickly the tables had turned. Outgunned and overwhelmed, they'd been forced to withdraw through villages and towns choked with refugees— Europe's displaced masses shambling somewhere, *anywhere* to escape the Bosch's boot heel. The Wehrmacht had defied all expectations. Exploiting an opening in the Maginot Line, they had pursued their quarry through France, routing the Allies north toward the only escape route left open: the port town of Dunkirk.

But there would be no *escape* for Jack if he didn't stop stalling.

Peering through the smoke, he saw the broken blade of a bayonet at his feet. He reached out, desperate, scrabbling for it with his right hand.

The boy stood beside him in the flames.

"*Get out of my bloody head*," Jack growled.

Touching the bayonet, he fingered it into his palm, slid the blade through the handcuffs and strained to break the lock.

It stubbornly refused to yield.

The truck lurched again as another support shattered.

He had minutes now at best.

With gritted teeth, Jack balled his left hand into a fist. *'Least I won't have to crawl far to cauterize it*, he thought grimly as the blaze around him intensified. Coughing, he slid the blade over his wrist and slowly applied pressure.

Jack hesitated.

Breathing shallowly, he exhaled and closed his eyes. Sweat dripped from his brow. *Come on*, he thought, *just twenty seconds of bravery…*

Another support splintered, showering him in cinders.

Forcing the blade down, Jack started unzipping his wrist—

"Oh, come now, Corporal."

Jack recognized the voice—and the feel of a cold revolver muzzle resting squarely against his neck.

"Let's not cheat the hangman. Drop the blade, Jack, there's a good chap, and turn around—*slowly*."

Dropping the bayonet, Jack reluctantly complied.

Lieutenant Walter Smiley leered at him.

*Could this day get any worse?*

"Get me out of these 'cuffs!" Jack demanded.

" A pleasure to see you too," Smiley said. The truck pitched again. "I see your luck hasn't changed."

*Smiley*—Jack despised the man. He was a jumped-up little shit with dreams of advancement far beyond his capabilities. Unfortunately, Jack had voiced this opinion loudly on several occasions—under the influence of alcohol—which had only served to fuel Smiley's ceaseless harassment, resulting in Jack's subsequent arrest on a trumped-up charge of desertion.

"What was it you said when we last met?" Smiley enquired.

"I believe it was kiss my arse, sir," Jack muttered. "I've always been one to turn a phrase."

"Assaulting your senior officer's no laughing matter," Smiley spat. "You've been a thorn in my side since boot camp—you *and* Briggs. Well, we've unfinished business, you and I." Smiley broke open the barrel of his revolver. "One in the chamber, Jack. Fate perhaps?"

Jack frowned.

"Given our diminishing odds of survival," Smiley sneered, "I feel it my duty to forgo the formality of your inevitable court martial and dispense just punishment here."

"*What?* You don't have authority! Cavandish said—"

"Cavandish is dead."

"Mutiny's the only crime that warrants a death sentence!"

"What can I say? The truck crashed, you jumped me for my sidearm and in the ensuing struggle, well... I acted *honorably*, old boy."

"You're mad," Jack spat. "It's bad enough the Krauts are givin' us a poundin'—now you're peggin' your own men?"

"Oh, you were never a man of mine." Smiley cocked his revolver.

Jack watched the boy glide toward him through the flames.

"Goodbye Jack Stone." Smiley said with finality. He levelled his gun and started to squeeze the trigger. "Give *Danny* my best."

The boy in the flames screamed!

Jack lashed out with his right hand, batting the revolver from Smiley. It discharged with a crack, striking sparks above his head.

"You insolent sod!" Smiley hissed. He gripped Jack's throat with both hands, slamming him into a support which gave way. The truck lurched again as Jack tried desperately to defend himself, but Smiley's assault was relentless and Jack could only use his right hand. "You're no use as a soldier," Smiley sputtered, "no use to anyone! That business in Belgium tipped you over. Always trouble and always you—you and bloody Briggs! *Intoxication, disobedience, insubordination—*"

"Best add *striking a superior officer* to that list o' yours," muttered a new voice from behind Smiley.

Jack recognized *that* voice too.

Smiley spun, his jaw connecting with a meaty right hook which knocked him out cold.

"Then you can shove it where the sun don't shine!" said the fist's owner.

"You took your time!" wheezed Jack, slumping into the arms of his best friend, William Briggs.

"What am I gonna do with you, eh?" said Billy, grinning. He was short-haired, portly and quick to lose his temper, but in a war where soldiers were wary of growing close to anyone lest they lose them, Jack and Billy had been firm friends since the beginning.

The truck groaned again as another support gave out.

Billy picked up Smiley's revolver and pulled a set of keys from his belt. He unlocked Jack's cuffs and heaved him over his shoulder, then stepping over Smiley, carried Jack from the truck.

Smiley groaned behind them.

Billy re-entered the vehicle, grabbed Smiley's webbing and dragged him from the wreckage as the ruined vehicle collapsed.

. . .

Jack gasped for air, his lungs burning. He opened his eyes and saw the pall of thick black smoke surrounding him slowly lift, revealing the blasted panorama of Dunkirk beach.

Hell.

Men cowered as explosions tore up the dunes and tracer and incendiary fire strafed wildly overhead.

"*This isn't over!*" he heard Smiley yell nearby. "*Not by a long chalk!*"

"That's another one you owe me," Billy said, reappearing at Jack's side.

"Where the hell've you been?" Jack coughed. He wiped his streaming eyes.

"The front line don't hold itself, mate! While you were busy gettin' yourself clapped in irons some of us were—"

"How'd you find me?"

"I followed Smiley," said Billy, ducking as a mortar exploded nearby and showered them with earth. "After Cavandish copped a bullet that tosser was next in line. I knew he couldn't resist finishin' what you started."

Suddenly nauseous, Jack rolled onto his belly and vomited. As the feeling subsided, he caught sight of his reflection in the truck's fractured wing-mirror. He looked gaunt and weak. Broken. The cocky young corporal who'd arrived in Europe with Billy seemed a long-distant memory now. At just twenty-two he'd been lean, tough, and spoiling for a fight. The reflection staring back at him was a different man altogether. His hair, a tousled mass of strawberry blond, was soaked with blood and sweat. His features, typically boyish, keen and square-set, were smothered in smoke and frenzy, and a livid scar ran diagonally down his right cheek courtesy of a German blade in Belgium.

Yes, the war had taken its toll—a fact Jack became painfully aware of as he staggered to his feet.

"How're the lads?" he said, ignoring the ringing in his ears.

"How d'you think?" Billy ducked as a shell whistled overhead. "Exhausted, demoralized, an' I can't say I blame 'em!"

The BEF had been pounded by the Germans for days. On their arrival at Dunkirk, the Allied survivors had scrambled frantically to mobilize, digging into the dunes. But exposed on all sides they had fallen prey to relentless waves of Stuka dive bombers, launching death from above. Despite the best efforts of the medics left alive, the injured and dying littered the beach and the broken men of a once-proud army now clung desperately to life amid ruined vehicles and machinery. While the determined fought on, with neither supplies nor ammunition Jack knew they would soon lose the fight.

*Damn the High Command*, he thought. *Damn Churchill!*

"Corp!"

Jack looked around and saw Charlie Mason, a young ashen-faced wireless man, hugging his set in the lee of a vaporized wreck. He flinched as shells ricocheted around him, but his spot was safer than theirs, out in the open. Charlie beckoned them over frantically.

Nudging toward the wreck on their elbows, Jack and Billy joined him.

"Listen to this," Charlie said. He handed Jack the receiver, his filthy hand shaking.

Covering his left ear, Jack heard a crackle of white noise, then: "… *is HMS Defiant … miles from your … If you can read me, we're …*"

Jack recoiled as a deafening burst of static disrupted the broadcast.

Charlie snatched back the receiver, spinning dials on his set in an attempt to regain the transmission. "Repeat again, *Defiant! Defiant*, do you—"

"*Down!*" yelled Billy as a volley of machine-gun fire kicked sparks across the wreck around them.

Jack grabbed Charlie's webbing to yank him down but with a ding, the boy's helmet indented, smoking. Charlie slumped; his expression frozen in shock as a crimson tear slid down his forehead.

Jack lowered his head and did the only thing he could, rolling the boy gently onto his back he untied Charlie's leather dog tags and stuffed them into his tunic pocket, closing the boy's eyes. "God's speed, son," he said quietly.

"*Bastards!*" growled Billy.

"*… Dunkirk defense do you … over?*" crackled the wireless.

Pulling on Charlie's headphones, Jack grabbed the receiver. "This is Corporal Jack Stone," he shouted over the blasts exploding around them.

"*… Reading … Corporal. This is Admir … Steadwell of his majest … Destroyer Defiant!*"

"Can you give us an ETA on evacuation, sir?" Jack yelled. "We're gettin' thrashed out here!" He ducked as dirt showered over them.

"*We're … all we can, Corporal, but … our own problems right now. RAF support's … beating. Without them we can't—*"

The ground rocked as a nearby blast nearly toppled the wreck. Feeling a sting, Jack looked down and saw a jagged splinter of shrapnel pinning the receiver, now silent, to his palm. Its tip jutted red from the back of his hand. Wincing, he eased it loose. Billy pulled the camouflage net from around his neck and bound the wound tightly.

"They're out there," Billy said, gazing toward the ocean. "They're bloody out there!"

After weeks of morale-sapping hopelessness, Billy's words seemed impossible. But as Jack peered into the mist beyond the shoreline, he saw flashes in the distance accompanied by the muffled crump of explosions.

"So we just 'ave to stay alive long enough for 'em to get here!" Jack said, rummaging through the backpack beside Charlie.

"Ah, we've had no help from the RAF since we got 'ere," Billy muttered. "Why should the Navy be different?"

"Don't count 'em out." Jack pulled a battered pair of binoculars from the backpack. "Not yet!" He'd seen more than his fair share of death on their doomed campaign, but he wasn't about to give up now, not with salvation so close. Despair could kill a man quicker than any bullet. "Chin up, Billy." He dropped onto his belly and peered around the wreck. "We've been in tighter spots than this."

"*Mont Cavalier?*" Billy exclaimed. "Oh yeah, that was a doddle. I've still got a bullet in me arse!"

"Then don't say I never give you nothin'," Jack chided, squinting through the binoculars.

"Remind me to say *thanks* when they cart us off to Colditz," Billy sighed. He scanned the beach. The Allies' armor was destroyed or discarded. The survivors had nothing now but small arms, Brens, and ammunition in dangerously short supply. The Royal Navy might be near, but with the Luftwaffe keeping the RAF at bay, there would be no air support for evacuation.

But Jack was a fighter.

His insanely heroic actions at Mont Cavalier had proved that, as had his exploits on so many other occasions. And while events had taken a dark turn in Belgium, for the first time in weeks, Billy felt a renewed sense of purpose in his friend along with a glimmer of hope that with Jack back in the game, they might just make it out of this mess alive.

Despite Billy's misgivings, he had to believe that.

Focusing his binoculars on the town, Jack watched a convoy of German Opel trucks bounce across debris. They stopped by a cluster of machine-gun nests facing the beach and their rear doors swung open, releasing dozens of German troops who scuttled eagerly over the sandbags like ants—young men fresh from the Fatherland, keen to fight for their Führer. Prepping tripod mounted Spandaus, the Germans looked to be gearing up for a push.

To make matters worse, a column of panzers rumbled through smoke to their rear. As Jack turned his attention toward them, he saw the hatch of the lead tank swing open and saw a man emerge from the turret.

Jack's blood ran cold.

The stakes had just been raised.

"What is it?" Billy said, sensing his friend's unease.

"It's him, Bill," Jack said, his voice wavering. "It's Mörder."

# 2

## CRY HAVOC

———

**F**ROST-BLUE EYES stared glacially across the dunes. Raising a clenched fist, General Ernst Mörder halted the panzer column to his rear. Chewing earth, the armored tanks ground to a halt, belching diesel and smoke like a pack of iron beasts.

Mörder, too, was a beast: solid and threatening, impervious to assault from all but the hardiest opponent. He was meticulously dressed and decorated; his features typically German. Gaunt aristocratic cheekbones framed a long slender nose perched above a slightly offset jaw. His hair, slick and blond, was trimmed high above his ears, but his most prominent and unsettling features were his eyes—like two piercing sapphires. Examining Mörder's face one gazed across a great alpine wilderness, its landscape vivid and wild with danger.

*The Jackal of Danzig* had gained notoriety during the Great War, his moniker wholly earned, thanks to his random acts of brutality, though many in Hitler's circle observed he was far more cunning, and certainly more carnivorous, than his canine namesake. Such observations were lost on Mörder, however. To his mind, he was simply a general in Germany's Wehrmacht, who ruled with a will of iron and obeyed his Führer's commands.

And his orders today were to eradicate the BEF.

"*Mensch!*" he barked from his turret.

In the tank to his rear, a handsome young man, his face flecked with dirt, looked up and removed his headset. "They're encountering resistance in town, Herr General!" The man's complexion flushed with panic. As Mörder's adjutant, Colonel August Mench was well aware of the consequences an ill-received answer could incite.

"Lay down suppressing fire when I give the command," Mörder barked. "I want them locked in like rats before the column advances!"

"Sir, it may be some time before we can—" Mench hesitated; he'd seen men shot for less. "The Allies are trying to break through, sir!"

"In number?"

"Unconfirmed. Poor visibility and the RAF are hampering our ability to—"

"Equip all batteries," Mörder snarled, "and prepare to fire on my mark. Cut down anything that sticks its head above those dunes!"

"Yes, sir," Mench pulled his headset back over his ears and relayed Mörder's orders.

Mörder gazed across the beach, redoubling his determination to destroy the Allies. There would be no escape for that scum, not this time, with victory so close that he could smell it. Crushing the BEF here would secure Great Britain for the Führer, cementing Mörder's seniority in Hitler's new world order.

"I will erase you from the face of the earth," vowed Mörder quietly as he scanned the dunes, "and by dusk, have your heads on pikes!"

. . .

Soldiers scattered as a Stuka's whine grew louder. Bursting through cloud it fired a volley of machine-gun fire that raked dual plumes of death along the beach. Scrambling into the charred shell of a medical truck, Jack and Billy watched it roar overhead releasing its payload. Men screamed, blown into the air and landing in pieces around them.

"These defenses are on their last legs!" Billy yelled, flinching as earth showered over them.

"Once those panzers move in, we've 'ad it!" Jack yelled back.

"What d'you suggest?" Billy ducked as a firestorm of mortars pummeled the dunes again.

"We do what we always do!" Jack yelled in reply. "Get stuck in 'n' raise hell!"

"I was afraid you was gonna say that!"

Jack scanned the beach and spied something. Staying low, he crawled around the wreck and returned seconds later, dragging a beaten-up messenger motorcycle. "We gotta buy these boys time to fall back," he shouted. "If we don't take the fight to the Krauts, we'll be dog meat when their armor rolls in!"

"Don't s'pose this has anything to do with Mörder?" Billy replied.

Jack cast a glance toward the town. Given half a chance, he'd raze it to cinders to put Mörder six feet under, but while thoughts of retribution were tempting, German E-boats were blocking their fleet and they had no air cover. Nothing short of a miracle could save them now.

But he had to try.

Righting the motorcycle, Jack climbed onto the saddle and flicked its fuel gauge. There was fuel, but was it enough?

"Just do what you need to do 'n' get back in one piece!" Billy yelled.

"We ain't missin' a boat back to Blighty, not now!"

Jack kickstarted the bike. It protested, then idled irascibly. "You're coming with me!"

"What?"

"You're a crack shot, Bill! I can't do this without you."

Billy sighed. He knew the look in Jack's eyes meant he was committed now, all the way. "What's the plan?"

"*Plan?*" Jack said, his smile grim. "Just try to keep 'em off me 'til I reach their line."

It was easier said than done. He handed Jack his grenade bandolier and a revolver. Freeing the bike's throttle, Jack rocketed across the beach.

Crouching beside Charlie's body, Billy examined his rifle. He glanced up at the scattered remains of the BEF around him, men now seemingly condemned to death.

But Jack gave him hope.

No, it wouldn't end this way—not on his watch. And if they were to die, then let them die fighting on their feet, not on their knees as prisoners.

Raising Charlie's rifle, Billy fired off a shot. "All right, lads, the fleet's on its way!" he yelled, bullets searing the air around him. "Let 'em 'ave it!"

Buoyed by the hope of a miracle, the men yelled battle cries, and charged across the beach behind Billy.

. . .

Jack gunned the motorcycle and hurtled toward the town. He saw something protruding from the beach and slowed to pluck it from the sand —a mortar rifle. He cocked the barrel and was relieved to see it was loaded. Perhaps his luck had turned.

Pushing the bike on, he roared over a dune and bounced onto the beach —in plain sight of the Germans, who immediately opened fire. As the beach erupted in his wake, Jack pressed on. It suddenly occurred to him that this was either the most brilliant plan he'd ever had, or a suicidal act of stupidity.

Perhaps both.

...

*"General!"*

Mörder looked up from a map and raised his field binoculars in the direction Mench was pointing.

"He's insane!" Mench cried.

Through the binoculars, Mörder saw the blur of a motorcycle speeding toward them and behind it, dozens of Allied troops cresting the dunes in a charge, giving the biker covering fire. They flooded the beach and advanced toward the town.

The ill-founded optimism of his enemies never ceased to amaze Mörder. What would it take for these fools to accept defeat? Well, if an example was needed, then he would be only too happy to oblige, and obliterating this upstart's act of defiance would serve as a starter.

Descending into the turret, Mörder ordered his panzer forward.

...

Hungry German Spandaus chattered death at the advancing horde.

Billy marked a particularly keen gunner tracking Jack's progress through his rifle sights. Crouching, he aimed and pulled the trigger, shooting the man through the eye just as Jack sped by. Reloading, Billy gave chase, dropping only briefly when a burst of machine-gun fire felled the line of men ahead of him. He staggered to his feet, leapt over their bodies, and continued after Jack with his comrades.

"I'm gettin' too old for this shit!" he gasped, pushing on through the chaos.

...

Drawing the Germans' fire, Jack searched for a chink in their armor. Skidding parallel to their line, he rode at full speed, hurling grenades from Billy's bandolier, which detonated behind him in a chain of devastating explosions. Machine-gun crews scattered as ammunition boxes erupted, their bullets whistling wildly through the air.

Hearing a cheer, Jack glanced back and saw Allied troops giving chase and covering fire. He whooped a wolf howl, raised his mortar gun, and arced the bike back toward them. So close to death, he had never felt more alive. He saw Billy up ahead and grinned—but his smile evaporated as Mörder's panzer crested a dune and smashed onto the beach between them.

Jack skidded to a stop and stared defiantly at the tank, his bike revving an angry dare for his nemesis, the general, to advance.

The tank's turret rotated to target him.

It was as if all the anger, all the rage Jack had felt since Belgium, exploded in this one desperate chance to exact revenge against the man who had destroyed his world.

Mörder.

"*C'mon!*" Kicking the bike into gear, Jack sped toward the panzer which juddered and ground toward him, machine-guns blazing as the turret's cannon leveled.

...

Billy sensed the inevitable seconds before it happened. With Jack in its sights, the tank fired a blast so powerful that it bounced the beast on its tracks.

The ground ahead of Jack erupted, pitching the front wheel of his bike into the crater and bucking him skyward. Yet even as he tumbled, airborne, Jack aimed his mortar rifle and pulled the trigger.

The mortar shot through the air, clattering down the tank's cannon into its guts.

Jack felt the shell explode with a thump as he landed on the panzer's deck plate. The tank swerved to a stop, the men inside screaming as they fried. The turret hatch swung open, releasing a plume of black smoke and the muzzle of Mörder's Luger.

"*Damn you!*" bellowed the general, rising like a phoenix through the flames.

Jack drew his pistol and pulled the trigger.

It clicked, empty.

Billy had given him Smiley's revolver!

Defenseless, he threw the pistol at Mörder, who took aim as the flames rose around him.

A single shot echoed in Jack's ears.

Jack flinched, certain he was hit, though he had felt nothing. Then he saw Mörder staring at him, incredulous. The Luger dropped from the general's hand, and he slumped backward out of the turret.

"A bloke can get 'urt around you!" Billy said, his head popping up beside Jack.

"You're still alive, aren't you?" was all Jack could muster.

"Not for much bleedin' longer," Billy muttered, looking around. Mörder's panzers were demolishing the Allied defenses. In spite of a brave countermove, they'd fought a losing battle.

"Bill, I—"

"Stow it, you sloppy sod," said Billy gruffly.

As he and Jack climbed down from the tank, Billy dropped several Germans before his pistol clicked. "I'm out!" he yelled over the battle's clamor.

A fresh wave of Stukas burst through the clouds above them. Billy and Jack glanced at each other. No words were needed now.

It was over.

They braced themselves for the inevitable.

Then with a roar, RAF Spitfires exploded through cloud behind the Stukas and opened fire, obliterating them. Swooping like hornets above the panzers, they sprayed the tanks with machine-gun fire, and right on their tails, a familiar drone announced a squadron of Allied bombers.

"Bloody 'ell!" Billy cried, euphoric.

"Better late than never, eh?" Jack said, grinning ear to ear. "C'mon!"

Jack started to run, and then realized Billy wasn't beside him. He turned to see his friend slumped against the crippled panzer, clutching his gut.

"I never even felt it go in," Billy said, shocked.

Jack threw an arm around him, and together they staggered through the firestorm. The beach was a hail of tracers, incendiaries, and mortar bombs cutting down men around them. The bedlam extended to the skies, where Stukas and Spitfires were engaged in a series of vicious aerial dogfights.

"We're almost there!" Jack yelled amid the chaos.

Ahead of them, the mist that had obscured their view of the ocean for days had finally lifted, revealing a flotilla of naval and civilian vessels, and on the horizon, Royal Navy destroyers. A wave of relief washed over Jack at the sight of the powderpuff bursts of smoke appearing from the destroyers' massive artillery batteries. Their shells whistled overhead, bombarding the German line.

All around, Jack saw the able-bodied carrying the injured out to sea in desperate snaking lines—thousands of men treading water in a last ditch bid to escape the carnage onshore.

Jack pushed on, dragging Billy alongside him.

"I can't do it," Billy gasped. He stumbled, almost bringing them down. Breathless and exhausted, he fought Jack's grip.

"Don't give up on me now!" Jack said, chancing a look back. "We're almost home!"

A wave of Stukas roared overhead trailing Spitfires in hot pursuit. The Stukas opened your fire on the men in the surf, spattering death into the ocean around them.

Jack saw a lone Stuka break away from its pack and scream toward them. "Keep going!" he rasped, dragging Billy after him.

The Stuka's guns sang and a dual hail of bullets tore into the beach behind them. Jack pushed on, every step taking him and Billy closer to the water and their only chance of escape. *Nearly there*, he told himself, *we're nearly—*

The beach erupted beneath them.

The Stuka must have dropped its bombs as it soared overhead. Jack and Billy were blown into the air, then hit the ground hard. Jack gasped for air, winded, his ears ringing. Laying nearby, Billy groaned.

Bruised and bloody, Jack crawled to Billy's side. "Get your arse up, Sergeant," he said, grabbing Billy's webbing. "Pubs close in 'alf an hour!"

Billy smiled unconvincingly through a layer of blood and dirt. "A bloke can get 'urt around you," he gasped, weakly.

"You're still alive, aren't you?" Jack muttered, clambering to his feet.

As he moved to pull Billy after him, he heard a whine. The Stuka had come around and was returning to finish the job.

"Christ, how much more can they throw at us?" Jack yelled.

Looking around, he spotted a Thompson sub-machine gun, its owner's hand still attached. Jack snatched the gun up and took aim.

"Jack," Billy gasped, "we ain't got time!" He tried to stand.

"I'm done runnin'," Jack growled.

He took aim and opened fire on the approaching Stuka.

The bomber was unfazed. Its bullet trails ripped along the beach—and through Jack's right leg. Spinning like a top, he hit the ground with a thud.

The Stuka screamed overhead but a destroyer's shell clipped its wing sending it spiraling into the dunes.

Billy had gotten to his feet. Though he was still clutching his gut with one hand, he somehow managed to grab Jack's webbing and hoist him over one shoulder. Now it was his turn to help a wounded friend. "We ain't.. missin' a boat back.. to Blighty," he muttered with grit. "Not now!"

Billy staggered into the surf and waded out to sea, joining the exodus of men escaping toward salvation.

The last thing Jack saw before he succumbed to darkness was the boy in his mind's eye. He stood on the beach in infinite calm amid the chaos, watching Jack leave.

France was lost.

Great Britain would be next.

It was only a matter of time before the remaining Allied resistance had neither the strength to fight, nor the will to maintain a defense. And when they fell, Germany would eliminate the final obstacle in its master plan for world domination.

A stubborn little island across the English Channel.

An island which now stood alone.

Great Britain.

# 3

---

# THE BRITISH BULLDOG

L ONDON'S DRAB, GRAY SKY mourned another night's destruction. It had rained for two days straight, a final insult to beleaguered Londoners who again that morning, were forced to circumnavigate fresh destruction wrought by the previous night's bombing raid courtesy of the Hitler's Luftwaffe.

Craters punctured the streets, many opening up tube tunnels, which gushed water from broken pipes as electricity cables sparked. The immolated shells of cars and buses lay on their sides like broken toys among ruined buildings, slumped together like Friday night drunks. And all around lay huge mounds of rubble and wreckage. Going about their business as best they could, the capital's populace meandered through the devastation that had become a part of their daily commute. Sidestepping dead animals, they pitied the weeping families, and prayed for the teams of firemen and air raid crews scaling mountains of bricks and debris in search of the missing.

*Blitz* raids were unrelentingly merciless.

Barrage balloons swayed listlessly above Big Ben as the great clock chimed the hour. It was a somber reminder that, for now, at least, life would continue as normal, in all its awful reality. Or as near to normal as could be managed given the circumstances.

. . .

Winston Churchill sighed as he watched the hands of an antique grandfather clock stutter.

"Does nothing in this infernal building work?" he muttered irritably. Taking out his pocket watch he checked the time, swung out the grandfather clock's glass door and adjusted the faltering hands.

But it wasn't just the clock that irked the prime minister.

The men seated behind him at the oak table in the center of his war room were equally unreliable.

Snapping shut his pocket watch, Churchill returned to his chair and looked around the table at the generals and assorted military brass of the British High Command. The prime minister sighed, musing that they were just as dusty a collection of dinosaurs as could be viewed on any given day at the Natural History Museum—one of the few buildings, observed Churchill with grim irony, that had thus far been spared the Luftwaffe's attention.

But that was not his focus today.

Three days had passed since he'd sanctioned what the press were now referring to as the miracle of Dunkirk.

*Miracle?*

The tension in the war room was palpable. Allowing it to mount a little further, Churchill took a long Maduro cigar from his jacket pocket, toyed with it for a moment, then snipped off the tip. He struck a match on the table—much to the annoyance of the older generals—lit the cigar, and puffed on it thoughtfully. Then with the cigar lodged between two fingers, he reclined, exhaled a great plume of smoke, and gazed sternly around at the fossils.

*Not a man jack among 'em willing to voice an opinion*, thought Churchill despondently.

It occurred to him that the men sat around him were much like the war room: polished but faded, and twenty years well past their prime. His heart sank. One of the youngest men to ever become a British prime minister, he was popular with the people, who admired his courage and undeniable sense of purpose—but behind closed doors, his suitability was questioned by Conservatives who had opposed his ascension. Indeed, there were many around the table who thought him a warmonger upstart. Well, he'd taken their counsel, and look where that had landed the country.

*His* country.

*Well, best get it over with*, he thought.

"France has fallen," Churchill boomed finally through a haze of cigar smoke. "And I find myself in the unenviable position of having to wage modern warfare with ancient weapons, namely," his gaze swept over the generals, "this High Command."

Sensing the timbre of the meeting was about to change, the men shifted uncomfortably.

With another puff on his cigar, Churchill continued. "For years, we've considered ourselves invincible. *An empire!* This fiasco at Dunkirk has proved otherwise!"

"We're at war, Prime Minister." General Cavandish Gort could always be relied upon to disagree. "Dunkirk was—"

"The worst of beginnings!" countered Churchill. "Wars are not won by evacuations! The British Expeditionary Force was sent to Europe unprepared and ill-provisioned, not to mention poorly led." He rose, strode across the room to a huge map on the wall, and slammed his fist against it. "The *wolf* is loose in Europe! Poised across the Channel to leap at our throats. And we sit here defenseless! *Alone!*"

A door behind Churchill opened, and his Military Chief of Staff General Hastings Ismay entered. "Good morning gentlemen," he said calmly. "Sorry I'm late; there's a war on." Taking a seat beside Churchill's chair, he opened his briefcase and looked up expectantly. "Have I missed anything?"

"Not one of you has had a single original idea beyond the same crippling strategies that failed us in 1918," Churchill continued, ignoring Ismay.

"Ah," said Ismay, clearly realizing exactly what he'd missed.

"Given the *obvious* lack of leadership for the prosecution of this war, I have today assumed the secondary position of Minister of Defense."

"This is preposterous!" said Gort, standing. "The purpose of this Command is to—"

"Our priority now is to buy time," Ismay soothed with diplomatic balm. "To re-equip the BEF."

Fuming, Gort resumed his seat.

"To that end," Churchill said, "my first order is to authorize the reactivation of some old friends."

"The GB Mark Ones," Ismay added, shuffling papers.

The declaration was greeted by stunned silence.

"Is that wise?" asked an elderly general. "Given their age, I doubt they could make *real* impact?"

"Not much different from yourselves then, eh?" Churchill snapped. He stubbed out his cigar and smiled. "You needn't worry, Worthington. I've someone in mind who can lick them into shape."

"Who?" asked Gort with suspicion, his eyes narrow.

"*Some—one*," Churchill replied, beginning to lose patience.

"Prime Minister, if you intend to wake up those antiques, I think we have a right to know who—"

"You have a right to know *nothing*, Gort," spat Churchill.

Ismay intervened. "Striking out with the Mark Ones now will buy the time we need to get back on our feet," he said calmly. "And as time is of the essence gentlemen, are there any further questions?"

The silence was thunderous.

"Very well," said Ismay cordially. "Same time tomorrow then. That will be all."

The men filed quietly out of the room. Ismay closed the door behind them and returned to the table.

Gazing contemplatively out of a window, Churchill said nothing.

Ismay knew it was always best to allow the PM time to diffuse after such meetings which had a tendency to be volatile, particularly if Gort was present.

"Was that wise?" said Ismay at last. "Gort, I mean. He has some of them in his pocket."

"Gort's the least of our worries," Churchill said, gazing up at the sky. The weather outside was still drab, still gray, and much like Churchill's mood, growing darker by the minute. It was as if a great coffin lid were closing inexorably over the capital. *But behind every cloud*, Churchill thought, *sunlight…*

Ismay frowned. "Someone in mind, you say?"

"Yes," the prime minister said, returning to the table. "He received dispatches for bravery in Europe, and some *lunatic* bloody action at Dunkirk." He slid a dossier down the table to Ismay. "I think he may be our boy."

Ismay examined the dossier's contents. "*Jack Stone…*" He looked up, surprised. "A corporal?"

Churchill returned his attention to the grandfather clock.

"I'll grant you he's the right material for promotion," Ismay said, scanning the papers. "A field commission, even. But he's young, Winston." He looked at Churchill. "The odds are against this."

"They always are," Churchill said, staring absently at the grandfather clock's face.

"It says here he's over at Chatham," Ismay said, sliding the dossier into his briefcase. "I'll have him brought in."

"See to it personally, would you, Hastings?"

"Of course." Ismay nodded. He was about to say more, but sensing Churchill's mood thought better of it and left the room.

As the clock chimed the quarter hour, Churchill checked his pocket watch again. Was he right to place the nation's fate into the hands of one so young? Only time would tell, but therein lay the problem—time was running out fast.

...

Morphine, antiseptic and shock choked the hospital corridor. Seated with his back to a wall, Billy drew up his legs as an exhausted orderly passed by pushing a gurney carrying a stunned young man. The man's face was blank, unemotional—he seemed oblivious to the loss of his legs.

Feeling his stitches pinch, Billy winced. He glanced around the corridor at the other men lining the walls. Survivors, like him, staring vacantly into the void; broken, injured and numb to the chaos around them as nursing staff and orderlies rushed about carrying bad news and bandages.

Billy reached into his pocket and pulled out a hip flask with a bullet lodged in its center; a couple of inches lower and the shell would have punctured his vitals. As it was, the bullet had hit the flask and fractured a rib. *But that's nothing compared to what some of these poor sods've been through*, he thought bleakly. He'd been lucky, wondering if that's what it took to survive now. Maybe, but all the same he *was* lucky, and so was Jack, who they had gotten to Chatham just in time, thank the Lord.

Now it was a waiting game.

Billy poured a capful of booze from the flask, raised a toast to Lady Luck, and swigged it back.

"Still here I see, Sergeant," said a sharp-looking man in a Scottish brogue. "What is it now, three days?" Raising an eyebrow over his horn-rimmed spectacles, Doctor Edward McKenzie looked down at Billy and smiled. "You're more tenacious than Greyfriars Bobby."

"How's Jack?" Billy asked, quickly concealing the flask as he eased himself up the wall.

"He won't be doing the quickstep any time soon, but he'll live," McKenzie said. "The shells passed straight through his leg."

"Will he lose it?"

"I doubt it, unless infection sets in. He's a fortunate young man."

Billy felt lightheaded, his relief for Jack suddenly quashed by an all-consuming hatred for an enemy who could maim and kill so senselessly. And for what? *Breathing room*. That's what Hitler had called it—the need for Germany to repatriate its borders following the sanctions imposed by the Treaty of Versailles.

Billy realized the doctor was still speaking. He tried to focus.

"I said, would you like to see him, Sergeant?"

Billy nodded.

"Then you have five minutes," said McKenzie, checking his watch. "Your friend needs rest—and lots of it."

...

The boy in Jack's mind's eye screamed!

Jack's eyelids snapped open.

The room he was in was dark and quiet, save for the sound of muted activity outside. Inhaling deeply, he smelled disinfectant and clean linen. He cautiously raised his head to look down the bed at his right leg, nervous at what he might see. It was elevated and bandaged. Exhaling relief, Jack let his head fall back onto his pillow. *We made it*, he thought.

But then he realized Billy wasn't with him. What if he hadn't reached the boat? What if the Hun had shelled their transport?

Jack spotted his tunic slung over a chair beside his bed. He reached for it, but still weak, his bandaged hand missed its mark. His fingertips connected with its pocket, releasing a cascade of embossed leather dog tags, many stained with dried blood. Jack stared at them, numb. *So many*, he thought. Yes, he might have made it, but a lot of lads hadn't.

And where the hell was Billy?

As if in answer to his question, the door opened slowly and Billy's head appeared. Jack's fear for his friend's fate evaporated.

"Hey," Jack croaked, his throat dry.

Billy came to stand at the foot of his bed. For a moment he couldn't look at his friend, then: "You look bloody awful," he said, forcing a smile.

"Thanks," Jack replied. It hurt too much to smile back. He sat up slowly, stiffening as pain coursed through his leg.

Billy pulled the flask from his pocket and shook it enticingly.

"Lucky sod," Jack said, noticing the flask's bullet. "No thanks."

Billy pocketed the flask and sat down hard on Jack's mattress.

"Jesus, Bill!" Jack complained through gritted teeth.

"Sorry." Billy rifled through a fruit bowl. "Ain't you got no grapes?"

"Don't you know there's a war on?" Jack said. As usual, Billy *had* made him smile, though it hurt like hell to do so. "How's your belly?"

"Ah, just a scratch." Billy looked at his friend. "So.. we made it."

"Yeah."

Billy's eyes turned toward the dog tags on the chair but he said nothing.

"The unit," Jack said suddenly. "How many of the boys made it 'ome."

Billy's forced smile reappeared. "You've been out for two days straight —missed a lot of pretty nurses!" Billy winked, but his joke fell flat.

"Billy—"

"Some of 'em were right bobby dazzlers, too!"

"How many, Bill?"

"The press've been tryin' to get in. Hey, there's talk you'll get a medal!"

"How many?"

Billy swallowed, looked away. "*None*," he said quietly.

Jack stared at him in shock.

"None of 'em made it back." Billy looked squarely at Jack. "It's just you 'n' me now."

Jack felt hopelessness wash over him. Overwhelmed by grief, he shifted painfully on his mattress to look out of a window. Droplets of rain flecked onto the glass.

Billy pulled the dented flask from his pocket once again. "You fancy that drink now?"

Jack shook his head slowly.

Billy nodded. "Well. If you need me, I'll be..." He trailed off, then stood and backed toward the door. "Jacky, I—"

"I'm *tired*, Bill."

Billy nodded dolefully. He reached for the door, but it opened on its own, revealing a general between two burly soldiers.

"Corporal Stone?" the general said.

Jack nodded, saluting the rank painfully.

Doctor McKenzie forced his way between the soldiers. "I really must protest, General..."

"*Ismay*," the general said.

"Sir, this man is in trauma recovery," said McKenzie, "Whatever you want with him will have to wait!"

"I'm afraid it can't, Doctor," Ismay said soberly. "You see, this man has an appointment with Winston Churchill."

# 4

## HOME FIRES BURNING

**T**HE **BLACK GOVERNMENT SEDAN** rumbled through blasted ruins. Despite McKenzie's protestations that Jack wasn't fit to travel, he'd been bundled into the vehicle with Billy. They sat quietly in the rear of the car, glancing unease at each other. General Ismay had not disclosed the purpose of their abduction, nor had they asked.

*Whatever it is, it can't be good*, Jack thought.

"What the 'ell," Billy said, leaning forward suddenly to look outside.

Following his gaze, Jack stared wide-eyed at the devastation gliding by. The capital he remembered had been strong and thriving; what he was looking at now was a burnt-out carcass. In the skeletal remains of a church he saw a congregation singing to the silhouette of St. Paul's Cathedral through the charred beams of the roof. A distraught young woman passed by cradling a doll; an upturned pram nearby covered in rubble. The sedan slowed as up ahead, ambulance crews carried stretchers through a crowd to a line of bodies on the pavement. A priest moved among them, offering hope to some, the last rights to others. And all around wandered dazed Londoners caked in brick dust like ghosts drifting through eerie, smoking streets.

Jack saw the boy in his mind's eye atop a mound of bricks, watching the sedan rumble by before disappearing into the haze.

"You okay?"

Jack saw that Billy was watching him. "Yeah," he replied, trying to keep it together, "'course."

Billy's eyes narrowed, then he nodded.

Ismay turned to look at them from his seat beside the driver. "Another bad one last night," he said, returning his gaze to the road. "Welcome to London, gentlemen."

Coasting on through the smoke, the car finally reached Downing Street.

Seeing the vehicle slow, soldiers manning a checkpoint circled it suspiciously. A young duty-sergeant leaned in through the driver's window and scowled at Jack and Billy, then bumped his head in surprise when Ismay leaned over and handed him papers. He withdrew hastily, saluted, and nodded hurriedly at his men, who scurried to raise the barrier. The sedan passed through the checkpoint and rumbled on into Downing Street.

The area was a hive of activity. Weary air-raid wardens were sandbagging doorways, taping X's onto the few remaining window panes that weren't shattered, and clearing debris scattered about the street. They looked up, watching the sedan with interest as it drew to a stop outside Number Ten.

Billy exited the vehicle first, then turned to help Jack out.

"I'm fine!" Jack hissed. He clambered out behind Billy, begrudgingly using a stick that McKenzie had given him, along with stern instructions not to put too much weight on his leg. It was advice he was beginning to appreciate, as every step he took sent waves of pain coursing through his muscles. With the aid of the stick and finally Billy's shoulder, he limped to Ismay and looked up at the barrage balloons floating above them.

"Even Whitehall isn't immune to the Luftwaffe these days," Ismay said, following his gaze. Turning on his heel, he moved under a wrought iron arch toward two sentries guarding the door.

"It's smaller than I thought it'd be," Billy whispered in Jack's ear.

The sentries snapped to attention and saluted Ismay. He reciprocated, then reached out to grasp a black lion's-head knocker but the door swung in, revealing a small, impeccably dressed man in a black morning coat and gloves.

"Inches," Ismay said warmly.

"Good afternoon, General," the man said. He glanced over Ismay's shoulder at Jack and Billy with a look of severe disapproval. "I believe he's expecting you, sir. This way."

The three men stepped into the entrance hall. Jack marveled at the chandelier, the marble walls and the gilded portraits which were a stark contrast to the ravaged landscape outside.

"The PM's in his study, sir," Inches said to Ismay. "May I take your coat?"

"Thank you." Ismay shouldered off his raincoat. As he handed it to Inches, his gaze fell on the butler's trembling hands. "Something the matter, Inches?" he asked, frowning.

"*Bugger it!*"

The exclamation came from a room off the entrance hall, followed immediately by a crash.

"*Ah*," Ismay said sympathetically. "How long has he been—"

"Ever since France capitulated, sir," Inches whispered. "To be honest with you, General, it's rare these days that he isn't in one of his... *moods*."

"Chin up, Inches," Ismay said. "These chaps may just lighten his disposition." Then to Jack and Billy, he said: "Follow me, gentlemen."

Leaving Inches behind, Ismay led Jack and Billy to a door at the end of a long corridor. He cast a cautious glance at the boys and knocked twice.

"*Enter!*" Churchill barked from the room beyond.

"Just.. be yourselves," Ismay said. He opened the door.

Winston Churchill stood hunched over a map spread out across his desk. He trailed a finger down a long line of swastikas dotting the French coast, muttered a silent curse, then looked up.

"Well now," Churchill said, peering at his guests over brass half-moon spectacles. "You look like men in need of a drink." He opened a cabinet under his desk and produced a near-empty crystal decanter. "Brandy?"

Jack knew that Billy was about to say yes, so he quickly spoke first for them both. "*No*. Thank you, sir."

Jack ignored Billy's scowl.

"Just me then," Churchill said. "Ah, well." He filled his glass to the brim. "You know, as a young man I made it a rule never to take strong drink before luncheon. Given our country's predicament however, I've changed that rule so I now never do so before breakfast!"

In spite of the pleasantries, Jack felt Churchill was assessing him, his abilities, potential. But for what? The old man could see Jack's stick and his injuries, but made no reference to them. What the hell did the old man want?

"The tales of your exploits are inspiring, Corporal," Churchill said. "Your appearance confirms they're no exaggeration."

"You wanted to see me, sir?" Jack said.

"To the point, that's good," Churchill said. "Well, let me be equally blunt. British freedom hangs by a thread. One organized push from the Nazis and we'll be occupied in days."

The weight of Churchill's words caught Jack off guard. Had he just heard the old man right? He was standing in the study of the great British bulldog, the resolute, steadfast leader who embodied such an overwhelming sense of defiance in the face of seemingly insurmountable odds, and the man had just admitted to Jack that the country was on the verge of defeat?

"Great Britain's resolve is waning," Ismay said. "Our people need *hope*."

"I'm not sure I follow, sir," Jack said.

"The courage which makes a fellow a hero isn't always equaled by ability," Ismay said carefully. "You appear to be the exception."

"An exception I've been looking for, for quite some time," Churchill said. "The BEF was repelled from Europe, Corporal, routed and largely destroyed. While Dunkirk's evacuations saved thousands, invasion *is* imminent. We're short on men, munitions and morale. We're woefully unprepared. Standing upon the brink, we stare into the abyss."

He picked up a dossier from the side of his desk and flicked through its pages. "I've read your combat history. You're arrogant, impetuous and stubborn, with a total disregard for the rules or your chain of command. In short, Jack…" Churchill winked at Ismay. "You're *my* kind of soldier."

Jack was lost. "Sir, I don't know what you think I can—"

"The press hailed Dunkirk a miracle," Ismay said, "but the British aren't fools."

"It's my opinion," Churchill said, "that one must learn to draw from misfortune the means of future strength—for strength is granted to all, when needed to serve great causes."

Billy looked at Jack, bewildered.

"It's *you*, Jack," Churchill said. "*You* who has that potential—or at least, you will by the time we're through with you. Y'see, the Hun expects us to play by the rules, but it's my opinion that your *penchant* for recklessness could be the key to our salvation. The country needs you, Jack. *I* need you." He glanced at Billy. "*Both* of you."

"Why?" Billy asked, his respect for rank all but forgotten now his interest was piqued.

"We've recently established an elite military division," Ismay said. "The Commando. It's our intention that they be at the core of our future offense strategy."

"To do what?" Jack asked.

"Take the war to the Bosch," Churchill said proudly. "With a fully trained team, you'll set Europe ablaze with butcher 'n' bolt tactics!"

As if sensing Churchill was getting ahead of himself, Ismay cut in. "To be more specific, Corporal, we want *you* to lead the first team."

"I don't believe this," Jack said, looking at Billy.

"Obviously with the assistance of the sergeant here," Ismay added, "who I'm given to understand is, at times, *equally* reckless?"

"Only on my good days, sir," Billy said with a grin.

Ismay gave him a slight nod. "Once fully trained, Commando units will disrupt enemy lines across all German-occupied territory. By keeping the Nazis engaged, you'll enable our boys to secure another foothold in Europe, launch a second assault."

Churchill downed the last of his brandy and lit a cigar. "No more *Dunkirks*, Jack."

Jack and a lot of other boys had suffered as part of the BEF in Europe. He'd been knifed, shot at, bombed, and practically crippled. And now they wanted to send him back?

"With respect, sir, I lost men in Europe. *Good* men. I lost my— *I…*" Pain throbbed through Jack's leg. He was suddenly overwhelmed by the memories of his recent experiences.

Billy stepped in. "Training new lads'll take time."

"Your team would be comprised of experienced veterans who've all seen active duty," Ismay said.

"How many?" Billy asked.

"Four initially, plus yourselves. The first group is currently being," he glanced at Churchill, briefly, "*assembled*."

"Jack, I need a man with pluck," Churchill said, "with the spirit to get the job done. I've chosen you as I want them to fight with guts— *conviction!* To use skill beside courage in battle, and to kill, I won't say without mercy, God forbid we ever part company with that, but with zeal —and not altogether," he focused on Jack, a glint in his eye, "without a little *relish!*"

The pain in Jack's leg intensified as his heart beat faster. He leaned hard on his stick, beads of perspiration escaping his brow. Jack summoned all of his strength, there was no other way to say it.

"I'm sorry sir but, I ain't your man."

Billy looked at him sharply. "Jack, just think about it. It's our chance to hit 'em, hit 'em back for Dunkirk, for all of it!"

Ismay folded his arms. "The British aren't fools. We know Hitler's winning the war. Most of Western Europe's already fallen. It's only a matter of time before we fall too. What then?"

"What then indeed," Churchill mused. "Jackboots on Whitehall, eh?"

He scrutinized Jack's reaction through a cloud of cigar smoke.

Jack suddenly found himself the center of everyone's attention: Billy, clamoring for bloody retribution; Ismay calmly studying Jack's response; and Churchill, the prime minister of Great Britain, calling him to arms. The carriage clock on the mantelpiece seemed to slow, ticking into eternity. Its bell chimed a duet with the muted clangs of Big Ben in the distance.

*This ain't how it's meant to be*, Jack thought. He'd seen things in Europe, *terrible* things that he'd buried, that he just wanted to forget. He'd been strong for Billy, for them all, but he'd made mistakes, stupid mistakes; mistakes that had cost him dearly for others had paid the price— others who haunted his dreams. Jack had nothing left to remember them by now but dog tags and nightmares. They slept in eternity, their eyes upon him too.

Jack flinched as Churchill snapped his pocket watch shut. "Give you a chance to get your own back, wouldn't it, *Captain?*"

"Captain?" Jack exclaimed.

Churchill nodded deliberately.

"Well, that's it then," Billy said, rubbing his hands together. "Where do we sign?"

"Now 'ang about, Bill, I'm not—"

"Have you seen this morning's headlines?" Churchill snapped, snatching a newspaper from his desk. "Jerries went after a munitions factory in the East End last night, overshot their mark and hit a hospital—a *children's* hospital." He held up the paper with a photograph of the devastation. "Poor little buggers never knew what hit 'em! Twenty-two kids whose remains wouldn't fill a tin bucket! That's on my head, Corporal—*yours* too if you refuse a direct order."

"We're running out of time," Ismay said. "RAF reconnaissance reports increased naval activity along the occupied French coast."

"Invasion?" Billy said, suddenly alert.

Ismay nodded solemnly.

"I need your help, son," Churchill sighed.

"Sir, I—"

An air raid siren wailed in the distance.

Jack found himself with his back to the wall; he had nowhere left to go. The pain in his leg was excruciating, and he felt nauseous. He staggered forward on his stick and fell to one knee. Billy stepped forward to assist him but Jack raised a hand and shook his head.

"What's it going to be, Jack?" said Churchill, staring down at him. "Die on your feet for your country, or cower like a dog on your knees as a slave?"

With his senses screaming at him to do everything to the contrary, Jack nodded, resigned.

"Bravo, Jack... bravo." Churchill returned to his desk.

As Billy helped Jack to his feet, Inches appeared at the door behind them holding tin helmets.

Churchill poured the last of his brandy, then signed a slip of paper. Inserting it into Jack's file, he passed it to Ismay. "You'll see my physician this afternoon, and then several days' respite should set you straight after which, you'll be flown to Achnacarry in the Scottish Highlands. Brigadier Hastings there will brief you on the team."

Jack and Billy saluted and left the room. Inches lingered at the door. "I'll be along presently," said the prime minister. With a reluctant nod, Inches closed the door, leaving Churchill and Ismay alone.

"What do you think our young captain will make of his new *men?*" Ismay asked the prime minister.

"Why, I expect him to make *soldiers* of them," Churchill replied, resolute. "It takes a young pup to breathe life into old dogs."

"But will they let him? It's a hell of a risk, Winston. He has questionable leadership experience."

"I have *experienced* men; all they do is debate." Churchill returned to his map.

Ismay thumbed through Jack's dossier again. "This business with his brother. You don't think it could compromise the—"

"We need *action* Hastings, and the boy's the best chance we have. He's the *only* chance we have besides *them.*"

"And you think they'll accept his authority?"

"This country's on the brink of invasion, my High Command are incompetent and the BEF's in tatters," Churchill said. The words tasted sour. "With time running out, we have no choice."

Resigned, Ismay knew he was right. The undulating wail of the siren continued outside. "We'd best get below," he said, heading for the door.

"I'll be along presently," Churchill muttered.

Ismay frowned.

"That's an order, Hastings."

Ismay nodded and left the room. Churchill reclined in his chair and gazed up at the portraits of his peers staring down at him; distinguished leaders who had carried Great Britain to victory time and again, and who now looked to him to safeguard their sacrifice. The weight of their expectations and the desperate hopes of a nation weighed heavy on his heart. In these final desperate days with Germany hammering at the door, he had nothing left to give save words—words, and the hope that a reluctant young hero and a team of old warriors could succeed where all else had failed.

*The Commando*, Churchill thought, *a new breed of heroes. My mongrels'll set Europe ablaze, their battle cries heard above the melee— casting light into darkness once more!*

But could Jack make it work? Could Great Britain make one last defiant stand and show the enemy that it was still a force to be reckoned with? Churchill had never backed down from a fight in his life, and he wasn't about to do so now. He'd see it through to the end, just as he always did; either the end of the war, or if he failed, his life.

Looking down at the swastikas dotting the map, Churchill stubbed out his cigar.

"Britannia's waived the rules," he muttered.

He rose and left the study. Behind him, wisps of smoke curled from the map where the cigar's tip was rammed into the lair of Churchill's nemesis, and the beating heart of Germany…

*Berlin.*

# 5

## HEART OF DARKNESS

**W**ITH WINGS SPREAD WIDE, the mighty granite eagle towered above a sea of fluttering swastikas. Adopted in 1935 from the standards of Holy Roman Emperors, the *Reichsadler* had been appropriated by the Third Reich as its emblem, and a symbol of national unity. Clutching a wreathed Swastika in its talons, the eagle's aerie crowned the peak of the Reich Chancellery at the center of Germany's capital—testament to the will of its master, Chancellor Adolf Hitler.

In just three years, the Führer had stabilized Germany's ailing economy—lifting it from the ashes of defeat during the Great War and the crippling sanctions imposed by the League of Nations—and created the wealthiest country in Europe. He had banished the rot of a vacillating Reichstag, replacing it instead with himself: a leader whose vitality, strength of will, and utter conviction were totally unsurpassed. No longer would Europe sit in judgment of Germany's fate; nor its ambitions be stifled as its people begged for scraps in the streets.

Hitler had shown Germany the way, and the Fatherland had followed him willingly.

Ascending through a firestorm of political turmoil, Germany's youngest chancellor had declared that his country needed to reclaim its borders. Such expansions were often costly, but not for Germany. On the first of September, 1939, Poland was first to fall prey to Hitler's *Blitzkrieg* —his lightning war. By June the following year, the Allied forces sent to quell the Fatherland's insurgence had been all but decimated.

While the eagle soared, Hitler would continue to conquer, defeating enemies to the west while reclaiming Germany's lands in the east.

Dominating Berlin's skyline, the *Reichsadler*—symbolic guardian of the Fatherland's new emperor—was the embodiment of Hitler's supremacy, and a constant warning to all who sought to oppose him.

...

Flames danced within a great marble fireplace in the study of Adolf Hitler.

Upon entering the room, one would be forgiven for thinking they'd descended to Hades: the blaze casting an eerie *danse macabre* of shadows across an eclectic assortment of iconography, statues and paintings resonating dark power and Teutonic myth. Most prominent among these was a black marble bust of the chancellor emanating diabolical strength.

Hitler gazed at an ornate German clock on his mantel. With a case housed in walnut and gilded gold, it ticked an ominous duet with the Führer's machinations.

What to do with Great Britain.

When France fell, Hitler would ensure that the British came to heel. The island fortress could ill afford to blunder into another endless war, for not even Britannia's robust economy could withstand a second conflict.

As for Churchill, he'd be a fool to think he could weather the swell of Hitler's ambitions. Even if Roosevelt managed to rouse Washington's sluggish senate to arms, Hitler would refuse to capitulate.

*Never.*

Germany had destiny on its side. And if the unthinkable happened, Hitler would drag the world screaming with him into the flames. Either the Fatherland would be a world power, or it would not *be* at all. Hitler refused to be a pawn to public opinion; on the contrary, he would *dominate* it. He swore that Germany would never again be a slave to the masses—but their master.

Force ruled Europe now. Force *was* law.

And Great Britain?

A single decisive blow would destroy the country's resolve and secure the Reich's foothold to America.

Norway.

Norway's secret was the key—but who to trust with such a task for there were precious few in Berlin that Hitler could send, fewer still capable of achieving success outside of the capital. The only men Hitler had ever found useful were those who could fight, but Norway required subtlety—a *tactician's* mind.

Gripping the mantel with his right hand, Hitler clenched his left tightly behind his back, and within it, the source of his rage and salvation. He closed his eyes and exhaled, allowing the flames to fan his appetite for destruction.

A knock sounded at the door.

"Enter," Hitler said, his voice soft, low.

The blaze danced higher as if heralding the visitor's approach.

"Joachim," Hitler said without turning.

"My Führer," said the man behind him. "France has fallen." Hitler's foreign secretary, Joachim Von Ribbentrop, was cautious, even when delivering good news.

Hitler studied a portrait above the fireplace. It depicted the chancellor clad in gleaming medieval armor astride a great white steed. He clenched the horse's reins in one hand and held the haft of a banner in the other, its gilded tassels fluttering from a Swastika flag overhead. The Führer's expression was stoic, and why shouldn't it be? He was supreme commander of the Third Reich, the mythic warrior emperor, the epitome of Aryan supremacy.

"Do you believe in destiny, Joachim?" Hitler said.

Von Ribbentrop swallowed nervously. The question had caught him off guard. One could never be sure what direction such enquiries might take when the Führer was absorbed.

"I believe that you are my Führer," Von Ribbentrop said cautiously. "That you *are* Germany."

"I am the strength that the Almighty has bestowed upon our people," Hitler said. "In me and through me, they will wage the battle of our time. But while others in conflicts past have not received the Almighty's blessing, my Germany fights for freedom, so that our people may fulfill the Creator's mission."

"Europe *bends* to your will, my Führer."

"But not the world. And if the world will not help Germany, then Germany *must* help itself."

"The people trust you, Führer, they *idolize* you. You are a national hero. You alone can lead us to victory."

"Our borders won't be won by appeals to God or the League of Nations, Joachim. Only by force of arms will we reclaim our rightful lands, and when the world kneels at my feet, a thousand-year Reich will rise. My new empire—*Germania!*" Hitler stared into the flames, his eyes burning with zealous frenzy, then: "What news of General Mörder?"

"He's being treated. A burns hospital in Hamburg, I believe."

"And his family?"

"His wife resides here in Berlin. His daughter studies at Himmler's SS Academy in Wewelsberg, a most promising pupil by all accounts."

*Himmler.*

Hitler's monster had proven useful in the early days, during the riots and the Beer Hall Putsch. But now? Hitler trusted him less with each passing day. In just ten years, Heinrich Himmler, renowned for his ruthless efficiency, had ascended the Nazi ranks from a hired thug in a brown shirt to become the head of the SS Gestapo. A former friend and advisor, he was just another shell in the Führer's magnificent arsenal.

No, if Norway required subtlety, it could not be assigned to Himmler. Hitler needed a steady hand; someone he could rely on. Someone he could trust.

Mörder?

Since their service in the Bavarian Reserve, Mörder had been a devoted supporter of the party, and a close friend and ally. Indeed, it was Mörder who had led the charge through Belgium into France with such deadly precision, outsmarting the Allies at every turn. It was man's most sacred right, Hitler believed, to till the earth with his hands, and his most sacred sacrifice to shed blood on that earth. Hitler had shed blood with Mörder, first in the fetid trenches and wastelands of the Western Front in 1914, and then, later, in the crazed streets of Berlin during the uprisings in the early days of the party.

Yes. Mörder could be his man.

Von Ribbentrop watched as Hitler turned from the fire and smiled. Von Ribbentrop never felt truly comfortable during such intimate conversations with the Führer. And despite his recent promotion to Hitler's inner circle and his familiarity with the chancellor's routine, he chose to move largely unnoticed through the halls of power—to be a ghost among the beasts.

"The Allies have something new," Hitler said, his eyes glinting unnaturally in the firelight. He raised his left hand and opened his fingers, revealing a crumpled communiqué. "A classified weapons project."

"The resolve of the British is crumbling," Von Ribbentrop said. "Whatever meagre resistance they can muster will be a fruitless gesture."

"Go to Hamburg, Joachim. Bring home the general."

"But I understand his injuries were all but—"

"Spare no expense."

That was the end of it. To disagree with the chancellor was dangerous; a contrary opinion could be shared only with those one could trust—or one's life could be forfeit.

"Of course," Von Ribbentrop said. "At once."

"With Mörder guardian to our assets in Norway, Germany will achieve a final *decisive* victory in the battle for Great Britain, the submission of its empire and the enslavement of its people, and then, Joachim…*America*."

"Heil Hitler," Von Ribbentrop said, saluting. He turned deftly on his heel and left the room.

Hitler looked down at the crumpled communiqué. "When diplomacy ends," he whispered, "so *war* begins." Tilting his hand, he let the crumpled paper roll into the flames, and watched them devour it ravenously.

…

A former mental institution, St. Sebaldus Hospital had been seconded by the Reich in 1939 for the war effort, its residents long since deported to the east and an unknown fate. Now modernized and refurbished to accommodate state-of-the-art medical facilities, the hospital had brought many men back from the brink.

But not, it seemed, tonight.

Deep in the building's bowels, Joachim Von Ribbentrop leaned against the doorway of a dimly lit room, at the center of which a long cylindrical chamber was bolted to the floor. Beneath the chamber snaked a network of tubes and hoses, connecting the cylinder to a fluttering bellows and complex array of breathing apparatus.

Stepping aside to allow a distraught young nurse to leave, the Reich minister craned his head in a futile attempt to see through a porthole on the chamber's surface, the only window to the occupant within.

Ernst Mörder.

The general, screaming wildly, had hammered dents into the walls of his confines.

Von Ribbentrop winced. He had listened to the man's cries for hours in response to the pain coursing through his broken body.

It had been several days since Von Ribbentrop had received his Führer's order. In that time, he'd learned that the general's wife, Magda, had refused to see her husband, and certainly didn't want their daughter Ilsa to be updated on her father's condition. Having heard rumors of the Jackal's atrocities in Danzig, Von Ribbentrop couldn't help but think that there was a certain poetic justice to the general's current condition. But could he recover sufficiently as to be useful to the Führer? The answer eluded Von Ribbentrop, but in the end, it did not matter. His chancellor's decree had brought him to this ungodly place and he would dutifully carry out his orders.

Von Ribbentrop removed a small silver case from his pocket and opened it. He took out a slim Eckstein cigarette, closed the case and tapped it lightly on the lid.

"Allow me, Reich Minister," said a voice by his side.

Turning, Von Ribbentrop saw a benign-looking man in a white coat and spectacles. The man struck a match and offered it up to Von Ribbentrop.

"Thank you, Doctor…"

"*Schtein*," the man said.

Von Ribbentrop nodded, cupping Schtein's hand and puffing on his cigarette. Exhaling smoke, he returned his attention to the chamber.

"How we fight it," marveled Schtein, shaking his head in wonderment. Thunder rumbled overhead as Mörder's screams reached a crescendo.

"There's a storm coming," Von Ribbentrop observed. "What's his condition?"

"We initially considered him untreatable," said Schtein, "a hopeless case, incinerated beyond all recognition. Given the Führer's directive, however, we—"

"Will he live?"

"Difficult to tell. Reconstruction has proved problematic. He's going through hell in there, despite enough morphine to drop a horse." Schtein checked a clipboard. "Third degree burns to over ninety percent of his body, a near fatal bullet wound. He *should* be dead."

"The desire for retribution can transcend many obstacles, Herr Doctor."

Von Ribbentrop took a single, long drag on his cigarette before discarding it and entered the room. He took a red leather case, embossed with a golden eagle, from within his trench coat as he approached Mörder's chamber.

"General?" he said quietly. Opening the case, he removed an object. "Your Führer has need of your skills. He vows to do all he can to aid your recovery, and has asked me to bestow you, with *this*."

Von Ribbentrop set the object, a Grand Iron Cross, down onto the glass porthole.

The rage in the chamber subsided; the fluttering bellows calmed.

From the darkness behind the porthole, charred fingers rose beneath the glass like blackened twigs to caress the medal. As the fingers applied pressure, the vaporized crust on what little flesh remained cracked open revealing glistening sinew beneath.

"Are you with us?" asked Von Ribbentrop, pushing aside his revulsion.

For a moment, the bellows accelerated, then the fingers retreated from sight.

"General?" Von Ribbentrop whispered.

Leaning over the porthole he peered into the chamber but could see nothing. For the first time in hours, the room was silent—save for the bellows, which fluttered rhythmically like a diabolical heartbeat.

Silence.

Then Von Ribbentrop inhaled sharply, recoiling as Mörder's fist announced his rebirth to the world—it erupted violently through the porthole in an explosion of glass, the charred fingers gripping Von Ribbentrop's throat and squeezing it. The bellows rasped a frenzied accompaniment as the Reich minister gagged, struggling to break free. Finally escaping Mörder's grip, he staggered back into Schtein.

Mörder's blackened arm stiffened into a Nazi salute. "*Seig heil!*" he screamed. "*Seig heil!*" And then sickly, psychotic laughter.

Rubbing his throat, Von Ribbentrop looked past Schtein to the six uniformed officers entering the room. All wore Death's Head insignia above grim emotionless faces. One produced a syringe, grabbed Mörder's flailing arm, and injected a pale blue fluid. With a final burst of obscenities, Mörder's scorched arm sagged as his rage subsided. The officer pinched Mörder's wrist and checked his watch.

"Well?" Von Ribbentrop demanded, picking the medal up off the floor.

Feeding the arm back into the chamber, the officer nodded.

"Get him prepped," Von Ribbentrop said, "I want him back in Berlin tonight!" Turning on his heel he left the room and strode back up the corridor.

"Herr Minister!" Schtein shouted as the officers unbolted the chamber. "He's in no fit state to travel!"

"That is no longer your concern, Herr Doctor." Von Ribbentrop rounded a corner.

The officers shoved Schtein aside as they carried Mörder's chamber from the room.

Thunder rumbled again.

*Von Ribbentrop was right*, thought Schtein, as he watched the men carry away Mörder. *A storm* was *coming*.

9

# INTO THE BREACH

S OARING ABOVE THE HIGHLANDS, the battered *Halifax* fought to stay aloft as a blizzard opposed its advance. The aircraft dipped suddenly into the darkness, its engines shrieking above the elements to compensate as the bomber struggled for altitude.

Jarred by the sudden drop, Jack awoke to see Billy gripping a bucket and vomiting.

Billy looked up, groggy. "Bleedin' bombers!" he slurred, wiping a dangle of spit from his lips. The *Halifax* lurched again and Billy dry heaved. He looked thoroughly miserable.

"*Apologies, gents ...*" crackled the pilot over the com. "*Haven't seen it this bad in a while ...*"

"Shoot me now," Billy groaned dolefully. "Get it over with!"

"Ah, you'll live," Jack said, smiling.

Jack twisted in his seat and wiped the ice from his window, straining to see through the driving snow outside. He glimpsed stygian peaks gliding silently by beneath them, protruding through the darkness like great snow-capped islands on a sea of bruised cloud.

It had been several days since their meeting with Churchill, time enough for Jack to have received some of the finest medical attention a lowly squaddie could hope for. Indeed, his leg felt considerably better, though he still relied on the stick given to him by McKenzie, along with a hell of a lot of pain killers. Their journey from London to the airfield at RAF Croydon had been uneventful save for a squadron of long-range German *Dorniers* flying reconnaissance over the capital. RAF Spitfires had given chase, but Jack and Billy had lost sight of any fracas as they'd left London with Ismay.

"Good luck, gentlemen!" the general had shouted on the airstrip above the roar of the bomber's engines. "The nation's hopes go with you!"

*What the hell're we getting ourselves into?* Jack had thought, as he'd shook Ismay's hand and saluted. He'd shouldered his pack and boarded the Halifax with Billy, smiling at his friend's sudden confession that he hated heights. Jack told him it was his fault they were in this jam in the first place—called it *poetic justice.*

Exhausted, the boys had settled in for the long haul. As Billy grew quiet and queasy, Jack had brooded on how he'd allowed himself to be press-ganged into such a disquieting mission. Who was Hastings? And why the hell were they being flown up to Scotland, as opposed to any of the military training schools closer to the capital?

It wasn't his *destiny,* thought Jack, to make decisions or lead a team; that was for other men, *better* men. He hadn't been a hero in France—just a soldier too afraid to run. And now? They were here, shivering their arses off in the belly of this rusty old clunker on their way to God knew where, and all the time the Krauts creeping closer across the Channel. And what of the mysterious *team* Ismay had mentioned? Four men—*just four!* Seeing as how Germany had smashed its way to victory through Europe in a matter of weeks, these *veterans* would have to be pretty bloody special to withstand that kind of ruthless efficiency, especially if the Jerries launched a British *Blitzkrieg* any time soon.

"*We're currently over Gairlochy ...*" crackled the pilot above the clangor. "*ETA five minutes ...*"

The metal-ribbed walls of the fuselage shuddered and rattled.

"If we don't hit something first!" Billy muttered, spitting into his bucket.

Jack rubbed his hands together in a futile attempt to keep warm.

Through the window, he saw the cloud disperse as the *Halifax* plunged into mountain passes chiseled through deep cragged valleys. *We're a long way from home,* he thought, pulling the collar of his great coat up around his neck. He and Billy had crossed into another world—one it seemed, where even mother nature opposed their advance. But while Jack didn't know what lay ahead, he felt certain it couldn't possibly be as bad as what they had already endured.

Billy groaned, vomiting again.

"Still up for this job then?" Jack chirped perkily.

"Oh, you're just *lovin'* this, aren't you?" Billy growled, leaning over the bucket.

"Just strikes me as funny you were so keen on doing this," Jack said, "an' now? Well ..."

"*Buckle up, gents ...*" yelled the pilot over the com. "*Looks like we're in for some chop …*

Jack gripped his seatbelt, and Billy clung on to his bucket as the fuselage clattered violently. The bomber's dual piston engines reached an ear splitting crescendo as they fought to push on through the storm.

"I could just eat a nice juicy chop," Jack mused casually.

"Don't…" Billy gulped. He started to perspire and turn pale.

"A great—*big—salty* one," Jack added, "with all the trimmings." He winked at Billy.

"Oh, *God!*" Billy's face flushed green. He heaved again, then wiped his lips with the back of his hand. "When we land," he snarled, trying to regain his composure, "I'm gonna punch your bleedin' lights out!"

Jack grinned and returned his attention to the window. What little could be seen of the landscape below was rushing up to meet them at breakneck speed. *One way or another*, Jack thought, *we'll soon be on the ground.* He said a silent prayer.

"Hold on to your backsides, *boys* …" yelled the pilot. "Here we go!

…"

A shrill whine rose through the fuselage, followed by a resounding clunk indicating the bomber's landing gear had reassuringly locked into position. Outside the window, Jack saw frozen ground whooshing toward them, and briefly glimpsed the silhouette of a huge structure rising through the snowstorm into the night.

The *Halifax* struck the ground with a brutal jolt. Clinging to canvas webbing lining the bomber's walls, Billy flashed panic at Jack as the impact bounced their backpacks from compartments above their heads. The packs hit the deck, sliding toward the tail end of the fuselage as the bomber skidded, then shuddered into a crawl, and finally an abrupt stop— its engines winding down.

"Well now …" said the pilot perkily, "another *happy landing. Welcome to Achnacarry, gents!* …"

Heaving aside the access door, Jack was hit by a blast of cold air that whipped snow inside the bomber. He looked down and saw that the *Halifax* had stopped at the end of a frozen airstrip.

"Charming," said Billy. He jumped down, took their backpacks from Jack and helped him onto the runway.

Jack's boots crunched ankle deep in snow. He took his backpack from Billy, then turned to get his bearings.

"*Bloody 'ell…*" Billy muttered, as the blizzard calmed momentarily, revealing the ramparts and battlements of an ancient stone fortress—presumably Achnacarry Castle, looming before them into the darkness. In the distance beyond, all around them in fact, lay a dark forbidding mountain range.

Jack's suspicion that this might just be the worst decision he'd ever made was instantly reaffirmed. "What the hell have we gotten ourselves into?"

"Dunno," murmured Billy, "but it don't feel like army to me."

"I say, *hello!*"

The voice, the epitome of civility, was decidedly out of place in such brutal surroundings. Barely audible in the gale, it issued from the castle's main gate through which a figure approached, fighting to stay upright in the storm. Peering through the blizzard Jack saw it was an officer. As he neared, the man's great coat billowed out behind him revealing his collar rank insignia.

"Brigadier," Jack said, saluting wobbly on his stick.

"Charles Hastings!" the officer yelled. He returned the salute, nearly losing his footing on the icy causeway.

"The stick tells me you're Captain Stone," Hastings said, smiling. He turned to Billy, clamping a hand over his cap to prevent the wind stealing it. "Which makes you Sergeant Briggs?"

"Yes, sir," Billy said, snapping to attention and saluting.

"At ease, boys," Hastings said. "It's too cold out here for formalities. Good to meet you both; I've heard a great deal about you." The wind picked up suddenly, nearly blowing Hastings off his feet. "I say, shall we go inside. Phipps has just put the kettle on."

Jack and Billy nodded gratefully. Shouldering their packs, they followed Hastings back to the castle.

. . .

Flames.

Deep in his subconscious, Mörder recalled the aluminum components housing the dials of his panzer's control board melting; he recalled shooting each of his three loyal crew members in the head, and then shoving the Luger's barrel into his mouth; and he distinctly remembered the sound of his own flesh sizzling, spitting, like bacon on a skillet.

But the Jackal had never been one to shy away from seemingly insurmountable odds. Recalling his beloved daughter's face, he had summoned all of his remaining strength to rise through the inferno from his commander's seat and open the turret hatch above. He recalled the astonished face of a young British soldier on his deck plate, and the sound and impact of a bullet which had propelled him in flames from the tank.

Human physiology, Mörder had once been told, can tolerate no more than ten degrees above the body's core temperature—at which point the dermis converts the sensation to pain. And that at one hundred and thirteen degrees, proteins fall apart and thermal injury begins.

In Mörder's panzer, the temperature gauge on his board had exceeded five hundred degrees before it had fractured, sagging from its housing.

After being shot the general had hit the beach, his clothes incinerated, of course, save for a small patch on his back where the metal seat had protected him from the blast. With his skin charred and blistered, swinging in smoking folds around his limbs, he'd staggered across the battlefield in a daze. Barely able to see through boiling, swollen eyes, Mörder had been rescued by stretcher bearers and taken by truck to a field hospital in Ostend. The rest had been forgotten in a fog of pain and sedatives. He vaguely recalled a man's face looking down at him through gauze, and something *glinting* on glass?

But Mörder's overriding memory was that of the young man on his deck plate; the young man who had ridden mayhem through his ranks.

It was apparent to Mörder that wherever his body was now, his doctors had attempted some kind of skin-grafting procedure. He'd vaguely heard voices discussing it as he'd faded in and out of consciousness, and recalled a number of eyes examining him, devoid of any optimism. Mörder's life as he had known it was now changed forever, and for a brief second, he regretted not pulling his Luger's trigger when he'd had the chance.

His thoughts, incoherent as they were, were interrupted as a shadow fell over him. And the last thing Mörder saw before he surrendered to the sedative's void was the face of the young man on his deck plate—the young man who had stolen his life.

...

Jack and Billy watched Hastings' aides-de-camp, Alexander Phipps, pour tea from a steaming pot into two china cups. The ADC stirred in powdered milk, offered sugar, and then slid the cups on saucers across the brigadier's desk to Jack and Billy.

"Will there be anything else, sir?" Phipps asked.

"No. Thank you Phipps that will be all," replied Hastings, taking a pipe from his desk draw.

Phipps nodded and left the office.

"Well gentlemen, a little colder than London, I imagine." Hastings flicked ice irritably from his moustache.

"Yes, sir," Jack said. He slid his fingers around his tea cup, grateful for its heat.

Hastings smiled and carefully tamped tobacco into the pipe.

"Bit out of the way here, isn't it, sir?" Billy said.

"It's Commando boot camp, Sergeant. You expected maybe Gibraltar?"

"I just meant—" At a look from Jack, Billy fell silent and slurped his tea.

"There are some rather *particular* reasons why the Highlands were chosen as our location, Briggs. Not least of which, as I'm sure you'll appreciate after your flight, is that we're *isolated* here from the prying eyes of any would-be German informers."

"*Quislings?*" Jack said. "I thought they were a myth?"

"Quite possibly, Captain." Hastings said, sipping his tea. "But while the rest of the country sees Nazis in their soup, we can ill afford a breach in security. If one word of what's going on here reaches Jerry High Command, it could destroy the only chance we have to prevent an invasion. If we succeed however, then we'll be able to give the Germans a bloody nose, make the Wehrmacht think twice before going on a little *day-sailing* across the English Channel."

Jack glanced at Billy. Hastings words were sobering, and certainly brought home the magnitude of his new commission.

"Is there any chance we can meet the men now, sir?" Jack said. "We're keen to get—"

"Afraid not," Hastings said, a little too quickly for Jack's liking. "We still have a few preparations to make." He slid a plate of biscuits toward them. "I imagine you're both exhausted. Drink up, get some rest, and we'll talk in the morning." Hastings rose from his chair. "I'll see if Phipps has your quarters ready." He strode from the office.

Once the door was shut, Billy grabbed a handful of biscuits and stuffed them into his mouth like a starving hamster. He noticed Jack staring at him. "*What?* I'm 'ungry!"

"Anything about this seem off to you?" Jack said, glancing around Hastings' office.

"Everything," Billy said, spitting crumbs. "But let's eat first, eh?" He swiped another handful of biscuits, stuffing them into his pockets of his great coat. "Tomorrow's another day."

# 7

## WHAT LIES BENEATH

**A** **CHNACARRY CASTLE** was an obvious location for the first of Churchill's Commando camps. Bordering Lochaber's Northern Mountains with the forest of Locheil to the south, the castle overlooked the shores of Loch Arkaig and a road that meandered lazily from the Great Glen to Strathan. Concealed in the wilds from all but the most curious onlooker, the fortress had been the ancestral seat to the chiefs of Clan Cameron for over one hundred years; though now the clan's only remaining presence were the ruins of an ancient chapel and burial site on a small island jutting from the Loch's eastern shallows. The castle's sprawling estate neighbored the village of Spean Bridge, whose residents, while exhibiting the requisite amount of polite Gaelic curiosity, remained blissfully unaware of Achnacarry's true objective—a fact that Churchill had counted on.

...

Deep beneath the castle, Hastings led Jack and Billy through a series of winding tunnels. Preceding their passage, rats scuttled through pools of flickering light cast by a network of rusty lamps dangling above their heads. Jack had slept fitfully, and his suspicion that Hastings was hiding something increased steadily as they moved through the underground labyrinth. He could see that Billy was also uneasy. As Hastings regaled them with the castle's colorful history, the boys eyeballed an unspoken warning. If their time in Europe had taught them anything, it was to expect the unexpected in even the most seemingly benign situation.

"And so the estate," continued Hastings with the air of a practiced tour guide, "became home to Clan Cameron."

"And now?" Jack asked.

"Now it's home to a different if not, equally ferocious, breed of warriors who thankfully this time around…" He paused, as if selecting his words carefully. "Well, let's just say that this time around, they're on *our* side."

As they rounded a corner, Jack saw a huge circular door filling the wall ahead of them. It was nearly ten feet high and possibly as wide, with a wheel at its center through which passed two vertical steel pillars filling holes bored into the tunnel's stone floor and ceiling. The door was flanked by two sentries who snapped to attention as Hastings approached.

Hastings clearly wanted nothing to get in—*or out*, Jack thought uneasily.

"Well," Hastings said, "here we are."

"Impressive," Jack observed.

"What's the big secret?" asked Billy.

Hastings smiled thinly. "Best you see for yourselves." He nodded at the sentries who shouldered their Sten guns, gripped the wheel, and heaved it counter-clockwise. As they turned, the bars retracted from the floor and ceiling with a grating metallic screech.

Finally, the door split down its center and swung inward in two halves. The room beyond was shrouded in darkness.

"After you," Hastings said.

Peering into the gloom, Jack took a cautious step forward.

Billy grabbed his arm. "You sure about this?" he said apprehensively. "It don't smell right."

"I needn't remind you both that you're under a direct order from your war minister," Hastings said, his tone stern.

Jack looked at Billy, then back into the gloom beyond the doorway. There was no backing out, not now, and despite his senses telling him to turn back, Jack was suddenly overcome by an overwhelming wave of curiosity. He raised his boot and stepped warily into the darkness.

The room was silent but for the dull hum of what Jack assumed was a generator. He squinted and saw vague shapes in the shadows, noting the smell of diesel, grease, and the tang of electrical discharge mixed with something else; something familiar...

Perfume.

It was *Soir de Paris*. Jack recognized it as the favorite scent of a girl he'd gone steady with before being called up for service. As he took another step forward, something crunched underfoot. He crouched and picked up the object, holding it up to the light from the doorway.

A large rusty bolt.

"I can't see a bleedin' thing in 'ere!" Billy muttered, bumping into him.

Jack dropped the bolt, and it clattered across the floor into the darkness.

"Sir, this is— What *is* this?" Jack said. "I thought—"

"Patience, Captain," said Hastings, entering the room behind them. "All will be revealed. For now, *let there be light*, as they say." Jack heard him flip a switch, and a dirty yellow strip light flickered on overhead, illuminating their section of the room.

They were stood in what appeared to be a large, untidy garage. Shelves were crammed full with machinery and stripped-down engine components. A nearby workbench was piled high with manuals and schematics, and beside them sat what appeared to be a Vickers heavy machine-gun. An antique from the Great War, its trigger and belt feed looked like they had been modified with an oversized magazine and butt-stock. Jack was intrigued by the craftsmanship of the update, but the thing was just so damn big. He had trained briefly with the now obsolete Thompson sub-machine gun before being posted to Europe, but its superiority even to his old bolt-action Lee-Enfield was questionable, and the monster on the table before him would take two men to lift it, or at the very least, a reinforced tripod mount to support its weight.

"Now, what you're about to be shown here is strictly classified," Hastings said.

"*Shown?*" Jack said. "I thought we came 'ere to meet men."

"Take a seat, Captain, please."

"What *is* this place?" Billy asked. "Looks more like a workshop than a barracks."

"It's *both*," chirped a woman's voice from the shadows. It sounded young and confident, *American*, and its tone was playful. "This is where the *magic* happens!"

A lamp clicked on in the darkness, revealing long slender legs draped casually over a desk. Chasing them to their source, Jack saw a striking young brunette grinning back at him. Similar in age to Jack, she wore goggles pushed onto her forehead, above vivid green eyes that sparkled like emeralds in the gloom.

"Welcome to Winston's toy shop, boys," said the woman.

"Bloody 'ell," Billy said, giving Jack's shoulder a spirited nudge.

"Allow me to introduce our project engineer," Hastings said. "Doctor Camilla Sullivan."

The woman stood and crossed the room toward them. She wore fitted denim dungarees over scuffed service boots and a red check shirt, its sleeves rolled up. Jack noted with surprise that she had a loaded tool belt slung around the slim curve of her waist. While she might not have the appearance of a doctor, even in such utilitarian attire, Jack thought she was the most beautiful girl he had ever seen.

"Please," she said, holding out her hand which Jack noted was smeared with oil, "call me Cammy. It's great to finally meet you both. I've heard a lot about—"

"Why an *engineer* for a combat team?" Jack asked, turning to Hastings.

"No pulling the wool over your eyes, is there, Captain?" Hastings said. "Sit, *please*. Shocks are so much better absorbed with the knees bent." He gestured toward two chairs.

"Best do as he says," Cammy said, amused. She popped a stick of gum into her mouth.

As Jack and Billy complied, Cammy joined Hastings.

"Now, as you're both painfully aware, we're in no state to launch a second offensive this side of Christmas," Hastings said. "It's imperative therefore, that we're afforded time to reorganize—and in his wisdom, the prime minister authorized the reactivation of the GB Mark Ones."

Jack glanced at Billy, suddenly aware that proceedings had taken a very different direction to the one outlined by Churchill.

"The original 1915 models while effective, were really rather primitive," Hastings continued.

"Their greatest victory was at Ypres," Cammy interjected. "More than two hundred men were rescued in an afternoon."

"By what?" Billy said, frowning.

Hastings ignored the question. "The war was over by 1918 however, and the project was mothballed."

"What project?" Jack said, unable to restrain himself any longer. "Just what're you up to here?

Backing up beside a generator, Cammy snapped on her goggles. "With your help, we think these weapons could tip the scales of the war in our favor."

"*Weapons?*" Jack said, standing. "Look, we were told—"

"I've upgraded the Mark Ones to give 'em strength, agility, and firepower," Cammy said.

"Now 'ang about," Billy said, rising to stand beside Jack. "We're talkin' about, what? *Weapons? Machinery?* I thought we came 'ere to meet *men?*"

"Two out of three, Sergeant," Hastings said. He turned to Cammy and nodded.

Cammy gripped a lever attached to the generator. "Churchill wants a weapon of resistance, boys," she said, slamming the lever forward. "*I've made you four!*"

The generator started to hum, then whine and vibrate, as rapid pulses of high voltage electricity discharged from a series of tesla coils connecting it to thick insulated hosing which extended back from the generator into the shadows behind Cammy and Hastings.

Jack looked up as the strip light overhead flickered.

The generator's motor rose to a shriek, and it started to buck in its housing like an angry bull. Jack and Billy ducked as bolts popped from the metal casing, whooshing across the room like bullets and embedding in the masonry.

"What the hell's going on?" Jack yelled above the clamor.

"Don't you feel it?" Cammy yelled back with a grin. "*Hope!*"

Crackling into the darkness, electricity illuminated four huge silhouettes. Jack gaped.

"*Men?*" He looked at Cammy, horrified. "You're *frying* men?"

"Not men, Captain," Hastings shouted, flinching as the generator emitted a shower of sparks. "*Super-men!*"

Cammy and Hastings backed up to Jack and Billy as a tesla coil exploded with sudden ferocity, and unrestrained electricity arced wildly above them, illuminating the room in a crackle of blue corona.

"Oh, I don't like the look o' this!" Billy coughed, covering his mouth as smoke from the generator billowed around them.

The strip light above them exploded in a shower of glass and sparks. Jack reflexively threw his arms around Cammy just as the generator burst from its housing and blew across the room, crashing against the wall.

Then darkness.

A defiant burst of sparks erupted from the strip light, and a red emergency beacon flickered on overhead, lending the room an eerie unnatural hue.

Jack slowly opened his eyes.

"Didn't know you cared," Cammy said, looking up at him.

"What? Oh, sorry…" Jack muttered awkwardly, removing his arms from around her. "I—"

"C'mon," said Cammy quietly. "It's time to meet your men."

Moving through the smoke, Jack followed her and gazed up at the four enormous figures towering above him. A pair of blue pinprick irises winked on in each giant's head, expanding to brilliant discs of light.

"*What the bloody 'ell...*" Billy muttered, trailing off.

"My God," Jack said, as he realized what he was looking at. His mouth gaped, and his knees threatened to buckle.

Cammy approached the nearest machine and leaned against its armor casually, folding her arms. In response, the giant craned its head toward her with a clang.

"What—what *are* they?" Jack gasped in shock.

Chewing her gum, Cammy grinned. "Jack Stone—meet the *Tin Can Tommies.*"

# 8

---

# CLOCKWORK MEN

CRACKLES OF BLUE ELECTRICITY backlit smoke which curled from the giants' armor. Crowned by vented Mark I Brodie helmets, the machines stared silently at Jack through bright binocular eyes that protruded from faces of sculpted metal, each different from the next. Their armor, bolted together in plates and fashioned to resemble British infantry battledress, was dented, rusty and speckled with a rainbow of patina. Oversized Webley Mark IV revolvers were holstered at each hip on worn leather gun belts, slung beside an array of tarnished equipment including modified Fairbairn Sykes fighting knives, cartridge belts, and khaki utility pouches. The machines' enormous feet resembled armored hobnail boots with what appeared to be a tread of reinforced tank track beneath. Their barrel chests, each emblazoned with a mottled chrome V, swelled with pride, and Jack noticed they all bore dented bronze plaques engraved with their specs, ranks and serial numbers. At over eight feet in height, each figure was undeniably impressive and imposing.

"*Lancaster!*" Hastings barked.

Jets of steam vented from the joints of the machine beside Cammy. It ground up its gears, ratcheted itself to its full height, and saluted Jack and Billy with a clang.

"Mark One serviceman—designation sergeant, *sir!*" boomed the giant through a face grille that resembled a gas mask. To Jack's surprise, the voice was crusty and old, with just a hint of irritation. And was that a *cockney* accent?

"*Hurricane!*" Hastings continued.

"Mark One serviceman—designation infantryman, *sir!*" The second machine, bulkier than the first and seemingly more powerful, snapped to attention. Its voice gruffer, confident—cocky, even.

"*Mosquito!*"

"Mark One serviceman—designation sapper, *sir!*" The third machine's voice was cooler, more thoughtful and measured, and its design sleeker.

"*Spitfire!*" Hastings yelled, completing his roll call.

The fourth machine, benign looking and smaller than the others, stood motionless, staring vacantly into space in an apparent daydream.

"*Spitfire!*" Hastings repeated, glancing at Cammy irritably.

Putting a thumb and forefinger in her mouth, Cammy gave a shrill, ear-splitting whistle.

The smallest robot started, snapped out of its stupor and stared at her. Cammy jerked her head toward Hastings.

"Uh? Oh, Mark One serviceman—designation medic, *sir!*" The smaller machine's voice was lighter, musical, almost childlike.

"*Atten—tion!*" Hastings barked.

In unison, the four machines raised their right legs and smashed their armored boots onto the workshop floor with a resounding clang and a subsequent cloud of dust. Turning their heads as one, each of the giants stared expectantly at Jack.

Jack looked at Billy, then returned his gaze to the machines in utter disbelief. *Men. Clockwork bloody men.* No wonder Hastings had been so slippery about the goings on here at the castle.

"I don't believe it," Billy gasped, collapsing onto his chair.

"Neither will the Hun when they see these boys in action," Hastings proclaimed proudly.

"Er, perhaps they could introduce themselves, sir?" Cammy offered.

"An excellent suggestion. Sergeant?"

Jack noticed the machine called Lancaster glance at Cammy. She raised an eyebrow like a stern school mistress. Clearly this had been rehearsed, but Jack sensed Lancaster's unwilling participation in the game.

"Well," Lancaster said at last, coughing a deep baritone rumble. "Sergeant Lancaster, reporting for duty—" He cut himself short and looked at Cammy, who glared at him disapprovingly.

"*Sir!*" Lancaster muttered bitterly. He saluted again, and bolts popped from a plate of armor on his rear which fell off, clattering on the floor. "*Bloody 'ell!*" he mumbled. When he stooped to pick it up, another piece of his backside dropped off. Clumsily fumbling for the armor with his oversized fingers, Lancaster picked up the plates and passed them to Cammy. Then he resumed his stance in line, attempting unsuccessfully to retain a modicum of dignity as Hurricane, Mosquito, and Spitfire sniggered beside him.

"These machines," Hastings said, ignoring their amusement, "have been modified to outclass the enemy in every way. They lack, however, the.. *spontaneity* shall we say, that makes your prowess on the battlefield unique."

"Warfare's changed since these guys last saw action," Cammy added. "By teaching them your skills, you'll be giving them the edge they'll need in combat—a *human* edge."

"You want me to *train* 'em?" Jack said, stunned. He looked up at Lancaster. "I don't think—"

"Look, I dunno what these *things* are," Billy said, crossing his arms defensively, "but we put our faith in machines back in Europe. Tanks, navy—*the bleedin' RAF!* And we barely got out alive!"

"I've 'eard enough of this bollocks!" growled Hurricane. Breaking rank, he balled his fists and stormed toward Billy.

"Get back 'ere now!" Lancaster snapped.

"An' you think we're 'appy backing you up, do you?" Hurricane growled, leveling a huge finger at Billy accusingly. "What 'appened to your last unit, eh? *Missin'? Dead?* Don't exactly qualify you in our eyes either, *chum!*"

"Hurricane!" Cammy said, grabbing his arm in a futile attempt to restrain him.

Billy toppled back off his chair, then picked it up and leveled it defensively like a lion tamer.

Lancaster stared down Hurricane. "Back in line, Private, or so 'elp me, I'll—" More armor pranged from his rear. "Oh, for the love of—"

"Yeah, we lost men," Billy spat, "good lads. Now we're talking about, what? Replacing 'em with this—these—*slot machines*?"

Mosquito placed a hand on Hurricane's shoulder. "C'mon, H, orders is ord—"

"Get your bleedin' hand off me!" growled Hurricane, shrugging him off.

"Best do as he says," Billy said defiantly, "or I'm gonna punch your *off* switch!"

Spinning, Hurricane fixed his gaze on Billy. "Oh, that does it," he growled. "I'm gonna introduce you to my *teaching* fist, boy!" He batted the chair from Billy's hand and advanced, raising his fist. "Pick a window, son, you're leavin'!"

"'kay guys, time out!" Cammy stepped between them; her arms outstretched.

Hurricane lunged threateningly, making Billy flinch.

"Hey!" Cammy yelled sternly, trying to push him back.

Glaring at Billy, Hurricane stubbornly stood his ground.

Cammy took a deep breath and exhaled. "C'mon, man," she whispered to Hurricane, conscious that Hastings was watching. "Don't do this to me."

Hurricane continued to stare down Billy.

"*Please, H*," Cammy implored.

Hurricane appeared to think about it for a second, then: "All right, doll. All right." He backed up slowly and resumed his place in line with the other machines, ignoring Lancaster, who shook his head.

"See?" Billy yelled, clearly rattled. "Can't control 'emselves in 'ere, and they want us to trust 'em in the field. No way, Jack! *No bleedin' way!*"

Fuming, Hastings turned to Cammy. "I thought you rehearsed this?" he hissed, then glared at Lancaster. "Is *that* what you call discipline?" Lancaster hung his head with a creak.

Cammy scowled at Hurricane.

"What—this is my fault?" exclaimed the machine.

Cammy maintained her glare.

"Yeah, right, this is my fault," Hurricane muttered grumpily. With a reluctant stride he approached Billy again. "Look, I—I forgot myself for a minute there, mate." The machine extended a huge hand. "No 'ard feelings, eh?"

Billy stared warily at the enormous open palm hovering before him, then flashed a glance at Jack, who in turn looked at Hastings and Cammy. Despite feeling that he and Billy had been tricked into their current predicament, Jack found the girl intriguing. "I guess we have no choice," he said finally.

With a sigh, Billy reluctantly placed his hand on Hurricane's palm. He winced as the machine's giant fingers encircled it.

"Apologies, Billy," rumbled Hurricane.

Billy nodded awkwardly and shook the machine's hand.

Releasing Billy, Hurricane turned on his tread. "*Billy bleedin' Bunter*," he spat cockily.

Spitfire elbowed Mosquito and stifled laughter.

"Oh, the bigger they are, *Frankenstein*," Billy growled, rolling up his sleeves, "the 'arder they fall."

"Billy," Jack warned.

"Ooh, I'm shakin'," Hurricane muttered sarcastically. He paused with his back to Billy. "And just what're you gonna do abou—"

Billy vaulted onto Hurricane's back and covered the machine's eyes with his hands.

Whirling blindly, Hurricane crashed into Lancaster, sending him reeling into the workbench.

"Get off!" Hurricane yelled as Billy clung on for dear life, smashing his fists against the giant's helmet. "*Get him off!*"

"Well," Hastings said, fuming. "Meeting adjourned, I think."

"This was never gonna be easy," said Cammy defensively. "A project this complex was always gonna have teething troubles."

"*Teething troubles?*" Hastings seethed, ducking as Hurricane's flailing arm swept overhead. The machine clattered about the workshop with Billy still on his back. "That's what you call *this?*"

Cammy watched as Jack, Lancaster, Mosquito, and Spitfire attempted to break up the fight.

"Boys will be boys," she offered, weakly.

Hastings' face flushed red. "Lock them down *now!* And get this bloody mess mopped up!" He stormed from the workshop.

Nursing a dent in his forehead, Lancaster joined Cammy.

"Not quite the *historic* foundation of the Commando he envisioned," she said.

"An' you still think this'll work?" Lancaster replied. "Well, I won't say I told you so, Camilla, but…" He turned to watch the madness unfolding before them.

At that moment, Billy was thrown from Hurricane's back into Spitfire, knocking him to the floor. Mosquito reeled, staggering back into Jack and carrying him over Cammy's desk in an explosion of paperwork.

Cammy sighed. She may have been the darling of her faculty's science department back home, but this was something else entirely. Sensing the dawn of a migraine she rubbed her temple and sighed.

This was going to be a hell of a lot tougher than she'd thought.

…

"General Mörder?"

The words sounded hollow, as if down a well.

"Can you hear my voice?"

Fingers snapped somewhere nearby; their sound painful.

"Herr General, can you—"

Mörder tried to open his eyes, only to realize with horror that in the absence of his eyelids, they were already open. He felt a sting as something cold dripped onto his eyeballs, then bright light assaulted them and his kaleidoscope vision focused.

Mörder made out a man and woman standing before him, the man in a white coat, a black uniform beneath, and the woman in white.

"Ah," said the man, stepping back as if to admire a portrait. "There you are. How do you feel? Comfortable I hope. We've given you quite the cocktail, General. My name is Metzker. Doctor Hans Metzker."

Opening his mouth to reply, Mörder heard his flesh rustle like dry leaves, then he coughed.

"Easy," said Metzker. He turned to the woman, who poured water into a glass from a pitcher on a table by Mörder's bed.

"You've been through quite an ordeal," Metzker said, returning his gaze to the general.

Craving fluid, Mörder gagged.

"Don't excite yourself, there's a good fellow." The doctor stepped aside to allow the nurse to approach. She offered Mörder the glass with trembling hands, carefully avoiding his gaze.

As Mörder raised his hands to accept the glass, he saw that they were bandaged tightly, as appeared to be the rest of his body. He touched his face and was shocked to discover that he couldn't feel it.

"Yes, your face is covered too," Metzker said. "Now, prepare yourself, General. You've suffered extensive third-degree burns. Had it not been for explicit orders from Berlin, we would have long since given up hope." The doctor paused, then: "The deep skin containing your free nerve endings was all but destroyed in the blaze. I know this isn't easy for you to hear, but your ability to feel pain, to feel *anything* in fact, will now be significantly diminished." The doctor checked a clipboard on Mörder's bed. "You've been through a number of skin grafts already, and on Berlin's insistence we've scheduled many more." He smiled at Mörder. "That said, with what you've experienced, you're a very lucky man."

*Lucky?*

Where was Mörder's Luger when he needed it?

Once more raising a bandaged hand to take the glass, he found that, save for a dull sensation of contact, his fingertips were devoid of any feeling. But Mörder cupped the glass numbly and leaned forward to drink. He sensed the coolness of the water on his tongue—then felt it seep between his teeth through holes where his cheeks should have been. It dripped from his facial dressings, pattering onto his bandaged legs from whatever his mouth had become.

"Well, one thing at a time, eh?" said Metzker sympathetically. "Your wife is here, General. I imagine you'd like to see her?"

*Magda?*

Mörder hadn't imagined she'd be there. He'd been away for so long on campaigns that he'd barely had time for his family. The thought of seeing his wife, of her seeing him, had never occurred to him until now. The war had taken its toll on their marriage, and while he and Magda had grown distant in recent years, Mörder realized that he was going to need her now more than ever. And then of course there was their daughter, Ilsa. The repercussions of what he'd endured, and the implications to his family, suddenly overwhelmed him. He retched on the water.

"*Not heeer—*" he hissed. "*Not... like thiss!*"

"Nonsense," said the doctor, taking the glass. "No time like the present, eh? It may take a while for your wife to acclimate to your appearance, but in my opinion that's exactly why you should—"

A gasp sounded behind Metzker.

Looking up, Mörder saw Magda stood in the doorway. Every inch the general's wife, she was beautifully dressed and manicured, a credit to bourgeois Berlin.

"Ah, come in, my dear," urged Metzker.

Magda took a hesitant step forward.

"I was about to show your husband his new face. I think you'll be quite impress—"

"Ernst?" Magda gasped. "Is it—you?" Her concern was visible beneath the black net of her wide-brimmed hat. Her trembling hands clutched her purse. She was clad in scarlet, with a fox fur around her neck —a gift caught by her husband during Göring's last hunt near his lodge in Schorfheide forest.

It had been months since Mörder had seen her, but she was still beautiful. He opened his mouth to speak but managed only a cough as he gagged again.

"Easy," Metzker said, placing a kidney dish containing surgical tools on the bed beside Mörder. "Seeing one's new face for the first time is no small thing," the doctor said, taking a scalpel from the dish and carefully cutting the bandages behind Mörder's head. As he slowly unraveled them, he looked back at Magda. "But fear not, Frau Mörder, we're trained to deal with every eventuality."

Mörder could not see his own face, but he could see Magda's reaction, could watch her recoil as the doctor unraveled a line of bandage from what he was now sure must be a blackened jawbone, all flesh incinerated from it.

"I think you'll find that while your husband's appearance has changed somewhat," Metzker continued, "he's still very much the same man you marr—"

Mörder grabbed Metzker's hand and glared rage from behind his bandages.

"I appreciate this is a shock," Metzker said shakily. Standing, he collected himself and turned to Magda. "I'll give you both some time." He left the room abruptly. The nurse looked relieved to follow.

"*Maghda*," wheezed Mörder. "*Wiffe…*"

A glimmer of recognition flashed across Magda's face, consumed quickly by disgust and then revulsion.

"*Can you sstill… love me?*" Mörder rasped.

"Love?" Magda looked suddenly nauseous. She turned away, ashamed. "I *never* loved you!"

It was a lie, of course. In the early years of their marriage Magda had been deeply devoted to her husband, but as his career had become his mistress, so too had Magda's dependence on her husband's ambition to maintain their affluent lifestyle. After the birth of their daughter, the couple had become distant, cold, and their love turned to resentment. Bonded by an unspoken pact, they had remained together for party appearances only, and for Ilsa who favored her father's devotions over her mother's dependence on the bottle. In Magda's eyes, her marriage had become a charade, and her husband the pathetic monster who now gawked helplessly at her with wide, unblinking eyes.

"*Maggda?*" Mörder edged himself off his bed and tried to stand, but his legs betrayed him, and he collapsed to the floor, reaching out. "*Pleasse!*"

Magda stepped back, horrified. She held a silk handkerchief to her mouth, tears flowing uncontrollably. What her husband had been, and what he'd now become. She had no words. Magda turned away, unable to look at him.

Metzker appeared at the door.

"I can't do this," Magda said. "I didn't want to come here. I need to leave. Now."

"*My... Magdda*," Mörder hissed. He reached out for her again, but his fingers raked her skirt like dry twigs.

Magda cried out, retreating to the door.

"Your reaction is perfectly normal," Metzker soothed. "In time, many wives learn to—"

"That *thing* is not my husband," Magda choked, her eyes wet, bloodshot.

"*Maggda!*" begged Mörder, trying desperately to claw across the tiled floor toward her.

"I want to go now," she said, staring at Metzker. "*Please.*"

With a reluctant glance at Mörder, the doctor pursed his lips, then nodded and stood aside as another figure appeared at the door.

"Magda, my darling, are you—" August Mench, his arm bandaged, stared in shock at his general.

Blood drained from Mench's face. "*My God...*"

Mörder's eyes widened at the sight of his adjutant. "*Menchh!*"

"Frau Mörder," the doctor pleaded. "I implore you to please reconsider."

"My husband is *dead*, Doctor, do you hear me?" She shot a look back at Mörder. "He's dead." Another wave of tears assaulted her and she turned to Mench. "Take me home."

"Of course." Mench took her hand and glanced back at his former master, then escorted her from the room.

Metzker collected his thoughts, then: "Well, I understand this must be quite distressing," he said, crouching beside Mörder. "Let's get you back into bed and we can—"

"*What haffe you done?*" Mörder hissed, gripping the doctor's wrist.

"Herr General," Metzker gasped. "I merely wished to—"

Mörder grabbed him with both hands, pulling him to the floor.

"*Basstard!*"

"*Herr General!*" Metzker choked as Mörder's hands encircled his throat, then he flailed, snatching a handful of Mörder's bedsheets and sending the surgical tray clattering onto the tiles. His hand found the scalpel, and he grabbed it, thrusting the blade into Mörder's back.

The general paused as he felt the impact, but no pain. Then he rose up over Metzker, gripping the man's head with both hands, and drove his thumbs deep into the doctor's eye sockets. Blood oozed up around them as Metzker shrieked. Mörder raised the doctor's head and smashed it onto the floor, cracking the man's skull, and the tiles beneath it, with a sickening crunch.

Metzker's thrashing ceased.

Gasping for air, Mörder slid from the doctor's body. He wrenched the scalpel from his back and examined the blade.

No pain. Fascinating.

"I just saw Magda," said a familiar voice.

Von Ribbentrop stood in the doorway. He took a silver case from his pocket, opened it, and removed a cigarette. "And I understand how you must feel." He closed the case, lit the cigarette, and handed it to Mörder.

Mörder took a drag, coughing as if it was his first. He felt the smoke invade his lungs, robust and heavy, enticing him to take another hit as his muscles slowly relaxed.

"They say the heartache you feel today is the strength you feel tomorrow," Von Ribbentrop mused. "I'm here at the Führer's request, Ernst, to offer you that *tomorrow*. A second chance."

Mörder exhaled smoke, his labored breathing subsiding.

"Do you accept your Führer's command?"

Mörder stared at Metzker's corpse. The man's death had made him feel *alive*. And the scalpel? It appeared his misfortune at Dunkirk had rendered him *invincible*. What strength! He'd picked the man's skull apart like warm strudel. And now that he had this power, Mörder intended to use it: against his enemies in Berlin, the Allies, against his bastard opportunist of an adjutant and yes, even against that bitch whore of a wife who had denied him. He would make them all suffer just as he suffered; destroy them as he'd been destroyed.

Mörder nodded slowly.

"Then welcome back to the land of the living," said Von Ribbentrop. He smiled; his master's task accomplished.

Mörder noticed that he was surrounded by a pool of Metzker's blood. The gore had permeated his dressings like ink on litmus paper, turning the cotton scarlet.

It was a baptism.

Mörder was ready to see his Führer.

The Jackal of Danzig lived—and the world would hear his howl!

# 9

---

# KEEP CALM AND CARRY ON

**H**ASTINGS FUMED SILENTLY behind his desk, the tips of his oiled moustache ticking involuntarily.

"You are the pathfinders for an *elite*," he said firmly. "Act as such, or you're out on your arses, is that understood?"

"Sir," Billy said, his right eye purple and swollen.

"Yes, sir," Hurricane muttered, his left eye lens dangling on a stalk of colored wires.

Hastings glowered at them. "You're both damn lucky I don't throw you out and be done with you." He shuffled papers irritably. "Hurricane, I'm placing you on stand down."

"*What?*" Hurricane protested. "C'mon Brig'!"

"Order in the ranks there!" Lancaster growled, standing nearby with Jack.

"Briggs, I'm demoting you to *private* status, effective immediately."

"You what?" Billy said.

"Henceforth you'll report to Sergeant Lancaster."

Billy's eyes widened. He darted a glance at Jack.

"Something to say, Captain?" Hastings said, an eyebrow raised.

Against Jack's better judgment, he held his tongue—for now.

"No, sir."

"But Jack—" Billy protested.

Hastings put down his paperwork. "Dismissed."

Billy and Hurricane stamped to attention and saluted.

"About turn," Lancaster ordered. "By the left... left, right, left, right, left—"

Marching out double time, Billy and Hurricane stomped toward the door—and wedged beside each other in its frame.

"Out of my way, *Private!*" Hurricane growled.

"Bloody *private!*" Billy spat. "This ain't over, dustbin!"

Forcing himself through the door, Hurricane chuckled, a deep throaty rumble that continued until he walked into a wall. He cursed as his eye lens detached from its wiring, bouncing across the floor and rolling into Billy's hobnail boot.

Billy picked it up and dangled it in front of the machine like a conker on a string. "*Lookin'* for something?" he said, pleased to finally have the upper hand, even if it was a bad joke.

"Oi, that's me eye!" Hurricane snapped. "Give it 'ere!" He snatched his eye from Billy's hand, and tried unsuccessfully to screw it back into its housing. Billy walked off down the corridor.

"Yeah, keep walkin', soldier!" Hurricane yelled, following. "You gotta get up pretty early to get one over on old Hurric—" He smashed into a low beam and crashed onto the floor.

Hearing the clatter, Billy sighed. The machine was bloody annoying, but he was also a fellow soldier. "You're going soft Billy, my lad," he muttered to himself.

He turned and walked back down the corridor. "C'mon," he said, extending a hand. "I'll 'elp you back to the workshop."

"I'm fine!" Hurricane growled, feeling his way up the wall and finally standing with his back to Billy.

"Just shut it and let me 'elp you, or you'll be 'ere all bleedin' night."

"I said—I'm *fine!*"

Billy ducked as the robot spun around, nearly knocking him off his feet. Stumbling, Hurricane staggered headfirst into another wall.

"Sure you are, *Hawkeye*." Billy took his arm. "C'mon!"

Protesting, Hurricane finally allowed Billy to lead him up the corridor. "*Dustbin?*" Hurricane muttered. "Cheeky bleeder!"

Billy smiled. This contraption was no Enigma machine, but against all better judgement, he was beginning to warm to this strange mechanical soldier.

. . .

Hastings looked from Jack to Lancaster, who stood before his desk.

"I needn't remind you both of the importance that this team succeeds."

"Hurricane's headstrong, sir," said Lancaster, "but he'll fall in line."

Hastings looked expectantly at Jack.

*Play the game*, Jack thought. "When it comes down to it, sir, Billy— *Private Briggs*—will do the same."

"There," Hastings said. "Common ground at last. No hard feelings on Briggs' demotion I hope, Captain?"

"None sir," Jack lied.

"We can't have two sergeants in the same team now, can we?"

Jack felt Lancaster stiffen in preparation for his response but he held his tongue.

"Good show," said Hastings. "Training commences at oh six-hundred hours, gentlemen. That will be all."

With a salute, Jack and Lancaster stepped out into the corridor.

As the door closed behind them, Lancaster started to walk away.

What a mess. Jack forced himself to offer an olive branch.

"Look Sergeant, I—"

"I've got work to do," Lancaster muttered without turning. He marched off up the corridor.

Alone now, Jack looked down at his boots. They'd only been there a day, and already Billy had been demoted and Jack was being forced to calm the waters with a bolshy bloody machine.

A storm outside howled through the fortress's battlements.

"*Bugger…*" Jack said to no one in particular. He thrust his hands into his pockets and stormed off in the opposite direction to Lancaster.

. . .

Cammy looked up from her welding as Billy entered the workshop supporting Hurricane. She switched off her blowtorch, pulled an oily rag from her pocket, and wiped her hands.

"Good day, boys?" she asked, pushing her goggles up onto her forehead.

"I've 'ad better," Hurricane muttered, groaning as he leaned against the door.

"Me too," Billy said, loosening his tunic collar and taking a seat at the workbench. He took Hurricane's eye lens from his pocket and gently placed it down.

"Hastings tear you a new one, huh?" Cammy said.

"Not 'alf," Billy replied wearily.

Cammy pulled a flashlight from her tool belt and looked at Hurricane. "Okay ol' timer, lemme take a look at that eye."

"Oi, less of the *old*, kid!" Hurricane exclaimed.

Cammy grinned as she grabbed Hurricane's collar armor and pulled him toward her. Standing on tiptoe, she clicked on her flashlight and shone it around the Tommy's eye socket. "Man, that is one jacked-up eye!" she said, shaking her head. "You've got a hell of a dueling scar, boy." She looked at Billy. "You did quite a number on him, Sergeant."

Billy winced apologetically. "It's *Private* now, actually," he muttered.

Hurricane chuckled—a baritone rumble that echoed around the workshop.

"*Shut it!*" Billy snapped, but Hurricane's laughter was contagious, and Billy started to chuckle as well. "I s'pose it *was* a bit of a scene," he said, smiling.

"I'll say." Cammy patted Hurricane's breastplate. "Okay, honey, go get into your cage."

Hurricane took several steps back and mounted a raised metal grid running the length of the workshop wall which glowed orange, humming faintly. Above it was welded four enclosed sections of caging, a ladder beside each one, and Hurricane slotted himself into a section and seemed to exhale. Mosquito and Spitfire stood motionless in sections of their own further along the wall.

"Evenin'," Billy said to the other Tommies.

"They can't hear you," Cammy said with a smile.

Billy frowned. "Why not?"

"They're on stand down," Hurricane said. "*Sleep*. Gives Cam 'ere time to poke around our innards in the name o' science."

Cammy unbuckled his gun belt.

"Wax 'n' a polish while you're down there, love," Hurricane said, the blue of his one good eye winking off and on cheekily at Billy.

"You wish," Cammy said, grimacing as she lifted his enormous gun belt up onto a hook. She pulled a wrench from her tool belt and climbed the ladder beside Hurricane's cage until she was level with his head, then, leaning across his shoulder, grabbed two recessed handles on the upper portion of his helmet and heaved it back on a rear hinge, exposing the inside of Hurricane's skull—a complex collection of cogs, brass mechanisms and electrical wiring.

"Don't go messin' with nothin' you might break!" Hurricane said grumpily.

"Your faith in me's overwhelming, pal."

"Sorry," Hurricane said, then he looked down at Billy. "An' I'm sorry about—"

"Save it," Billy said. "Me too."

"See you at roll call?"

Billy nodded.

"Sweet dreams, champ," Cammy sighed, reaching inside Hurricane's head with her wrench.

"G'night darlin'," Hurricane replied.

Cammy twisted the wrench, and Hurricane's lone headlight dimmed, shrinking to a pinprick and winking out with a compressed hiss.

"Looks like you made a friend," Cammy said, descending the ladder. "That's no small thing with my man here."

"He's all right," Billy said.

"All right?" Cammy exclaimed, raising an eyebrow. "He's *magnificent*."

"You're proud of him?"

"Of them all." Placing her wrench on the workbench, Cammy picked up Hurricane's eye lens and examined it. "This has to work, Briggs. You know that, right?"

"Call me Billy," he said, offering his hand. "And yes, I do. Look I— I'm sorry about earlier. I use my gob before my brain sometimes, y'know? No 'ard feelings, eh?"

Cammy suddenly felt enormous sympathy for the man. Having worked with four rusty metal ones, she knew what an effort it took for a soldier to apologize to anyone, let alone a *woman*.

She took his hand and shook it firmly. "*No 'ard feelings*," she growled, in a gruff approximation of Billy's accent.

Laughing awkwardly, Billy shoved his hands into his pockets. "Well, I'd best be off." He headed for the door.

"Billy?" Cammy said.

He turned to look at her.

"Thanks. Thanks for bringing him home."

For a second, she saw Billy's expression soften. Had she broken through? Gotten him on-side? If so, then Captain Stone would surely follow? Time would tell.

Billy smiled, nodded, and left the workshop.

Cammy exhaled. The room was silent again save for the humming of her freshly repaired generator. She picked up Hurricane's detached lens and spat on it, polishing it on her dungarees, then grabbed her wrench and started up the ladder.

"Not often I see him stuck for words," said a man's voice.

Startled, Cammy twisted and lost her footing, toppling from the ladder into Jack's arms.

He put her down gently and smiled.

Cammy struggled to regain her composure. "You make a habit of sneaking up on defenseless women, Captain?"

"Defenseless?" Jack said, nodding at the wrench in her hand. "I think you're the kinda girl who can take care of herself."

Cammy straightened her clothes, suppressing a smile. "An' don't you forget it." She started back up the ladder.

Jack looked around the workshop and approached a tarpaulin covered object in a corner. "What's under here?" he asked, curious.

"That?" Setting her wrench on Hurricane's shoulder, Cammy slid down the ladder and joined him. She heaved off the tarp revealing a battered MK-1 tank.

"You got a *Matilda?*" Jack said, fascinated.

"You know tanks?" Cammy exclaimed; the young soldier had just gone up a notch in her estimation. "They sure don't make 'em like this baby anymore."

"For good reason," Jack scoffed.

"Don't let the boys hear you say that," Cammy said. "They're older than she is." She patted the tank affectionately. "And just like them, this girl's seen her fair share of action."

"It's falling to pieces," Jack said, sliding his finger through a bullet hole in the tank's armor.

"I like to fix broken things," said Cammy, "make 'em better than they were before, y'know? You just gotta see past the damage—see the beauty within." Cammy ran her fingers lovingly over the tank's freckled patina.

"You really love this stuff, huh?" Jack said.

"How can you not? She's *kick-ass*, Captain." Cammy took a step back and gazed at the machine. "A real *trench-stomper!*"

Jack shook his head. "I'm glad you're on our side, lady."

"I told you already, call me Cammy."

"And you might as well call me Jack, since we're knee-deep in this mess together now."

"Mess?" Cammy smiled. "Oh, you ain't seen nothin' yet." She picked up the tarp and started to re-cover the Matilda. Jack took a corner and helped.

"Thanks," Cammy said when they'd finished. She returned to Hurricane and swung up his chest plate like the hood of a car.

Deep within his workings, Jack saw what looked like a modified motorcycle petrol tank.

Cammy pulled a hose from a fuel bowser beside the cages, unscrewed the cap on Hurricane's tank, then inserted the hose nozzle and depressed the trigger, releasing fuel.

"They originally used these as a power source," she explained as she repeated the process with Mosquito. "That's why I built the cages, an' fitted the boys with batteries so they can charge up quicker for longer. But they still like to stay topped up, for old times' sake I guess."

Jack gazed up at the Tommies. The potential of what stood before him was more than anything he'd ever dreamt of, and they were *his* to command. Jack thought about the day's events and realized he'd been everything his record had accused him of.

*You're arrogant, impetuous and stubborn, with a total disregard for the rules or your chain of command…*

Churchill had been right, lauding Jack for those qualities but that didn't make him feel proud, and somehow in Cammy's presence, Jack wanted to appear worthy of the responsibility he'd been given. Despite Lancaster's resistance, Jack *was* beginning to see a bigger picture, and the possibilities of what might be achieved with these machines.

Jack noticed Cammy studying him. She looked away quickly and shivered. "Cold tonight." She rubbed her hands together and blew into them. "I got a flask of hot chocolate—you want some?"

"Please," Jack said gratefully.

Cammy took a battered tin thermos from her desk drawer, sat and poured chocolate into two chipped enamel mugs.

She flinched when Jack draped his great coat around her shoulders.

"It's just a coat," he said gently. "Keep you warm."

"Thanks." Cammy smiled, a little embarrassed. "Maybe Hastings got you all wrong."

"Yeah?" Jack said, taking a seat opposite Cammy. "So what'd he say?"

"That you're young, inexperienced."

"Ah," Jack said, looking into his mug. "Anything else?"

"Oh yeah," Cammy said. "But I like to form my own opinions."

"Good," Jack replied, enjoying the game. "How am I doing?"

"That remains to be seen," Cammy said. "But you get bonus points for tank knowledge."

Jack grinned.

"I like your friend Billy."

Jack nodded, still looking into his mug.

"How're you holding up?" Cammy asked.

"Me?" With all the madness of the day's events, Jack hadn't had time to think about it. He changed the subject. "How'd you get involved in all this anyway?"

"Believe me, I've asked myself the same thing," Cammy said. "I studied at Princeton under a genius. Churchill asked Roosevelt for a quantum engineer—I drew the short straw on his recommendation. Six weeks ago, I hauled these guys outta crates at the MOD and was flown up here to the back of beyond with 'em." She looked at the Mark Ones affectionately. "Now I've got over the shock, I've grown quite fond of these knuckleheads, despite their sass." She took a sip of her chocolate. "Your turn, Captain."

Jack shook his head and sighed. "I was never much good at school, but I was always good in a fight. Ah, I dunno—*guns*, *men*, I understand. But *this*? What the hell are they anyway?"

"Honestly? I still don't know. Hastings limits my access to their records. But as far as I can tell, everything in those heads is as it was mothballed in 1918. I figure they feed off've some kinda *sentience* engine, but as to what the source material was?" Cammy shrugged.

Jack's leg ached, and he rubbed it and winced.

Cammy caught the movement. "You've seen action?" she asked.

"Yeah. Yeah, I was posted to Norway, well, me 'n' Bill."

"What happened?"

"The Nazis. Routed us back through Belgium into France, then they tore us a new one."

"I read about the things you did. The men you saved."

"I couldn't save everyone," Jack said quietly, lost in a distant memory. He looked beyond Cammy at the empty cage beside Hurricane. "You're missing one."

Cammy followed his gaze. "Lanc? He's usually last to roll in. Probably still in his garden."

"His what?"

"You'll have to ask him about that. Hastings turns a blind eye. Lanc keeps to himself at stand down, guess it's a rank thing." Cammy leaned forward and topped up Jack's chocolate. "You know," she added, "this is kind of historic. What you're about to do here, I mean. We should toast the occasion, don't you think?"

"A toast?" Jack said in surprise.

"You're a limey, man," Cammy joked. "Didn't you guys practically invent toasts."

"Well, I know one," Jack said, rising to her challenge. He held up his chipped mug and smiled. "Here's to those who wish us well, and those who don't can go to hell!"

Cammy smiled and raised her mug, clinking it against Jack's, and joined him in downing her chocolate.

Jack looked at her expectantly, a thick moustache of chocolate lining his upper lip.

Cammy laughed.

"What?" Jack said, pouring more chocolate. "C'mon, a toast!"

"Okay, okay, I got one," Cammy said, raising her mug. "Here's to the changes life may bring even through the toughest trials. May we always do our best and then if not? Embrace denial!"

"Yes!" Jack hammered the table with his fist. "I mean *deep*—but yes!"

Their laughter subsided, leaving the workshop silent but for the heartbeat throb of the generator.

"And this *will* be tough," Cammy said, suddenly serious. "You know that, right?"

Jack looked from Cammy to the Tommies. On the strength of day one alone it wasn't going to be easy, and the odds were loaded against them, *impossible* even, but in the presence of this amazing woman Jack felt that somehow anything might be possible.

So perhaps there was hope after all.

Jack nodded. "Maybe for now we should just say—good luck."

"Amen to that." Cammy raised her mug, clinked Jack's, then drained it. She tipped her thermos to refill it, but it was dry.

"Ah, it's getting late anyway," Jack said, rising. "I'll see you tomorrow?"

"Are you kidding? After today, I wouldn't miss it." She stood to remove his great coat.

"Keep it," Jack said softly. "Cold in here."

Cammy nodded gratefully. "Thank you again."

For a second their eyes met, lingered—the young man whose achievements belied his age, and the woman whose age belied her achievements.

"Well, g'night," Jack said. He turned and left the workshop.

Cammy pulled his great coat around her. The room had grown a little warmer for Jack's company, she thought.

She climbed the ladder beside Hurricane and picked up her wrench from his shoulder. Noticing a blemish on his faceplate, she pulled the rag from her pocket and buffed the mark.

"Looks like we all made a new friend today, huh pal?"

...

Night was drawing in as Jack crossed the parade ground. The blizzard had subsided and the air was chill and crisp. He paused as he heard a curious digging sound, then followed the noise along the corrugated wall of a Nissen hut and peered around its corner.

Lancaster was crouched in front of a rose plant in what appeared to be a crudely dug allotment. Wiping snow from its base, the machine gently spaded mulch over the roots, then picked up a child's watering can and sprinkled water.

"Digging for victory, Sergeant?" Jack said, stepping out.

"Eh? Oh…" Startled, the old machine clattered to his treads. "Yes sir, very good."

"Sullivan said you might be out here. I hear you like gardening?"

"I like to grow things, sir," Lancaster rumbled. "Roses, mostly." He noticed Jack staring at the orange blossom beside him. "This is *Autumn Sunset*—she's a hardy climber." He cupped the plant's leaves softly in his huge iron fingers. "I call 'er *Molly*."

"She's beautiful," Jack observed awkwardly. Spending time with Cammy had changed him in some way. He felt different. As if he now owned the situation and had to make the best of it.

His interest appeared to buoy Lancaster's enthusiasm. "Y'see, even 'ere in this bleak bloody place, she can still survive a winter or two. Gives me 'ope."

"Hope?" Jack frowned.

"That life can adapt, sir, *survive*. There's magic, don't you think, in giving life, not takin' it."

"I can't argue with that," Jack replied, encouraged by the tone of their discourse; it was almost conversational.

"You just 'ave to nourish 'er, see? Feed 'er, give 'er space to grow, and that's always best done," Lancaster turned his back on Jack, "by a *seasoned* hand."

*Oh, here we go*, Jack thought. "Look, Lancaster, I know you don't agree with my command."

"You'll pardon me for saying so, Captain, but—you're a *young* man."

"Meaning?"

"I 'ave doubts, *serious* doubts, about your ability to lead this team."

"Anything else?" Jack said. He was done playing the nice guy.

"I hear you take chances, sir—*risks*. In my day, men was disciplined; they followed orders."

"Blindly."

"We got the job done," Lancaster said soberly. "My lads follow my orders—*my* orders. And that's the reason we're still operational. The thought of you taking chances with 'em, well…"

"Look, Lancaster, my job here's to do just that—but I've no intention of losing anyone along the way."

"Let's 'ope so."

Lancaster ratcheted himself up to his full imposing height, folding his arms disapprovingly.

Flecks of snow drifted between them as a bugle in the distance sounded the "Last Post."

"Time to *stand down*, sir," Lancaster said finally, handing Jack his watering can. "G'night."

Whistling a tune through his grille, the old sergeant sauntered back to the castle.

# 10

## BOOTNECKS

THE MORNING SUN GLITTERED across Loch Arkaig as lapwings hailed the dawn.

At the edge of the tangled forest which bordered the castle's estate, stag and red deer grazed on dew-laden heather in the shade of pine and spruce while black grouse bobbed through the bracken chittering gossip.

Closer to home, the castle's human inhabitants awoke, just as they always did, to the ceremonial skirl of a Great Highland bagpipe sounding "Reveille" from the castle's courtyard, stirring them to another day's labor.

...

As Achnacarry drew slowly to life, Hastings stood at his office window and watched a tattered Union Jack fluttering wildly from the castle's battlements. Much like the country, it was holding on by its fingertips.

The Brigadier, shouldering a mountain of concern, had been awake since daybreak completing the new team's training roster. *Commando One* as this first unit was to be called, would be led by Jack Stone with Lancaster as its Sergeant. The rest of the group, all specialists in their field, would provide additional back-up and support.

But Stone wasn't the leader for this team, Hastings thought, and the qualities extolled by Churchill in the boy would have had him kicked out of Hasting's army were it not for the old man's backing. Still, it was the PM's decision to make and that was the end of it.

Hastings sipped his tea and winced. It was lukewarm.

He noticed Cammy crossing the courtyard, struggling with an armful of papers. Wading ankle-deep through snow, she headed toward the stairwell which led to her workshop, and disappeared from sight.

Hearing a knock, Hastings turned to see Phipps in the doorway holding a tray.

"Good morning, Brigadier," chirped his ADC. "I've made you a fresh cup sir, just as you like it: Earl Grey, hot, with a dash of lemon."

"Thank you, Phipps."

The ADC's disposition was at times, a little *too* sunny given the gravity of their country's predicament, but his intrusion this morning was a welcome one.

"Will there be anything else, sir?" Phipps said, placing the tray on Hastings' desk and offloading its contents.

The Brigadier said nothing. Preoccupied, he stared at the flag.

"Sir?" Phipps repeated.

Hastings turned. "No. Thank you Phipps that will be all."

"Very good, sir."

Phipps closed the door. Hastings sat and poured his tea. He glanced up at a filing cabinet in the corner of his office. Much like any other, it was tall, grey and dinged here and there.

And within it—the Tommies' files.

Files that Sullivan had so frequently pressed him for.

It was also a cabinet, Hastings mused with mild unease as he quietly sipped his Earl Grey, that hid a secret.

A secret that could win the war.

. . .

Deep beneath the castle, Cammy stepped into her workshop juggling coffee, schematics and a whirlwind of concern. A slice of toast was clenched between her teeth.

When she reached her desk, she let the papers slide from her arms but they hit her coffee mug splashing a steaming wave of joe across her notes.

"Aw, shit!"

She wiped the coffee from her desk with an arm, then picked up her dripping paperwork and draped it over a heating pipe beside her newly installed generator. She threw the generator's lever and sent crackles of electricity coursing into the cages.

"Rise 'n' shine, boys!" she shouted.

The machines shuddered to life, their pinprick irises expanding to brilliant blue headlights as each Tommy looked in turn at their neighbor, then at Cammy.

Lancaster rubbed the back of his squeaking neck and reached for an oilcan. "Good morning, Camilla," he said, then glanced down the line at the other machines. "All right, you scruffy 'erberts—let's be 'avin' you!"

The other machines shook their heads.

"Ain't you ever off duty?" Hurricane muttered.

"England expects every man to do his duty," said Lancaster, "just as I expect you to do yours. Do that private, and victory is assured."

Hurricane rolled his eyes but said nothing.

"Big day today, Lanc," Cammy said, approaching the cages. "You ready to roll?"

"As I'll ever be," Lancaster grumbled despondently.

Cammy lifted a flap beneath his arm and plugged an oil feed into his torso, then sidestepped to Hurricane. His newly repaired eye flickered to full brilliance as he stared down at her.

"See you survived the night, bruiser," Cammy joked. "Shoulda nicknamed you Joe Louis!"

"That big jessie?" Hurricane boomed, as if his manliness was affronted. "I'd have 'im on the ropes any day!" He jabbed the air like a boxer, ducking blows from an invisible opponent. There was a rattle in his skull, and he shook his head irritably from side to side. "You sure nothin's loose up there?"

"Aside from the screws?" Mosquito mumbled to Spitfire.

"I 'eard that, nonce!" Hurricane growled. "That's strike one, you got two more!"

Hurricane had never gotten along with Mosquito. Truth be told, he'd never really liked the machine who appeared to be closer to Spitfire in age and temperament. He felt equally uncomfortable at times with Lancaster, who could be obstinate and irascible. In fact, he realized that based on the previous day's events he actually felt more of an affinity with the newcomer, Billy Briggs, than he did with his fellow machines.

Cammy pulled him down toward her and shone her flashlight into his ear grille. "Ah, that's where my spanner got to," she said. "Well, it'll do no harm; I'll get it later." She moved over to Mosquito. "How 'bout you, Moz? She plugged in his oil feed. "Ready to wow 'em today?"

"I was born ready!" he said coolly. He polished his armor with a rag while checking his reflection in a piece of broken mirror. "Not sure I can top 'urricane's little show yesterday though."

"*Strike two, sapper!* You're gonna be pickin' up your nuts with a broken arm in a minute!" Hurricane swiped at Mosquito.

Mosquito recoiled from the blow. "'Ere now, watch me finish! I'm buffin' here!"

"Bugger your bloody buffin'!" Hurricane growled. If he'd had sleeves, he would've rolled them up and gone to town on the vain hunk of scrap.

"Order in the ranks!" Lancaster yelled.

Hurricane and Mosquito reluctantly resumed their stance.

Cammy rolled her eyes. They hadn't even gotten to the parade ground yet and the boys were already at each other's throats.

"Allo, beautiful," Mosquito said, admiring his reflection in the mirror.

"That bleedin' face'd make onions cry," Hurricane said.

"You've no class, Hurricane," Mosquito replied, admiring himself. "No *joie de vivr.*"

"Bloody frog lingo!" said Hurricane. "You're meant to be a soldier, son—*a killin' machine!*"

"Don't you worry, H," said Mosquito, "When it comes down to it mate, I'll do my bit. Just you wait n'see. I'll—"

Hurricane swatted Mosquito. Mosquito swatted back.

"Oi, I said order!" Lancaster yelled. "Order in the—"

Cammy left Lancaster to referee them, and sidestepped to Spitfire. "How you doin', honey?"

"Cam, how comes I'm the youngest?" chirped the machine in its childlike voice.

"Huh?" The question caught Cammy off guard. She'd always viewed the Tommies as being different ages, with Spitfire the youngest and worthy therefore of a little more attention than the others. He was inquisitive with a real love of nature, plus he was also the least *soldierly* of the four, who were all so different in attitudes and temperament. Spitfire had never commented on this fact before, and his sudden realization implied significant self-awareness. Deep down, perhaps, he possessed some long-forgotten knowledge of their genesis; knowledge that had thus far eluded Cammy. She'd wanted to know more of course, but Hastings had always denied her, claiming that all records other than the ones she'd been provided with were on a strictly *need to know* basis. *Goddammit*, Cammy thought, looking into Spitfire's blue eyes, *I need to know!*

"The others're so much… *older* than me," Spitfire continued. "How comes I, I'm—"

Standing on tiptoe, Cammy put a gentle hand on his faceplate and whispered into his ear grille. "I don't have all the answers yet, baby, but I'll let you in on a secret." She looked down the line at the other machines, who continued to argue. "You're my best boy. *Perfect*, just as you are."

Spitfire turned bashfully away, shuffling from tread to tread.

Cammy returned to her desk with a smile. "Okay, boys, play nice," she said, checking her watch. "You got half an hour to prep." She bit her lip in trepidation of the day yet to come. "Then it's up 'n' at 'em!"

...

Slumped on the end of his bunk in threadbare long johns, Billy yawned. He was hungry, having long since polished off the biscuits he'd pilfered from Hastings' office, and the remains of his daily rations. He was also bloody cold, having spent the night shivering in the tin pot Nissen hut that Phipps had given the boys to bivvy in. His terrible night's sleep had been compounded by Jack's foul mood after returning from his chat with Lancaster—a *mood* that had resulted in Jack pacing back and forth most of the night like a lunatic.

And now he was ranting about it all over again.

"I still can't believe it!" Jack raved. "The old bugger stared me down last night bold as brass! *Bold as bloody brass!*" Jack cursed Lancaster and every other machine he'd ever encountered.

"Look, all I'm saying," Billy said, "is that we're 'ere now, aren't we? So we should try 'n' make the best of it."

"You've changed your tune!" Jack said.

"Yeah, well, that 'urricane's not such a bad lad," Billy said. "And the girl—"

"Cammy."

Billy smiled.

Jack glared. "What?" He turned away. "That's her name, isn't it?"

"As if you didn't know," Billy said. "She's nice."

"Yeah," Jack said, calming. He gazed out of the window toward the castle. "She's all right."

As if struck by some new resolve, Jack opened a cupboard beside his bunk and took out his freshly pressed uniform. He noticed Billy watching.

"Well, what're you waiting for, Bill? Let's get fed 'n' watered. We're gonna show that old bugger what it is to be *real* soldiers."

...

At oh six hundred hours, Commando One stood in formation in full battledress on the parade square before Hastings. Behind him stood a rugged-looking man who appeared to be made from the same grit and granite as the mountains surrounding the castle. Seemingly impervious to the cold, he wore standard khaki uniform from the waist down, and braces over an undershirt, with his sleeves rolled up to his elbows revealing muscular forearms covered with tattoos.

"Today, a new era dawns," Hastings said with military bristle. "And a new breed of soldier is born: *The Commando*."

Looking down the line, Jack saw Lancaster watching him. The machine quickly faced forward again.

"The gentleman to my left is Sergeant Mungo McNulty," Hastings declared. "For the duration of your training here, he will be your drill-instructor, and he will treat you all as regular privates, irrespective of rank."

"You may be special forces, boys," McNulty growled, "but you ain't *that* special."

"Make us proud, Commando One,' Hastings said, "and good luck to you all."

Hastings strode from the parade square and joined Cammy on its periphery.

McNulty's gaze swept over the team like a searchlight, taking in the measure of each man, each machine. "All men are created equal, boys," he said, "but then *some* become *Commando*." His stance relaxed, and he gave an unsettling grin. "So, you're my raw materials, eh?" He folded his arms, and Jack watched the tattoos bulge and swell as he paced back and forth. For a man of his years he looked remarkably fit.

McNulty walked down the line, inspecting each of the team diligently, ignoring their obvious differences and picking out minor imperfections in their appearance, kit or stance.

"Looks like I got me some big tall lads," he said, craning his head to look up at Lancaster, "an' I got one big *wide* lad." He stopped in front of Billy and prodded his belly with his pace stick.

Billy winced and tried unsuccessfully to suck in his gut. He grimaced as he heard Hurricane stifle laughter.

"But while you're different on the outside, boys, like it or not you're now not one but many—not man or machine but a *team*. And in action, you'll only be as good as the soldier stood next to you. It's my *proud* duty to mold you goons from the rabble that stands before me, into a crack fighting unit. An' lookin' at the state of you I reckon I've got my work cut out. Make no mistake, training under ol' Mungo will be both physically and mentally demanding. You'll learn a lot about soldiering, you'll learn a lot about each other, and you may just learn a thing or two about yourselves."

McNulty resumed his position at the front. "Be confident, boys. Trust in your abilities. Believe in yourselves and each other. Remember that you're here for one reason and one reason only: Churchill wants warriors. So do I. Make me proud."

As Hastings and Cammy watched the proceedings, Hastings whispered, "How are they doing?"

"They're doing well," Cammy said, shivering. "But…"

He looked at her expectantly.

"They ask questions," Cammy finished, recalling her conversation with Spitfire. "Questions I can't answer. I wondered, since you have their records, if there's more that I should know?"

"Doctor, we've already been through this. Their records are restricted. Off limits. You're just their engineer so for now, concern yourself with the job at hand. Keep them operational."

"So, in order to gauge your abilities," McNulty was now saying, "we're goin' on a yomp. It's a bit like a nature hike, but with pain 'n' sufferin'!"

Mosquito snorted.

"You've somethin' to say, Private…?"

"Mosquito, sir. Nothin' to say."

"Really?" said McNulty, hands on his hips. "You see, it strikes me, Private *Mosquito*, that you've got plenty to say. It strikes me that you're seein' ol' Mungo here and you're thinkin' 'This senile old fart's for the knacker's yard, so why should I bother?' aren't you, Private Mosquito?"

"No, sir, I never—"

"But you *did*, Mosquito. Not in so many words to your pals standing beside you, but in the disrespectful way you comport yourself on my parade square, and in the cocky tone o'your voice, 'cos you think your shit smells better than everyone else's, don't you, son?"

"Sir, it's impossible for us to sh—"

"Get down on the ground now 'n' give me a hundred, Private Mosquito!" McNulty screamed. "By the time I've finished with you, son, you'll be beggin' me for an oil can!"

Mosquito dropped to the ground and commenced his punishment; the weight of his massive frame popped bolts from his joints.

Spitfire opened a red-crossed box on his chest plate and took out a screwdriver. He broke rank, starting down the line toward Mosquito.

"And just where the bloody 'ell d'you think you're going, laddy?" yelled McNulty.

"He can't fix 'imself, Sarge," Spitfire said. "I'm the medic, well, more of a mechanic really, just not as good as Cam—"

"*Get stompin'!*" McNulty yelled.

"But Sarge, I only—"

"That goes for all of you!" McNulty screamed at the rest of the team. "Five times 'round my parade square, then I want you back 'ere in full kit 'n' gear. And you can thank Privates Mosquito and Spitfire for the exercise!"

Mosquito paused, then looked up at Jack for assistance.

"Did I give you permission to stop, boy?" McNulty shouted.

"But Sarge, it's against the Geneva Convention, this is!"

"Aye, laddy," said McNulty. "So's *this!*" He stepped onto Mosquito's back and produced a stopwatch from a cord around his neck. "Crack on, Private Mosquito, only ninety-eight more to go!" He clicked the stopwatch. "*What're you lot gawkin' at?*" he yelled at the rest of the team, who stood watching the punishment in shock. "*Move your arses!*"

Commando One scrambled to comply.

Cammy winced as Mosquito popped more bolts. "A little harsh, don't you think?" she whispered to Hastings.

Jack, Billy, and the Tommies jogged by. Jack winked cheekily.

"Do I sense disapproval?" said Hastings, unamused.

Aware that yet another argument with the brigadier was futile, Cammy bit her lip.

"Look, you know how this works," Hastings said. "We have to break them down to build them up."

"Just don't break them down *too* much," Cammy said bitterly. "I'm short on spare parts."

"There's a war on, Camilla," Hastings said. "You'll just have to do what the rest of the country's doing."

"And what's that?"

"Make do and mend," Hastings said, smiling, then he walked brusquely back to the castle.

Cammy returned her gaze to the torture. "*Asshole,*" she muttered quietly.

. . .

"You look well, Ernst."

Snapping the heels of his boots together, Mörder saluted. His veined, lidless eyes watched his Führer. "It iss my honor to serve Germany," he said, annoyed to hear his teeth clicking together beneath the bandages still covering his face.

"I have need of you once again, old friend," Hitler said, stepping around his desk and clasping Mörder's hand.

"My panzer korpss?" Mörder hissed.

"Something new, something far more ingenious," Hitler said. "*Living* armor."

While he found the concept intriguing, Mörder said nothing.

"To achieve this," continued Hitler, "I need you to obtain two assets from our agent in Great Britain and bring them to Berlin. You'll then oversee phase two of our project in Norway."

"Norway?" Mörder rasped. "But Norway hass fallen."

"This mission, and the need for your presence there, will be disclosed in due time."

"As you wissh, my Führer."

"I understand from Von Ribbentrop that you acquired a somewhat *unique* anomaly from your injuries?"

"Anomaly, Führer?"

Hitler picked up a silver letter opener from his desk, handing it to Mörder. "Show me."

Taking the blade, Mörder nodded obediently. "My life for ssacred Germany," he swore solemnly, then stabbed it into his leg without flinching. It was a curious sensation, thought Mörder, to wound oneself without feeling pain.

Hitler smiled, nodded, then looked down at a globe beside his desk, spinning it idly. "Soon, my friend, you shall lead an army of men in your likeness—an army of invincible warriors!" He slammed a hand down hard on the globe, his fingers encircling Great Britain. "And when all of our enemies have fallen, Germany shall rise to reign supreme. A thousand-year Reich."

"A thousand-year Reich," Mörder repeated.

"You have my directive, old friend. Begin phase one. Retrieve our assets from Great Britain—return them to me here in Berlin."

"Heil Hitler!" Mörder said, saluting. He strode from the chancellor's office.

He would do his master's bidding—but first he would attend to some loose ends.

. . .

Snow drifted down as Commando One returned to the castle.

Worked beyond exhaustion by McNulty, Jack, Billy, and the Tommies were ready to drop. If Jack thought he'd had some choice instructors in the past, they were nothing in comparison to the old drill sergeant, who despite his declining years had a seemingly inexhaustible supply of energy. Now feeling the full weight of their packs, Jack and Billy could barely stand. The Tommies were flagging too, courtesy of the iron equipment cases bolted onto their backs by Cammy at McNulty's request.

As they stood on the parade ground, a robin fluttered onto Lancaster's helmet, then flew away leaving a gooey white drip on its rim. *Serves him bloody right*, Jack thought.

"All right, Commando One," McNulty said, clicking his stopwatch. "I'll admit I'm impressed, but I want better—and I warn you, I *will* get it. Follow me."

The team followed McNulty across the estate to a round hole in the ground about twenty feet wide and ten deep.

"What's this, Sarge?" Hurricane asked.

"The bear pit," McNulty said. "Before your training comes to an end, each of you will stand toe-to-toe with an opponent down there."

"That's milling, that is," Billy said. "Did it in me old unit. Two men in, one out, eh, Sarge?"

"The pit's not about how hard you can punch a man, Billy. It's a test of mettle, *grit*. It's about how hard you can take a punch and keep moving forward. Out there..." He pointed at the Black Mountains surrounding them. "Out there, you'll learn to bond with each other, but down there," he pointed into the pit, "is where you'll come face to face with yourself. Unadulterated hand-to-hand combat, boys, as dirty as it gets. And I guarantee you won't come out the same man as goes in. There's gonna be blood 'n' oil spilt—and I have to confess, boys..."

McNulty looked around at the group, his eyes wild. They settled on Jack and Lancaster. "I cannae wait!"

# 11

## LORD OF WAR

**M**EANDERING DRUNKENLY along the street, Magda Mörder stifled laughter. August Mench staggered drunkenly in her wake.

"Magda? Wait!" Mench said, stumbling off a curb.

Teetering on heels too high to be home before midnight, Magda spun, nearly falling over as he reached her. Smiling sympathetically, she laughed and straightened his collar.

"Always my smart soldier," she said proudly, looking from Mench's ribbon bar into his eyes.

"My siren," Mench whispered, caressing her cheek with the back of his hand. Though many years his senior, the woman still had much in the way of her looks, and this evening a cocktail of schnapps and the Berlin moonlight had transformed her into a goddess.

Mench leaned forward and clumsily tried to steal a kiss.

"Not here," said Magda, withdrawing. She put a hand on his chest and looked about.

"I—I'm sorry." Mench stared down at his boots like a sullen child. "After what you said at the hospital, I thought—"

"Oh, August," Magda chided, stifling a giggle. "*So* serious. I said not *here*, didn't I?" She took a set of keys from her purse. "What happens indoors is, well…" She jangled the keys enticingly. "An altogether *different* affair."

She turned and meandered on. "Are you coming, Colonel?"

· · ·

The intruder moved silently through the house. The rooms were large and opulently furnished, and while each was lit only by the lamps in the street outside, the man moved with an obvious familiarity with his surroundings, easily navigating obstacles.

The intruder continued into the sitting room and approached a large glass cabinet. Pausing to examine its contents, the figure trailed a black gloved finger down the gilt etch of the cabinet's glass door, and then swung it open.

Inside, photographs and mementos of numerous military campaigns were neatly arranged around a large and impressive collection of eclectic military artifacts. Guns of varying shapes and sizes were displayed amid an assortment of ancient weapons: Madagascan tribal spears, Zulu iklwas, even a ceremonial Amazonian bola. The dark centerpiece of the collection was a grotesque crimson samurai mask that stared defiantly at the intruder. Hook-nosed and hateful, its mouth yawned wide in a grimace of awful fury.

The intruder reached into the cabinet but paused, transfixed by the darkness within the mask's eyes.

Laughter sounded outside, then a key scraped in the lock of the front door.

Reaching silently into the cabinet, the man, the mask, and the darkness became one.

...

Magda and Mench stumbled through the doorway into the entrance hall. Magda sighed as Mench pushed her against the wall, kissing her lips and throat passionately, his hands roaming over her body with frenzied expertise.

"You're sure about this?" Mench looked up suddenly.

"You saw him," Magda said. "Ernst can't even stand, let alone return to duty. As far as I'm concerned, he can rot in that hospital."

Mench stared into her eyes. "And us?"

Magda smiled coyly. Her husband's adjutant might be young but he was handsome, ambitious, and in Ernst's absence, her position in Berlin's societal hierarchy was assured at Mench's side as she shared his ascension. She smiled and nodded.

"Then we need a drink to celebrate!" Mench said, overjoyed.

Climbing the staircase, Magda removed a clip and released a cascade of flowing blond hair. "Don't keep me waiting, liebchen."

Mench eagerly kicked off his boots and staggered into the sitting room. He opened the door of a drinks cabinet and poured cognac into two crystal glasses. As he did, he noticed a framed photograph of Magda stood beside Mörder and a young girl in a Hitler Youth uniform. Magda was young and beautiful, and her husband calm and composed, very much the general in waiting. The girl, who greatly resembled her father, wore an odd, disconcerting expression far beyond her years.

Then Mench noticed something glinting on the table top beside it. Picking up the object, he saw it was a medal: A Grand Iron Cross.

"Your conduct is unbecoming to an officer of the Wehrmacht."

Mench spun, dropping the medal. He saw no one in the darkness. "Show yourself," he hissed, drawing his Luger. "I warn you; this is loaded!"

"August, I'm waiting!" called Magda from the landing.

"As was I," whispered the ethereal voice.

A demonic face slowly formed.

"Hello, August," said the mask, appearing to float in the gloom.

"How do you know my name?"

Mench saw a flash of the general's ribbon bar beneath his leather trench coat and knew instantly whom he faced. But it was too late. Mörder lunged and gripped his throat.

"*Ach, Herr General I—can explain!*"

Mörder's eyes stared at Mench, wild with rage. "We're beyond that now," whispered the general frenziedly from behind the mask. He felt his adjutant's spine crumble between his fingers. "You *betrayed* me, August."

Mench flailed impotently in wide-eyed terror, then slumped dead.

"What's taking so long?" Magda shouted.

Mörder dropped Mench's body. He noticed the photograph beside the cognac and picked it up, his mask glinting in the darkness.

"Ilsa," Mörder whispered, tracing a finger tenderly over the young girl's image. "Papa's home." Then he turned his attention to the image of his wife beside her. "And *you*—"

"August, it's getting late," Magda shouted from the landing. "If you don't hurry, I shall just go to sleep."

"And so you shall, my love," Mörder whispered, squeezing the frame. The glass fractured across Magda's face. "*So you shall…*"

. . .

Magda sashayed from the bedroom in a white silk negligée. She crossed the landing and peered over the banister into the entrance hall, squirting perfume from a bottle.

"August?"

Silence.

Magda frowned. "This isn't funny."

Movement.

Relieved, Magda smiled as a figure appeared through the gloom. "I thought you'd gotten lost."

The figure stepped out into the light, and the samurai mask stared up at her. "In *my* own house?"

In shock and terror, Magda dropped the perfume bottle over the banister; it shattered on the tiled floor below.

Mörder ascended the stairs. "Why my dear," he hissed, "you've gone quite pale."

"You— You can't be—"

"Oh, but I am—*wife!*"

Mörder swiped at her, but Magda fell backward, screaming. She scrambled back on all fours as he lunged again, grabbing a handful of her negligée.

"Is *this* what you've become?" Mörder spat. "Whore!"

Magda flashed a glance downstairs.

"Yes, your lover's down there in the sitting room," Mörder hissed. "I'm sure he'll be great solace—if you can piece him back together!"

"*Bastard!*" Magda sobbed, glaring hatred at the mask. Tears streamed down her cheeks.

The force of Mörder's fist sent her reeling.

Spitting blood and several teeth, Magda tried to stay conscious, kicking out at the general. He grabbed her ankle and hauled her back toward him.

"Your face—" Magda whimpered as the mask drew her close.

"Yes," Mörder said. "Let me show you *my face!*"

Mörder removed his mask, and Magda recoiled in horror, her screams lost in the undulating wail of an air raid siren.

. . .

Seagulls cawed, scattering as Commando One staggered across a beach.

"Come on, boys," McNulty yelled, from his vantage point on a rock. "Daylight's wastin'!"

Jack appeared first through the mist, leading Lancaster and Spitfire. The struggling trio carried a huge twelve-foot log over their shoulders. The second team—comprised of Billy, Hurricane, and Mosquito—followed behind, carrying a similar-sized log. It looked like both teams would finish the race with the same number of bearers as had started, but they were clearly exhausted.

"That's it, ladies," McNulty said. "You're simulating the movement of supplies and ammunition retrieved from an air drop. If you need a further incentive, just imagine a hundred Jerries firing mortars at you."

They had traveled for two miles uphill, fighting for every step, and it had taken its toll.

"I want maximum determination to the end!" McNulty yelled. "Even if your arms are dropping off an' your bodies are screaming for you to stop —push on! And if a hundred Jerries don't inspire you, just imagine my boot up your arses if you fail this task!"

Arriving at McNulty's rock, Jack, Hurricane, and Spitfire threw down their log.

"Och, my gray-haired old mammy could run a quicker time than you slovenly drovers," McNulty grunted. He clicked off his stopwatch as Billy, Hurricane, and Mosquito arrived.

Jack gripped his knees, his chest burning as he filled his lungs with the fresh loch air. Billy collapsed breathless beside him.

For three weeks they'd prospered and thrived under McNulty's watchful eye—and they had, Jack felt, finally turned a corner, though it hadn't been easy. They'd been woken every night, torn from their beds and cages by seemingly endless orders to turn out their weapons and kits for inspection. McNulty had told them there would be times when they'd wish they were dead, and Jack had to agree—but as the old drill sergeant had said, when they were out in the field with the Hun about to skewer them on bayonets, with a little luck and their training, they'd be the last men and machines standing.

In addition to the basics, McNulty, along with his skilled team of training staff, had taught them a number of tricks and techniques for survival in the wild behind enemy lines. They'd learned about field explosives and demolitions, close-quarter combat and holds, sabotage, knife work, signaling, and all manner of shooting techniques. On the mental side they'd received training on nutrition—or in the Tommies' case, the various forms of petrol and engine lubricants available to keep them going in the field. The team had also been taught about heat and fatigue resistance, airsickness, seasickness, and survival in all manner of climates. The final phase of their training had consisted of a series of psychological tests, including a grueling two-day session designed to test their resistance to interrogation. It was safe to say that to a man, and machine, they were trained but ready to drop.

"*I think... I'm dyin'!*" Billy gasped.

"Dyin's easy, Billy-boy," McNulty said, jumping down from his rock.

"It's livin's the hard part!"

"Too bloody right," Hurricane muttered.

"What are you talkin' about?" Mosquito said. "You ain't *livin'*—you're a machine, just like us!"

"I'm runnin' around this beach, ain't I?" Hurricane reasoned, "Feelin' just as knackered as you lot, ain't I? *That's* livin'!"

Any further philosophical conversation was quashed as McNulty blew his whistle. "All right lads, pipe down. Now it's your last day of training, and I'm proud to say that you've all done everything asked of you. 'Cept the bear pit, eh, Jack?"

While everyone else had been in and, with the exception of a few cuts, bruises or dents had survived the experience—more or less—Jack and Lancaster had not yet had the pleasure. McNulty had made the team draw lots for the pairs, and of course Jack was paired with Lancaster. *A right stitch-up*, Jack had thought, as McNulty feigned surprise. Their turn was yet to come.

"Your old uncle Mungo's got y'all a present to say, 'Thanks for the memories!'" McNulty smiled.

"Easy, lads," Billy said. "He's got a crate of stout stashed away somewhere!"

Jack and the Tommies laughed.

"Ever the joker, eh, Billy?" McNulty said. "You can have yours first then."

Bristling with bravado, Billy smiled and approached McNulty.

"What the 'ell d'you think you're doing, Briggs?" McNulty snapped, suddenly serious.

"But you just said—"

"You think old Mungo's gonna buy you a beer 'n' give you a pat on the back? *Bollocks!* You're Commando!" McNulty pointed to a jagged black spike of rock jutting from the cliff face above them. "Dronna's Tower!" he shouted. "The objective's simple, boys: reach the peak, 'n' once there you help the next man up!"

With a collective sigh, the exhausted team looked at each other.

"Typical," Mosquito said. "Just when I thought things can't get no worse!"

"Not much worse than having to climb that thing!" Spitfire craned his neck to stare up at the cliff face.

Thunder rumbled overhead. A single drop of rain pinged off

Mosquito's shoulder plate. "You were sayin'?"

"Flesh or steel, boys," McNulty said. "It's time to see what you're *really* made of." He raised his whistle and blew a piercing shriek that echoed across the beach. At that same moment, the heavens opened.

"This don't look so bad," Jack said. "I mean, how 'ard can it be?" He walked to the rock face and tried to get a foothold but slipped back off the slick rock.

"Need a hand, sir?" Lancaster asked.

"No thanks," Jack said dryly.

"Suit yourself then." Lancaster raised his left hand and spread his fingers wide. "Anchors aweigh!" A miniature grapple hook shot from his palm in a burst of compressed air. It curled up onto the cliff face, trailing a steel cable from within his forearm.

Hurricane looked at Jack. "Grapple 'ook, boss. We all got 'em."

Lodging in a crag on the cliff face, Lancaster's grapple hook cable drew taut. The other Tommies fired their own grapple hooks, then their backpacks concertinaed open, and they reached over their shoulders and pulled out oversized climbing picks.

"Came in handy, did these," Mosquito said.

"Those Kampfwagens near Langemark?" Spitfire asked.

"Nah, it was Hotsa," Hurricane said, then to Mosquito: "You blew up the ammo store, you dozy sod!"

"Only 'cos I tripped on a—"

"Let's get to work," Lancaster said, all business. He turned to Jack. "See you up top, sir." He ratcheted the cable into his forearm and slowly began his ascent.

Billy looked at Jack. "Shouldn't we just—"

"Bloody Lancaster!" Jack seethed through gritted teeth.

One by one, the Tommies followed Lancaster up onto the tower. Hurricane looked down at Billy and extended a hand.

"Jack?" Billy said, wary of his friend's reaction.

Jack sprang up onto the tower and scrabbled after the old sergeant. Billy moved to stop him, but McNulty placed a hand on his shoulder.

"Better here than in the bear pit," he said, wiping rain from his eyes.

Thunder boomed again as Jack scaled the cliff face. Lancaster ignored him, carefully continuing his ascent at a steady cautious pace, using his pick and then ratcheting the cable into his arm.

"Lancaster?" Hurricane shouted. "They need our 'elp!"

"This ain't your fight!" Lancaster muttered, determined.

"This isn't a *fight!*" Spitfire yelled. "We're a *team!*"

"Sarge's right," Mosquito said, climbing beside him. "They need to stay our pace!"

"No," Spitfire argued, "we have to help each other!"

Climbing faster and with less care, Jack drew even with Lancaster.

"Jack, slow down!" Billy shouted, straining to see his friend through the rain as lightening arced overhead.

Lancaster tried to climb faster, but eager to press his advantage, Jack scrabbled ahead of him. He looked down and smiled cockily, then reached out for a ledge, but his fingers slipped on the wet rock, and at the same time he lost his footing.

He fell.

Then a huge hand gripped his forearm, taking his weight.

Jack swung wildly in mid-air.

Lancaster glared down at him, rain cascading from the brim of his iron helmet. "This don't change nothin'!" he growled, lifting Jack back up onto the rock face.

Thunder boomed again.

"That's it, boys!" McNulty cried. "You're *Commando*—Commando don't fear the storm!"

Lightening cracked the sky above them.

"Commando *are* the storm!"

Glaring at each other, Jack and Lancaster reached the summit. When the rest of the team had joined them, they watched McNulty scale the cliff, unaided and with ease.

"What are you, boys?" he shouted, reaching the top.

"Commando!" shouted the team.

Jack shouted it too, but he felt as uncomfortable as Lancaster obviously was. Jack had to concede though, they *had* achieved something.

"Can't 'ear you!" McNulty cried.

"*Commando!*"

"*Again!*"

"*COMMANDO!*"

"*Yes!*" McNulty yelled; his fists raised to the heavens.

# 12

## PASSING OUT

**M**CNULTY LADLED steaming spoonfuls of stew into three bowls from a tin pot. A campfire crackled beneath it illuminating the camp on Dronna's Tower. "Grub's up boys," he said heartily. "Come 'n' get it."

Sat nearby, Jack and Billy took their bowls and tucked in. Impervious to the chill night air or the lure of the campfire, Hurricane, Mosquito, and Spitfire sat nearby playing cards quietly recanting adventures.

Lancaster gazed out across the loch from a bluff above the camp. Seemingly preoccupied, he'd been distant since the incident with Jack earlier that afternoon.

Jack was quiet too and had so far refused to thank Lancaster for his assistance. Billy had sensed the friction and had asked his friend about it, but Jack had snapped at him and Billy had retreated to the Tommies' company, making Jack feel even more isolated.

"I'm starvin'," Billy said, wolfing his food. "What is it, Sarge?"

McNulty picked a small bone from his teeth. "Rat."

Billy sputtered, coughed, and gobbed out a mouthful of food.

"What's wrong with you, son?" McNulty said. "That's good Scottish rat, that is!"

"I've suddenly lost my appetite, Sarge."

Jack rolled his eyes as Billy got up and rejoined the Tommies. They welcomed him into their circle, laughing and joking. Watching his friend, Jack felt a stab of jealousy for Billy's popularity within the group. He seemed to just fit in with ease among the old soldiers, whereas Jack, well… He looked up at Lancaster. How the hell could he make this right? Even if he did go and speak to his rusty sergeant, the prickly old git would probably rebuke Jack for his impetuous actions.

"So," McNulty said, following his gaze, "think you're ready?"

"I didn't ask for this." Jack said, staring into the campfire's flames. "An' no matter how hard I try, I— *he*… ah, I dunno."

"What is it, son. Lancaster? Och, he's an old soldier like me," McNulty said. "Stubborn as they come. You'll work it out."

"I have—*doubts*."

"There isn't a soldier alive that doesn't," McNulty said. "Jack, leadership's about suppressing *doubt* and *fears*, and believing in your abilities. It's about resilience, determination and the raw courage, or the sheer bloody stupidity sometimes, depending on the situation, to step into the unknown, irrespective of the odds. It takes courage to look your enemy in the eye, Jack—but sometimes more so a friend. You need to conquer those doubts. Go 'n' talk to him."

Without waiting for a response, McNulty picked up his backpack, climbed a ridge, and took out a set of old Highland bagpipes. "Tonight, boys, we honor the fallen brave, that they might give you the strength to prevail in the dark days ahead." Wedging the tartan bag under his left arm, he held the bagpipes' drone reeds with his right and blew gently into the mouthpiece, playing a melancholy tune over the popping and crackling of the campfire.

Jack thought it sounded beautiful, and sad, and he looked up again at Lancaster.

The Tommies and Billy grew quiet, glancing at each other uncertainly as Jack climbed the bluff.

Jack still had reservations, but if his team was to succeed, he had to swallow his pride and fix the rift.

"I join you?" he said, approaching Lancaster.

The old sergeant said nothing, just stared out across the loch.

"Still haven't thanked you for saving my arse out there today."

Lancaster remained silent, motionless.

*Ah, sod it*, thought Jack. *I dunno why I even—*

"I've 'eard about the men you lost," Lancaster said quietly, "and I've known boys like you. Seen 'em cut down in action draggin' good lads to their graves. A true leader, a leader of *men*, needs perspective to see the 'ole battlefield. You've fought in the dirt for so long that you've lost yours." He stared directly at Jack. "You ain't a leader—you're a *liability*."

"You're wrong," Jack said, earnestly. "I came here to *lead* this team."

Lancaster started past him toward the camp, then turned and looked up at Jack, his blue eyes burning. "Then I'm sorry you've wasted your time." He continued down the hill and joined Billy and the Tommies.

McNulty finished playing his pipes. "Stand down, boys," he said, descending into the camp. "Tomorrow's a new adventure."

Jack joined him and watched them scuttle about, keen to obey his command. Whatever magic the old man had in keeping this group on track had so far eluded Jack. Lancaster had clearly made up his mind, and while the others, Hurricane and Spitfire certainly, had done their best to integrate themselves into a wider unit, Mosquito resisted Jack's command as well.

But they'd made it through basic training—and that had to count for something.

"Together you prevail, Jack, remember that," McNulty said. "I've taught them all I can."

"And now?" Jack asked uncertainly.

"Now it's *your* turn," McNulty replied, a glint in his eye.

. . .

"No," Hastings said.

"Why not?"

"You know damned well why not."

"But they deserve some recognition!" Jack said. "Passing out, the pipe parade, it's a traditional part of—"

"Don't presume to lecture me on *tradition* at Achnacarry, Captain."

"Look I admit when I met 'em I had doubts," Jack said. "I was wrong. If Churchill wants symbols of resistance why shouldn't it start here? Now?" He looked past Hastings to McNulty. "You can't agree with this, Sarge?"

"What I do and don't agree with isn't in question here, laddie." McNulty folded his arms.

Hastings gave Jack a smug *I told you so* look.

"But for the record, Brigadier," McNulty said, "I think it's bureaucratic bollocks!"

Jack shot Hastings a look of triumph.

"Captain, this is a *covert* team," Hastings said, irritated. "That means *Top Secret*. The Tommies may, in time, buoy British moral as the PM intended, but for now it's my job to ensure that their existence here remains strictly confidential—concealed from the public eye—is that understood?"

Jack was about to counter Hastings but caught a stern look from McNulty and remained silent.

"Now you and Briggs may of course take part in the parade," Hastings continued, "but until such time as I receive further orders from London, the Tommies are to remain stood down."

"But—"

"*Dismissed*, Captain."

Jack stormed from Hastings' office and headed toward the workshop. If he was going to unite his team, it would take a monumental gesture of goodwill—an olive branch that not even Lancaster could fail to be impressed by.

"So, what'd he say?" Billy said, hurrying to match Jack's stride.

"What d'you think?" Jack muttered.

"Look, we've come this far, 'n' I wouldn't have put odds on that! Don't go upsetting the applecart now, eh? Get us thrown out."

"Oh, I ain't gonna upset it, Billy."

"Well, thank god for that!" Billy breathed a sigh of relief.

"I'm gonna kick the bleedin' thing over and stamp all over it."

Billy stopped dead in his tracks as Jack strode off down the corridor. "*Jesus*," he muttered, then ran after his friend.

...

Cammy raised her welding mask. "You want what?"

"All I need to know is if you can do it, Cam?" Jack said.

"Well, yes, but I don't think Hastings is gonna—"

"He's not," Jack said, leaving the workshop. "But we're gonna do it anyway."

A thought suddenly occurred to Cammy. "Jack? *What about Lancaster?*"

...

Lancaster looked up from his roses. "*Absolutely not!*"

"God, Lancaster you are so—" Taking a deep breath, Jack closed his eyes and tried to remain calm. What was it about this crotchety old machine that pushed all the wrong buttons with him? If this was going to work, he had to get Lancaster on side. "Look, Lanc, I'm doing this for the boys, so just for once stop being so *bloody* stubborn and try to see it from my—"

"I've run a steady ship 'ere for these lads!" Lancaster levelled an accusing finger at Jack. "And I don't want *you* causing trouble for 'em now, 'specially on the eve of us getting back into action. And besides, it's against orders!"

"All the best things are," Jack said, hands on his hips.

"Look Captain your methods, they— they just *ain't* mine."

"The boys're passing out tomorrow, Sergeant, and so are you!" Jack said firmly as he strode back to the castle. "And that *is* an order!"

Lancaster sighed, looked down at his watering can, then he kicked it across the parade square.

...

The following morning was bright and warm, the perfect day for a parade. In the workshop beneath the castle, Jack and Billy, dressed in full ceremonial attire, dipped their green berets in and out of hot water, just as McNulty had instructed, then wrang them out.

"That's it, boys," McNulty said, as they pulled them down over their heads, and pulled the excess material to the right, respectfully smoothing it down. "Wear your green berets with pride, and be proud of what you've achieved." He pinned on their silver unit badges—a fist gripping a lightning bolt within a cog—to the left of each man's beret, then straightened Jack and Billy's collars.

"What about us?" Mosquito grumbled. "Don't we get nothing? I mean, my hats stuck on me 'ead!"

"Don't worry Mosquito," said McNulty. "You boys have something too, courtesy of the good doctor here." He winked at Cammy.

She smiled, relieved at last to be able to reveal her secret and pulled open her desk drawer. She took out a tray with four oversized bronze unit badges laid upon it.

"Lummy!" Spitfire said in wonder, as Cammy laid the tray on the workbench. She picked up her soldering iron.

"All for one, boys," Jack said, smiling.

McNulty gave a satisfied nod.

"An' one for all," Billy said. "Eh, lads?"

The Tommies, with the exception of Lancaster, agreed.

One after the other, Cammy soldered the unit insignia to the Tommies' shoulder cogs.

"Feels good to belong to something again," Hurricane said.

"Not half," Spitfire added.

"Yeah, not too shoddy," Mosquito conceded, checking himself in his mirror. "What d'you reckon, Sarge?"

With a burst of sparks, Cammy finished welding the last emblem to Lancaster's shoulder. He looked down at it, and for a moment appeared to be speechless, then: "All right, you 'orrible lot, get yourselves buffed up, your best spit 'n' polish jobs."

McNulty took Jack to one side and clapped him on the back. "You made it, Jack," he said quietly. "You're finally on your way!"

...

Commando One stood expectantly on the parade square.

"Congratulations, gentlemen," Hastings said. "You've passed your basic training. You now belong to the finest, and most pioneering troop in this war: The Commando. No one has gone before you. You are the first, the legend, and the benchmark by which future generations of soldiers will measure their achievements. The badges you wear don't just carry the crest of your unit; they carry the hopes and prayers of the British people. I trust you'll keep that in mind."

He stepped back formally and saluted McNulty.

McNulty took a step forward and gazed at the team with pride. "When we first met, I told you that all men are created equal, 'n' then some become Commandos. That day has finally come. You stand before me now a little older, a little wiser, and ready to face the enemy. I also said when we met to be confident and trust in your abilities—to believe in yourselves and your team. Churchill wanted warriors, and I can see that's what you've become. Now when it's time for you to face the 'un, and they see the determined glint in your eyes and the cold steel of your bayonets, they're gonna drop their machine-guns, and run like bloody 'ell!"

Laughter, tinged with sadness to be leaving their mentor, rippled down the line.

"I'm proud of you boys," said McNulty. "All of you. And I know you'll make this work not because you *have* to—but because you *must*. You're the line in the sand now; beyond you, this country has nothing left to defend itself with but sharp sticks 'n' rocks—so good luck to you all."

Saluting the team, he strode to the sidelines and Cammy.

"Nice speech," she whispered.

"I was up all night writing it!" McNulty replied.

Striking up a stirring rendition of a well-known Scottish marching tune, a pipe and drum band marched forward to honor the newly graduated team and, as was tradition at Achnacarry, lead them in a procession from the castle into Spean Bridge village.

"Well, I think that went rather well, don't you?" Hastings said to Cammy and McNulty. "Get the four of them back in their cages. I'll contact London and see what they want to—"

Cammy's eyes widened as Jack led Billy and the Tommies past

Hastings and out through the castle's main gate.

"Something the matter, Doctor?"

"I think the, er, cat's out of the bag, sir," McNulty said.

Turning, Hastings saw Spitfire, last in line, trying to keep pace with the others now disappearing through the gate. The little Tommy looked back at Cammy and waved enthusiastically, before vanishing as Hurricane grabbed his collar armor and dragged him outside the walls.

"What the bloody hell are they doing?" Hastings yelled.

Beyond the gate, he heard a great cheer go up.

"Did you know about this?" Hastings spat, staring daggers at Cammy.

"Me?" Cammy said innocently. "I'm *only* their engineer, remember?" She flashed a glance at McNulty.

Seething, Hastings turned and ran for the gate.

"Och, this ain't gonna be pretty, girl," McNulty said, grinning. "*Come on!*"

. . .

Boots crunched on cobbles as the pipe band played on, leading the soldiers out of the castle. Villagers from Spean Bridge cheered them on, their flags and banners fluttering above their heads. Local press photographers moved among them, jostling for the best position to set up their cameras, keen to secure a front-page photograph.

The pipe music reached a crescendo as the band led the men out of the gatehouse, into the sunshine, and across a bridge toward the village. The crowd quieted as Jack and Billy emerged, followed by Lancaster, who sheepishly led out the other Tommies. The machines waved to the crowd, their insignia gleaming in the sunlight as their chests swelled with pride.

The cheers diminished as the villagers reacted in shock to the machines now walking toward them. The pipe band looked to their rear, then slowed and fell silent in an untidy mess of noise.

"*Stop!*" Hastings yelled, sprinting from the gate house into a crowd of silent shock.

His steps faltered as he was suddenly aware of the eyes, and cameras, now upon him. He looked across the crowd. Men muttered suspicion to each other, and women clasped babies to their bosoms. Children stood aghast at the strangely magnificent machines marching as part of the parade.

"Get them back inside!" Hastings yelled.

Lancaster turned to face him. "Now Brigadier, just wait a—"

Hastings spun to Jack. "And as for you, *Captain*—I'll have your arse in a sling for this!"

Jack took a step forward. After weeks of butting heads with the officious pen-pushing toff he was done mincing words, irrespective of the consequences. "All due respect, sir, but why don't you go and take a flying fu—"

"Jack!" Cammy shouted, appearing behind Hastings with McNulty. She pointed at a little girl who had broken from the crowd and was approaching him.

The girl carried a tattered teddy bear in one small hand and a paper flag on a stick in the other. She nervously held the flag out to Jack.

"Thank you," he said, taking it.

Then the little girl looked up at Lancaster, towering above her. She reached up, grabbed one of his huge fingers, and tugged at it. Lancaster looked down at her, and then uncertainly at Jack, who smiled.

Crouching, the old sergeant looked at the girl. "Now then," he said gently. "Who might you be?"

"My name's Morag."

"Morag, is it?" Lancaster pointed at the bear. "And who's this then?"

"Davey."

"Davey? Well, that's a grand name for a bear, isn't it?" He shook the bear's paw. "Pleased to make your acquaintance, Davey."

The child touched Lancaster's face-plate, hesitantly at first, then with more confidence. "Are you going to hurt us, mister?"

"Hurt you?" Lancaster said, taken aback. He looked up as murmurs of suspicion rippled through the crowd.

"That what you think, is it?" Jack yelled. "That they're here to hurt you? 'Cos I can tell you they ain't. Don't be afraid of 'em, none of you. They're the *Tin Can Tommies*, and they're on *your* side—here to fight for *you!*"

The little girl smiled and kissed Lancaster's face plate, and to Jack's surprise, he gently picked her up.

"Now what say we finish this march, eh?" Jack yelled.

The little girl nodded enthusiastically, and the crowd erupted in spontaneous cheers and applause.

Jack winked at Cammy, who wiped a tear from her eye. Then he slid the paper flag into his tunic pocket, nodding at the lead piper who struck up a jaunty tune.

"Come on, boys," Jack shouted above the noise, then to Hastings: "Excuse us, Brigadier!"

Furious, Hastings stormed back into the castle.

Jack and the Tommies marched on to the flash and pop of cameras committing the revelation to eternity.

"Best find your tin hat, lassie," McNulty said to Cammy. "There's gonna be a reckonin'."

. . .

"I want you out of this castle by oh five hundred tomorrow," Hastings snapped.

Standing beside him, McNulty winced but said nothing.

"For the record," Jack said, "I'd like to state that Miss Sullivan knew nothing about—"

"You can rest assured that I'll deal with Miss Sullivan once I've processed your court martial."

"And Bill—*Private Briggs*. He had nothing to do with—"

"Briggs will remain here to await the team's new commander."

"But—"

"Not so amusing now, is it Captain?"

Hastings' phone rang. He snatched the receiver irritably. "*I thought I said no inter*— Ah, yes, sir. He's here with me now. I've already—" Hastings looked uneasy. "Oh, yes, of course."

He held the receiver out to Jack.

Frowning, Jack took it. "Hello?"

"This is bad form, Jack," Churchill said sternly down the line.

. . .

Ismay pawed through a pile of newspapers on Churchill's desk, a horrified expression on his face.

The Tommies' photographs were printed on every front page.

Churchill snatched one and grimaced as he read its headline: ***TIN CAN TOMMIES ON THE MARCH—WHITEHALL SILENT!***

"Now see here, Jack, we can't just go parading our military secrets in public for all to see, eh?" He sighed and threw the newspaper into a bin beside his desk. "Imagine Hastings is none too pleased?"

. . .

Jack looked at Hastings.

"Oh, he's positively fuming, sir."

Hastings tried to remain calm as McNulty snorted back a laugh.

"Put him back on, would you?" Churchill said down the line.

Jack handed the receiver to Hastings.

"Hello sir," Hastings said. "Now I—but—" He exhaled. "Yes, yes of course. As you wish."

He replaced the receiver. "Dismissed."

"Sir?" Jack said, surprised.

"Get out of my office, Captain!"

Jack hesitated for a second, then spun on his heel and left the room. McNulty followed him and closed the door behind them.

"That's another bullet dodged," McNulty said with a smile.

"Only a million more to go," Jack said. "Thank you, sir, for everything."

"Remember the tower, Jack. Together you prevail." He saluted smartly and held out his hand.

Returning the salute, Jack shook it and watched the old drill sergeant march off down the corridor.

Command of the team was his now.

He was finally on his own.

# 13

## MOONLIGHT AND MUSIC

THE WOMAN IN THE MIRROR smiled at Cammy as a dreamy tune drifted from her wireless. Applying her best black-market lipstick—a rich ruby red—she returned the smile wistfully. It had been a while, she thought, since she'd taken time to pamper herself. Her usual effort consisted merely of scraping grease from under her fingernails or scrubbing crud from her hair with carbolic soap.

But that wouldn't do this evening.

Leaning forward, she examined her reflection. *Talk about needing camouflage*, she thought, wondering what had happened to the wide-eyed girl from Idaho who had swapped the obscurity of her late father's ranch for a redeye to Washington and an internship at Princeton University.

The study of applied quantum mechanics hadn't been foremost on Cammy's mind while threshing crops in her youth, but after each day's labor, she'd immersed herself in the science books she'd borrowed from school or her town's small library. Fascinated by mechanics, she soon gained notoriety as the best engineer in Cottonwood, and it wasn't long before local farmers were paying for Cammy's assistance to fix vehicles and machinery in need of repair.

At Princeton, the teenager's talents soon caught the eye of her faculty. One professor in particular took her under his wing, mentoring her, cultivating Cammy's insatiable thirst for knowledge, particularly in the field of quantum mechanics and the study of subatomic particles. This faculty member, a former professor at the Berlin Academy of Sciences, was called Albert Einstein.

Einstein had only recently stepped off the boat from Berlin, having fled Germany after Kristallnacht—the night of broken glass. In a series of coordinated attacks carried out by Hitler's brutal paramilitary, German authorities had turned a blind eye as dozens of synagogues and hundreds of Jewish-owned buildings were destroyed. Einstein had sensed the inevitable and escaped to the United States. After disembarking at Staten

Island in early 1940, he opened a dialogue with Roosevelt on the rising danger in Europe and took a position at Princeton's Institute for Advanced Study where, amid a sea of physicists and mathematicians, he'd discovered Cammy.

It was strange, Cammy thought, how these distant events and chance meetings had ultimately led her to the Tommies. She vividly remembered the first time she'd seen them. Bone-shaken from a ten-hour journey from the states, she'd arrived at the MOD to find four huge crates in their archive. On arrival at Achnacarry she'd scoured the notes given to her by Hastings, and after recovering from the shock of seeing the machines, had successfully managed to reactivate the old warriors—and was astounded by their capacity for artificial intelligence.

Cammy remembered Lancaster, so serious at first. She had immediately gravitated toward his almost fatherly manner. Cammy had only a distant memory of her own father and found the machine's concern for her deeply affecting. How unexpected, she thought, given that Lancaster had no more of a heart than her mother's harvester back home. She had become obsessed with discovering whatever it was that drove these amazing machines but thus far, the secret of their creation had eluded her.

The wireless music changed pace to swing, waking Cammy from her daydream. She glanced at the clock on her bedside table and realized she had better hurry.

Pouting, she touched up her lipstick one last time, then straightened to examine her reflection again. *Hope you appreciate this, Jack*, she thought, picking up her clutch purse. *These nylons cost a goddamn fortune!*

...

A glitter ball revolved above the castle's banquet hall, shimmering flecks of light about the room. Adorned with streamers and bunting, it was home to a gathering of uniformed men, women, and locals who whirled a foxtrot on the dance floor while a singer crooned on stage with a swing band. The youngsters laughed and danced, enjoying each other's company and for this moment at least, forgetting the war. It was a time for celebration, and, as was always the case after a passing out parade at Achnacarry, the Cèilidh was in full swing.

Standing at the bar, Jack laughed as Billy chugged beer through a bullet hole in an upturned German helmet. They were joined by Hurricane, Mosquito, and Spitfire as Billy finished. He held the helmet aloft triumphantly to the cheers of his team.

"Don't look too 'appy, does he?" Billy said, nodding at Lancaster, who stood at the far end of the bar keeping his distance. The old sergeant was staring dejectedly into a pint of Vickers gun oil which, Jack had been told by Cammy, was the Tommies' poison of choice having gained a taste for it in France during the Great War.

"Does he bloody ever?" Jack said, curling his lip.

Billy looked uneasy. "We should really ask 'im over."

"What?" Jack said. "I ain't *that* drunk! Get a grip, Bill!"

"Oi, Lancaster!" Billy yelled across the bar.

The sergeant looked up from his oil can.

"What the hell're you doing?" Jack growled.

"We're a team now; it's time to start acting like one! Lancaster, get over 'ere, big fella!"

Jack grabbed Billy's arm, but Billy shrugged him off.

"C'mon, Sarge, get that rusty arse over 'ere!" Billy yelled.

"I'm gonna kill you for this, *Private!*" Jack snarled.

"What harm can it do?" Billy said. "Let's build some bridges, eh?"

Lancaster joined them, unenthusiastically, but he and Jack refused to look at each other.

Hurricane downed his oil. "Next stop, the Siegfried Line, eh?" He balled a fist, and Spitfire slapped him on the back with a clang. "Payback time for old Adolf!"

"Yeah, cold steel," Mosquito said. "Right up his *jacksy!*"

As they laughed, Lancaster crossed his arms disapprovingly and looked over Jack's head. "That's your influence rubbin' off on 'em, that is."

Saying nothing, Jack turned his back on Lancaster and leaned against the bar.

"C'mon, Sarge, it's a celebration," Billy said.

"I don't hold much with these types of functions," Lancaster muttered. "They make a mockery of—"

"God give me strength," Jack said, turning. "Are you *ever* off duty?"

"See?" Lancaster said. "That's exactly the kind of attitude that'll send us to the wall!"

"Ah, go boil your 'ead!" Jack said.

"C'mon, Jack, what you doin'?" Billy pleaded. "Wave a white flag, eh? We're off duty."

"Not according to the *expert!*" Jack spat, jerking a thumb at Lancaster.

"*You're—too—bloody—reckless!*" Lancaster said, jabbing a finger at Jack.

Jack downed the last of his pint and looked at Billy. "I don't 'ave to stay 'ere 'n' listen to this." He pulled his beret from his shoulder strap. "G'night, lads."

"C'mon, Jack, where you goin'?" Billy shouted as Jack walked away. "*Jack?*"

Jack pulled on his beret and made his way through the crowd, relieved to be away from the walking, talking pain in the arse that was his sergeant. He'd go and find Cammy; maybe she could give him some advice. More and more these days, she seemed to be his confidante, a rock of calm and wisdom in the mess that had become his life.

"You gonna buy me a drink then, Captain?"

Jack turned and saw Cammy had found him first. The crowd parted as she approached, stunning in a scarlet evening dress.

"Close your mouth, Jack," Cammy said, a little embarrassed. "You're catchin' flies."

…

"I'm sorry about Jack," Billy said. He tipped his pint-pot and finished the last of his beer.

"Boy's a maverick, William," grumbled Lancaster. "Ain't no place in a team for one o' them."

"Give 'im time," Billy said. "He'll come around. There's more to Jack than meets the eye."

"Oh, I *seriously* doubt that," Lancaster said.

Billy was out of excuses. What more could he possibly do with the pair of them? For all their differences, he knew that the same stubborn streak running through Jack also ran through Lancaster. He sighed and looked around the room. The Tommies were surrounded by fans, and the dance floor crowded with party goers as the swing band struck up another tune.

Billy heard a tapping sound, looked down and saw the tread of Lancaster's boot bobbing in time to the rhythm.

"You like music, Sarge?" he asked tentatively.

After a pause, Lancaster looked down at him. "I'm partial to the oldies," he replied, taking a sip of his oil. "Being one o'them."

"Yeah?" Billy said with genuine surprise. Then, seeing a new side to the machine, a grin slowly spread across his face. "Me too!"

...

"You look good," Jack said.

"Thanks," Cammy replied, "only thing I had that wasn't covered in oil."

"You should wear girl's clothes more often."

"Don't get cute." A smile crept across Cammy's face.

"So, what're you having?" Jack said, as the barman nodded.

"Bourbon. *Neat*."

Jack raised an eyebrow.

"What?" Cammy said, laughing. "It's been a hell of a day."

"Tell me about it," Jack said. "And a pint," he added, to the barman. He looked at Cammy. "You ain't a cheap date, Sullivan."

"That what this is?" Cammy smiled. "You're getting a little ahead of yourself."

"Oh, I dunno." Jack was enjoying their banter and as usual, Cammy had lifted his spirits. "Good-lookin' girl like you? Handsome devil like me? Plus, you lumbered me with Lancaster—should be *you* buying *me* a drink!"

Cammy laughed. There were few things in the world Jack had ever thought to be beautiful, but Cammy's smile was one of them.

The barman slid them their drinks.

Sipping her whisky, Cammy wrinkled her nose. "I got better booze than this in the workshop."

"Now that *does* sound like a date," Jack said wryly.

Cammy downed her whisky, smiling flirtatiously. "Maybe."

Jack was punching above his weight, and he knew it. What could Cammy possibly see in him, when she could be with any of the society types—hell, anyone at all for that matter? He didn't know the answer, but it wasn't going to deter him from trying. *Maybe tonight won't be so bad after all*, he thought, lost in Cammy's eyes.

...

Lancaster jabbed a finger at Hurricane, Mosquito, and Spitfire. "And just 'cos you lot've got the night off, don't mean you're off duty!"

As he continued the tirade, Billy mounted the stage behind him and took the microphone from the crooner.

"Er, testing, testing," Billy said, tapping the microphone.

"What the 'ell?" Lancaster spun toward the stage. "William?"

"We got a new act in the castle tonight folks," Billy said, self-consciously. "Been a while since he's been on stage, so he's a little bit *rusty*." The drummer stung his cymbals, completing the joke. "Er, cheers," Billy said, nervous.

The audience laughed and began to form around the stage.

"But seriously, folks," Billy continued, "he's been stood at the bar all night, so at least now he's *well-oiled*." The drummer stung his cymbals again.

"What the 'ell's he up to?" Lancaster turned to the other Tommies. "Are you lot in on this?"

"So let's hear it for the man himself," Billy shouted. "Give him a big hand to go with the two he already has—*Sergeant Lancaster!*"

The audience laughed and cheered as Hurricane, Mosquito, and Spitfire dragged Lancaster across the dance floor to the stage.

"I'll make your lives bloody 'ell for this!" Lancaster yelled.

. . .

Disturbed by the noise, Jack looked across the bar. "What the hell…" he muttered in disbelief.

Following his gaze, Cammy saw the Tommies pushing Lancaster up onto the stage. "Oh no…"

. . .

"All right boys, crank it up!" Billy said to the swing band, twirling his finger in the air. As the band struck up again, he grabbed Lancaster's hand.

"Briggs, what the hell're you doing?" the sergeant growled.

"Just follow my lead," Billy said. "You'll be fine." He placed Lancaster's hand on his shoulder and started to bob across the stage, singing.

"That's bloody awful," Lancaster said.

"You can do better?" Billy challenged. He swung around, put his hand on Lancaster's shoulder and pushed him in the opposite direction. To his surprise, Lancaster started to croon the second verse, interrupting himself only to curse as a piece of his backside dropped off.

The audience cheered and applauded as Billy and Lancaster got into their groove, playing to the crowd and waving to the other Tommies.

. . .

Unable to hold back laughter, Jack wiped a tear from his eye. He noticed Cammy studying him. "What?"

"Nothing," Cammy said. "Not often I see you smile is all." She took a swig of his beer. "You should do it more often, looks good on you."

"Yeah?" Jack said, putting his hand on hers. "Well, it happens occasionally, when you're around." It was a risky move, but the beer had given him Dutch courage, "or when Lancaster's arse drops off," he added.

Cammy smiled again.

"Seriously?" Jack said. "You can't fix that?"

They were enjoying each other's company, free from responsibility, if only for the moment; if only for the night.

"That was a wonderful thing you did for them today," Cammy said. "For Lancaster too. In time he'll appreciate it."

"The only thing he'll appreciate is me packing my bags," Jack lamented.

"You'll win him over," Cammy said.

"That remains to be seen."

"Give him a little longer, huh? For me."

Jack's eyes narrowed as he studied her. "You aren't like any engineers I've ever known."

"So, that's a good thing, right?

"Definitely. Most of 'em were six-foot with chest hair."

Cammy laughed.

"But yeah…" Jack took her hand again. "That's a *very* good thing."

Oblivious to their surroundings, their conversation continued as they stared into each other's eyes and the band played on.

# 14

---

# SCRAP

**M**OSQUITO LAUGHED as Billy and Lancaster continued their duet. Feeling the warm buzz of his oil, he cheered them on—and staggered into an American pilot, drinking shots at the bar with his back to them.

"Sorry mate," he said.

"Can't a guy get a drink in peace around here without some Limey —?"

"Hey, watch your mouth, *Yank!*" Hurricane growled.

"What're you even doing here?" Mosquito muttered to the pilot. "You ain't even in this war. Maybe if you drank less and got down off that fence stuck up your country's arse, you'd be useful!"

"C'mon, Moz, leave it," said Spitfire. "Let's go 'n' find Cammy."

"Sullivan?" the American remarked without turning. "I brought that kitty over here on a B-52. Man, she's a fox, but… women 'n' machinery, y'know?" He shook his head. "And those freaks she hangs 'round with—"

"Oh, that does it!" Hurricane growled, balling his fists. "Don't make me jump, boy, 'cos if I do, it's gonna hurt!"

"Yeah?" the American said cockily. "You 'n' who's army?" Turning, he looked up at Hurricane, then gritted his teeth and landed a punch square into the robot's middle—with a resounding clang. Screaming silently in pain, the pilot—an oily looking rat of a man—gripped his damaged hand.

Mosquito balled his fist and raised it. "I don't need no army for what I'm gonna do to you," he said, swinging.

· · ·

Lancaster and Billy heard a commotion coming from the bar.

"What's that?" Lancaster said, bumping into Billy.

"Dunno, but it ain't good," Billy muttered, watching a pilot fly across the bar into a table of US Rangers. The Rangers rolled up their sleeves and converged on Mosquito and the Tommies. More soldiers around them piled in on the brawl on either side cheering, or jeering, as fists flew from every direction. Whatever was going on, Billy's mates were smack in the middle of it.

He leapt from the stage and waded into the brawl.

"William?" Lancaster yelled. "Get back 'ere!"

. . .

"I'll 'ave your guts for garters!" Mosquito shouted, as several Rangers fought to restrain him.

"Bring it on, trash can!" yelled the pilot, wiping the blood from his split lip and leaping at him.

. . .

"This is all *your* fault," Lancaster said, appearing between Jack and Cammy.

Jack rolled his eyes as the romance of the moment shattered.

"We need to break this up," Lancaster added.

Lifting his glass casually, Jack watched an American pilot slide along the bar. "Off duty, Lanc. So're the boys. Let 'em blow off a little steam."

"Camilla," Lancaster said, "I strongly advise—"

Cammy was tired and tipsy, and she held up an abrupt hand.

Annoyed at being silenced, Lancaster left them and entered the fray. As he attempted to round up the team, a whistle blew, and military police flooded into the room—to the whoops and cheers of the brawlers.

Jack shielded Cammy from a chair flying overhead. It shattered a mirror above the bar with a crash. "I think that's my cue to leave," she said, downing the last of her drink.

"I'll see you back to your quarters," Jack said.

"Uh-uh, Captain, they're your boys now. Duty calls." Cammy dodged a fist. "Stick around, soldier," she kissed him gently on the cheek, "and remember you owe me a dance!"

Jack watched her leave. Then, sighing, he got up to wrangle his team.

. . .

Cammy shivered as she crossed the parade ground. A chill wind was blowing down from the mountains, whipping powdery snow around her ankles. She pulled Jack's great coat around her, grateful again for its warmth, much like the young captain himself. Her relationship with Jack still confused her, and while at times she might not have agreed with his methods, she had to admit he got results—which reassured her for the future.

She had grown close to the young captain, attracted to both his vulnerability as well as—she hated to admit—his cockiness and over-confidence. The combination both confounded and annoyed her. She was a woman of science and hard fact, not *emotion*. But she found the brash young soldier intriguing. Only time would tell if Jack was an asset to the team or a burden, but for now, she was glad to have him around.

Feeling payback for her bourbon, Cammy stumbled and paused to inhale the cool night air. It diminished her drowsiness, and she continued on her way.

A light flickered on in the castle's administration block.

Hastings…

Cammy cursed him. For months he'd stonewalled her requests for the Tommies' files, and until now she'd toed the line. But if her boys were going to see action, then surely it was her *duty* to know everything she could about them, to give them the best possible chance of survival. And if that meant a little skullduggery along the way, well, then so be it.

Whether it was the bourbon or the renewed sense of defiance Cammy felt following Jack's parade ground act of rebellion, she resolved that the moment had finally come. *Tonight*, she thought, *I'm gonna damn well get what you've denied me*.

Cammy glanced about furtively and saw sentries doing their rounds, and dozing in the snug of their watchtowers. She slowly changed direction and headed toward the admin block.

Her journey through the castle was quiet until she reached the main corridor. A group of off-duty clerical staff came along, gossiping, and Cammy had to shrink into an alcove. She hugged a wall as they passed by, then peered around the corner.

The corridor up ahead was quiet.

A lightbulb dangling from a ceiling cable above her flickered. The wall Cammy clung to was damp, and she shivered in the silence.

Then she took a step forward—

Hastings' door opened, and he stepped into view.

Cammy quickly withdrew once more into the alcove.

She heard the distinct sound of Hastings locking the door behind him, and then his footsteps headed her way. Wide-eyed, she held her breath and retreated further into the shadows.

He was almost upon her. Just a few more feet, and then—

"Brigadier?"

It was Phipps and by the sound of it, he was stood at the far end of the corridor.

"London's on the wire, sir."

Hastings' footsteps stopped. "At this hour?" he said irritably.

"It's SOE, sir," Phipps said. "Would you like me to—"

"No," Hastings said. "No, I'm coming." Hastings muttered something to himself, and his footsteps retreated back down the corridor.

Exhaling relief, Cammy was alone once again. For an instant, she was pricked by her conscience. Hastings had said the Tommies' files were off-limits, and who could blame him? There was a war on, and everyone was suspect, even the individual who'd reactivated the machines. She imagined the consequence if she were caught. She could be thrown off the project, imprisoned—or worse, accused of being a quisling. Suspicions of collaboration could end her career. They could also end her life if she were convicted of treason against the crown. *And these limeys love their damn crown...*

Common sense—*all* of her senses for that matter—screamed at Cammy to turn tail, call it a night, and go sleep off her bourbon. *But I won't get a chance like this again.*

With the odds of success stacked against her, she made the only rational decision a girl in her position could make.

*Screw it!*

She crept stealthily down the corridor toward Hastings' office.

...

Hurricane played a piano beside the bar and crooned to the assembled crowd of former rioters. The men joined in, sloshing their drinks and cheering noisily as military police moved among them taking notes. Mosquito and Spitfire sat at a nearby table playing cards.

Spitfire slapped down his hand and sat back jubilantly. "*Snap!*"

"What d'you mean, *snap?*" Mosquito muttered, spreading out Spitfire's cards. "This is *Rummy*, you pillock!"

Jack finished his conversation with a senior military officer and returned to the bar. He was tired, and he'd run out of beer and patience. It was time to call it a night.

"Captain?" Lancaster said, appearing behind him. "We need to talk."

"Tomorrow," Jack snapped. He found the cantankerous old machine exhausting.

"Tomorrow I'm seeing the brigadier," Lancaster said. "To inform him that I refuse to recognize your command."

"Fine, *whatever*," Jack said, immediately regretting the response.

At first Lancaster lingered, staring at Jack. But the officer who had spoken to Jack beckoned Lancaster over, and he left Jack alone at the bar.

Jack looked at himself in what was left of the shattered mirror above the bar.

What a bloody mess.

Reaching for his pint-pot, he noticed Cammy's clutch purse beside it on the bar.

...

Cammy pulled a small tortoiseshell clip from her hair, bent the wire, and slid it into the keyhole. Breathing erratically, she glanced up and down the corridor, then twisted the wire abruptly.

A click. Then another.

She heard the lock mechanism slide back.

*Bingo!*

...

"Cam?" Jack peered through the gloom of the parade ground.

He was alone.

He looked down at her purse in his hand. Much like Cammy's touch, it felt soft, offering warmth and reassurance. She had taken him by surprise at the Cèilidh. The most beautiful girl in the room, her dress a stark contrast to the practical clothes she wore about the castle. For the price of a great coat on his arrival, Jack had made a good friend in Cammy—and he hoped, after her parting kiss, maybe more.

*Remember you owe me a dance.*

Jack smiled, and then, looking around the castle grounds, frowned. Something was off. He couldn't put his finger on it, but as Billy so often said, it didn't *smell* right.

A door flew open behind him shattering the silence, and a crowd of men and women staggered drunkenly out into the moonlight, giggling and singing. It seemed everyone was having a good time tonight, except maybe the sentries who had to stay sober.

The sentries!

That was what was off. Jack peered at the guard huts and watchtowers. There were *no* sentries. And the usually floodlit parade square was shrouded in darkness.

Jack cautiously raised the wrist-wireless Cammy had given to him and Billy. "Lancaster?"

There was a brief pause, then: "Captain, if this is about—"

"Just shut up and listen. I'm out on the parade square and no one's on the watch. There a drill tonight?"

"Not that I'm aware of."

"Then you'd better get out here."

"On my way."

Peering into the darkness, Jack spotted a figure slumped in the shadows behind the nearest guard hut. He ran over and crouched beside it.

A pool of blood crept black across the cobbles from the sentry's open throat.

"And Lanc?" Jack said, standing. He cautiously unclipped his revolver. "Best bring the boys."

...

Clenching a mag light between her teeth, Cammy cursed. Hastings' office door had been easy to crack, but his filing cabinet was a whole different ball game.

She withdrew her hair clip from the keyhole, snapped it in half, and bent one piece into a hook. Then she reinserted both wires, using the hook to pull back the locking cylinder while aligning the pins that stubbornly prevented her access.

Cammy glanced toward the door as voices passed by. When she was satisfied it was safe to continue, she slowly rolled the tumbler and said a silent prayer.

Nothing.

Cammy rolled it again, applying more pressure, but the lock remained in place.

"C'mon," she hissed, rattling the drawer in annoyance. Then she hit the lock with her palm. "*Goddamn it!*"

With a click, the tumbler rolled and the drawer sagged under the weight of its contents.

Cammy quickly pulled the drawer open. Inside were dozens of tattered brown files, many stamped *TOP SECRET*. Cammy's eyes were drawn to a dog-eared old file at the back of the drawer. It was covered in tape to keep it together, and the faded dates stamped across it indicated it was nearly forty years old. A name scribbled on the folder read '*Gustav Lotz*'.

Who the hell was Gustav Lotz?

The file was heavy. As she rested it on the drawer to open it, Cammy dropped her hair clip. With a curse, she crouched to retrieve it, moving her hands in slow circular motions over the cold stone floor, searching.

To her surprise, her fingers slid over deep arc-shaped grooves in the floor. She traced them from the corner of the cabinet diagonally toward Hastings' desk. Even in bright light, the groove was probably invisible to the naked eye, but it was clear to her fingertips, and just as clear was what it meant: this cabinet had been slid away from the wall a number of times.

Cammy closed the drawer, gripped the cabinet, and heaved it in the same direction as the grooves. It swung aside easily, revealing a small alcove. The alcove contained a transmitter, the model of which Cammy didn't recognize, and a number of small books.

Cammy opened one of the books which contained code.

*German* code.

The muzzle of a revolver kissed her cheek.

"Don't make a sound please, Doctor," Hastings said.

"*Traitor!*" Cammy spat. "You won't escape!"

"Oh, that's exactly what I intend to do. And you're coming with me."

"What?"

"Not only will the Führer get the Mark Ones' schematics, but their caretaker to boot. I'd say my place at his side is well won, wouldn't you?"

"You're insane!"

"No more than Churchill thinking he can stave off an invasion."

"You can't win," Cammy said. "Jack'll kick your—"

Coldcocked at the base of her skull, she slumped.

Standing over her unconscious body, Hastings holstered his revolver. "No, he won't."

# 15

## THE ENEMY WITHIN

**BILLY AND THE TOMMIES** joined Jack and Lancaster on the parade square.

"She ain't in the workshop," Billy said, breathless.

"Her quarters're empty too," Mosquito added.

"You hear that?" Spitfire looked toward the airstrip.

The rising drone of engines echoed in the distance.

"There!" Hurricane whispered. He pointed at the lights of an approaching aircraft above the mountains south of the castle. He leaped up onto the ladder of the nearest watchtower. The metal slats of his irises drew wide. "It ain't one of ours."

The parade square dimmed as a light flickered off in the admin block.

"Hastings," Jack muttered.

"You don't think…" said Lancaster.

"Sound the alarm!" Jack took off toward the castle. "Get McNulty!"

. . .

Hastings took the file from Cammy's hand, along with several others from his cabinet, and slid them into a briefcase. He looked up as Phipps appeared in the doorway.

"They're on approach, sir."

"Right." Hastings looked down at Cammy, who was slowly regaining consciousness. "Help the good doctor, would you?"

Phipps grabbed Cammy's arm roughly and hauled her to her feet. Woozy, she tried to take a swing at Hastings who deftly stepped back. Phipps restrained her.

"Now behave yourself, Camilla," Hastings said, closing his briefcase. "It's time for us to leave."

Klaxons wailed as Jack and Billy crashed into the administration block, revolvers drawn. The Tommies brought up the rear welding their Webleys. As they rounded a corner, the group saw Hastings and Phipps at the far end of the corridor dragging Cammy.

Spinning, Hastings aimed his revolver.

"Brigadier?" Lancaster said, aghast. Just as Hastings opened fire, Lancaster stepped forward covering Jack and Billy; shots ricocheted off his armor.

"This mean he ain't on our side now?" Jack yelled.

"I'd say that's a *yes*, wouldn't you?" Billy replied.

"Good," Jack said, gritting his teeth. "I've been lookin' to drop that posh sod since we got 'ere!"

Hurricane, Mosquito, and Spitfire returned fire as stonework exploded around them.

Hastings dragged Cammy into an alcove while Phipps sprayed gun-fire down the corridor. The Tommies returned fire.

"Easy boys," Jack yelled above the clamor. "You'll hit Cam!"

Hastings stepped out behind Phipps and dragged Cammy toward a door.

"Jack!" Cammy cried. She struggled against Hastings as he kicked the door open, dragged her outside, and slammed the door shut behind them, leaving Phipps to cover their escape.

"Brigadier?" yelled Phipps, continuing his fire. He started to back up the corridor.

"That door leads to the airstrip!" Spitfire cried.

"The aircraft!" said Mosquito.

"He's gonna fly her outta here!" Lancaster yelled, reloading.

"Then we'll just 'ave to beat him to it!" Jack said.

"Remember Alsace?" Lancaster said, nudging Hurricane.

Hurricane nodded. "How could I forget?" He drew his second Webley as Lancaster dropped into a crouch in front of him. Hurricane leapt over his head and charged down the corridor at Phipps, both guns blazing.

Phipps reached the door but found it was locked. "Brigadier?"

His machine-gun clicked emptily.

"Oh, no," Phipps whispered, as Hurricane smashed into him, carrying Phipps on through the door and into the compound beyond.

Hurricane shook splinters from his joints as Jack, Billy, and the other Tommies joined him.

"You've got Phipps on you," Lancaster said, pointing to a bloody smear on Hurricane's chest plate.

"We've got company!" Mosquito yelled, ducking as the compound erupted with the chatter of machine-gun fire. They were surrounded by assailants dressed in British infantry uniforms.

"Take cover!" Jack shouted.

"Where did this mob come from?" Billy yelled.

"Must be the ones who took out the sentries," Spitfire said.

They returned fire. Jack could see Hastings dragging Cammy toward the airstrip, but they were pinned down, unable to give chase.

"Jack?" Billy shouted.

"What?"

"When we took cover, did you look at what it was we were taking cover behind?"

"Why?"

"Take a look Jack, just— *take a look.*"

Jack took a look.

They were crouched behind a fuel bowser.

*Oh, this just gets better 'n' better*, he thought, then he let his guns sing.

. . .

Lights appeared over the airstrip as Hastings dragged Cammy to the runway. A Junkers 927 cargo plane skidded down onto the ice with a screech. Cammy resisted Hastings with every step, but still light-headed from the concussion was unable to break free.

"Why're you doing this?" she demanded.

"You'd be a fool to think Germany doesn't have friends in this country."

"A fifth column?"

The cargo plane's lights illuminated the runway as it rumbled down the track toward them.

"Please!" Cammy pleaded. "Don't do this!" She pulled free for a second, but Hastings grabbed her again and dragged her back into his arms. He hauled Cammy onto the airstrip and stumbled toward the aircraft, which was rumbling along beside them.

With a clang, the fuselage door slid open.

. . .

"We're running out of time!" Jack shouted.

"And ammunition!" added Lancaster.

"Not to mention we're sat on top of a bloody great bomb!" Billy yelled.

"We're what?" Hurricane said.

Rattling under the bowser, an unpinned grenade rolled to a stop at their feet.

Mosquito's irises widened.

"*Fire in the hole!*" Spitfire cried.

The team dove for cover as the grenade blew the bowser.

...

Cammy flinched as a fireball erupted from the compound, and panic set in. Fighting Hastings' grip, she pulled his hand to her mouth and sank her teeth into it, raking them over his knuckles.

"*Bitch!*" Hastings yelled, recoiling in pain. He spun around and slapped her to the ground. Torn between his prize and the Junkers that had now moved ahead of him, he reluctantly released Cammy and ran after the aircraft.

...

Lancaster landed hard, releasing Jack, who rolled from his smoking armor.

"C'mon, boys!" Jack yelled.

He got to his feet and sprinted toward the airstrip with Billy. Shells whiffled through the air around them. The Tommies walked backward, laying down covering fire and methodically taking down Hastings' men.

...

Hastings reached the Junkers and climbed into the fuselage. "Where the hell've you been?" he said. "The Führer won't take kindly to—"

The mask lunged from the darkness and snatched his briefcase.

"Did you *really* think you'd be of use to us in Berlin?" Mörder said, his Luger leveled.

Hastings' jaw dropped.

"Auf Wiedersehen, Brigadier."

With a *crack*, Hastings was blown from the fuselage. His body hit the runway and rolled to a bloody stop in the snow.

...

Jack skidded to a stop beside Cammy. "You okay?"

"He's got a briefcase," she said, gasping for air. "It's everything we have on the boys!"

"Stay with her, Bill," Jack said, as Billy joined them.

Jack took off after the Junkers.

...

From the fuselage door, Mörder saw a figure sprinting after the aircraft. A soldier. A *soldier* Mörder recognized.

He took aim, and slowly squeezed the trigger.

...

McNulty stepped onto the airstrip ahead of the Junkers. He raised a machine-gun and opened fire.

The Junkers' windshield fractured in a spatter of blood on the navigator's side, and the aircraft veered wildly as the pilot fought to regain control.

...

Mörder fired at the boy but his shot went wide as he was nearly thrown from the fuselage. He cursed and took aim again, but the soldier was too far away.

...

The Junkers' pilot corrected his takeoff and drove the aircraft at McNulty. McNulty bounced off the fuselage and was thrown back just as the aircraft took to the skies.

...

Jack cursed, watching the Junkers disappear into the night.

The pain in his leg was excruciating. As his running slowed, he cursed his body for letting him down. Jack holstered his revolver. Breathless, he doubled over and gripped his knees.

"*You'll fail…*"

Jack looked up and spotted a crumpled figure on the runway. He limped toward it and saw that it was Hastings.

Cammy, Billy and the Tommies arrived at the spot with him.

"*All of you…*" Hastings wheezed, coughing blood. "*I'm not… alone.*"

He dislodged a tooth with his tongue and crunched down on it—then convulsed briefly before slumping, motionless. Snowflakes drifted onto his wide, dead eyes.

"Well," Hurricane said. "That's done for 'im."

"Where's McNulty?" Billy said, looking about suddenly.

"Fan out," Jack said. "Find him."

Billy and the Tommies followed Lancaster into the snow.

Cammy swayed and Jack took her arm. "I'm okay," she said. Touching the back of her head she winced. "I found a file in Hastings' office."

"A file?"

Cammy nodded. "And a name—*Gustav Lotz*.

"Mean anything?"

Cammy shook her head. "I don't know."

"Well, a file we can locate," Jack said. "At least you're still here in one piece."

"Captain?" The alarm in Lancaster's voice was evident.

Jack ran to him and saw McNulty at his feet. Jack skidded into the snow by his side and took his hand.

As if blind, McNulty looked beyond him and smiled. "*Jacky? That you, boy?*"

"It's me," Jack said. Cammy knelt beside them to examine McNulty's injuries.

"*You 'n' these boys,*" McNulty gasped, squeezing his hand. "*You're gonna save the world.*" He fought for every breath. "*Remember… what I told you… on the tower?*"

Jack nodded. "Yes, sir."

Cammy worked desperately to stem the blood from McNulty's wounds, taking bandages and dressings handed to her by Spitfire.

"*Make me proud, son...*"

McNulty's grip weakened.

"Sarge? Jack said, tears in his eyes. "You can't die!"

"*Dyin's easy, Jack,*" McNulty wheezed, the fog of his breath slowing. "*It's livin's… the hard part.*" He coughed blood. "*Keep 'em together, keep 'em… alive, and… you'll win this war.*"

Jack looked up at Billy, at Lancaster and the Tommies, but there was nothing they could do. "Cam?" Jack said helplessly. "Can't you—"

McNulty's eyes grew wide, and he exhaled one last time.

Cammy leaned forward, tears streaming down her cheeks, and closed the old man's eyes, kissing him gently on the forehead.

"*No.*" Jack said. "Come on, Cam, you can do something, you can—"

Cammy shook her head silently and stood. Lancaster put a comforting arm around her.

"But we can get him to the infirmary, can't we?" Jack said. "We can —"

"Jack." Billy put a hand on his friend's shoulder. "He's gone."

. . .

Mörder clasped the briefcase and seethed.

So, the boy had survived Dunkirk. Well, his luck would soon run out and when it did, Mörder would be there to claim him.

For now, he had his mission to accomplish. He would be patient, and return to Berlin with his prize. But when this was over and Great Britain a part of the Reich, Mörder vowed that he would find the young soldier who had destroyed all that he had ever held dear.

And when he did, Mörder would have his revenge.

# 16

## TANK GIRL

**J**ACK GASPED FOR AIR in the bear pit and wiped blood from his lip with bruised knuckles. He lurched forward, ankle-deep in mud and drenched in the pouring rain; his fists raised and ready.

"Come on then, 'obnail," Jack spat, wiping blood from the cut above his eye. "Do your worst!"

"Captain," said the shirtless giant stood before him. "Please. Don't make me—"

"*Do it!*" Jack yelled.

Towering above Jack, Pieter "Hobnail" Jadinski, a huge Polish soldier who had earned his nickname by owning the first pair of size thirteen boots in the camp, flexed bloody fingers painfully.

"I can't—"

"You're through when *I* say you're through," Jack growled, his feet unsteady. "*C'mon!*"

Jadinski glanced up at Billy and Lancaster above them, and reluctantly moved in. He dodged Jack's fist with ease, counterpunched him in the gut, then clipped his jaw, sending him reeling into the sludge.

"I'm sorry, Jack," Jadinski said, exhausted. "I'm sorry about McNulty —but I'm done." He climbed out of the pit.

"I dunno what you're trying to prove," Billy said from above.

"I ain't trying to prove *nothin'*," Jack said, rolling onto his back. He gasped for air, bruised and bloody.

"Well, he's proved one thing," Lancaster said, beside Billy. "He's proved you can't send a boy to do a man's job." He started back to the castle.

"Where you going?" Billy asked.

"I think it's time to put an end to this mess, don't you?" Lancaster paused, then walked back to the pit, and looked down. "Get out and get cleaned up."

"Get *out?*" Jack yelled from below. He limped to a near empty beer bottle and drained it. "You're just too afraid to get *in!*" He staggered, collapsing back into the mud.

"D'you know something, Captain?" Lancaster said. "For a minute the other night in that carnage, I thought, 'Now there's a man I can follow—a leader.' But then I look at you now. I told you on that tower: you've been down in the dirt for so long you don't 'ave no perspective. I can see now I was right. Stay down there, son, 'cos it's where you belong, isn't it? Anything else'd be too much 'ard work."

He glanced at Billy. "Get him out, William, 'n' get him back to the workshop."

"Rusty git," Jack muttered, trying to stand. "*You rusty git!*" He threw the bottle out of the pit in disgust.

Lancaster shook his head and disappeared from sight. Billy went after him.

Jack stared up at the heavens. The sky, much like his future, was clouded. When Jack had first arrived, he'd thought himself a man and Lancaster the machine. Now it seemed their roles had reversed. He'd seen another side to the sergeant. Lancaster had genuine concern for his men, for Billy too—whereas Jack had just wanted to score points, without emotion. Again, it came down to Lancaster, *always* bloody Lancaster. And with McNulty gone, there seemed nothing for him now in Achnacarry. His team felt like a ship without a rudder.

"He's right, you know."

Jack looked up and saw Billy. "About what?" Jack said, climbing from the bear pit. He pulled on his tunic.

"About you."

"If you've got somethin' to say, Bill, just say it!"

"Cam's worried 'bout you." Billy paused, then: "So am I."

"I'm fine."

"I've 'eard that before."

Jack looked away.

"When you dragged 'alf the kids in our squad into hell 'cos of Dan—"

Jack spun and hit him.

Billy rubbed his jaw. "Feel better now?" he said.

Jack started back toward the castle.

"Jack! You lost Danny, 'n' that weren't your fault. But if you ain't careful, you're gonna lose Cam 'n' all, and that *will* be."

"Sod off, Billy," Jack said, without turning.

But he knew his friend was right. It had been a week since McNulty's death, time enough for Jack to get steaming drunk and challenge every man in the castle to a fight. He felt anger, and helplessness, and in spite of Cammy's counsel, utterly lost.

He turned to say more, but Billy tripped him with his boot and pushed him onto his back.

"Get a grip," Billy said, "an' stop wallowin'. There's a war on if you hadn't noticed, 'an we've got work to do."

Jack watched him walk back to the castle. He felt cold sludge permeate his tunic. He squeezed his eyes shut, his chest heaving. He'd been defeated. Without McNulty's encouragement, he was directionless, without purpose. He couldn't do this on his own. Even Billy, the one person he could rely on, had turned away from him. When the hammer fell, Jack knew it would be on him to lead the team—but it was a team that so far remained divided. Jack hadn't asked for this command; had never *wanted* it.

He wished it all away.

"Hey soldier," chirped a voice above him.

Jack opened his eyes to see Cammy's silhouette standing over him.

"Boy, you took a spankin'." She took his hand and helped Jack to his feet.

"He's gone, Cam," Jack said. The pain in his leg had returned. "I just can't do it."

"McNulty went down fighting," Cammy replied. "We're all gonna die, Jack. But it's how we *live* that defines our lives."

She was right of course, but Jack's faith had been shaken.

"That *thing* tellin' you that you can't do this?" Cammy said. "It's fear. It's pain and exhaustion. And yes, they're a part of you, Jack, but they're not *you*. You've still got *fight* in you, I know you have, 'n' I know you're tired, 'n' I know you feel you can't go on... but this was always a long shot. It was never gonna be easy." She levelled her gaze at Jack. "You got a purpose here, man. *Real* purpose. And if there's one thing I know, it's that when life knocks you down, you gotta land on your ass, 'cos if you can *look* up, you can *get* up."

"And if I fail?" Jack muttered.

"Then fail *better* next time, dammit, 'cos I can't do this without you!"

Cammy teared up and stormed away.

"Cam?" Jack staggered after her. "Cammy, come on." He stumbled and fell.

Cammy sighed. How could she make this right? She returned to Jack and crouched at his side, wiping mud from his forehead.

"An' I thought Lancaster was tough," Jack said.

Cammy smiled sympathetically. "C'mon." She helped Jack to his feet.

"Where we going?"

"All work and no play, Jack, makes you a *very* dull boy." The sparkle in her eyes intrigued him. "You ready for a *real* challenge?"

. . .

"It's true I tell you!" said Spitfire, cleaning his gun in the workshop.

"What? Cam 'n' the Cap?" Hurricane said, surprised.

"Nah." Mosquito buffed his armor. "He's not her type."

"An' you are I s'pose?" Hurricane glared at Mosquito.

Mosquito ignored him and continued to buff his armor.

"Ah, I dunno boys," said Billy, "between McNulty and Lancaster, I think he might be losing—"

A lone binocular lens suddenly appeared behind Billy's shoulder, attached to a small but perfectly machined skeleton resembling a wasp. The segmented sections of its thorax, expertly welded together, were connected to a mass of intricate brass legs that ticked as a motor within its shell hummed.

"What the bleedin' 'ell's that?" Billy gasped.

The automata hopped up onto his shoulder and stared at him, whirring mechanically.

"Ah, there you are," Spitfire said. "Cam calls him a *drone*."

"Says he's the future of reconnaissance," Hurricane added.

Spitfire coaxed the little machine from Billy's shoulder onto his finger. It hopped on with a motorized whir of the miniature propellers in its wings, it's lens glowing as blue as the Tommies' eyes.

"An' what do *you* call 'it," Billy asked.

"A royal pain in the arse," Mosquito muttered. "Left oil in me crank shaft last week!"

"Oh, good lad," Hurricane said.

Mosquito tossed an oily rag over his head. "Watch it, Sapper!" he growled.

"Ah, he don't mean nothin' by it," Spitfire said, stroking the little drone's lens. The machine purred appreciatively. Spitfire looked at Billy. "I call him *Bug*."

"Soft git," Mosquito muttered.

Spitfire raised his finger, examining the little machine.

"Funny lookin' blighter, isn't he?" Billy said, fascinated.

"Cam made him for me, he's part of my kit. She said he might come in handy one day."

"Well, I can't see it myself," Billy said, leaning in close to peer into the drone's pulsing lens. "Ain't much goin' on in there, is there?" The drone stared at him curiously, its miniature propellers angling in their wing housing, buzzing in tandem with its movement.

"Least he knows where he came from," Spitfire sighed. "Who made him, I mean."

"And you don't?" Billy asked.

The Tommies glanced at each other.

...

Cammy picked the padlock securing the castle's vehicle compound.

"Isn't this risky?" Jack asked.

"If life's got no risk, then what's the point, right?"

"Look, Cam, I appreciate this 'n' all, but—"

"C'mon Jack, live a little." Cammy removed the chain and stepped into the compound, beckoning for Jack to follow. "Just be quiet about it. They don't like me snoopin' around down here unsupervised; think I'll scavenge parts for the boys from their toy tanks."

"And would you?"

"In a New York minute!"

Jack followed her along rows of training tanks, landing craft, and assault vehicles to an open space where two mounds were covered by tarpaulin.

"Lanc said you needed perspective," Cammy said. "I figure the only way you can get it is by taking you outta the castle, and up there." She nodded toward the black, snow-capped mountains surrounding the estate.

"It's a helluva distance."

"Sure is," Cammy said, pulling away the tarp. "Which is why we'll need *these*."

Jack gaped in astonishment at two monstrous motorcycle frames housing an intricate network of cylinders, grilles, and engine components. Each vehicle was encapsulated by a single thick caterpillar track.

"I call 'em *crawlers*," Cammy said proudly. "You like 'em?"

Jack approached the nearest crawler and crouched to examine the engine. "You *built* these?" he said, running his hand respectfully over the bike's sculpted innards.

"Half a ton of grease, guts 'n' gasoline."

Jack shook his head, awed by the workmanship.

"What can I say?" Cammy said. "While the boys pop bolts on the parade ground, I have time on my hands to tinker. That old Matilda back in the workshop's the tip of the iceberg. These babies are the only way to traverse the Highlands, and they *move*. Full tilt, they can get up to seventy miles an hour—providing nothing shakes loose."

She unclipped a pair of goggles from her utility belt, pulled them on, and swung a leg over the saddle of one of the crawlers. She gave Jack an amused smile. "First to the Chieftain's Gorge?"

"Hell yeah," Jack said. He knew the place from his yomps with McNulty.

His morning's despair was suddenly forgotten at the prospect of escaping the castle with Cammy. A pair of scuffed goggles dangled from the second crawler's bars, and he pulled them on as Cammy kick-started her machine. It roared then rumbled irreverently, spitting diesel from dual tailpipes.

Jack clambered onto his crawler, wrestling to keep it upright. "There a trick to these things?"

"Sure is," Cammy said. She gripped her bars, leaned forward, and revved the engine. "*You try to keep up!*"

She thundered out of the compound and across the courtyard.

"Yes, ma'am," Jack said, kick-starting his crawler and hunkering behind his bars. Dumping the clutch, he roared after Cammy in an unholy blast of acceleration.

The gate sentries barely had time to raise the barrier as Cammy zoomed beneath it in a deafening blur, hurtling down the lane beside the loch. This wasn't the first time Doctor Sullivan had given the sentries a fright, but they weren't expecting her to have company. They were already pulling down the barrier again when Jack blasted by, ducking beneath the barrier and missing it by inches.

...

For the first time in weeks, Jack felt free. Free from the drills and procedures of his training, free from the rank and responsibility he'd fallen into, and—*thank God*—free from Lancaster's ceaseless disapproval.

Jack sped over a humpback bridge, gaining in confidence on his crawler. As the vehicle's tread slammed onto the cobbles beyond, he gunned the engine. Up ahead, he saw Cammy hang a right off the road and into the wilderness of the lowlands. Braking as late as he dared, Jack slung his weight sideways and heaved his crawler after her.

Cammy flashed a glance back and grinned. Veering left and right, she blocked his advance and splashed across a brook in a spray of water and shingle, then sped up the opposite bank. Behind her Jack churned earth, struggling to control his machine. Cammy raced through heather that shimmered in waves across the landscape.

Growling across the mountainside, Cammy hung a left, forcing Jack to slam on his brakes. She mounted a ridge and soared over a drystone wall, then bounced down into a field on the other side. Roaring across it, Cammy scattered a herd of sheep, who bleated terror in her wake.

Jack smashed through the wall behind her, crisscrossing the pasture to avoid the sheep—as well as an angry crofter who emerged from a barn, red-faced in anger, to take a swipe at him. Jack banked left to avoid the crofter but sideswiped a haystack. Up ahead, he saw Cammy accelerate and thunder across a ravine, barely making the other side.

Spitting straw, Jack gritted his teeth and took full control of his crawler. Tightening his grip on the bars, he screamed across the ravine and bounced down behind Cammy. His crawler ploughed dirt as he accelerated to overtake her. As he pulled up alongside her, he leaned over his bars, glanced at her, and grinned—then whooped a cry of freedom as they roared in unison across the mountainside.

With the wind whipping her hair, Cammy joined him in his exultation, hollering wildly as the first rays of sunlight broke through cloud and rolled across the highlands.

Together they glided across the landscape, the race and the war forgotten as they weaved a diesel-fueled ballet over bracken-swathed fells into the mists beyond.

Their eyes locked as they approached the peak ahead. Neither refused to back down or brake, but each dared the other to do so. Chieftain's Gorge approached, and beyond it, Jack knew, was a sheer drop into the valley below. He put his foot down, roared forward, and cut his crawler in front of Cammy—then swerved to a stop just inches from the abyss.

Exhilarated, he pulled up his goggles, allowing the dawn sun to storm his vision. "Not bad," he said, sitting back in his crawler's saddle.

"Your first time out," Cammy said, dismounting. "I let you win."

Jack smiled.

"You like how she handles?"

"Feels good to have something you've made behave itself for a change," Jack said.

Punching his arm playfully, Cammy gazed out across the highlands. "When I'm out here it's like… like the war, like the rest of the world, it doesn't exist, y'know? It's like I'm free."

Her eyes sparkled in the sunlight. Even covered in smoke and dirt, she was still the most stunning girl Jack had ever seen. Following her gaze, he looked across the landscape, at the stark beauty of its heather-covered peaks and abandoned crag-top castles shimmering in the mist.

"It's beautiful."

"Yes, it is," Cammy said. "Worth fighting for."

There it was. Jack knew if he left now, this moment would be the last he'd share with a woman he'd grown to respect, to admire, and maybe more.

"McNulty had a dream," Cammy said.

"McNulty's gone," Jack replied. "The dream died with him."

"It's alive, Jack, inside *you*. You just gotta make it reality."

"And Lancaster?"

"Never said it'd be easy. But you *can* make this work, I believe that."

Jack sighed. "You like to fix broken things, huh?"

Cammy smiled. She linked his arm, resting her head on his shoulder and together, they watched a new day dawn.

# 17

## HELLFIRE CORNER

**MULCHING COMPOST** around the roots of his rose, Lancaster gazed skyward.

The undercarriage of a B-24 Liberator rattled overhead and descended toward the airstrip. As he watched it disappear behind the castle, he heard the crawlers' engines. Jack and Cammy roared into the castle's courtyard and headed for the vehicle compound.

He shook his head irritably and returned to his gardening.

"Sergeant Lancaster?"

Angus McGregor, a portly senior comms officer from the castle's transmitter room, puffed red-faced across the parade square bearing a folded piece of paper and a mild expression of unease. "I'm terribly sorry to bother you, sir," he said, handing Lancaster the message. "We've just decoded this from Combined Ops," McGregor fought to catch his breath, "in London, sir. *Code red.*"

...

"And that's about all any of us can remember," Hurricane said. "The Western Front, I mean. Before that, well, we dunno."

Billy looked from Hurricane, to Mosquito and Spitfire. The Tommies' recounting of their history had been a sad one; of allies saved and enemies defeated yes, but also of friends, *men*, lost along the way. After his experiences in Europe, Billy now felt a kinship with these machines. They were pawns—all of them—shuffled around a board, sacrificed by old men hundreds of miles away from the action for the sake of other pieces, old men prepared to fight to the last drop of everyone else's blood to secure victory at any price. Billy felt sorry for them. The Tommies had been created as weapons of war, manufactured for a single purpose, living, if such a term could be used, with the ever-present knowledge that they were nothing but cannon-fodder, expendable.

The Tommies were undoubtedly machines, but in Billy's estimation, they were so much more.

"I'll talk to Jack," he said, "see if he can find anything out."

"Oh, would you?" said Spitfire. "That'd be-"

"A complete waste o'time," said Lancaster, entering the workshop.

"Why?" demanded Spitfire. "Why can't we know where we came from?"

"I think you'd better cool down, son," Lancaster crossed his arms like a stern father, "have a think about what rank you're addressin'."

"Kid's right, Lancaster," said Hurricane, "Things are changing round 'ere. It's time you changed too."

"Any more back-chat an' I'll—"

"But Sarge—" Mosquito pleaded.

"I don't want to hear no more about—"

"About what?" Jack said, entering the workshop with Cammy.

"All right?" said Billy awkwardly.

Jack glanced at Cammy, then nodded. "Look, boys I, uh… I know we've had our differences over the last few weeks, but I just wanna say that from now on, we're gonna—"

"Captain," Lancaster interrupted. He held out the slip of paper. "You need to read this."

Jack took the paper and read.

The team watched him expectantly. "Well, what does it say?" Billy asked.

"Best pack your buckets 'n' spades, boys," Jack said, looking up. "Looks like we're off to the seaside."

...

At the southern end of the Kent downs sat an elevated spit known as Shakespeare Cliff. Owing much of its striking façade to a composition of white chalk and flint, it ran east to the town of Dover, and west to the town's seaport. It was visible from the French coast, as it marked the point where Great Britain was closest to Europe across the Channel. The white cliffs of Dover had long formed a symbolic bulwark against countless invasions throughout history, and as Jack was driven along the coast road to meet his contact, he knew it might well have to do so again.

As his car slowed, Jack felt renewed vigor for whatever trials lay ahead. The rest of the team had been taken to Hawkinge Air Base and he would shortly join them, but first, he needed to know why they'd been summoned.

Jack got out of his car and saw a jeep parked nearby. Beyond it, a uniformed man stood at the furthest point of a cliff, tracing vapor trails in the sky through binoculars.

Jack dropped his haversack and approached.

"Admiral Dowding?"

"Captain Stone," said the man without turning. "Welcome to Dover. Your presence here is some much-needed good news. Something we've been in rather short supply of along the south coast of late."

"That's rationing for you, sir," Jack quipped, following Dowding's gaze.

Dowding lowered the binoculars, noting Jack's interest. "Just watching one of our boys take a pop at a Jerry raiding party. Care to take a look?"

"Please," Jack said, keen to see the dogfight in more detail.

He took the binoculars and located the vapor trail, then traced it up through cumulus until he found a lone wounded Spitfire trailing black smoke. It was zipping through cloud with two Heinkels on its tail. Propellers whirling, the pursuers fought desperately to track the little fighter. Then Jack saw flashes and heard the distant pea-shooter chatter of machine-gun fire.

Jack marveled at the skill of the pilots as they dipped and weaved suicidally through cloud, seemingly defying gravity and the laws of physics. He wondered for a brief second what it must be like to fight for your life alone in aerial combat. *Not for me*, he thought. It was hard enough staying alive on the ground, never mind in the air

"They call this place 'Hellfire Corner,'" Dowding said, fighting to light his pipe in the gale. "Believe me, it's well named. There isn't a day goes by that Nosy and his boys aren't up there defending our convoys."

"Nosy?"

"Alan Parker, commander of 2 Squadron RAF at Hawkinge." Dowding squinted skyward as a Heinkel exploded in a brilliant white flash. "Rather turned the tables on them, what?" he said proudly. "Good show, Nosy."

The wreckage spiraled into the ocean. Jack scanned the sky for the pilot, but couldn't see a parachute.

"They seem to want to go down fighting rather than live to fight another day," Hastings said, frowning. "Funny lot, the Germans." He finally lighted his pipe, and puffed on it thoughtfully.

Parker's Spitfire corkscrewed toward the ocean. "He's hit!" Jack cried.

"No, he's not," Dowding said calmly without even looking.

The remaining Heinkel was in hot pursuit, but with the Spitfire plummeting and apparently a goner, the Heinkel peeled away and started back to France.

"But how do you—"

The little Spitfire nosed up into the air, performed a perfect loop, and brought its guns around to bear on the Heinkel's rear. Machine-guns blazing, the little Spitfire scored a direct hit on its opponent's back quarter. The Heinkel's entire right side erupted in a ball of flame and debris. The Spitfire banked hard and looped back toward the coast as, trailing black smoke, the Heinkel spiraled into the ocean.

"Impressive," Jack said, lowering the binoculars and handing them back to Dowding.

"It doesn't always end so well," Dowding said solemnly as Parker's Spitfire approached. "But now we have you boys, eh?" He waved as Parker soared overhead, dipping his wings triumphantly.

Jack gazed across the ocean toward France.

"You know, it wasn't so long ago that Drake looked out there and spied the Spanish armada," Dowding said softly, "and before them the Normans, and before them the—well, you get my drift. Now it's Göring's bloody Luftwaffe. There's something really rather tiresome about being the only child in the playground with the toy that everyone wants."

"I'm just not sure where we fit in, sir."

"Walk with me, Jack."

As the sea battered the rocks beneath them, Dowding walked along a narrow coastal path. "Unlike the Hun, we currently have neither an airborne assault force nor facilities to train one. I met with the PM last week, and he's ordered me to remedy the situation—starting with your boys. Alan Parker's base at Hawkinge has been nominated as your test center, and Alan's currently prepping a roster for your training."

"What kind of training?" Jack asked.

"The kind involving parachutes."

Jack imagined Billy's reaction to that news.

"I suspect the PM's order is in preparation for some clandestine party he has planned, but I know neither where nor when. I do, however, know that when the time comes, you'll need to be as good in the air as you are on the ground. In spite of our totally inadequate resources, Nosy will get you through, but you'll be covering in six weeks what Jerry's had six years to perfect. In essence, you're starting from scratch, so it's a leap into the dark for us all—quite literally, I expect, for your boys. But if Nosy can teach you the basics in what little time we have, then I don't think we can ask for much more."

Jack felt his hackles rise, yet again it appeared something was afoot, and he'd be the last to know.

"I'll have my man take you to Hawkinge," Dowding said, "your team should already be there. I understand those machines of yours are extraordinary. Let's hope we don't break any."

Dowding led Jack back to his jeep. The driver's door opened, and a pretty young woman, a WAAF corporal, got out and saluted.

"Captain Stone?" she said, stifling a smile as she saluted. "Corporal Polly Dunston, sir. Pleased to make your acquaintance."

Jack saluted and moved to pick up his haversack, but Polly beat him to it.

"I drove Miss Sullivan to Hawkinge earlier, sir," Polly said, heaving the sack into the jeep. "She told me all about you."

"She did?" Jack said suspiciously.

"Well, only the fun stuff." Polly suddenly seemed aware that her enthusiasm had exceeded her rank. "I'm sorry, sir." Avoiding Dowding's gaze, she climbed into the driver's seat.

Bashing the Digger Flake tobacco from his pipe, Dowding pocketed it. "I'll be honest, Jack, this whole thing seems a little fanciful, and quite over my head of course, but if you can achieve what Winston thinks you can achieve, well…"

"We'll do our very best, sir," Jack said, saluting.

"The way things are going," Dowding replied, glancing skyward, "you may bloody well have to." He returned Jack's salute and walked to the other car. "Good luck, Captain."

Jack climbed into the jeep beside Polly, then realized she was staring. "Er, something to say, Corporal?"

"I hear there's never a dull moment around you, Captain," Polly said, as she turned the key and revved the jeep's engine. Vera Lyn blasted from the wireless.

"You could say that!" Jack yelled over the music.

"Then if that's true, sir," Polly yelled back, "you're going to love it 'round here!"

Jack was about to reply, but Polly shouted, "Buckle up, Captain, and hold on!"

Clinging to the dashboard, Jack said a prayer as they sped off down the lane.

# 18

## THE BRYLCREAM BOYS

**R**AF **HAWKINGE** lay three miles inland from the south coast between Folkstone and Dover. Renowned as the nearest Fighter Command station to enemy-occupied France, its pilots had endured relentless swathes of attacks, and were a mere ten minutes response time to the Luftwaffe's air fields in France's Pas-De-Calais. The station, also used as a forward base by other squadrons, enabled the dogged RAF to intercept Luftwaffe squadrons approaching the south-east coast as soon as they were detected by British radar. But it was this issue of proximity to the action, that had also made Hawkinge vulnerable to attack.

As Jack crossed the airstrip with Billy he saw the base had been subject to the same long-range cross-Channel shelling as many of the battle-scarred towns Polly had driven him through. If Jack had thought London was in bad shape, his journey through Dover, a town so often referred to as the lock and key to the kingdom, had opened his eyes to what the Germans were truly capable of: mountains of rubble and cratered streets were the grim harvest of destruction reaped by the Nazis' guns. Jack had read newspaper accounts of the mighty German shore batteries stationed along the French coast, and as Polly navigated the rubble strewn airstrip he made a mental note to pay them a visit some day with the Tommies for a little late-night sabotage.

Looking around the airfield, Jack knew in these final desperate days it was the RAF, not the Tommies, who were Britain's last line of defense. But while the RAF's ground crews and pilots maintained a stalwart round the clock vigil protecting Great Britain's shores, *surely*, Jack thought, *we can take the fight back to the Nazis*.

They had to buy some time.

. . .

"You what?" Billy said, wrenching Jack from his thoughts.

"I said, you're a dark horse," Jack said, amused.

"Dunno what you're on about," Billy replied dismissively.

"Yeah? I saw the way Polly looked at you."

Billy said nothing. He'd hit it off with her during their journey to Hawkinge after learning that she was from Bramley, the same village in Surrey where he'd grown up with his grandparents. As Jack had exited the jeep, Billy had hung back to talk to the sweet young WAAF, leaving her giggling churlishly.

Jack grinned.

"Well, I got news for you *hero*, you ain't only stunner 'round here! Anyway, what about you 'n' Cammy? You've been hittin' it off pretty good of late."

Jack ignored him.

"Oh, the *silent* treatment now, is it?"

"Ah, I dunno, Bill, me 'n' Cam, it's…"

"Ah, don't tell me it's complicated. You're a bloke, she's a bird… Twenty seconds o' bravery, isn't that what you always tell me?"

Jack wanted desperately to really *talk* to Cammy, tell her how he felt, but right now he had other priorities. Dowding's revelation about the team's future had given him cause for concern.

He picked up his pace as he strode toward a group of scruffy young pilots idling outside a battered canteen shed, where a tattered pair of long johns fluttered from a windsock mast. The men—or rather *boys*, Jack noted—were lounging in an assortment of deck chairs, old sofas, and hammocks.

Jack approached the nearest pilot, whose face was obscured by a comic. "All right, son?" he said.

As Billy reached for the comic, a scruffy three-legged terrier bolted from beneath the hammock, growling territorially.

The comic slid aside to reveal a handsome young man in his late teens. He smiled affably and raised an eyebrow, allowing the aviator sunglasses on his forehead to slip down over his eyes.

"We're lookin' for Alan Parker," Jack said.

"Oh, he's around here somewhere, I shouldn't wonder," the young man replied.

The other pilots sat up, smirking and digging each other.

Billy scowled, his feathers ruffled. "Now let's not get off on the wrong foot 'ere, sunshine."

The young man sat up and swung his right leg around to the ground. "Many a true word, Private," he said jovially. He used both hands to lift his left leg, swung it down, and knocked on it three times. The hollow sound indicated it was wooden.

"Heard you were heading our way," said the boy, turning to the other pilots. "Heads up, boys, it's the rest of Churchill's likely lads!"

The pilots gave a lackluster cheer.

"Parker?" Jack gasped.

"*Squadron Leader* Parker, to be precise." He picked up a cane and leaned on it to stand. "But the boys here call me Nosy," he said, smiling. "And if the first pint's on you tonight, then you may do the same." He untethered the terrier's leash.

"But you're just a kid!" Billy said. "How old are you?"

"Old enough to fly a Spit, old boy," Parker said, limping toward the canteen shed. The terrier trotted obediently at his heel. "Care for a spot of tea?"

Jack and Billy followed Parker back to the shed. Jack noticed Lancaster's rose in a pot beside the door.

Billy saw it as well. "Don't waste no time, does he?"

The interior of the canteen shed was spartan. A lone tea urn sat on a table among dirty tin mugs.

"Has Miss Sullivan arrived?" Jack asked as Parker poured their tea.

"She's prepping for our briefing." Parker handed Jack a mug.

Jack nodded thanks and looked out the window. The Tommies were admiring Spitfires near the airstrip, and behind them, a group of young pilots were admiring the Tommies.

"Your chaps seem to've settled in nicely," Parker said. "They're beautiful machines. Perked my boys up no end."

Still looking out the window, Jack saw Cammy entering another shed carrying something covered in sacking. "Yeah, beautiful."

Parker handed Billy a mug, then eased himself into a chair and patted the terrier's head as it sat beside him. He sipped his tea, then winced and rubbed his leg.

"What 'appened?" Billy asked.

"Dunkirk," Parker said. "Minor disagreement with a Messerschmitt, took a bit of fire." He scratched the terrier's head, and the dog closed its eyes appreciatively. "I got off lightly. My pal? Well, he wasn't so lucky."

"I'm sorry," Jack said.

"Not your fault. I gather you boys saw some action of your own in that mess?"

Jack nodded.

"Well, we all carry the scars of our experiences, don't we?" Parker said. "And this?" He tapped his wooden leg with his cane. "Gets me to the front of the queue where the ladies are concerned so, every cloud, as they say." Parker set down his tea. "Now. I understand from the powers that be, your boys need parachute training?"

"You—wait, what?" Billy said, his mouth falling open.

"My pilots won't be happy nursing greenhorns."

"*Parachute training?*" Billy exclaimed, grabbing Jack's arm.

"Miss Sullivan says she may have something to placate them," Parker continued, ignoring Billy's outburst, "but unless it's Adolf's head or a barrel of best bitter from The Crooked House down the road, I have my reservations. We've precious resource here at Hawkinge, and we're desperately overstretched as it is to spare men or materials."

"Orders *are* orders," Jack said.

"Indeed they are," Parker replied amiably, "just don't expect my boys to like them." He checked his watch. "Well, Miss Sullivan's briefing us shortly. Excuse me, gentlemen, I'd best go and wrangle my pilots." He stood and limped to the door, then: "A remarkable woman, Miss Sullivan. Quite the little firecracker."

Jack's face flushed red. He downed his tea.

Parker smiled knowingly. "Bottoms up, old boy," he said, winking at Billy. Then he limped from the hut.

As the door closed behind him, Billy turned to Jack.

"Don't even think about it," Jack growled.

...

The briefing shed was musty with a lingering smell of men and apathy. Cammy strode through the funk to join Jack and Parker at the head of the room. Before them sat two rows of pilots chattering expectantly, and behind them stood Billy and the Tommies.

Billy looked down at Parker's terrier, which was yapping at his feet. "Cute little mutt," he said, bending to muzz the terrier's chin. "What's 'is name?"

"Rusty," Lancaster replied, scooping the little dog up.

Billy smirked.

"What?" Lancaster stared at Billy blankly, clearly missing the irony.

"All right boys, settle down," Parker said finally.

The pilots continued their chatter.

Cammy jammed two fingers into her mouth and blew a shrill ear-splitting whistle. The chatter in the room fell silent.

"Good-oh," Parker said. "Now, you've all met Miss Sullivan—"

An explosion of wolf whistles and cheers drowned him out.

"Pipe down, you animals!" Parker yelled, grinning.

Billy noticed Jack shift uncomfortably.

"Now, Captain Stone and his team are here at the old man's request, so listen up." Parker gestured for Jack to step forward.

"You've all met the Tommies," Jack said, a little nervous. "They're an iron in the PM's fire called the Commando, and it's up to us to get in, raise hell, and get out before Jerry even knows he's been hit. In order to do that, one of the methods we need to master is the aerial drop."

"Now the last time these boys were operational," Parker interjected, "the Royal Flying Corps were still running biplanes over the Somme. So as such, they're new to aerial combat. And that, 2 Squadron, is where we come in. We're going to teach these old dogs some new tricks."

"This is bloody rich," Hurricane muttered.

"In essence," Parker continued, "we've been asked to achieve something that's never been done in the history of the British military: the creation of *paratroops*, a unit of airborne soldiers who can be dropped in front of, over, or behind enemy lines at a minute's notice."

A gasp swept through the crowd, not least from Billy, who was still in shock at his prospects.

A chair creaked, and a young pilot not much older than Parker stood and smoothed his uniform.

"Yes, Dicky?" Parker said.

"With all due respect, Skip, that's impossible."

"Maybe so," Parker replied calmly, "but still and all, we have six weeks to achieve it."

Another pilot stood and took the pipe from his mouth. "We're Home Chain's number one squadron, Nosy. Why do *we* have to assist?"

The other pilots muttered agreement.

Parker looked to Cammy, who took a step forward.

"Radar—"

The sound of disapproval continued.

"*Radar!*" Cammy shouted.

The room fell silent.

"Radar only covers the south coast's defense chain above five thousand feet; below that you're blind as bats. In exchange for your assistance, I'll help you plug the gaps, deal with incoming strays sneaking in undetected. Once the Krauts know it's not an option, you'll find those low-level raiding and reconnaissance parties who've been kickin' your asses recently diminish real quick, as will the numbers on your casualty board."

"And how d'you propose to get *them* airborne?" asked a skinny young pilot with an eye patch.

"Yeah," Hurricane said. "We weigh more than Billy!"

Embarrassed, Billy tried to suck in his gut.

"They're too big for Spits, Nosy," said another young pilot.

"The answer's twofold," Cammy said. "The reinforced chutes for the Tommies won't be here for another week, so in their absence, they'll use *these*." She reached under a bench and pulled out the covered object Jack had seen her carrying earlier. Removing the sacking like a magician's assistant, she revealed a sturdy leather harness attached to two large battered cylinders.

"What the 'ell…" Mosquito muttered.

"I call it the Heaven Stormer," Cammy said proudly. "It's developed primarily for short-burst jumps: rivers, gorges, that kinda thing. But in the absence of chutes, I've adapted it for aerial drops."

"A jet pack?" Spitfire gasped.

Cammy looked at the Tommies. "So what d'you think?"

The Tommies stared at her, aghast.

"O—kay…" Cammy continued, "two engines take you outta the aircraft, one gives thrust, the other brakes. Opening the thrust'll give you a descent speed of roughly two hundred feet a second, after which you kick in the gas."

"Gas?" Jack asked.

"Yeah, nitrous."

"Oxide?" Billy stared at her wide-eyed.

"Okay, so it's still in development," Cammy admitted defensively. "I haven't worked through the kinks."

"*Kinks?*" Lancaster blurted.

"Comforting that, innit?" Hurricane said, giving Spitfire a dig.

"Is it safe?" Jack asked.

"I think so, although it may be a little unstable at altitude."

"And you're putting them in the air?"

"Only to nine thousand feet. At that altitude they'll be fine, I'm sure."

"You're *sure?*" Mosquito blurted.

"This is insane," said a pilot in the front row.

"No, it's not," said another. "They can easily drop from three thousand —"

The pilots started to argue with each other, while Billy and the Tommies bickered over the viability and reliability of the stormers.

"Knock it off, you bozos!" Cammy yelled.

The room grew quiet.

"Like it or not, boys, this is it," Parker said. "We run them through chute training, they help us with our blind spots. Now I've jumped previously, which is why I'll be lead instructor." He looked at a pilot in the front row. "Flynn, you'll be my second." The man rolled his eyes and nodded. "Though we may lack the experience, manuals or special equipment—" Parker continued.

"This gets worse by the minute!" Lancaster said.

"We're keen, enthusiastic, and we're willing to give it a go."

"I'll be honest, he's not selling it," Mosquito groaned.

"Thank you," Jack said to Parker as the group filed out of the shed.

"Don't thank me," Parker said. "Let's just make sure they can do it."

Jack nodded, then: "Cam, you said there were *two* solutions to getting the boys in the air. What's the second?"

At that moment, a deafening bass drone sounded outside. Cammy looked at Jack and smiled. "She's right on time!"

# 19

## FLIGHT OF THE VALIANT

**A** **HUGE SHADOW RUMBLED** overhead, its silhouette obscuring the sun. While it resembled many of the American bombers Jack had seen in newsreels, the aircraft on approach to Hawkinge was far larger and vastly different. Two tiers of wings housed eight sets of huge whirling prop-rotors mounted on individual engine pods. They protruded from either side of a double-decked fuselage that rattled above them as the massive battleship droned through the cloud and descended onto the airstrip.

"What the 'ell..." Billy gasped as the bomber screeched onto the runway in a great plume of dirt and debris. It bounced twice, corrected course, and roared past the crowd outside the shed, clattering debris in its wake.

"She's beautiful, right?" Cammy was unable to conceal her excitement.

"*She?*" Jack asked.

"She's got curves an' can kick ass, Jack. 'Course she's a girl!"

"Christ, it even makes the jet pack look safe," Mosquito said, watching the fortress groan around and arc toward them.

"What the 'eck is it?" Spitfire asked.

"A bleedin' wreck," grumbled Hurricane.

"She's the first tilt-rotor super-fortress," Cammy said proudly.

"Looks like our lend/lease agreement with Roosevelt's paying off," Parker remarked. "I've heard rumors of such things, but I never thought —"

"I call her the *Valiant*," Cammy said, then to Jack: "She's our new mobile command."

"This don't look good," Billy whispered in Jack's ear. "It's in worse shape than the Tommies!"

"I 'eard that." Hurricane gave Billy a shove.

The fortress ground to a halt, and Cammy crossed the airstrip. "Hey!"

she shouted as the cargo bay door in the fortress's rear end lowered and its pilot emerged onto the airstrip.

"Okay, people," he yelled. "Who's ready for the ride o' their—"

The pilot spotted the Tommies and stopped abruptly, then slowly removed his goggles revealing two bruised eyes.

"Oh, you got to be shittin' me!" Hurricane growled. "It's that arse'ole from the bar!"

"Hey, guys, c'mon," the pilot said, taking a nervous step back. "I mean, we're all on the same side here, right?"

"I'm gonna kill 'im!" Hurricane said. He stomped past Cammy toward the pilot.

"Oh, man," Cammy sighed.

"You know him?" Jack asked, joining her.

"Unfortunately. Sal Remmy. Back home they call him 'The Fixer.' He's one o' the best aviation engineers around, but…"

Hurricane closed in on Remmy.

"Hey, hey I dig machines, man, I swear!" The pilot backed up. He tried to run back into the fortress, but Hurricane snatched the scruff of his overalls, lifting him into the air.

"But?" Jack prompted Cammy.

"Hurricane called it," she said. "Guy's an asshole. Hey Remmy, where's my crew?"

"*Crew?*" Remmy laughed, still in Hurricane's grip. "What crew? I'm all ya got."

Jack groaned.

"Another Yank in the ranks." Parker glanced quickly at Cammy. "Apologies, Miss Sullivan, no offense intended."

"None taken." She turned to Hurricane. "H, enough already!"

"He started it!" Hurricane yelled back.

"Put 'im down for God's sake," Lancaster growled. "That's an order."

Begrudgingly, Hurricane dropped Remmy onto the asphalt.

"Well, I'd better go establish the pecking order," Parker said. "Excuse me."

He limped across the airstrip, Rusty trotting at his heel. As Hurricane stepped aside, Remmy stood and lit a stogie with a Zippo lighter. He pulled an oily rag from the pocket of his bomber jacket and wiped his hands on it.

"If it ain't the Brylcream boys," Remmy said as Parker approached.

"If it isn't John Wayne," Parker replied sourly.

"Heard you needed a hand, kid."

"Can't help what you've heard," Parker said, tapping a piece of the fortress's debris with his cane. "You plan on parking that thing here permanently?"

"Ouch, kid, that hurts," Remmy said. "She's the only transport we had with a big enough ass for your boys there." He nodded toward Hurricane and the Tommies. "I got orders here somewhere." He rifled through his pockets and cast a glance back at the *Valiant*. "She's unique, kid, one of a kind."

"Oh, she certainly is that." Parker eyed the fortress with disdain. "And it's *Squadron Leader*."

"Here they are," Remmy said, ignoring him. He pulled a crumpled piece of paper from his overalls and stuffed it into Parker's tunic pocket, leaving a greasy smear. "Oh, I'm sorry," he sneered. "Let me help you with that." He wiped the oily rag over Parker's pocket, making an even bigger mess.

"Shit," Cammy muttered.

"Well, I think this conversation's over," Parker said calmly.

"Me too, kid," Remmy said. "Hey, is your momma home? Maybe I could talk to her instead?"

Rusty started to growl.

"And tell *Lassie* there to cool it," Remmy said.

"Kindly remove your wreck off my strip," Parker snapped.

"I respectfully decline. Plus, you 'n' your boys are just kids."

"Oh, I wouldn't judge a book by its cover, old boy. Our bite's much worse than our bark." Parker smiled cordially. "Move your wreck now, there's a good chap."

Remmy wrinkled his nose.

"Why don't you go take a flying—"

Rusty leapt at Remmy, knocking him off his feet. Snarling, he tore into the pilot's boot.

"Get it off, man! Get it off!" Remmy yelled, trying to wrestle the dog from his boot.

"Welcome to England, old boy." Parker turned and limped calmly back to the briefing shed.

At that moment, a klaxon wailed across the airstrip, and Parker's attitude instantly changed. "*Scramble boys, scramble!*" he yelled, clanging a bell above the briefing shed door.

2 Squadron leapt into action, grabbing their gear and sprinting across the airstrip. They climbed into their Spitfires, slid their cockpit canopies closed and prepared to take off.

Remmy had finally shaken off Rusty. He staggered up onto the *Valiant*'s cargo bay door. "Hey, you coming or what?"

Cammy looked at Jack doubtfully. "Think we should stay put?"

"The cupboard's bare on the coast when it comes to anti-aircraft guns," Parker said, pulling on his leather flight helmet. "And what we do have is manned by men older than your machines. Plus, you've some awfully big guns on that crate of yours." Parker nodded at the *Valiant*'s turrets. It'd be a tragedy if your senior parachute instructor bit the bullet a day before starting your training."

Jack looked at Cammy. "Kid's got a point."

"Guess there's no time like the present then," Cammy said. "Let's go say hello."

"Oh, no," Lancaster said. "My boys ain't gettin' in *that* thing!"

"*My* boys," Jack corrected.

"*They* ain't goin' nowhere," Lancaster said indignantly. "Least not 'til those death traps Camilla's made 'ave been tested."

The *Valiant*'s bay door started to rise.

"You comin'?" Remmy yelled again, this time from the fortress's open cockpit window. The tilt-props had already started to rotate.

"Lanc, we don't have time for this!" Cammy shouted.

Jack called to the Tommies. "C'mon, boys, get on board!"

"Stay where you are," Lancaster countered, standing between Jack and the Tommies. "I said they ain't goin' nowhere!" He spun on his tread and headed toward the canteen shed.

"Sergeant!" Jack shouted. He stormed after Lancaster and grabbed his arm. "Get your rusty arse on the—"

Lancaster whirled, snatched Jack's tunic, swung him around, and hurled him through the air. Jack hit the shed wall above the door which crunched inward, then he peeled away and dropped to the ground, smashing Lancaster's plant pot.

Billy rushed to Jack's side and helped him to his feet.

Hurricane grabbed Lancaster's shoulder and shoved him against a wall. "What the 'ell are you doing?"

"I never meant—" Lancaster appeared shocked by his own behavior.

"The fight's out *there*," Hurricane spat. "It's out there, Lancaster, not 'ere! *You* might wanna get boxed up in that stinkin' warehouse for another twenty years, but *we* don't!"

Lancaster looked at Mosquito and Spitfire, then at Cammy. "Camilla, I didn't—"

Cammy's glare silenced him.

"All right, boys, show's over," Billy said. "Everyone onto the big scary machine, eh?"

He hustled into the *Valiant*'s loading bay, and Mosquito and Spitfire followed.

Still pinned by Hurricane, Lancaster watched Jack storm after them. "Captain, I—"

Jack spun. "Consider yourself stood down."

Hurricane shook his head at the sergeant. "Change is comin', Lancaster. You can be a part of it, or you can end up like *them*." He jerked a thumb at a group of burnt-out fighters beside the airstrip.

"I only—"

"Dammit, Lancaster, just do as Jack says!" Cammy yelled.

Lancaster watched as the others ran to the *Valiant* and disappeared into its belly. As the fortress charged her engines, he crouched to scoop up the remains of his broken rose.

"I'm sorry," he said tenderly, cradling the plant in his hand.

2 Squadrons' Spitfires took off, and the *Valiant* taxied toward the airstrip.

Lancaster looked at the rose. "What are we going to do, eh?"

. . .

The double-decked interior of the *Valiant* was huge and spot lit. Cammy's Matilda and the crawlers were secured to one side, and the Tommies' cages bolted to the other.

"Go lock yourselves in," Cammy yelled to the Tommies.

Hurricane ushered Mosquito and Spitfire to their cages. Jack followed Cammy up a ladder onto the flight deck. Remmy was in the pilot's seat with Billy standing beside him.

Remmy rolled his eyes. "You come to bury the hatchet?" His fingers danced frantically, but expertly, along a row of switches above his head.

"Don't tempt me," Cammy said. "For now, it looks like you got your hands full."

"Ain't you the forgivin' type." Heaving his wheel back, Remmy accelerated and launched the fortress skyward. "Buckle up, sweetheart, this could get a little rough."

Pulling on a headset, Cammy sat beside Remmy and flicked on the radio. It crackled to life.

"… home, do you read, over? Valiant, this is chain home, do you—?"

"Hey, that's Polly," Billy said.

"She's based at Bentley Priory," Cammy said, then into the radio: "*Valiant* receiving, over."

"Camilla? Sorry to break up the glee club. We've got a convoy of merchant ships carrying evacuees to Canada about fifteen miles south of your position. Our scouts report bandits converging on them, coordinates zulu victor two-one-seven, over."

Billy grabbed a crumpled map from the floor and opened it up. Marking their position, he nodded at Cammy.

"Roger that," she replied. "Parker, you get that?"

"*Loud and clear*," crackled Parker through her radio. "*We're on our way.*"

One by one, the Spitfires soaring ahead of the *Valiant* banked and swooped out of sight into cloud.

"An' he calls this a wreck?" Remmy said with contempt. "Watch *this!*" He palmed a switch, and the four engine pods on the *Valiant*'s upper wings ratcheted back and angled their tilt-props forward. With their plane of rotation almost vertical, the wings gave lift while the rotor blades below gave additional thrust, and as the props droned, the fortress's speed increased.

"*Yee-haw!*" Remmy yelled. He peeled the *Valiant* south after the Spitfires, then drove the fortress ahead of them. "British craftsmanship, my ass!" he yelled, as the *Valiant* spearheaded the vanguard.

"*Tell him I heard that*," Parker muttered dourly through Cammy's headphones.

"I'm no expert," Jack said, examining Billy's map, "but even at full speed, Parker's boys won't reach that convoy before the Germans."

"But *we* can," Cammy said. "So we use the *Valiant*'s guns, keep 'em busy 'til 2 Squadron arrive."

"Great idea, sweetheart," said Remmy, "'cept we don't have no guns."

"What?"

"The fore 'n' aft bathtub squirters ain't loaded. We got no ammunition."

"Why the hell not?" Cammy demanded.

"You can have quick or you can have ready, lady. Your boss wanted quick. I flew this bird across the Atlantic, just me on my own. How was I to know we'd get yanked into this mess minutes after she landed? The V ain't meant to see combat 'til you've made her fit for purpose."

"There are *some* guns on board," said a voice behind them.

Turning, they saw Hurricane's head sticking up through the floor hatch.

"But you aren't ready," Cammy said. "You—"

"Got any other ideas?" Jack asked.

"Look, we fly in low over the lead boat," Hurricane said. "Krauts'll hit it first to slow down the ones behind, make 'em easier targets. Get us in close enough, 'n' we can drop onto the deck using Cam's stormers. We'll get stuck in, keep 'em busy 'til Parker's boys arrive to dust up."

Cammy looked skeptical.

"What choice do we have?" Jack said. "Cam, there's gonna be kids on board. You gotta cut the boys loose sometime."

Cammy nodded, resigned.

"Then let's go get you prepped," Billy said.

Billy, Cammy, and Jack followed Hurricane down into the cargo bay. Cammy heaved the lid from a crate and pulled out the first of the stormers. She helped Mosquito into the harness.

"These things come with instructions?" he asked.

"Just punch your ignition to boost," Cammy said. "Then again to douse the jets. Angle your descent, and your body weight'll do the rest."

Jack was already helping Spitfire into his own harness. He noticed the little machine shaking, and put a calming hand on his shoulder. "Nerves are good, Spitfire," he said quietly. "Let's you know you're still alive!"

A burst of machine-gun fire rattled outside.

"I think we've found your Krauts!" Remmy yelled through the comm. "An' we're coming up on your boats, so whatever you're gonna do, do it fast!"

"No heroics, boys," Jack said. "Keep your heads low 'n' your spirits high!" He flicked a switch on the comm. "Okay, Remmy, they're ready."

The bay door lowered with a clang, and a gale blasted around them. The Tommies clawed their way along the webbing lining the fuselage to the bay door. The Channel roared by beneath them.

"Yea, though I walk through the valley o' the shadow o' death,"

Hurricane muttered, locking his stormer harness, "I will fear no evil."

"Just something he does before battle," Mosquito whispered to Jack. "Always was a superstitious bugger."

"For thou art with me," Hurricane continued, "thy rod 'n' thy staff, they comfort me."

"I like it," Spitfire said. "Makes me feel safe, like we're being watched over."

*Feel?* Could the Tommies feel? Jack made a mental note to ask Cammy. Were these machines truly *alive*?

"You prepare a table before me in the presence of my enemies," Hurricane continued. He turned to Cammy and caressed her cheek gently. "You anoint my head with oil."

The infantryman drew his Webleys and nodded. "Let's do this."

"Don't worry," Spitfire said. He hugged Cammy.

"We'll be fine," Mosquito added. He glanced at the ocean gliding by beneath them. "I think!"

"Right," Hurricane yelled above the cacophony. "Let's go drop some lead on 'em!"

"We're over the lead ship," Remmy yelled through the comm. "Get ready to jump in *three!*"

Clinging to webbing, Jack, Cammy, and Billy watched the Tommies prepare to jump.

"*Two!*"

"You lot look out for each other!" Hurricane yelled, glancing back at them.

"*One!* Go! Go! Go!"

Hurricane slammed his stormer ignition and blasted through the bay door into the void. Mosquito and Spitfire followed.

"Oh yeah!" Jack yelled as he watched them plummet toward the boat. "*Go get 'em, boys!*"

# 20

## DOGFIGHT

**C**LANGING DOWN onto the deck of the HMS *Ulysees*, Hurricane rolled into a crouch, his guns cocked and ready.

"Thought these things 'ad brakes!" he muttered as his stormer coughed and sputtered.

Mosquito and Spitfire slammed onto the deck beside him as the *Valiant* roared overhead and came about.

Chaos reigned on board. The ship's bell clanged, and passengers ran frantically about, fleeing for safety. Several German fighters had broken through the clouds, screaming toward the ship, but the sight of the Tommies only made the crowd grow even more hysterical.

Spitfire twisted a dial on his neck, ratcheting his eye lenses out on cylinders like two telescopes. "I got eyes on them," he said, focusing. "*Messerschmitts!*" he gasped, recognizing them instantly from the pictures in books Cammy had shown him.

"Watch your butts down there, boys," Cammy warned through their wrist-wirelesses. "Parker, where are you?"

"Two clicks away," crackled Parker's voice. "Be there in a jiff."

Hurricane raised his Webleys. "Easy boys," he said. "Wait for it."

"Been a while," Spitfire said. "Sure you two can keep up?"

Hurricane glanced at Mosquito and sniggered.

"Funny, innit?" Spitfire said. "Doin' this without the sarge."

"You don't get rid of me that easy!"

They turned and saw Lancaster on the level above them. He crashed down onto the deck, losing a couple of rear end plates in the process.

"But how—"

"I hitched a lift on that death trap," Lancaster said, drawing his guns. "And don't deny you couldn't do with my 'elp, 'cos last time I checked, half a ton of scrap don't float so good!"

"Oh, you've always got to bring that up, 'aven't you!" Hurricane muttered. "Egypt was a long time ago. An' anyway, it was your idea to swim out into the Nile and—"

"Just shut up 'n' shoot!" Lancaster growled.

The Tommies leveled their Webleys, and together they let them sing.

. . .

Peering through the *Valiant's* cockpit window, Cammy flinched.

"They've engaged," she said, nervously checking the skies. "Where the hell's Parker?"

Billy frowned. "Is that *Lancaster* down there?"

. . .

Passengers screamed and the Tommies leapt for cover as the deck exploded in a hail of gunfire around them. The Messerschmitts roared overhead and came about for another pass.

"Well this was a bleedin' good idea, I must say!" Lancaster yelled, passing a finger through a shell hole in his shoulder. "Didn't you idiots think to bring anything bigger than your Webleys?"

"Don't blame me," Mosquito yelled, brushing splinters from his armor. "This wasn't my idea!"

"Then whose idea was it?" Lancaster glared at Spitfire. "Come on."

"Oh, please don't make me dob someone in, Sarge." He cradled his left arm, which was riddled with bullet holes.

"It was me, okay?" Hurricane blurted. "Seemed like a good idea at the time."

"An' is *this* a good idea?" Lancaster said, grabbing Spitfire's arm and holding it aloft. "Look at the state of 'im! I ought to knock some sense into that thick bloody 'ead o' yours, *and* that kid what stole my command."

"Haven't we been through this already?" Hurricane said.

Swooping low above the ocean, the Messerschmitts bore down on the *Ulysses*, machine-guns blazing. The Tommies opened fire again, sending the lead fighter cartwheeling to destruction.

"I'm out of ammo!" Hurricane shouted, guns smoking.

"Me too," Spitfire said, panic creeping into his voice.

"Bugger this!" Mosquito tore a partially lowered lifeboat from its davits and flung it over the guardrail toward the cockpit of the nearest Messerschmitt. The fighter accelerated to avoid it, clipping its companion. The first fighter spiraled into the ocean, and the second was sent twisting into the side of the ship in a blast of orange flame.

Mosquito ignited his stormer, boosted over the guardrail, and landed on the fuselage of the rapidly sinking Messerschmitt. "Cooey!" He leered through the canopy at the terrified pilot within. He wrenched open the canopy, heaved out the pilot, and flung him into the ocean. "You're on private property, Fritz," he yelled, "so swim back to old Adolf!" He pointed across the ocean to France. "Tell 'im the Tin Can Tommies said *no trespassing!*"

As the pilot splashed frantically away to escape the talking machine, Spitfire boosted onto the fuselage beside Mosquito.

"Not a bad day's work for a load of old clunkers!" Mosquito said. "Just like old times, eh? I mean, shame there weren't a few more to go 'round, but—"

Eight Messerschmitts broke through the clouds above them and screamed toward the fleet.

"You had to go 'n' open your big gob, didn't you?" Hurricane shouted.

"We can take eight easy," Mosquito replied. "I can do that on my—"

The ocean bubbled and seethed beneath the Messerschmitt. It shook and rose slowly out of the water...

...atop the deck plate of a surfacing U-boat.

. . .

"Oh, this isn't good," Jack muttered, his eyes flicking between the Tommies on the U-boat and the fighters.

. . .

The submarine's klaxon blared, and a hatch clanged open on the conning tower as its crew emerged, armed to the teeth. More crew climbed out of the forward hatch.

"Moz?" Spitfire said quietly.

"Yeah?"

"I don't 'ave no more ammo."

Mosquito looked at the conning tower, noticing the deck gun bolted in front of it. "Here, take these," he said quietly, handing Spitfire his Webleys.

"What you gonna do?"

"Me?" Mosquito's lenses narrowed with determination. "I'm gonna go kick some 'arris!"

He leapt from the ruined Messerschmitt just as the crew on the conning tower opened fire. Mosquito pounded down the sub's deck, shells sparking off his armor, and skidded to a stop in front of the deck gun. He grabbed the stock and spun the gun ninety degrees to face the conning tower, opening fire on the German crew.

...

"We gotta get over there," Hurricane said, reloading.

Lancaster looked skyward as the second wave of fighters screamed toward them. Things were going from bad to worse.

"C'mon!" Lancaster boosted his stormer and shot through the air onto the U-boat's deck plate, Hurricane close behind, and together they joined the fray.

"*Tally ho, chaps!*" crackled Parker through their wrist-wirelesses.

Punching through cloud above the *Valiant*, Lancaster watched the 2 Squadron hit the Germans with all guns blazing, taking the Messerschmitts by surprise and scattering them.

"*About time, kid,*" Remmy yelled over the airwaves. "*I'm waitin' to be impressed!*"

"*Watch and learn, Remmy,*" replied Parker. "*Watch and learn!*"

...

Remmy ducked as a Messerschmitt roared out of nowhere and opened fire, fracturing the *Valiant's* cockpit glass. Moments later, the Messerschmitt exploded in a ball of flame, and Parker's spitfire soared through the blast.

"*Remember the Alamo, eh?*" Parker crackled through the radio.

"Nobody likes a smartass!" Remmy muttered, furiously rewiring a sparking panel.

"Cam! Come gimme a hand with this!" Jack shouted from the cargo bay.

Cammy looked at Billy, then clambered down the ladder and saw Jack stood by the bay door.

"The boys are in trouble down there." He started across the bay. "Come gimme a hand with this!"

...

The ocean whooshed as the sub spat a torpedo at the *Ulysses*.

Spitfire boosted his stormer and leapt onto the shell, riding it like a bronco.

Mosquito sprinted down the sub's deck plate and leapt, landing behind him. "What the hell're you doing?" Mosquito yelled.

"What d'you think I'm doing?" Spitfire replied, as the shell arced toward the Ulysses. "Tryin' to disable the thing!" The ends of his fingers spiraled out, and the tips split into small multi-purpose tools. "*Digi-tools,*" Spitfire said matter-of-factly. "Cam made 'em."

"I 'aven't got those!"

"'Course not. You ain't a medic!"

Spitfire deftly unscrewed the timer plate and tried to hotwire the torpedo. But with a spark, the cylinder made it clear it wasn't going to cooperate.

"Okay, Plan B."

"What's that?" Mosquito asked.

Spitfire gripped the shell and, using the weight of his frame, hauled it around in an arc on a trajectory back to the U-boat.

"You gotta be kiddin' me," Mosquito said, gripping the shell and heaving.

...

Pinned down on both sides of the conning tower, Lancaster and Hurricane fought back; Hurricane on the deck gun, and Lancaster blasting his Webleys.

As the sub's crew closed in, a shadow eclipsed the sun.

The *Valiant!*

It hovered above them, and a chain was hurled through the bay door, swaying wildly above them in the gale beneath the fortresses rotor-blades.

"Lancaster!" Hurricane yelled.

"Get outta here, I got this!" Bullets pinged off Lancaster's armor.

Hurricane looked at him reluctantly.

"I'll be right behind you!"

Hurricane leapt for the chain, grabbed it, and climbed toward the *Valiant.*

"*One's broken away from the pack,*" Parker crackled through Lancaster's wrist-wireless. "Bag him, Dicky!"

As Hurricane neared the bay door, the *Valiant* took a salvo across her upper wing from the rogue fighter. Two propellers stalled in a ball of flame. Groaning, the *Valiant* yawned sideways, away from the U-boat.

...

Sparks exploded from a panel above Remmy.

"Aw, no no no, this ain't happenin'!" He leapt from his seat, tore off a panel, and furiously rerouted circuits. "C'mon, baby, play nice for daddy!" He glanced over at Billy. "Take the wheel."

"What?"

"I said take the damn wheel!"

Billy slid into the pilot's seat and reluctantly gripped the wheel. "What now?"

Remmy ducked as sparks showered over them. "*Pray!*"

. . .

Machine guns blazing, the U-boat crew converged on Lancaster.

"Jack, they're killin' him down there!" Cammy yelled across the loading bay.

Following her gaze, Jack saw she was right. He hit the comm button. "Remmy! Can you get us in over that sub again?"

"What the hell are you doing?" Cammy yelled.

"*My job!*"

. . .

"Jack, whatever you're about to do," Billy yelled into the comm, "I'm coming with you." He moved to get up from the pilot's seat.

"No, I need you on the wheel!" Remmy snapped.

Nodding reluctantly, Billy sat down.

"*Just hold her steady!*" Jack yelled through the comm.

"He always this insane?" Remmy asked.

"This?" Billy sighed. "This is a *good* day!"

. . .

Hand over hand, Hurricane climbed the chain toward the Valiant. In the ocean below, he saw Spitfire and Mosquito riding the torpedo toward the U-boat—toward Lancaster—his armor now dented and smoking. The old sergeant was desperately crawling toward the bow as the sub crew's guns bore down on him.

. . .

With a roar, Jack burst from the fortress's loading bay astride a crawler. He clanged down onto the U-boat's stern and sped toward the conning tower. He hollered and palmed a switch on his crawler's dash. Two panels slid back on the vehicle's chassis revealing Browning machine guns, which rose and opened fire. The sub's crew scattered and dove for safety.

Jack swerved around the tower and saw Spitfire and Mosquito on a collision course with the U-boat.

He had seconds at best!

"Time to leave the party, boys!" he yelled into his wrist-wireless.

"*Affirmative, boss*," Mosquito crackled, dragging Spitfire off the shell into the water.

"Didn't I just ground you?" Jack yelled, skidding to a stop beside Lancaster.

"If there's one thing I've learnt from you, it's how to disobey orders!"

"Then there's hope for you yet! *Get on!*"

Lancaster climbed onto the saddle behind Jack who gunned the crawler toward the bow.

...

"Oh God, he's gonna—" Cammy hit the comm. "Remmy, get us in front of that sub!"

"In front now?"

"*Do it!*" Cammy yelled.

With a groan, the Valiant aligned her bay door with the U-boat's bow as the torpedo hit the sub.

...

Erupting behind the conning tower, the blast blew the sub's ballast tanks sending a chain reaction of shockwave explosions along the U-boat's hull, as if chasing Jack's crawler. As the fireballs increased in speed, Jack gunned his machine on toward the safety of the *Valiant's* bay door. He saw Cammy and Hurricane up ahead, watching their approach.

"Hold on!" Jack yelled.

"We ain't gonna make it!" Lancaster yelled.

"We'll make it!"

"No we won't, we—"

The bow erupted, engulfing the crawler in flames.

...

"*Hot damn!*" Remmy yelled through the comm, fighting to keep the *Valiant* aloft as it was buffeted by aftershock.

"Down!" Hurricane cried, dragging Cammy to the deck as Jack's crawler blasted through the inferno, flew into the bay, and crashed against the Matilda. The impact of the blast shook the fortress.

Below them, Cammy saw the U-boat fracture and slowly sink beneath the ocean, now slick with black oil. Crewmen leaped for their lives and swam for the safety of dinghies as the sub's giant stern section rose into the air, the propeller still churning.

"Jack?" Billy slid down the ladder.

"I'm okay!" he yelled from a corner, clinging to webbing. He raised his wrist-wireless. "Boys?"

"*Reading you, boss,*" Mosquito crackled.

"Spitfire?"

"*He's fine.*"

Cammy exhaled relief.

"*We, uh, borrowed a few life jackets from our friends down 'ere on the briny.*" Mosquito crackled. "*Bloody blast ruined my paint job, but nothin' Cammy can't fix.*"

Lancaster pulled himself up from a tangle of webbing, his armor smoking.

"You okay?" Jack asked.

The old machine checked his spare parts and nodded.

"We'll uh, give you boys a minute," Cammy said. She hustled Billy back up to the flight deck. Making himself scarce, Hurricane locked down the crawler.

"Y'know, for a minute there, Sergeant," Jack said, "it felt like we were both on the same side."

Lancaster appeared to contemplate his words for a second, then: "Y'know, you tellin' me to stand down back at the airfield?" The machine looked guiltily down at his treads. "That's the first order I've ever disobeyed, and it's somethin' I ain't proud of. I was taught to *respect* rank, to *obey* orders, without question. Today, you forced me into a decision to go against everything I was trained to believe in."

Jack smiled, putting a hand on Lancaster's shoulder-plate. "Then there's hope for you yet."

...

It was late afternoon when the *Valiant* limped back to Hawkinge for repairs. In the largest hangar the RAF could spare, the Tommies loaded ammunition and equipment into the fortress. Cammy watched Jack patch up the old bird with Remmy, both of them straddling the lower wing. Seeing her, Jack grinned and waved. She smiled and waved back, then turned and bumped into Billy, who was biting down on an apple.

"Reckon you got your work cut out there, princess," he said.

"The *Valiant?*" Cammy said, though she knew exactly what he'd meant. "Oh, I dunno—I like a challenge." She ran a hand along the fortress's fuselage, pretending to examine it. "She's in bad shape but, with a little care and attention…"

"I ain't talkin' about this bucket," Billy said. "Don't think you was neither." He winked cheekily. "See you later, darlin'." Whistling, he sauntered up into the fortress.

Cammy looked up at Jack and felt like a guilty teenager, realizing that she might just be falling for the dashing young captain. She chided herself, for now it was she who needed perspective. *Work.* Yes, she'd go back to her quarters and do something constructive.

"Pardon the intrusion, Miss Sullivan."

Cammy turned to see Parker and his crew stood behind her. Parker glanced about at his boys and smiled cordially. "We wondered if you chaps fancy a drink?"

# 21

---

# THE CROOKED HOUSE

**THE CROOKED HOUSE** was, as its name implied, lopsided beyond any stretch of the imagination. Originally a farmhouse, the pub's distinctive lean was caused by local tin mining operations; the building was so profoundly affected by subsidence that the entire left side of its foundations had sunk four foot lower than its right. When the structure was condemned as unsafe, the villagers in the surrounding area, fearing for the loss of their local watering hole, rallied together. They buttressed the pub with a network of supports and girders, eventually saving it—and quenching the thirst of many a farmer on a hot summer's day in the process. The resulting oddity of the pub's appearance made The Crooked House a home-grown attraction, beloved not only by locals, but by the staff and air crews at RAF Hawkinge.

The disconcerting skew of the building was enhanced further on the inside by a labyrinth of twisted doorways and windows, creating the illusion that one was about to topple over when standing perfectly upright. The odd slant also gave rise to optical illusions, including beer glasses that slid across level tables and marbles that appeared to roll uphill, amusing newcomers. The hostelry had a warm homely atmosphere and a smell of malted hops and sawdust.

A line of customers watched a tankard of bitter slide down the bar into Parker's waiting hand. Clasping the handle, he nodded at the barman and drank heartily. "Give 'em 'ell, Nosy!" said a ruddy-faced landlord.

"Always!" Parker said, grinning. "Cheers, Albert!" He downed his pint and slammed the tankard onto the bar.

Behind him, bemused locals marveled at the Tommies' engineering as Billy, Remmy and the young pilots of 2 Squadron compared war stories. Parker grabbed a couple of pints and waded through the crowd, joining Jack and Cammy at a table in the snug.

"Nice place," Cammy shouted over the din. "Wonky!"

Parker smiled as he set down the pint pots. "They say that when you leave, if it looks okay, you've had one too many!"

Jack smiled.

"So, Captain," Parker said. "Your boys were impressive today!"

"You sound surprised," Jack said defensively.

"I underestimated them."

"Maybe I did too," Jack said. "I thought we'd be back in France by now."

"Be careful what you wish for." Parker lit a cigarette. "You may be there sooner than you think."

"What do you mean?" Cammy asked.

"We had a call from High Command this afternoon," Parker said. "Very keen to see how your boys fared in our little fracas."

"You think we could be shipping out?" Jack asked.

"Why else would you be here for training? I've given up trying to second-guess Whitehall's machinations, but seeing your boys out there today? I think we might just have a chance of keeping the Bosch at bay." A shout went up from the bar. "Do excuse me, would you?"

Parker limped back to the bar and the Tommies. "All right you rusty old buggers, who wants to buy me a drink for saving your hides out there today, eh?"

The bar erupted in cheers and applause.

Cammy smiled. "Kid's got spirit," she said. "They all have."

"There's an old head on those shoulders." Jack looked distant.

"Hey, you okay?" Cammy asked.

Jack nodded.

"Then why do I feel we're at a wake? We did something today, Jack. We really *did* something."

"You mean *they* did something. Cam, the old man gave 'em to me 'cos he thought I could lead 'em, and for a while I thought maybe I could. But seein' 'em today…"

Cammy eyes bored into him.

"Ah, I dunno. Lancaster said—"

"The same *Lancaster* whose ass you rescued out in the Channel today?"

"He'll never accept me."

"He *needs* you, Jack. They *all* do. And yes, today was rough around the edges, but it was really something—a new beginning. And with training and determination, you'll push the fight back to the Nazis, and we can turn this war around. All of us, *together!*"

Jack watched the Tommies at the bar. "I dunno. Maybe Lancaster was right. What can I possibly teach 'em? I'm just another soldier."

"A damn good one."

"I could never achieve what they can."

"And they couldn't achieve it without you, don't you see? Jack, you saved Lancaster today, and he knows it. You're a hero."

Jack shook his head and looked into his pint. "Ah, I dunno."

"Heroes are made by the paths they choose, not the powers they have." Cammy downed her drink. "I don't know how this war's gonna end, but when the time comes, it'll be with Lancaster, Hurricane, all of 'em, and they'll follow you, Jack. You're their captain. Their leader."

"Tell that to the lads I left at Dunkirk."

"You can *do* this."

Jack looked unconvinced. Cammy pursed her lips. Would she ever get it through his thick head?

But this was her first night out since the Cèilidh at Achnacarry, and she was damn well going to enjoy it.

"Know what'll make you feel better?" she said.

Jack shook his head.

She snatched his green beret and pulled it on. Sliding a pack of cards from her sleeve, she shuffled them expertly. "You're in trouble now, boy. Wanna see some action, Stone, then batten down the hatches! The game's seven-card stud, blind draw's a three-round fill or a straight flush. Buy-in's a shilling, and *no* coffee housing!"

Jack couldn't help but grin. This woman never ceased to amaze him. Every time he thought he was down, Cammy pulled him back from the brink.

"C'mon, Jack, hustle," she said, dealing cards. "You got serious dough to lose tonight!"

Jack picked up his cards, and Cammy whistled across the bar. "Hey, Parker!" she yelled. "Hope you're feeling lucky tonight, flyboy. 'Nother round over here when you're ready!"

"Hey, what about me?" remmy yelled.

"Yeah, you too. Haul your skinny ass over here."

Laughing, a crowd of Tommies and pilots slowly formed around the table as Jack, Cammy, Parker and Remmy played poker, their camaraderie bolstered from the day's action. But the hour was late and eventually the landlord clanged a bell and yelled *last orders*. It was time to return to the air base.

As the patrons stumbled out into the night, Jack held the door open for Cammy. "Walk you back?"

"I'd like that," she replied.

...

Cammy linked Jack's arm as they strolled along a winding country lane in the moonlight.

In the group behind them, Parker gave a wolf whistle.

"You ain't too old to go over my knee, Squadron Leader!" Jack shouted.

Behind them the gang laughed, then began drunkenly slurring a song.

Cammy shivered. "Glad you loaned me your coat. I'm gonna have to get my name sewn into it."

"Ah, you never know," Jack said, enjoying the stroll. "We might get lucky, get stationed somewhere warm. I hear Italy's nice this time of year. 'Course there's the bombs 'n' the Nazis, but they say the food's very nice."

Cammy laughed.

"Think you'll stick around?" Jack asked. "When all this is over, I mean."

"Right now, that feels like a long way off," Cammy said. "I dunno. Always been a loner, never really fitted in anywhere, but here, with those guys?" Cammy nodded back at the Tommies. "It feels right, y'know? For now, my home's here, with them."

"Good."

Cammy noted his approval with a smile.

They rounded a bend in the lane and saw the air base ahead. "Well, thanks for walking me back," Cammy said.

They paused at the perimeter gate, and Parker and the others walked past them into the base. "Straight to bed now you two!" Remmy said quietly.

The group's laughter faded away, leaving Cammy and Jack alone.

"Back at the bar, you asked what you could teach them," Cammy said. "Maybe being here isn't about training them to be killers; God knows there are enough of those in this war. You want to teach them something? Teach them *humanity*. Teach them to be *men*."

Jack gazed into her eyes. He took Cammy's hand and linked his fingers with her own. Cammy stood on tiptoe, and was about to kiss him tenderly on the lips…

"Jack, you comin' or what?" Billy's voice echoed from inside the base.

Cammy pulled back abruptly. "I'm sorry, I shouldn't have—"

"No," Jack said. "No, I—"

"Jack?" Billy again.

Cammy turned and sashayed toward the base.

"Cam?" Jack called.

She turned mid-stride and smiled coyly. "G'night, Jack."

# 22

---

# A CHANGE OF PLAN

**A**S HE WALKED ALONE to his quarters, Jack pondered his conversation with Cammy. He had so many doubts—about everything. But in spite of the obstacles in his path, Cammy had driven home the fact that he *had* achieved something, and he knew there was no going back now. This admission both pleased and frightened him. Still, the evening's events had boosted his morale and yet again, Cammy had made him see sense. Yes, the odds might be against them, but if he just stuck with it, maybe this could all work out.

As for Lancaster? Was Jack breaking through the stubborn old sod's defenses? Jack didn't know. Although he had certainly seen a sea change in the way the sergeant regarded him. In turn, Jack realized that he himself now felt differently toward the Tommies. He was starting to see that there were more similarities than differences between him and these machines. He no longer regarded them as anything other than "the boys." *His* boys, in fact. And for the first time in a while, Jack allowed himself to feel good about that.

And she'd nearly kissed him.

Jack felt a long-forgotten glow. He felt pride, and not a small amount of amazement, that such a remarkable woman could see something, *anything*, in him. But did she? Was that what Cammy's kiss might have meant?

His head hurt, and the beer hadn't helped. He would have to ponder the confusion of their relationship another time. For tonight, he would sleep soundly, basking in the remembrance of her touch and the look in her eyes. And while Jack knew he still had a long way to go, with Cammy by his side he felt invincible.

Jack arrived at his quarters to find Billy waiting for him. He was stood awkwardly in the presence of a uniformed officer who had his back to Jack.

"Bill?"

Jack entered the Nissen hut.

The officer turned and smiled. It was Ismay. "Good evening, Captain. Are you ready to accept your first mission?"

...

The team—Jack, Billy, Cammy, and the Tommies—had assembled in the briefing shed with Ismay.

"At ease, Commandos." Ismay opened a briefcase and pulled out a tan file. "Well, I'm sorry to break up your evening, but I'm afraid Jerry's rather forced our hand." He took out a sheet of paper stamped *CLASSIFIED* in red above a number of signatures.

The air in the room grew tense, heavy with expectancy. This was it, Jack thought. His first mission as leader of Commando One.

"My condolences on the loss of Mungo," Ismay said. "He was a good man, and he had great faith in you all. I trust you'll honor his conviction." He looked around the room. "Well, the hour is late, so to business. In six days' time, you'll be air-dropped into Norway behind enemy lines, where you'll liaise with the Milorg."

"The what?" Hurricane asked.

"The Norwegian resistance," Cammy answered.

"Very good, Doctor. You have some knowledge of the organization?"

"Only the language, sir. My grandparents were immigrants from Narvik."

"Then that familiarity should serve you well."

"Cam's going?" Jack said, suddenly concerned.

"Miss Sullivan's the Tommies' engineer. There's no one who knows them like she does."

"Don't worry, Jack," Cammy said cockily. "I'll keep you safe."

The Tommies stifled laughter.

"Where's the party, sir?" Billy asked.

"Telemark. SOE would like you to affect Operation Ice Pick: the sabotage and destruction of the Norsk hydropower plant."

"What is it, sir? Munitions?" Hurricane asked.

"Something far more important," Ismay replied, "and potentially devastating should your mission there fail to succeed. We need you to put a stop to all German production of deuterium oxide."

"*Heavy water?*" Cammy gasped.

"What the 'ell's heavy water?" Mosquito asked.

"What've I told you about disrespectin' rank?" muttered Lancaster, then to Ismay: "I'm sorry, sir."

"That's quite all right, Sergeant. I had no idea what the bloody stuff was myself until I read the intel. It seems that in 1934 the Norwegians built their first commercial facility capable of producing deuterium oxide, a byproduct of fertilizer manufacturing. The substance, more commonly known as 'heavy water,' is a key component in the harnessing and manipulation of atomic energy."

"A bomb?" Jack said.

"Capable of leveling an entire city," said Ismay grimly.

"How far are they into production?" Cammy asked.

"SOE's source reports they're one week away from a shipment to Berlin. That's where you come in, Jack. Working with the resistance, your team will travel to the town of Rjukan, where SOE's source will make contact. From there, you'll be escorted to Vemork. But blowing the place won't be your only problem. Between you and Vemork, there's fifty miles of frozen terrain patrolled by Wehrmacht Alpen Korps, and another garrison stationed in the town."

"That'll be interesting," said Spitfire. "I mean, we'll kinda stick out at checkpoints."

"We've also received reports," Ismay continued, "of a heightened Gestapo presence in the region."

"Sounds charming," said Billy.

"So, we get in and blow the joint, no problem," Mosquito said. "I'm the best sapper goin', sir. In 'n' out, it'll be a doddle." He pulled open his breastplate, revealing several rows of plastic explosives, timers, and an assortment of colored wiring. "I got things in 'ere that'll go bump in the night for all occasions!"

"You mean you've been walkin' 'round with that lot inside you?" Lancaster said.

"I'm a sapper—where else am I meant to stick it?"

"I'll tell you where," Hurricane said, balling his fists. "Right up your —"

"Hurricane!" scolded Cammy.

"Thank you, Doctor," said Ismay irritably.

"And the factory?" Spitfire asked.

"Deemed inaccessible," Ismay answered. "Typically, it would require a battalion of men to take it. It's carved out of the mountainside with only a bridge and railway line as access, it's virtually impregnable to assault.

You'll have to scale the Rjukan waterfall, which, I'm reliably informed, should be frozen this time of year."

"Should be?" Billy quipped.

"Even SOE aren't infallible, Briggs. That's where you come in, Jack—that talent of yours for thinking *outside* the box." Ismay's expression turned dark. "But I won't deny this isn't tricky, and I won't lie to you: the stakes couldn't be higher. If Hitler creates just one atomic bomb, he'll set its sights on London—followed, no doubt, by the rest of the free world." He looked around at the team. "Humanity hangs in the balance, gentlemen. You'll either save it, or see it destroyed. Winston would obviously prefer the former."

"All in a day's work," Jack said, glancing concern at Cammy.

"Nervous, Captain?" Ismay asked.

"Too right, sir."

Ismay smiled. "That's perfectly natural; I would be too. Johnny Jackboot isn't just going to invite you in for a wink or a flash of ankle. But you're Commando. Your boys specialists in their field. If things go bad—and invariably they do—these boys will get you out. But *only* after you've blown the factory—is that clear?"

"Crystal, sir."

"Can't we just bomb the place?" asked Spitfire, nervous. "Call up a squadron of pathfinder Wellingtons and wipe it off the map completely."

Ismay smiled. "Excellent question, Spitfire, I'm impressed. The factory's fueled by a number of acid pipes, however, that carry chemicals as well as water down the mountainside to the factory. If we bomb Vemork, hundreds of gallons of it will end up in the town below. Wouldn't be too good for Anglo-Norwegian relations, I imagine. Any other questions?"

The team was silent.

"Excellent. You'll be jumping over the Hardanger Plateau. The Milorg there will be waiting when you land, and escort you to Rjukan. Once you've infiltrated the plant, SOE's source will guide you to the factory's water cells in the basement. After setting explosive charges, you'll light the fuse, run like hell, and blow the bloody place to kingdom come. At least, that's SOE's assertion."

"And what's yours, sir?" Jack asked.

Ismay considered his response, then: "A Norwegian team attempted something similar late last year," he said soberly. "They were captured by local Gestapo—and executed."

The room fell silent.

"Sounds like a one-way ticket," Billy said quietly.

Ismay reached into his briefcase and pulled out a small glass vial. "Did I mention you'll have cyanide?" he offered bleakly.

...

Jack and Cammy stood by the door as the team filed out of the briefing shed.

"When I was at Princeton," Cammy said, "my professor was Albert Einstein. He was forced to leave Germany when he saw the way things were going for the Jews. I'd heard rumors, but when Einstein told me what was going on there it chilled my blood. It was Einstein who alerted Washington to the fact that the Nazis were conducting research into the destructive power of the atom—and told them of Hitler's willingness to use it. Looks like Roosevelt listened—either that or he already knew —'cos the Senate announced a weapons development program codenamed 'The Manhattan Project' run by a guy called Oppenheimer."

"How do you know all this?"

"Because Oppenheimer asked me to work for him. At about the same time I was approached to come here 'n' help your government with these guys." She nodded at the Tommies who had huddled in the mist. "I chose to create, not destroy."

"And I'm glad you did," Jack said.

He moved to touch her arm, but she pulled away. Cammy was clearly rattled. Ismay's admission that Hitler was days away from Armageddon had understandably gotten to her. *First London, then America*, he thought.

"Jack, this mission can't fail. 'Cos if it does, the Nazis win the war. They'll drop a bomb on London that'll produce a blast equivalent to twenty thousand tons of TNT."

As Jack stared into her eyes, he felt Cammy's fear. Now was his moment to shine, to prove to Cammy that her faith in him wasn't misplaced. "Then we *won't* fail," he said with conviction.

Gazing up at him, Cammy nodded. "C'mon, let's go stand the boys down."

They joined the group, who were arguing in a huddle.

"Bloody cyanide?" Billy was muttering. "Did you see the state of Hastings?"

"That's enough, William," Lancaster growled. "Orders are orders."

"It's not a pretty way to go, Sarge," Billy said. "Just be thankful you boys 'ave off switches."

"What, you think that's a good thing?" Mosquito snapped.

"Hey," Jack said, silencing them. "Time to turn in, boys. Been a long day."

The huddle dispersed, and Cammy went with them, leaving Jack alone in the moonlight.

Ismay exited the briefing shed and stepped up beside Jack. "Not easy, is it? Being all things to every man."

A Spitfire took off from the airstrip. It launched skyward and disappeared into the night.

"Is there a chance, sir?"

"Oh, there's *always* a chance," Ismay said. "You just have to believe in blind luck. I'm a pacifist at heart, but I'm willing to fight for peace, whatever the odds. This mission *must* succeed, Jack."

"We won't let you down, sir."

"I know you won't. Now go and get some rest. It may be the last chance you get."

...

Moonlight glittered on the deserted snow-covered streets of Oslo.

*Curfew*, thought Mörder, as he gazed out the window of his staff car. His journey from Berlin had taken its toll, and his body was still recovering from the hell of the treatment he'd endured at the hands of Hitler's physicians on his return from Achnacarry.

But he felt strong.

As he passed by a factory, posters glowed in the lamplight, daubed with painted V signs and the initials of Norwegian King Haakon VII.

Damn the Milorg.

Fleeing to Great Britain when Norway's defenses collapsed, Haakon had established a government in exile, even as martial law was declared by his country's new masters. Nazi party official Josef Terboven, appointed Reichskommissar to Norway, allowed the civilian government to remain in power on the understanding that it only follow Berlin's orders. However, Germany's attempts to reshape Norwegian society had come up against stiff opposition, with its victors increasingly reliant on violence to maintain control.

Still, Germany dominated Europe from the English Channel to the Polish city of Warsaw, and it appeared unlikely to most Norwegians, despite the attempts of a growing resistance movement, that the Fatherland would ever be defeated.

His staff car slowed and stopped. Mörder's driver got out and opened his door.

Mörder looked up proudly at the swastika banners fluttering from the walls of the Victoria Terrasse complex. Formerly a government office block, the building had been appropriated by the Reich and now housed the headquarters of the Nazi Security Police and SS Intelligence agencies. The perfect white plastered façade crowned by fairytale towers and domes belied the building's true nature. Mörder had heard the rumors. In the three months since Gunther Schenk had become SD-Leiter of all Gestapo activities in Oslo, more prisoners had chosen to take their own lives than face interrogation in the building's basement.

But that was not Mörder's concern.

He was here to facilitate the first shipment of heavy water from Rjukan to Berlin, and nothing, neither Schenk nor the Milorg, were going to obstruct Hitler's command.

"Wait here," he said to his driver.

The lobby was quiet. The few administrative staff who were present disbanded at the sight of Mörder's nightmarish visage. He entered a lift, exited on the fifth floor, and followed the corridor to a large oak door. The brass plaque read SD-Leiter. Opening the door without pause, Mörder strode into the room.

A fat, red-faced man in a uniform two sizes too small sat behind a desk. He looked up from his conversation with two men in black suits and fedoras.

"I am here for information," Mörder announced.

"What is this?" Schenk yelled. "I'll have you court-marshaled!"

"You may try," Mörder said. "However, before doing so, you will procure for me all available intelligence on Milorg activity in the Rjukan valley region."

"I shall do no such thing," protested Schenk.

"To deny my request would be unwise, SD-Leiter."

"You can't just barge in here like an animal in a party mask making demands! Who the hell do you think you are?"

Mörder approached Schenk, grabbed his tunic, and heaved him from his seat to the floor. Then he sat in Schenk's chair, calmly picked up the phone, and tapped its receiver. "This is General Ernst Mörder. Connect me to the Reich Chancellery in Berlin. Yes, I'll hold."

"Who the hell are you?" said Schenk in shock. The men in black suits quickly left the room. "I wasn't informed—"

"What you have or haven't been informed of is not my concern."

"But what gives you the right?"

"The question is not *what*, SD-Leiter, but *who*." Mörder held up a finger, then into the phone: "Yes, connect me with the Führer's office." He paused, waiting. "Hello?" The demonic mask held the phone out to Schenk. "Perhaps you'd care to register your disapproval with the Führer personally?"

Schenk got to his feet and shook his head frantically.

"Good." Mörder replaced the receiver. "Now, as requested, you will have all available intelligence on Milorg activity in the Rjukan valley region taken to my car in the next ten minutes."

Schenk got it done in eight.

...

As his car left Oslo, Mörder opened the first file. He had over one hundred miles in which to formulate a plan that would ensure a successful mission. There was a saying in the Austrian army that the man on the ground knew tactics, but the man in the chair knew strategy. Mörder knew both. He began by reviewing the transportation of the heavy water inventory from the factory in Rjukan to the nearby port of Larvik. From there, the barrels would be transported by ferry across Lake Tinnsjø, then taken by rail to the open sea and Germany. Mörder factored in all possible scenarios for the shipment to be sabotaged en route, taking into account the locations of all known pockets of resistance. He would send a message to the Milorg that if they dared interfere with his mission, he would paint the snow red with their blood.

As the dawn sun rose over Oslo, Mörder looked out of his window.

It was going to be a beautiful day.

# 23

---

# HEAVY METAL

"**FOR THE NEXT FIVE DAYS** you are no longer Commando," Parker declared, as he paced back and forth on the airfield the following morning. "You are *paratroops*."

"What's the difference?" Billy asked.

"Paratroops have bigger balls," Parker said, smiling. "Present company excepted, Miss Sullivan."

Cammy nodded, amused.

"Now, I understand from Remmy that the *Valiant's* still incapacitated," Parker continued, "so in her absence, I'd like you to meet our new friend, the Whitley Bomber."

He stood aside as a long, twin-engine heavy bomber trundled down the runway toward them. "Since the military's never done what you're about to attempt, we've devised a method to get you and your kit into the air at altitude by cutting a hole in the Whitley's floor through which you will jump."

The team looked doubtfully at one another.

"We're nothing if not inventive," Parker said smugly. "Forming an orderly queue in the fuselage, you'll hook your para lines to a bar above your heads. After you've jumped, that bar will deploy your chutes in the aircraft's slipstream, carrying you away from Mr. Whitley—at which point it's hoped, not least of all by yourselves, that you'll float *gracefully* down to the drop zone and make textbook landings."

"You make it sound so easy," Cammy said.

"That's because it is. You just close your eyes, let go, and jump."

"Oh, I'll let go all right," Billy muttered to a ripple of laughter.

"Remind me not to jump before you," Jack said.

"Ah, the British capacity for arse jokes in the face of adversity never ceases to amaze," Parker continued. "Now, when you're up in the air about to jump, one detail to be aware of is that unless you maintain a perfectly rigid stance while stepping into the unknown, the slipstream beneath the aircraft will carry you backwards—and if you're lucky you'll break your nose on the edge of the exit."

"And if you're unlucky?" Spitfire asked.

"Thanks, Tufty," Parker shouted to a pilot climbing down from the Whitley. The young man turned and waved. He had a perfectly coiffed moustache beneath a hole where his nose should have been.

"We call it ringing the bell," Parker said dryly. "Luckily you don't need a sense of smell to be a spit pilot."

He took a stack of books from a table near the pilot's chairs and handed them out. "You'll be relieved to hear that there are no jumps planned for today, as I've scheduled lectures on parachute theory, PT training to loosen you up for landing practice, and a number of aircraft drills on board the Whitley."

"That's a relief," Billy said.

"Tomorrow, however, you'll make the first of three planned jumps in order for you to be deemed fit for your mission."

"Bugger."

"We're reliably informed by the met office that a bomber's moon is forecast for the Hardangervidda in four days' time, so God willing, that's when you'll make the jump."

"Bomber's moon?" Lancaster asked.

"A full moon, Sergeant. Perfect illumination for your landing zone."

"Four days?" Jack said, turning to Cammy.

"Ismay said the heavy water shipment leaves for Germany in seven," she replied. "That gives us three days to get to Rjukan and blow the factory."

"We're cutting it fine," said Billy.

"That's correct," Parker said, "six weeks has become four days team, so I suggest we crack on. If you remain calm at all times, listen to your instructors, and stay alert, I guarantee that most of you will come through this unscathed."

"There's optimism for you," Billy grumbled.

"Don't worry, mate," said Hurricane. "If your jump goes wrong, I'll scrape up what's left and bring you 'ome in a jam jar."

...

It had been a day since Mörder's arrival at Vemork, and already things were not to his liking. While heavily fortified on its exterior after the previous year's raid, the harsh Norwegian weather had taken its toll on the factory's concrete edifice, creating a series of nooks and crannies that could easily be exploited by potential saboteurs. After issuing orders to have them shored up, Mörder descended to the basement to check on the production's progress with the plant's manager, Tor Johanssen.

"The shipment will be ready in three days?" Mörder asked.

"Yes, General," Johanssen said nervously.

"Good. You are a local man, Johanssen, are you not?"

"Yes, sir."

"And are you aware of any subversive activity in this region that might affect this shipment reaching its destination?"

"*Activity*, sir?"

Noticing a photograph of a pretty young girl on Johanssen's desk, Mörder picked it up and examined it.

"My daughter," said Johanssen proudly. "Karina. She's seven years old now. How they grow."

"A very lovely child," Mörder said.

"Do you have children, General?"

"Once," Mörder said absently, then: "With regards to Milorg activity, Johanssen, let me rephrase my question. You see I am no fool, but you would be one to take me as such. So, if you wish for little Karina to remain as lovely as she is in this photograph, you will give me the identities and locations of all Milorg insurgents in this region, starting with their leader."

Johanssen stared at the general incredulously.

"You have thirty seconds," Mörder said, checking his watch, "after which I shall ask a unit of my men to visit little Karina's school with flame throwerrs. Do I make myself clear?"

Johanssen nodded, tears welling in his eyes.

"Now," Mörder said calmly. "A name."

Johanssen cursed himself, tears cascading down his cheeks. "Hellstrøm," he said at last. "His name is Magnus Hellstrøm."

…

Jump one took place one hundred and fifty feet above the ground from a platform tethered beneath a barrage balloon. The Tommies' parachutes had finally been delivered, heightening their anxiety further as the day of reckoning approached. The team were silent as the platform ascended, and Billy physically sick as Parker locked it off, and turned to them with grim expectation.

"Right. Now remember what I said," Parker yelled above the gale. "Jumping's the easy part. *Anyone* can jump. But you'll have ninety pounds of equipment strapped to your backs, the Tommies much more—and that's not even including your chute or its reserve. That's a hell of a lot of weight taking you down, and once you're outside the aircraft there'll be a hundred-and-twenty-knot gale to contend with."

"Then what?" Jack gripped the guardrail as the platform creaked and swayed.

"Then it's game on, old boy. Every man, woman, and machine leaps after you, and you pray to the Almighty that no one steals your air."

"I don't even want to 'ear this," Billy said.

"If the jumper beneath you steals your air, your parachute will fold," Parker said, "and you're liable to get caught up in your rigging lines. It's unlikely, but it does happen."

Jack gulped. With every training session that passed, their prospects were looking less promising.

"Now once you commit, there's no going back. You're fighting the odds just being up here, and there's no reverse gear on a parachute."

The platform tilted violently. Billy grabbed Hurricane's arm. "I think I'm gonna puke again!"

"Get a grip, will ya?" Hurricane muttered.

Parker opened a gate on the guardrail. "Let's get this show on the road. How about you, Camilla? Ladies first?"

Cammy looked terrified, but she nodded.

"I'll go," Jack said, stepping forward.

"No, it's okay," Cammy mustered all her determination. "I can do this."

"Of course you can," Parker said reassuringly as Cammy adjusted her leather helmet and stepped up to the gate. "Just remember your classes. You've checked your rig. Your main canopy D-ring's here, and the reserve's here. Your cutaway release is here in case your main chute gets tangled. Now you mentioned those wrist-wirelesses of yours contain a built-in altimeter—nice work by the way—and in the real world, you'll release your chute at no less than forty-five hundred feet. Terminal velocity's around one thousand, and that's it. Okay, let's put these boys to shame!"

Jack, Billy, and the Tommies could sense Cammy's fear, and while they were all equally nervous, each would have willingly traded their place with her—but this was something that had to be done if she was to join them on the mission. Without her, the Tommies would have no engineer. She was an integral component of the mission, and failing here would cause further delay. Failure, therefore, was not an option.

"Come on, Cam," said Hurricane. "You got this."

She glanced back at Jack. "Twenty seconds of bravery," he said, his eyes narrowing with conviction. "You can *do* this."

Behind him, Lancaster nodded reassurance.

"Go for it, Cammy!" urged Mosquito.

"Yeah, show us how it's done," Spitfire added.

"Okay, now imagine the red light's on," Parker said calmly. "Prepare to jump." He put his hand on Cammy's shoulder.

Cammy took a deep breath, then exhaled. She was scared as hell, but excitement consumed her too. When Parker yelled, "Green light, *go!*" she emptied her mind and stepped calmly into the void.

Her stomach lurched and the air rushed from her lungs. Instinctively she released her parachute, and feeling a jerk across both shoulders, she cried out. Looking up, she was relieved to see the silk of her deployed canopy fluttering in the air currents as she floated gracefully down to the airfield. She laughed out loud as she heard the boys above her cheering.

Aside from the kiss she'd nearly given Jack, this was the greatest thrill she'd experienced. It was a hell of a rush, and was certainly something she could get used to—which was just as well, given that two more drops were scheduled before the real deal in Norway. But that, she knew, would be a whole different ball game.

Cammy calmly surveyed the landscape as the airfield rushed up to meet her. Before she knew where she was, she'd landed with a bump on her backside. Exhilarated, she climbed to her feet and gathered in her canopy.

"She made it!" Jack said, turning to Parker.

"Of course she did," he replied, smiling. "You all will."

Spitfire jumped next, followed by Mosquito. Both landed safely and appeared to be just as elated as Cammy.

"Okay, Bill, you're up," Parker said, pulling on a harness of his own.

"Really?" Billy said nervously. He looked down over the guardrail and gulped, then looked up at Lancaster. "Age before beauty, eh?"

Lancaster stared at him blankly.

"Didn't think so." Out of options, Billy braced himself, and shuffled up to the gate gripping his harness straps. "This thing better bleedin' open!"

"Red light on, Billy," Parker said calmly.

Billy swallowed and said a silent prayer.

"Green light, *go!*"

Billy remained rigid, his knees trembling. "I can't," he said, squeezing his eyes shut. "I can't—"

"William?"

Billy opened his eyes and saw Lancaster looming over him.

"Yes, you can!" Lancaster pushed him off the platform.

Screaming through the air, Billy pulled his D-ring. His canopy deployed, and he floated smoothly to the ground.

"What the 'ell was that?" Jack yelled.

"He needed to get down, so I 'elped 'im!"

"Not by pushing him off the bloody platform! *Jesus!*" Jack shook his head in shock.

"Are you going to reprimand me *every* time I make a decision?" Lancaster snapped. "'Cos if you are—"

"See you on the ground, gentlemen!" Parker said, stepping off the platform. He expertly deployed his parachute, glided smoothly to the airfield, and landed deftly. Then he gathered up his chute and looked up at the platform. "Easy as pie, boys!" he yelled. "Who's next?"

. . .

"He just bleedin' jumped!" Lancaster said, gripping the guardrail.

"Yeah," Jack muttered.

"But that leaves us—alone—up 'ere."

"Yeah."

. . .

Cammy stormed up to Parker. "Hey, just what the hell—"

"Parachuting is a means by which you get to a battle, Camilla, not a means by which you fight a battle. Just like a balloon, the pair of them will descend from on high when they each run out of hot air."

. . .

"Well, this is bleedin' great, innit?" Lancaster yelled. "Stuck up 'ere with *you!*"

"You're stuck up, full stop!" Jack shouted back.

Lancaster balled his right fist.

"Oh, you're gonna hit me now?" Jack said. "Then take your best shot!

Shame you didn't have the guts to jump into the bear pit during basic! I could take you any day!"

"Yeah?" Lancaster yelled. "You 'n' who's army?"

"*My* army!"

"But they're *my* army, ain't they?"

"*Our* army, then! *Christ, Lancaster!* Is it gonna be like this every time we disagree?" Exhausted, Jack slumped against the guardrail. "You know what makes this worse? There are actually times I look at us all, and I know how formidable we could be! *You* know it, too—I know you do! With your experience 'n' my—"

"Hot-headed recklessness?"

Resigned, Jack looked at his boots and smiled. "Whatever we may think about each other, we just have to get past it."

"And why's that?"

"Because if we can't see something bigger than ourselves, we won't blow that factory. And if we don't do that, then we'll have no home left to come back to, even *if* we make it out alive. I don't want that, I know you don't either. It'd be the end of everything you know—the boys, Cammy…"

Lancaster looked out across the airfield. The armor on his shoulders rose and fell. He let out a frustrated sigh. "Agreed."

Jack looked up in shock. "What?"

"Don't make me say it again."

"Well then… What're we waiting for?"

"Want me to give you a shove?"

"I liked you better when we disagreed."

"You'd better get down there," Lancaster said. "Don't want to keep Camilla waiting."

"No. Together on three?"

Lancaster nodded. "*One—Two—Green on go.*"

Leaping from the platform, Jack and Lancaster soared toward the airfield, landing together with precision and relief.

"Nice of you boys to drop in," Parker said, lighting a cigarette. "Told you it was a piece of cake."

Lancaster nodded and quietly gathered in his canopy.

Cammy sensed a change in the old machine. "What's this?" she said, glancing at Jack. "A truce?"

"Yeah," Jack said, catching Lancaster's eye. "Peace in our time."

# 24

## BOMBER'S MOON

**I**T WAS NIGHT FOR MAN NOR BEAST as the Whitley prepared to take off from Hawkinge. The ground crew had attached a glider by a tow line, containing all the equipment the mission called for. Jack, Cammy, and Billy were all armed to the teeth in alpine camouflage assault suits and packs. The Tommies were ready too, sprayed grey and white in their own oversized jump gear.

The Whitley's engines coughed to life and its propellers started to rotate, and the group traipsed through the rain toward the fuselage door. As they reached it, Ismay's sedan drew up. He climbed out with his aide, who struggled to hold an umbrella above him in the gale.

"It's a hell of a thing to send men into the unknown," he said soberly, shaking each of their hands in turn. "Worse still that I have to send you, Doctor."

"Where they go, I go," Cammy yelled over the noise of the propellers.

"She'll be well looked after, sir," added Lancaster.

"I don't doubt it," Ismay nodded. "I hate to leave things on a macabre note, but—" He produced a small black box, slid back the lid, and took out three rubber-covered capsules—the suicide pills he had mentioned in their briefing. "If you get into trouble and the outcome looks bleak, well… I'm told it takes five seconds." He handed the pills to Jack, Cammy and Billy. "Sew them somewhere they can't be found."

"Understood sir," Jack said.

"And the Tommies?" asked Ismay.

"Each carries an incendiary device which I've fitted to their tanks," said Cammy. "We get into any scrapes; the boys know what to do." She looked down the line at the Tommies almost apologetically. They nodded their understanding in response.

"Good luck, Commando One. Your mission tonight takes you deep behind enemy lines. You are about to do more for your country than should ever be asked of a soldier, man *or* machine. Have courage and hold fast, you fight for freedom and for all that we hold dear. Godspeed Jack, and to all of you. I'll be praying for your safe return."

Ismay saluted. The team reciprocated.

"Right then," Jack said. "Let's get this show on the road. Lancaster, get the boys on board."

"Sir," Lancaster said efficiently.

Cammy looked at Jack in surprise. In fact, everyone seemed taken aback by Lancaster's quick willingness to comply.

Seeing the looks on their faces, Jack brought it home. "All right, you 'orrible lot, into that bloody death trap on the double! Hup to!"

"What the hell did you say to him on that platform?" Cammy said as she climbed into the fuselage with Jack.

"Just told him you'd kick his arse if he didn't start behaving himself."

"Come on, love, get a wiggle on," Billy muttered behind them. "It's pissin' down out 'ere, or 'aven't you noticed?"

"Permission to kick *his* ass, Captain?" Cammy said, narrowing her eyes at Billy.

"Granted, but after we get back, eh?"

"*If* we get back, you mean," Billy grumbled. "Come on, will ya, Cam? I'm soppin'!"

Cammy disappeared into the bomber, and Jack helped Billy up.

"S'pose there's no chance of a spot of leave before—"

Jack glared at Billy.

"Didn't think so," Billy said. He took his bucket seat with the Tommies inside the Whitley's fuselage.

A young sergeant air gunner named Stokes heaved the door to and hit a comm switch. "We're locked in, sir," he yelled as the engines rumbled. "Good to go for takeoff."

"Good show." It was Parker, via the loudspeaker. "Right-o, Commandos, I suggest you get comfy and snuggle up. We'll be flying at an altitude of ten thousand feet across the North Sea this evening to Norway's coastal belt. Once we get in over the mountains, we'll descend to a cruising altitude so Jerry can't track us. When we reach the Hardangervidda, your Milorg chaps should be waiting in an area called Skrykken, which will be your drop zone."

Jack pulled a block of chocolate from his pocket and offered it to Cammy. She broke a chunk off and passed it to Billy.

"Oh, one more thing," Parker said. "Your co-pilot this evening will also be your entertainment officer."

"What the 'ell's he on about?" Lancaster asked.

"*Evenin' ladies.*" Remmy now, through the loudspeaker.

"Ah, bloody 'ell," Hurricane growled.

"Where did I put that cyanide pill?" Billy shouted.

"We're gonna begin this evening with a little Glenn Miller to keep you limeys back there warm." Swing band music blasted through the intercom, almost drowning out the engines.

As the bomber taxied onto the runway, the team cast nervous glances at each other. The fuselage shook like hell, and the motors shrieked. Then the brake released with a clunk, and they accelerated like a bullet down the runway.

Cammy gripped Jack's arm as she felt the wings take their weight and heard the gear retract as the bomber ascended into the night. Jack closed his eyes and rested his head back against the side of the fuselage.

They were finally up in the air.

Now they just had to get back down.

...

Drifting in and out of sleep, Jack was reminded of his flight to Achnacarry. It felt like an eternity ago. His dreams merged with nightmares, and the boy in his mind's eye screamed.

He awoke suddenly.

Cammy had fallen asleep on his shoulder, and he looked down at her, watching her breathe, admiring the perfect contours of her face. *Beautiful outside as well as in*, he thought.

Billy was also dozing—while he still gripped a bucket, it looked like he'd finally overcome the airsickness he'd suffered so badly on board their old Halifax. The Tommies had also settled down after singing along to a few raucous songs played by Remmy. As for Lancaster? He appeared to have finally come around—for now at least.

"*Captain?*" Parker's voice cut through the chill air. "*A minute?*"

Jack unhooked his safety belt, gently eased Cammy's head from his shoulder, and made his way to the cockpit. Parker was leaning over his wheel and peering through the windshield into the night. Remmy chewed gum beside him. Both looked on edge.

"What is it?" Jack asked.

"Rather dashed bad luck, I'm afraid," Parker said, sitting back in his seat. "We're over the Hardangervidda, and while the Met office confirmed a beautiful bomber's moon, the cloud's so thick beneath us that we can't see your drop zone. As if that's not bad enough, we also appear to have piqued the interest of a passing Jerry Heinkel. It's currently sat on our tail trying to decide if we're friend or foe. So. Either we drop lower into cloud down there and risk hitting something snow-capped, or you make your jump up here and reveal all to Jerry."

"Or we call it off," Remmy added. "Turn tail 'n' live to fight another day?"

"Not an option," Jack said.

Parker nodded. "Then let's go see what's down there." He eased his wheel forward.

"Crazy damn limeys," Remmy muttered, shaking his head. He gritted his teeth and eased his wheel forward as well.

"You'd best go back and get hooked on, Jack," Parker said. "Just in case."

Jack returned to the fuselage and approached Lancaster. The sergeant's irises pulsed orange, an indication that he was on standby. Jack put a hand on his shoulder

Lancaster's irises flickered to blue discs, and he looked about nervously. "We there?" he muttered, half-powered.

"Not yet. As a precaution," Jack said, "get the boys hooked on."

Lancaster clambered to his feet. "All right you rabble, wake up 'n' get 'ooked on."

In a line along the cramped fuselage, Cammy, Billy, and the Tommies clipped their parachute catches to an overhead guide wire running the length of the Whitley's tail. Jack hooked his clip on beside Cammy.

Stokes put a hand to his headset. Parker was probably relaying the situation he'd outlined in the cockpit. The air gunner moved along the wire in a hurry, checking everyone's clips, then flicked the comm. "They're all on," he said nervously.

"Okay, I've dropped us a thousand feet," crackled Parker over the loudspeaker. "Still can't see a landing—"

With a screech, the bomber lurched sideways, then righted itself.

"What the hell was that?" Jack yelled.

"I think we just lost the glider!" Stokes replied.

"Yes, tow cable snapped," Parker said. "Must have frozen. Not our night, eh?"

"That glider was carrying our supplies," Cammy said.

"We'll figure it out," Jack reassured her, trying to sound calm.

Machine-gun fire battered holes along their fuselage. Cammy screamed as the last few shells punctured the hull and clattered off Hurricane's chest plate above her head.

"Looks like our friend in the Heinkel's figured we aren't friendly," Parker said.

"There's a *Heinkel* out there?" Cammy exclaimed.

With a whine, the Whitley nosed into a steep descent.

"Bloody marvelous," Billy said. "Just lost the glider, now we're gonna get shot up before we've even jumped! Why couldn't we just land like a normal bleedin' bomber?"

"You know why," said Hurricane. "I've brought that jam jar, by the way."

Billy stared at him incredulously as Parker crackled over the loudspeaker again: "We're flying blind through cloud, but we appear to have shaken our Heinkel—for now at least. I'm sorry, Jack, I'll have to get her clear or we're going to end up hitting something. Remmy and I will head back as soon as you've jumped, and happy landings! Three minutes, Stokes."

A bell rang and a red light flickered on above the exit hatch in the floor in front of Jack.

"Affirmative," Stokes said into his headset. He walked back up the line to the exit hatch. "Prepping for jump in three minutes!" he yelled.

"Good luck, you maniacs!" came Remmy's voice. "See you at the rendezvous point in three days!"

*God willing*, Jack thought.

Stokes heaved open the floor cover in front of him, and an arctic blast of wind whipped snow up into the fuselage, sucking away the last remaining warmth. He locked the hatch in place on a standing latch, then beckoned Jack forward. "First man out when the red light turns green," he yelled over the deafening clatter of engines.

A bell clanged twice, and the red light blinked above them.

"Two minutes!" Stokes yelled.

Jack gazed down through the hatch, hypnotized by the freezing darkness roaring by beneath them. Feeling Cammy shake beside him, he looked into her eyes, took her hand, and squeezed it reassuringly. It was a weak gesture through the thick standard-issue mittens they were wearing, but he hoped it was sufficient to give her the strength she needed. She squeezed his hand back.

The bell clanged again, and the red light blinked again. "One minute!" yelled Stokes.

"Still time to become a conscientious objector, kid," Mosquito said to Spitfire.

Spitfire said nothing, though his armor rattled faintly.

"Steady, lad," Lancaster said, putting a hand on his shoulder. "Just remember your training."

Jack looked up the line. This was finally it.

He caught Lancaster's eye and nodded; he was comforted to see the sergeant nod back. *'Least that's one less battle to fight down there.*

He looked up at the red light. The wait was excruciating.

And then with a screech, the floor of the bomber was shorn away right beneath their feet, exposing a long unfathomable drop into a freezing abyss. The Whitley had gone too low and scraped a jagged peak of rock. If not for their tether lines holding them in place, they all would have plummeted to their deaths; as it was, they dangled loosely, bouncing violently from one side of the fuselage to the other.

The aircraft went into a violent spin, klaxons blaring. Jack instinctively put an arm around Cammy's waist.

"Jack!" she cried.

Following her gaze, he saw Stokes, wide-eyed and clinging desperately to a shred of webbing in the tail section. The young man was the only one who hadn't been tethered in.

Jack stretched out an arm in a desperate effort to reach him, but the Whitley jolted violently and Stokes's webbing ripped away from the wall of the fuselage.

He was sucked into the ravening darkness below.

Aware that the same fate could befall his team, Jack unsheathed his commando knife and raised its blackened blade to his tether. *"Cut loose, boys! Cut loose!"* he shouted down the line.

The bomber whined as it entered a steep dive. Time was running out.

A thick, oversized Commando blade shot upward from Mosquito's wrist and locked into place. "See you on the ground, boys!" he shouted before cutting his line and dropping into the night.

"Take care of Cammy, boss!" Spitfire said. He cut his own line and dropped, roughly following Mosquito's trajectory.

"Cam, cut your—"

Jack's stomach lurched as he realized that she was dangling limply beside him, her forehead bleeding. He pulled off his mitten and checked the carotid artery in her throat for a pulse, overwhelmed with relief when he found one.

"You can't carry 'er and look after yourself too, boss!" Hurricane yelled. "We ain't got no time—here, give 'er to me!"

Jack knew Hurricane was right. If he was lucky enough to survive this, it would be by the skin of his teeth—and while he hated to admit it, he couldn't protect Cammy during the drop as well as Hurricane could. He slid her down the tether bar to Billy, who in turn passed her to Hurricane.

The machine wrapped an arm around her waist to secure her to his side, then ejected his own blade and cut Cammy's tether. "She'll be safe, boss. That's a promise!" He cut himself loose and dropped into the darkness.

"Get going, Bill!" Jack yelled.

"I ain't goin' nowhere without—"

Billy dropped screaming out of the fuselage. Lancaster had cut him loose.

"Together?" Jack yelled.

Lancaster nodded.

As the Whitley came apart around them, Jack realized that there was fear and there was stupidity—and he embraced them both.

They dropped from the stricken bomber, which shrieked out of sight behind a dark mountain range.

Their fate was now in the hands of destiny.

Wind whistled around Jack's ears. Checking the altimeter on his wrist-wireless, he saw that he was at five hundred feet. With a whoosh, he heard Lancaster's canopy deploy, pulling him up into the night.

Jack heard snatches of chatter from the transceiver on his wrist-wireless.

"*It won't open!*"

"*I'm gonna hit it!*"

"*'old on!*"

"*Jack!*"

Jack pulled the D-ring on his harness.

Nothing happened.

He tried it again. It came away in his hand.

The earth was rushing up to meet him.

Jack remembered his training and yanked on his reserve. He was overcome with relief when he felt himself jerked upward by his chute. But he could tell something was wrong. Looking up, he saw several tears in his parachute, and as he picked up speed, his canopy ripped open further as the sub-zero winds whooshed through it.

Jack felt panic, exhilaration and sadness that he'd never get to tell Cammy how he truly felt about her. The last thing he saw before unconsciousness washed over him, was the flicker of crimson flares on the snowy wastes below.

# 25

## ENEMY OF MY ENEMY

**MÖRDER LOOKED UP** from Hellstrøm's file as his telephone rang. Annoyed at the interruption, he snatched up the receiver.

"Herr General?" It was Weissner, a senior officer from the Rjukan garrison's barracks. "A reconnaissance fighter reported an unidentified aircraft over the Hardangervidda in the early hours this morning."

"Allied?"

"Unconfirmed, sir, but they think it was towing a glider which appeared to cut loose. They lost sight of it in cloud over Skrykken. Captain Kramer's unit from Jansbu is currently en route to investigate."

"Thank you."

Mörder replaced the receiver and contemplated the news. So, the Allies were making a play. It would have been foolish to assume otherwise, with resistance rife in the region. That the Allied High Command would attempt a sabotage operation against Vemork seemed perfectly logical given the stakes, but in order to do so they would need Milorg assistance.

Mörder took a map and compass from his briefcase and measured various distances. Skrykken was forty miles northwest of the factory. It was reasonable therefore to assume that the saboteurs, along with their Milorg accomplices, would trek southwest to Vemork. If so, then it might be possible to intercept them before they reached Rjukan.

He picked up the telephone. "Get me Weissner."

"Yes, sir."

The glider almost certainly contained Allied weapons and equipment. If it did, then the saboteurs' effectiveness would be compromised.

"General Mörder?"

"Weissner, I want maps and schematics detailing the topography between Vemork and Skrykken, and tell Kramer to report in as soon as he reaches the crash site."

"Very good, Herr General."

Mörder replaced the receiver, allowing himself a brief flush of satisfaction. This was going to be easier than he'd thought.

...

Jack felt it before he saw it, tugging at his boot.

Focusing, he looked down into the piercing amber eyes of a giant gray wolf. Panting hot breath, it leapt up, snarling through bared canines, to tear at his leg. Jack lashed out, kicking it with his boot, and the predator backed up growling, its hackles raised.

Jack slowly became aware of his surroundings. He was in a forest, swinging from the branches of a fir tree; apparently his canopy lines had gotten tangled. Beneath him, the gray's pack was circling his tree uneasily, their leader probing and testing the strange new meal that had crash-landed into their territory. This was the worst good news-bad news scenario Jack had ever heard of.

Jack fumbled for his revolver. His frozen fingers managed to slide the weapon from its holster, but they were unable to grip it, and it dropped into the snow.

The gray growled again and prepared to leap.

The sharp crack of a rifle echoed through the forest. The gray, along with its pack, fled to a nearby rise.

Three men came crunching through the snow toward Jack. The first, carrying the rifle, was a bear of a man, with wild blond hair and a beard that glistened with ice. The second man was tall and lithe, and he leapt up onto the trunk of Jack's tree and climbed expertly toward him. The third man had a huge moustache ending in icicles, and he and the first man stood beneath the tree and appeared to be joking in Norwegian.

The lithe man climbed up above Jack and looked down at him. His pockmarked face bore a deep scar above the left eye. "Wulff Larssen," he said, nodding. He drew the biggest knife Jack had ever seen and cut the lines to the canopy, sending Jack crashing into the arms of the men below.

The man with the icicle moustache set Jack on his feet and held out a hand. "Erik Kristianssen," he said cheerily.

"SOE sent me a boy?" said the man with the rifle, destroying the brief moment of cordiality. He looked up at Jack's parachute. "Not so impressive," he growled in baritone. His face was tanned and stoic. "Magnus Hellstrøm," he said. "Milorg." He grabbed Jack's backpack, spun him around, and examined it. "No equipment?"

"We lost our glider last night," Jack said. He was cold, hungry and his leg had started to throb.

"This was bad plan from beginning," Hellstrøm growled. "I tell SOE—they not listen!"

"Yeah, they're like that," Jack said. "Look, there were others, the group who jumped with me."

"We found some."

It was an open-ended answer. Concerned, Jack was about to ask more.

A twig snapped.

Hellstrøm brought up his rifle with lightning reflexes.

Jack spun to see Billy step into the clearing, arms raised.

"Easy," Jack said. "He's one o' mine."

"You're Stone?" Hellstrøm asked.

Jack nodded and offered his hand.

"I shake when factory destroyed," Hellstrøm rumbled. "Come."

He slung his rifle over his shoulder and strode from the clearing. Larssen and Kristianssen ushered Jack and Billy after him.

"Jittery buggers, ain't they?" Billy said.

They made their way through the forest and arrived at a derelict hut that had been overrun with moss and vegetation. Lancaster and Mosquito were waiting outside, guarded by two more Norwegians.

"Where are the others?" Jack asked, running to them.

"We only just got 'ere," Lancaster said. "Spoke to Hurricane on the way down, but I lost 'is signal."

"And Spitfire?" Billy asked.

Mosquito shook his head. "Kid's still out there somewhere. "I just 'ope he's all right."

"Dark soon," Hellstrøm muttered. "We go. There is shelter nearby to eat, sleep."

"Three of my team are still missing," Jack said.

"Then they're already dead."

Billy raised his Sten gun. "We ain't goin' nowhere 'til we find our people."

Lancaster loomed threateningly over Hellstrøm. The Norwegian looked slowly up at him. "I read of you in papers, Sergeant. You're far less impressive up close."

Jack saw that Hellstrøm's men had leveled their machine-guns. "Four against one," said Hellstrøm, amused.

"Make that four against four," Jack said, as Billy, Lancaster and Mosquito raised their guns behind him.

Hellstrøm frowned. "But that's only—"

In a blur, Jack pulled Hellstrøm's revolver from its holster and pointed it at the man's temple. "We look for my people, or we don't go at all," he said with deadly conviction.

A smile crept across Hellstrøm's face. "Good reflexes, boy," he chortled. "There may be hope for you yet."

"I'd agree with that," said a new voice.

Cammy stepped into view, her revolver drawn. Beside her was Hurricane, and he wasn't looking good. He was using the broken trunk of a fir tree for a crutch, and his leg was dripping oil.

"*A woman?*" Hellstrøm hissed, turning to Jack.

"Hey, *Norway,* I'm right here!" Cammy exclaimed.

"She's their mechanic," Jack said, nodding toward the Tommies.

"Where's Spitfire?" Cammy asked.

"We don't know yet," Jack said quietly. "We were just about to go look."

"My job is to get you to factory," Hellstrøm muttered, "not search the entire Hardangervidda for—"

"We can't leave him out here!" Cammy protested.

"The Hardangervidda covers two and a half thousand square miles," Hellstrøm said, "and after your light show last night, it will soon be crawling with Nazis."

"There aren't any Nazis for miles," Cammy said.

"What about that Heinkel?" said Lancaster.

"There is more to fear than Nazis out here, little woman." Hellstrøm jerked a thumb at the Tommies. "And your machines are no good if frozen! We have three days to reach Rjukan."

Jack put a hand on Cammy's shoulder. "What about Spitfire's tracker?"

She checked her wrist-wireless. "Still activated."

"Then he's okay," Jack said, though he was unconvinced. "Look, I don't like this any more than you do, but Spitfire knows where we need to be. If he can't communicate with us, he'll head to Rjukan and rendezvous with us there. Cam, we can't miss that deadline."

Cammy's shoulders slumped in resignation. "I know."

"Then we go," said Hellstrøm. He turned to Larssen and nodded. Shouldering his Sten gun, Larssen heaved a coil of oiled rope from his shoulder and started untying it.

With a smile, Hellstrøm tossed an empty hessian sack at Cammy. "We take you along to pick reindeer moss, little woman. Cook broth for the boys."

Cammy stuck out her chin. "Look, mister, who the hell made you king o' the hill, huh?"

Jack grabbed her arm and took her aside. "Turn it down a notch, will ya?"

"Says you!" Cammy spat. "Two minutes ago, you were ready to shoot it out 'n' come looking for me!"

"No time to argue—dark soon!" Hellstrøm shouted. "Tie them on, Wulff."

Larssen handed one end of the rope to Jack. "We trek single file, hide numbers from Germans."

Jack tied the rope to his belt, then handed it to Cammy, who did the same before passing it to Billy. When they were all tied in a line, Hellstrøm's men fell in behind them, and the column headed out across the glacier.

Bordering Buskerud, Hordaland and Telemark, the Hardangervidda was—as Hellstrøm had indicated—vast. This fact was sorely realized by Jack and the team as they trekked wearily across it several hours later. The vegetation was lush at first, but the barren terrain grew progressively more desolate and rocky as they climbed higher into the icescape. Jack had the uncomfortable sensation of being utterly exposed to both the elements and the enemy. The Highlands of Achnacarry seemed like a tropical paradise, a stark contrast to the rocky fells of the Hardangervidda, and despite the presence of his team, Jack felt cold, alone, and desperately concerned for Spitfire.

Hellstrøm regularly tested the ground ahead of them and often ordered them to veer left and right to avoid potential pitfalls and crevasses. Every so often he would cast a glance back at Jack and shake his head, muttering something about what SOE had sent him. Eventually he slowed, pulled a compass from his pocket, and checked their coordinates. He and Larssen yelled to each other in Norwegian, and Jack noted that there appeared to be a dispute about which direction they should go.

After a couple minutes of conversation, Hellstrøm turned to face them. "We head east. Germans will come looking for you. There is hunting lodge I know of which Germans don't."

"We've got three days to make Vemork," Jack yelled into the gale.

"We don't have time for—"

"You head east, boy, or you die, either in storm or when Nazis catch you." He started up an incline and heaved on the rope. "Your choice," he said without turning.

"Well done, sir," Lancaster said sarcastically. "A veritable master class in pulling rank."

"He's even more stubborn than you are," Jack muttered.

"Let's go," Cammy said. "I gotta work on Hurricane before his leg jacks in."

They marched for two more hours before they reached the lodge. It was little more than a broken down lean-to creaking in the gale, but to the weary and shivering raiding party, it was a welcome sight, and they rushed to get in out of the cold.

Hellstrøm packed kindling into a copper stove in the corner and lit it with a match. The warmth was felt immediately.

"What I wouldn't give for a pie 'n' a pint," Billy said, pulling off his gloves and wiggling his fingers in front of the stove's flames to warm them up. "The Crooked 'ouse'd be nice about now."

Hellstrøm beckoned Cammy over and gestured for her to hand him the hessian bag in which she'd begrudgingly collected moss from beneath the ice. "We make good stew, little woman," he said. "Reindeer moss, see?" He sprinkled the moss into the pot, then tapped snow from his boot and added a generous handful. Cammy didn't care what he put in the pot; she was just grateful for the stove's warmth—which appeared to be melting Hellstrøm's prickliness as well as the ice on his beard.

"Army marches on its stomach, yes?" Hellstrøm said.

"If that's true, we can jump on Bill's back 'n' bounce to the factory!" Hurricane said, taking a spot on the floor beside Lancaster and Mosquito.

"Count yourself lucky I'm too knackered to punch you," Billy said, wearily unshouldering his pack.

For the first time, the other two Norwegians, the men they'd met outside the hut in the forest, spoke, introducing themselves as Haakon and Seim. They, along with Larssen and Kristianssen, sat around the lodge's table.

Jack and Billy joined them. Jack pulled several packets of cigarettes from his pack and handed them out. In thanks, Kristianssen pulled out a flask, poured something into a rusty tin cup, and slid it to Jack. When Jack took a swig, he felt his lungs ignite; he coughed involuntarily, to the great amusement of Hellstrøm and his men.

"What is it?" Jack gagged, passing the cup to Billy.

"Is good, eh?" Hellstrøm said. "Karsk!"

"What's Karsk?" Billy said. He took a swig and coughed even harder than Jack. "*Jesus!*"

"Coffee and moonshine," Kristianssen said.

"And a spoonful of sugar," Hellstrøm added, winking at Cammy. He took the cup from Billy, sucked in a mouthful, then spat it into the stove, blasting the flames higher. "Is good for toilet clean too!"

"That figures," Billy said. "No wonder they mix it with coffee!"

"This," said Hellstrøm, "is why I asked for men. Yet they send me children. Children and machines."

"Well, if that's the way you feel about it, we'll sod off back where we came from," Billy said.

Hellstrøm smiled. "You've spirit, Briggs. Maybe we fight outside, but after you've eaten my soup first, huh? I'd hate for you to say you'd not experienced true Norwegian hospitality."

Billy was unsure whether to take this man seriously. "Is that what that was? Bloody funny way to show it."

"I like you, Briggs," Hellstrøm laughed. "Come. We eat now!"

...

The stew was disgusting, but it filled the gap. After their meal, while the Norwegians played another round of cards, Jack saw Cammy slip outside, and he followed.

He found her on a bluff, gazing out across the snowfield.

"He's out there, somewhere."

"We'll find Spitfire," Jack said. "I promise."

"Jack, there's something else. After Hurricane and I landed, I checked our chutes. There were tears in them. *Man-made* tears."

Jack's stomach lurched. "Mine was torn too. You're saying they were sabotaged?"

Cammy nodded.

"It couldn't have been Hastings. Who else had access?"

"The packs were in the *Valiant's* hangar all night before the drop. Anyone could've gotten to them."

"Let's keep this to ourselves for now, huh?" Jack said. "C'mon back inside."

...

It was late when they settled down to sleep with full bellies, topped by Karsk. Billy and Hellstrøm's men were snoring, Cammy was asleep, and the Tommies had been shut down. That left only Jack and Hellstrøm sitting at the table.

Jack looked about the room, bathed in the flickering glow of the boiler fire. The gale outside howled, and despite his blanket's warmth he shivered.

"You know," said Hellstrøm, "this will not be, how would your doctor say, 'a walk in the park,' my young friend. Whatever's going on at Vemork, it isn't just heavy water. Rumors dance on the wind like snowflakes. An *army*, they say, at Vemork." He waved his Karsk cup at the Tommies. "One much like your own."

"I prefer to believe in facts," Jack said. "Something I can see, something I can feel. Not rumors."

Hellstrøm smiled. "There was a time when your machines were just rumors, no? Can you deny *they* exist?"

"Whatever's at Vemork, we're going to blow it. *Period.*"

Hellstrøm stared into the boiler's flames. "Let us hope you are right, my young friend, for if we fail, the fate of Great Britain may soon be that of Norway."

"Never."

"There was a time when I thought like yourself. But how would you deal with an occupying enemy who attacks you with a smile?" Hellstrøm asked. "Would you spit in their face with your back to a wall against which you may be shot? No, Jack, you would do nothing—or at least be seen to do so. Resistance, my friend, takes time, organization, before it can be forged. My Norway *will* be free again, that I promise you."

Jack understood. *Freedom.* Men would fight for it, die for it even. Men like Hellstrøm.

"Skål," Hellstrøm said quietly. He raised his tin cup and downed the last of his Karsk.

"To freedom," Jack said, reciprocating.

"Now sleep, boy. Long trek tomorrow. Better keep up."

Jack nodded, drifting off to sleep as the gale howled outside.

# 26

## BRASS MONKEYS

**MÖRDER SURVEYED** the Rjuken valley from a balcony above Vemork's compound. All around, the ceaseless drubbing of the factory's industrial machinery pounded as its twelve massive penstocks, each with a six-foot diameter, carried thousands of tons of water from rivers above the mountainside to the factory below.

Mörder looked up as the dawn sun broke through grey clouds scudding overhead, obscuring the crowns of the factory's chimneys. If Kramer confirmed his suspicions today, then weather permitting, Mörder would be able to fly.

The general turned his attention to the compound below as his troops changed shift. In many ways, Mörder thought, no fortress was better protected by nature, or better located to withstand an assault. With only a single-track railway running along a narrow mountain shelf, and a slender suspension bridge crossing the gorge three hundred feet above the river Måna, the compound, now stationed with Mörder's sentries, checkpoints and machine-gun nests was a truly formidable stronghold. One might say, almost impenetrable.

Almost.

But Mörder had been entrusted with the key to his Führer's victory, and he would allow nothing to prevent him from fulfilling his mission. Gazing out across the valley, Mörder silently reaffirmed that oath.

"Excuse the intrusion, Herr General—"

Johanssen appeared timidly beside Mörder.

"Captain Kramer's on the phone, sir. He said it's urgent."

...

Mörder picked up the receiver.

"Kramer?"

"General Mörder? My men have found the glider's remains on the outskirts of Skrykken. We estimate from the debris field that the aircraft was headed due south when it hit the Hardanger. The reconnaissance aircraft which spotted their descent also confirmed this."

"And the glider's contents?"

"Weapons, explosives and ammunition. Damaged, but untouched."

"Without equipment, the saboteurs will need help from the Milorg," Mörder said, "and the Milorg will need friends and family." He examined the map on his desk. "How far are you from Gøystavatnet?"

"About twenty miles, sir."

"Then recall your men," Mörder ordered. "Make for Gøystavatnet. I'll rendezvous with you there."

"Yes, Herr General."

Mörder replaced the receiver. The plateau from Skrykken was barren and offered few opportunities for saboteurs to rest or provision themselves. But Hellstrøm's file stated that he had a sister who lived in Gøystavatnet, so it was likely that he would lead the saboteurs there to provision and re-equip before escorting them on to Rjukan.

When they arrived, Mörder would be there to take them. And if by some chance they evaded him at Gøystavatnet, well, he still had an ace up his sleeve.

Mörder gripped the balcony's iron railing with black gloved hands, and his heart sang at the prospect of killing two birds with one stone.

...

Jack and the group's trek from Skrykken in the early hours of the morning had been hard going across tough terrain, and everyone was fatigued. At any other time, a stroll across the Hardanger Plateau would have been a pleasant day out, but with the sun riding high, the ice fields were beginning to break up, turning snow into slush and sure footing into leaps of faith. Hellstrøm had told them that without effective weapons or equipment the party had no alternative but to push on to Gøystavatnet and provision before liaising with their OSE contact in Rjukan.

They descended through tall, snow-laden pine trees toward a ridge from which they could see a valley below. The Norwegian raised a hand for silence, then hunkered down and pulled binoculars from a satchel around his waist. The others crouched and looked about nervously while Hellstrøm powered forward on his elbows to peer down from the ridge.

Jack shouldered his Sten gun and crawled forward to join him. "What is it?"

"Gøystavatnet," said Hellstrøm, passing Jack the binoculars. "My home."

Peering through the binoculars, Jack saw a picture-postcard hamlet. A square at its center was surrounded by concentric circles of little wooden houses, raised high on slate bricks with steps leading up to their doors. The roofs were covered with moss, and smoke drifted lazily from stone chimneys. Chickens and geese wandered freely in the streets, and a field contained cattle and reindeer, separated from one another by a babbling brook. As Jack watched, a young couple dressed in silver and gold costumes were being led on horseback to the village square, followed by a procession of brightly dressed villagers.

"Astrid," Hellstrøm said. "My sister Vanja's girl. Today is her wedding day."

Jack watched the young couple mount a makeshift wooden stage adorned with flowers in the village square, where they clapped and whirled to a merry tune played by cheering fiddlers and folk musicians.

"Looks safe enough," Jack said, returning Hellstrøm's binoculars.

"This is Norway, boy," Hellstrøm muttered. "Appearances are deceptive."

"We're out of food and low on just about everything else since we lost the glider. Aside from what the boys have in their packs, I don't even think we have enough ammo for the raid." He glanced back at Cammy, Billy and the Tommies, then looked at Hellstrøm earnestly. "We're running out of options."

Hellstrøm drew his pistol. "We go take closer look."

. . .

Hellstrøm led the team down the mountainside toward the bank of a frozen lake. While it was easier to traverse than the plateau, the terrain was no less treacherous, especially for the Tommies, whose weight carried their momentum downhill at speed. Still, they took care to remain under cover as they crept through the fir trees and foliage.

When they reached the ice lake, Hellstrøm removed his backpack and snowsuit, collected an armful of logs, and piled them up in his arms, hiding his rifle among them. "Wait here," he said. Then he skated across the lake toward the nearest house.

As Jack crept back down the line Billy stopped him.

"You smell a rat?" Billy asked, watching Hellstrøm.

"I can't even feel my nose, mate" Jack said. He shivered and knelt beside Cammy, who was sat listening keenly into her wrist-wireless. As he moved to take her hand, she batted him aside.

"Hey, I'm just trying to help," he said gently.

"Well I don't *need* your help," Cammy said, wiping her nose. She shouldered off her backpack and threw it aside.

Jack took her hand, and this time she didn't resist. "I'm worried about him too," he said gently, "but he'll be okay."

"He's just so young compared to the others. The thought of him out there alone…" Tears welled in her eyes.

"Look, you fitted the boys with trackers. Just 'cos we can't see Spitfire's doesn't mean he can't see ours."

Cammy composed herself and nodded.

"Jack," Billy growled. "You need to see this."

Hellstrøm was skating back across the ice toward them. When he reached the group, he crouched down. "Okay, is safe."

. . .

A plump, kindly-looking woman with thick blonde braids was waiting for them at the outskirts of the village. Two dogs sat beside her, fat and sturdy, their tails coiled tightly around their backs. The woman smiled and beckoned for the group to follow her. "I am Vanja Hellstrøm," she said. "Welcome to my home. This village is loyal to my brother and the Milorg. You will be safe here, but please, we must get you out of sight."

She led them past the village square, where the celebration was in full swing. The villagers, all wearing brightly colored bunads and capes, were not taken aback in the least at the sight of the Tommies. To the contrary, they handed them flowers and shook their hands, kissing the Norwegians as they moved through the crowd.

They arrived at a barn in a quiet area. Vanja heaved open the door and gestured for the team to enter.

As Jack's eyes adjusted to the light, Vanja approached a large object covered by tarpaulin. "Our mechanic, Lars Nielsen, found it out on the plateau," she said. "When he told me about it I thought… well, Lars towed it back here."

Larssen and Kristianssen removed the tarpaulin.

"Spitfire?" Cammy gasped.

The little Tommy was in bad shape. His entire left side was dented, crushed, and his left eye lens fractured.

"Oh, no…" Lancaster said.

"Kid?" Hurricane gasped in shock.

Mosquito bounded across the barn and crouched beside his friend.

"C'mon, Spit, wake up!" He looked up at Cammy, panic-stricken. "You gotta fix 'im, Cam!"

Cammy walked right up to Vanja. "This Lars Nielsen," she said purposefully. "He got a workshop?"

. . .

Mörder strode across the landing pad as the propeller blades of the Flettner Hummingbird rotor-copter began to spin. Climbing into a seat beside the pilot, Mörder nodded, and the man heaved back on the stick. Buffeted by the wind, the Hummingbird rose shakily with a whine, nosing up through a whirlwind of snow.

As the icescape glided by beneath him, Mörder worked methodically through every tactical scenario that might present itself at Gøystavatnet, creating a counter-move for each situation.

He would eliminate the saboteurs at Gøystavatnet.

He would crush them under his boot heel.

. . .

Spitfire stood motionless in Lars Nielsen's workshop, his dead eye staring at the Tommies who talked quietly nearby. Cammy was sitting astride Spitfire's shoulders, his helmet hatch opened before her.

"You got a welder?" she asked Nielsen.

The mechanic, grizzled but kindly looking, frowned and scratched his stubble until Cammy pointed at a welding mask on a nearby bench. Nielsen nodded, taking an arc welder from a cabinet, and throwing it up to Cammy along with the mask.

"Thanks." She pulled on the mask, lit the torch, and got to work. A burst of sparks erupted from within Spitfire's head.

Hurricane flinched. "I don't fancy his chances."

"Don't count 'im out, boys," Mosquito said. "Not yet."

"Come on, lads," Lancaster said. "There's nothing more we can do for him."

"Yes, there is." Mosquito turned and left the workshop.

"He's takin' it bad," said Hurricane.

"It coulda been any one of us," Lancaster said. "The boy's in Camilla's hands now. C'mon." He pushed open the workshop door and left with Hurricane. Nielsen followed them with Vanja who promised to stay nearby in case she was needed.

Jack entered the workshop as they departed. "Hellstrøm's got guns 'n' explosives," he said to Cammy. "Should be enough to do the job. They're loading them onto a flatbed now."

Cammy, elbow deep in Spitfire's mechanisms, was utterly absorbed in her work. "Hand me a wrench, would you?"

Jack found one on the bench and handed it up to her. "His battery's damaged," she said, heaving against something awkward with the wrench.

Cammy climbed down, sniffed, and wiped oil across her nose. "I got fused wires, most of which I can't replace. A lot of his major cells've blown. If it wasn't for his tank... I mean, there's stuff in there I can't reach, 'n' even if I could I don't think—"

She slammed the wrench angrily back on the bench, knocking the contents of a tool tray onto the floor. "Dammit!"

She knelt down to clean up the mess, then paused and took a breath. "This is all my fault. He was scared about coming out here, y'know? I promised him he'd be okay, said I'd look after him." Tears streamed down her cheeks. "If I'd just made him stronger!"

Jack crouched beside her and took her hand. He wiped a tear from her cheek. "This isn't your fault," he said softly.

She pulled away. "Yeah, well, I got work to do." She retrieved a few tools and climbed back up onto Spitfire.

Jack stood and put a hand on the little Tommy's chest plate. "Come on, Spitfire," he said quietly. "*Fight!*"

...

As Mosquito entered the village chapel, he saw Billy on a bench in front of a wooden cross on the wall. He sat down beside him, the bench creaking under his weight.

"How is he?" Billy asked.

Mosquito said nothing, which told Billy all he needed to know.

"My old mum was a big churchgoer," Billy said. "She used to dress us up every Sunday for morning worship." He smiled reflectively. "I can still feel that shirt itch. Anyway, point is, I never much got it at the time. Religion, y'know? But here? Now?" He rose and put a comforting hand on Mosquito's shoulder. "Now I think I get it."

Billy left the chapel.

Clasping his hands together, Mosquito looked up at the wooden cross before him.

"I uh, I dunno if you can 'ear me," he said. "I dunno if me askin' even counts. Hurricane says we all 'ave souls 'n' that we... Well, it's a nice thought. And if it's true, I need your 'elp, 'cos it's all very well bein' the flash one with the big gob, but I can't do nothin' to help 'im 'n' you can. If you do this for me, I'll change. Be a better *man* like what Hurricane said. I ain't one, I know, but I can try. Spitfire? Kid didn't deserve this, 'n' he's my friend, see." Mosquito bowed his head. "So please…"

The bench creaked beside him. Looking over, he saw Lancaster and Hurricane had joined him. As dusk's dying rays pooled around them through the little chapel's stained-glass window, the three Tommies looked up at the cross and prayed.

...

Spitfire's blue eye winked on.

Jack took a step back in disbelief. "Spitfire?" he whispered.

A metal shutter closed over the lens and reopened. A *wink?*

"Cam?" Jack said.

"Huh?" She looked up.

With a groan, Spitfire stomped his right foot forward, then his left, and then, juddering violently, he staggered about the workshop, Cammy still on his shoulders.

Cammy plunged the wrench deep inside Spitfire's head. She gritted her teeth and heaved, and with a groan, Spitfire lurched forward and crashed down onto the bench.

Cammy skidded across the floor and hit the wall. Spitfire stared at her, his blue eye fizzling out.

"What the hell…" Jack said.

"I think, I think he's—"

Engines roared suddenly outside. Billy appeared at the door with Sten guns. "We got company."

...

A convoy of three German Opel trucks growled to a stop on the frozen lake. Their rear doors slammed open, releasing dozens of gray-green Stormtroopers. The men swarmed into Gøystavatnet, going straight to the village square, their machine-guns leveled. They herded the villagers toward the outskirts of the village as Mörder's rotor-copter descended in a tornado of snow nearby.

The general climbed from the aircraft as an officer approached him. Seeing the mask, the officer saluted warily.

Mörder returned the salute. "Kramer?"

The officer nodded. "I must say general, it's an honor to—"

Mörder ignored him and turned to survey the villagers. His gaze fell upon a little girl, watching him from behind her terrified mother's apron.

He crouched in front of her. "Such a beautiful child," he murmured absently, glancing up at her mother. "The face of an angel, yes?"

Petrified, the mother nodded agreement.

Cupping the little girl's face in a black gloved hand, Mörder caressed his mask, distant. *"An angel…"*

...

"Bucket 'eads!" Billy growled, peering through a crack in the workshop door.

He handed Jack and Cammy their guns and carefully slid a wooden block across the door. "Looks like the lid's just blown off the kettle."

"They must know we're here," Cammy said.

"Probably found the glider," Jack said. "Put two 'n' two together. Where're the boys?"

"In the chapel," Billy said. "Where's Hellstrøm?"

Jack slid a clip into his sten. "Left him loading guns."

Cammy squinted out the icy window of the workshop. It provided a good view of the village square. "That's a helluva lotta troops for a house-to-house. Who's the freak in the mask?"

"Does it matter?" Billy said. "There's more o' them out there than us, even with the lads' 'elp." He slid the safety back on his Sten gun. From the cover of the building they watched the soldiers scurrying between houses, banging on doors with the butts of their machine guns, and dragging out terrified villagers.

"I want Hellstrøm," Mörder yelled, drawing his Luger. "And those he brought here!"

The crowd remained silent.

Mörder checked his watch. "You have precisely one minute, after which my men will hang everyone in this village until they run out of rope. Anyone left alive after that will be shot."

"I am Hellstrøm."

It was Vanja. She stepped from the crowd defiantly, her hands on her hips, flanked by her dogs. The villagers laughed.

"So, a sense of humor," said Mörder, amused. He aimed his Luger and shot Vanja's dogs.

*"No!"* She dropped to her knees as the animals twitched and expired.

Shock swept through the crowd.

"What? No more laughter?" Mörder mocked. "I ask for the last time now—where is Hellstrøm?"

. . .

"We gotta get out there and 'elp 'em!" Hurricane growled, peering around the chapel door.

"And hand it to the Krauts on a plate?" Mosquito said. "Use your head, dummy."

"Easy now," Lancaster said, nodding toward the square. "Look."

Kristianssen emerged from the crowd. He threw down his rifle and stared at the mask. "I am Hellstrøm," he said. "I am the man you want."

Mörder regarded him. "So, it would appear the rumors are untrue."

"What rumors are those?" said Kristianssen.

"That not all Norwegians are cowards," Mörder scorned.

His soldiers laughed.

Mörder turned to Kramer. "Take him back to Vemork. Raze the village to the ground."

As Kramer turned, Kristianssen leapt for his rifle—but he didn't make it. He struck the ground with a bullet through his eye.

Lowering his smoking gun, Mörder addressed the crowd. "I grow weary of these charades. Give me Hellstrøm, or the fate of this man will seem like an act of mercy compared to what your children will endure."

The crowd shifted nervously, but still no one spoke.

"Very well." Mörder pointed his gun at the little girl, now in the arms of her mother. "Let's send the angel back to heaven."

His finger squeezed the trigger.

"*I'm Hellstrøm!*"

Hellstrøm stepped forward, arms held wide, palms up. Mörder nodded to Kramer, who barked an order. Soldiers moved in on Hellstrøm.

But Hellstrøm was prepared. He reached behind his back and pulled out two primed German stick grenades. Before Mörder was able to get a clear shot, Hellstrøm had wrenched the strings dangling from both sticks and lobbed them over the soldiers' heads.

They landed in the snow near the trucks and exploded impotently with a resounding boom.

"You appear to have missed!" Mörder sneered.

"I wasn't aiming for you!" Hellstrøm said, smiling coldly.

With an almighty crack, the plates of ice covering the lake shifted and came apart. Groaning, the Opel trucks upended and slid back into the water. The shattered ice sheets rolled beneath their weight, carrying

German troops with them. The men cried out as they sought desperately for sure footing. Some escaped to safety, but others slid beneath the ice into the freezing depths.

Larssen appeared from the crowd with Haakon and Seim. He threw Hellstrøm a rifle, then opened fire. Jack, Cammy, and Billy joined them as the Tommies burst from the chapel.

"What are you waiting for?" Mörder screamed, swaying as the ice shifted beneath him. "*Shoot them!*"

As his men returned fire, Mörder shot a glance at the crowd. Hellstrøm had vanished. Worse, the cracks in the ice were spreading. Soon they would take down his rotor-copter.

A scenario he hadn't envisaged? How could this have happened?

The ice shifted and fractured beneath him.

There would be time for analysis later. For now, it was time to fall back.

He strode to the Hummingbird and instructed the pilot to take off. What remained of Kramer's forces fell back under fire from the villagers, then they fled around the lake into the forest.

*This was a setback*, thought Mörder, *not a failure*. He would regroup, and when he did—

This wasn't over…

. . .

Hellstrøm joined Jack and the group at the workshop as the gunfire subsided. The Norwegian looked around at the village. "My people must leave now. *Reprisals*."

"What can we do?" Cammy said. "They know we're coming."

"Yeah, they do," Jack said, shouldering his Sten gun. "But we beat 'em. Now they'll *fear* us."

"Come on lads," Billy said. "Help me get the rest o'those crates stashed." He returned to the truck with Hellstrøm and the Tommies.

Cammy looked suddenly concerned.

"You okay?" Jack asked.

Cammy said nothing, looking over his shoulder.

"Cam?"

Jack heard a pistol click ominously behind him. He slowly turned to see Kramer, panic stricken, his Luger trembling. "Easy," Jack said, raising his hands.

Wide-eyed, Kramer's eyes darted from Jack to Cammy, then back to

Jack, then he suddenly took aim.

A great fist slammed down onto his head and he dropped into the snow with a crunch.

Spitfire stood hunched behind him, his one good eye flickering blue. He looked at Jack and Cammy.

"What'd I miss?"

# 27

## RJUKEN

**J**OHANSSEN'S OFFICE DOOR flew open and slammed against the wall cracking the plaster. Johanssen leapt to his feet and backed up to a window as Mörder stormed into the room.

"Gen—" Johanssen coughed, tugging at his collar. "General?"

"When will the shipment be ready?" Mörder demanded.

"The train is being prepared now. I anticipate that by later this evening the last of the heavy water will be loaded, and the barrels can be transported to the ferry port."

"I want to be informed as soon as everything's in place."

"Of course, sir." Then: "Was your trip to Gøystavatnet productive?"

Mörder took a threatening step forward. Cursing himself for his words, Johanssen shrank back.

"Be thankful, Johanssen, that due to your scientific expertise, you are —for now at least—a very necessary component in this process. Otherwise I would have you hanged from that bridge out there."

Johanssen gulped. His hand rubbed his throat.

"General, I gave you Hellstrøm's name. Was he not in Gøystavatnet? If I were a member of the Milorg, surely that would not have been so?"

"Possibly," Mörder said. In a blur of motion, his hand was gripping Johanssen's throat. "But irrespective of the Führer's directive, should I discover that you're connected with the Milorg in *any* way, neither you or your pretty daughter will live to see the dawn. Is that clear?"

Squeezing his eyes shut, Johanssen nodded furiously.

Feeling Mörder release his grip, he opened his eyes to see the general striding from the room.

"I'm doubling security on the bridge," Mörder said. "And men will be posted at every access point both in and out of this factory, around the clock, until those barrels are loaded!"

"Yes, Herr General."

"And Johanssen," Mörder paused in the doorway without turning, "don't fail me!"

. . .

Snow was falling softly again as the raiding party arrived at the base of a steep slope in Fjosbudalen. They hid their truck in the trees, gathered their guns and equipment, and made their way through scrub up an incline.

Hellstrøm stopped at a point overlooking a valley below. "Rjukan," he said, peering through his binoculars.

The town wound its way along the banks of a meandering river. The water sparkled with reflections of tiny lights flickering in the windows of houses, seemingly oblivious to any blackout laws, as the sun had begun its descent behind the mountains on the opposite side of the valley.

"How far's Vemork?" Jack asked.

"This valley curves west about a mile from Rjuken." Hellstrøm made a sweeping gesture across the town. "The plant's on the opposite side, just out of sight around that bend."

The snow was now coming down so fast, Jack couldn't even see the bend.

"We'll need to cross that river," Lancaster said.

"It don't look too frozen from where I'm standing," Hurricane added. He had extended his lenses for a better view.

"The Måna's thawing," Hellstrøm confirmed.

"Thawing?" Billy exclaimed.

"Crossing's not ideal," Hellstrøm continued, "but it *is* possible. Closer to factory, where ice doesn't see sun."

"Ismay mentioned a bridge," Jack said.

"And a rail track," Cammy added.

"The Germans have mined banks on either side of the Måna," Hellstrøm replied. "Even if you reached bridge, you'd only alert the guards in plant's barracks, who would call in the garrison stationed in Rjukan—probably Møsvatn, too. Once they closed in, no way off that bridge but down."

"What do you propose?" Jack asked.

"The valley beneath Vemork's in shadow all year round—the ice on the Måna should be thick enough there for us to cross," Hellstrøm said.

Jack nodded.

"If the banks're mined then we'll need to pass straight through Rjukan to get through," Billy said. "Either that, or we waste time scrabbling about these slopes."

"We don't have a choice Bill, we have to meet SOE's contact," Jack said.

"Looks awfully busy down there," Cammy said, gazing at the town through Hellstrøm's binoculars.

"No risk, no reward, eh?" Jack muttered.

"Is hunter's lodge down this slope," Hellstrøm said. "Seldom visited, empty this time of year. We stay there to prepare, then move down into town after dark, meet your contact."

"Okay," Jack nodded. "Let's go."

...

Stars twinkled above Rjuken as dusk stretched tentative icy fingers across the valley. Much like the group's first shelter, the lodge was a rickety derelict but it offered cover close to the town before their mission began in earnest. To the best of their knowledge, the group's descent into the valley had gone unnoticed, and on arrival at the lodge they had blacked out its windows and stuffed moss into every crack and cranny to avoid their light being detected.

Hellstrøm's men had snared a couple of hares which the group, now seated around a table, devoured hungrily by the light of a flickering stove.

"It's agreed then," Jack said. "We climb the gorge up to the factory."

"Germans think anything other than bridge assault's impossible," Hellstrøm said. "They won't be looking for mountaineers, so God willing, we get in unnoticed. Those slopes are near vertical, so we travel light: arms and explosives only."

"What about getting back?" Lancaster asked.

"The slope behind the factory's too sheer," Seim said, glancing at Hellstrøm.

"Then we get out the way we came in," Jack said.

"After blast," Hellstrøm said, "the town garrison will head to factory. By the time they get there, we'll be long gone."

"So we blow the place and meet back here," Jack said, "then grind the truck onto the Hardanger."

"Where my men build strip for your transport," Hellstrøm said.

The team looked doubtfully around the room at each other.

Jack unbuttoned the top of his snow suit. Underneath it was a German uniform provided by Hellstrøm's people in Gøystavatnet. There had been enough for all human members of the raiding party; Jack hoped it would keep them from drawing unwanted attention in Rjukan.

"I don't like it any more than you do," he continued, "but we don't have a choice. Once we reach the plant we'll split into two teams. I'll lead the demolition party with Lancaster, Mosquito, Cam and Hellstrøm. Billy, you'll lead the covering party with Hurricane, Spitfire, Larssen, Haakon, and Seim. If anything happens to us, you're to act on your own initiative, continue the mission as planned, is that clear?"

Billy nodded, though he looked rattled by the prospect.

"If we can't get into that factory," Jack continued. "Moz will need to blow the doors, and if that happens, you need to be ready for anything."

Billy nodded.

"Once we get inside the high-concentration room, Mosquito will set the charges." Jack turned to Mosquito. "How long will it take?"

"Well, we got eighteen canisters to destroy, so I'd say twenty minutes tops once we're in, boss. We just need to strap on the jelly 'n' light the fuses, then we make a run for it."

Jack nodded. "Will the wrist-wirelesses work in the complex, Cam?"

"Depends on how thick the walls are," Cammy answered doubtfully.

"Assuming they don't," Jack said, looking at Billy, "the only sure sign we've been successful will be the sound of the detonation."

"It'll be a hell of a firework when it goes up," Cammy said.

"And during the confusion, we fight our way out," Hurricane added. "Sounds like a plan."

"Carry your guns with their magazines filled, boys," Lancaster said, "but no shells in the chamber—can't risk a miss-fire givin' the game away to the Krauts.

"Whatever happens," Jack said, "our priority is to blow those cells, is that clear?"

The group nodded agreement.

"And if anyone's taken prisoner…" Jack said. He took a deep breath. "Then we take our own lives." He looked at Hellstrøm. "Ismay gave us—"

"We use bullets," Hellstrøm said. "Much kinder than Gestapo."

"I, uh… I've told the boys how to detonate their tanks," Cammy said. "But hey, that ain't gonna happen, right?"

"No." Jack looked around the table at each member of the party in turn. "No, it's not. See, it all comes down to tonight. When those cells blow, we'll have the biggest fight of our lives to break out. It's a huge risk —we all know it. But so what? We *take* that risk, and we keep takin' 'em, willing to sacrifice ourselves, to sacrifice what we *are*, for the hope of what we can *achieve*. Rise to this challenge, boys. *Rise!* And we'll defeat the greatest enemy the world has ever known. Tonight, we choose to fight —whatever the consequences!"

Hellstrøm raised his Karsk. "Whatever the consequences!"

The others joined him in his toast.

Jack checked his watch. "Okay, check your weapons, packs and equipment. We leave in one hour."

Jack watched the group disperse with a renewed sense of optimism. He saw Cammy watching him. She smiled and nodded, then turned to check the Tommies.

"Sentries change shifts every two hours at factory," Hellstrøm said.

"Then we'll hit 'em at half past midnight," Jack said. "Give the relieved men time to relax, and the fresh troops time to let their guard down."

Hellstrøm nodded, quietly impressed by the young man's conviction. He returned to his men who were checking their weapons.

With their plan finally settled, the group ate—mostly the last of the hare and some reindeer meat, plus a little chocolate from Gøystavatnet— then they sat around the stove with coffee and cigarettes, sharing stories.

After a while, Jack slipped outside to gaze down on Rjukan. He heard footsteps crunching through snow. Cammy appeared at his side.

She offered him her coffee cup. Jack took it and drank. "Nice speech back there," Cammy said. "Very *rousing*. I even think you've gone up a notch in Lanc's estimation."

"That good, huh?" Jack smiled.

"Ah, he needs your recklessness just as much as you need his restraint."

"Funny, isn't it? The thought that this might be the last drink we ever share."

"I'd rather drink Hurricane's cold joe over Hellstrøm's Karsk. I've filled the boy's tanks with better fuel."

"Skol," Jack said, raising the cup.

Looking up to the night sky, they saw a shimmering green light start to form. It undulated eerily in diffuse parallel waves above the valley.

"What is it?" Jack said.

"The Northern Lights," Cammy replied. "Beautiful, aren't they? My grandfather told me about them when I was a kid. He said that a long time ago, people believed they were reflections from the armor of the *valkyrja*."

"The what?"

"Norse goddesses. With the power to decide who lived and died in battle."

"Then let's hope they're on our side tonight." Jack took another sip of coffee and handed the cup back to Cammy. Looking up at the stars, he felt all the world's possibilities within himself. But he also felt sadness.

"You know, it's okay," Cammy said, turning to face him. "To *miss* him, I mean."

The statement caught Jack off guard. "You know?"

"I read your file before you arrived at Achnacarry. You're a nice guy, Jack, but there's sorrow in you too. We've all got scars, but they'll never heal unless you tell people about 'em. People who care."

"I'm not one o'your tanks that you can fix up good as new."

Jack looked down at his boots. This wasn't somewhere he wanted to go, not now, but then again, there'd never be a right time. Jack had locked it all away, tried to forget it.

"You can only skate around the truth so long before the ice breaks," Cammy said. "C'mon. Let me in."

Looking down at her, Jack knew it was time.

"Danny was always a good kid," he said quietly. "A good little brother. We never knew our parents, but we were in the same orphanage together, thick as thieves, and he stuck to me like glue. We were lucky enough to be posted to the same unit in Belgium. I tried to look out for him, y'know? Then the order came through to fall back, and on our way out, we got trapped in a factory south of Mortsel. The place'd been shelled by the Germans for days, but it was a fortress, and we weren't coming out, not 'til the reinforcements we'd been promised rolled up.

"Anyway, days passed, still no reinforcements. I argued with our CO Smiley about it, I mean, we were losing men fast and he just froze, blocked us out. After I decked him, he had me locked up in a store room for dissension. Turns out he'd only promised us the cavalry was coming while he'd been panickin', tryin' to figure out his arse from his elbow. Trouble is, while he was doing that lads were dying—good lads.

"Well then this high-ranking panzer commander turns up, Mörder his name was, turns up with a plan to bomb the shit out of the place so his toy tanks could get through. Danny should've been on sentry duty, but he'd disobeyed Smiley's orders, snuck out with a couple of grenade bandoliers and a plan to blow up the Germans' tanks. Kid tripped a wire 'n' they caught him. Mörder, bastard that he is, had Danny tied between two tanks, threatened to rip him apart unless Smiley flew the white flag. The kid told Smiley not to surrender."

Jack paused. His breath caught in his throat at the thought of what his brother must have endured.

"I didn't see it, but when he died, I *felt* it, you know? Like a light had gone out forever. After that, I didn't care. I went after Mörder with every gun I had, every man I had. An' I lost 'em. Bill said it wasn't my fault, but..."

Jack looked up at the stars. "When the old man asked me to lead this party, I was scared, Cam. Not of the enemy. Of myself."

"But you fought on." Cammy took his hand. "You survived. It's only when you've seen the deepest valleys, that you can know what it's like to stand on the highest peaks. And look where we are, Jack."

He turned to face her. "I miss him, Cam. He was the only family I had."

"Not anymore." She caressed his cheek tenderly. "Don't you see? *We're* your family now."

Jack wanted to tell Cammy how he felt, but yet again, now wasn't the time. Would they ever get a break? He gazed into her eyes.

"Hey," she said, as if snapping out of a daydream. "I made you something."

She pulled an object from her pocket and put it around his neck. It was a dog tag, metal like his own, but engraved with his brother's name. "I figure now he can always be with you. Close to your heart."

Jack examined it, speechless. "I don't know what to say. Thank you."

Cammy nodded, then turned and walked back to the lodge.

"Cam, what if history repeats itself? What if—"

She stopped and turned to look back at him. "Y'know, my grandfather used to say that we all have two wolves on our back: one good, the other bad, an' they both wanna eat. You just gotta feed the good wolf a little more." She smiled and disappeared inside the lodge.

Alone, Jack looked down at his brother's dog tag beside his own. It was time to go to work.

# 28

---

# ZERO HOUR

**THE STREETS WERE DESERTED** as the raiding party made their way through the shadows. The buildings around them were typically Norwegian: sweeping rough-hewn chalets with sloping eaves and ornate carved oak balconies. They were old and low, and with the street lamps now switched off the group had only the moonlight and stars to guide them.

Jack was grateful for the solitude, courtesy of the cold weather and the allure of the Rjuken's many hostelries. But their luck couldn't last forever. Tonight was the night they'd worked toward for the last few months, and everything had to go like clockwork.

Casting a glance at Hellstrøm, Jack saw that he was tense. "Where we headed?" Jack whispered.

"The Bear and Boar. A beer hall, on eastern edge of town."

As the raiding party moved silently through the streets, they steered wide of hotels and restaurants, all doing a roaring trade courtesy of the Fatherland. But they were close enough for Jack to hear the babble of conversation, laughter, and voices singing to accordion music. He smelled hot food wafting on the breeze, and for a moment, wished he were back at The Crooked House with Cammy and the boys, enjoying each other's company.

They finally arrived in front of a large log building with a swinging, snow-covered sign carved with a bear and boar. Hellstrøm turned to the group. "Jack and I will go in," he said, looking furtively around the street. "There is wood shed to rear of building. Follow my men. We'll meet you there shortly."

As the others disappeared around the hostelry, Jack followed Hellstrøm up the steps into the beer hall.

A huge wood-burning stove in the corner threw out such heat that Jack immediately started perspiring. The oak beams above it were darkened with smoke and age. Swaying oil lamps illuminated a crowd of German soldiers three deep at a solid oak bar. They laughed and yelled for service, waving their empty steins in the air. More troops sat in thick hand-cut chairs at tables scattered all about, singing, laughing, and joking with each other. Accordion players moved among them playing Germanic folk music.

"This was a *bad* idea," Jack muttered.

"Nonsense," said Hellstrøm. "We're two faces amongst two dozen."

"What do we do now?"

"We do what everyone else is doing!" Hellstrøm smiled heartily. "Our man's in booth over there," he said, nodding toward a timid-looking figure in spectacles. "Go and swap code words while I get us something to drink."

Elbowing his way toward the bar, he left Jack alone.

Jack fought his way to the half-booth. As he reached it, the man looked up nervously. "Busy tonight in Rjukan," he said, nervous.

"Trafalgar Square's busier," Jack said.

"Four lions sleep there."

"But now the lions are awake," Jack said, completing the code.

Standing, the man extended a hand, which Jack shook.

"Johanssen," he said, introducing himself warily.

"Jack Stone."

Hellstrøm joined them holding two frothing steins. He set them down on the table, and the three men sat.

"Good to meet you, Captain Stone," Johanssen said. "When I heard about Gøystavatnet, I feared the worst."

"Word travels fast," Hellstrøm observed, sipping his beer.

Johanssen glanced nervously about the beer hall.

"Something on your mind?" Hellstrøm said.

Johanssen looked down at the table. "Magnus, I... I am a *weak* man."

Hellstrøm's eyes flared with realization. "You ratted us out?" He reached for his pistol.

"Easy," Jack cautioned, raising a hand to calm him.

"*Coward!*" Hellstrøm snarled.

"Maybe so," said Johanssen, "but I'm a coward bearing the key to the plant's production area." He pulled a key from within his jacket and passed it to Jack beneath the table. "I also have a plan of the factory and this evening's guard roster." He looked at Hellstrøm. "Believe me Magnus, I had no choice. He *threatened* Karina's life!"

"Who?" Hellstrøm said. "The mask?"

Jack recalled the German general in Gøystavatnet.

Johanssen nodded. "He threatened my daughter. I had to give him something real so he wouldn't suspect my involvement!"

"So you gave him *my* village?" Hellstrøm hissed.

"Hey," Jack warned, then to Johanssen: "What can you tell us about him?"

"He was sent from Berlin to facilitate the water's transport. The man's brilliant, but *quite* insane."

The door of the beer hall creaked open, and more soldiers stepped in out of the cold, preceded by a blast of snow.

"How many more of these boys are there?" Jack asked.

"After this afternoon's skirmish, more troops were drafted in from Møsvatn." Johanssen kept his eye on the soldiers approaching the bar. "Rjukan has eyes and ears everywhere now. The Gestapo seek to infiltrate the resistance with undercover informants. A number of triple-zero agents have already been arrested and imprisoned. Many more will lose their lives if your mission here fails tonight. We must be cautious."

"*You* lecture *me* on caution?" Hellstrøm's eyes narrowed.

Johanssen continued. "When I left Vemork this evening there were twenty armed guards in the barracks and two patrolling the bridge. Tonight's guard roster states that the sentries will change shift at midnight. If an alarm is triggered, the men from the barracks at the factory will search the plant, while the garrisons here in Rjukan will scour the valley with the aid of floodlights from the bridge. The factory also has two Norwegian night guards who patrol the plant's interior."

"They are of no concern," Hellstrøm said, "and will not put up any resistance if we encounter them."

"Gøystavatnet put the Germans on high alert. It's possible they could change their routine."

"Then you've damned us all to hell!" Hellstrøm growled. "I ought to snuff you out right here!"

"Easy," Jack said. German faces were observing them.

"I told you I had no choice, Magnus!" Johanssen whispered. "If the general hadn't believed me I'd be dead already, and you would have no keys."

Jack checked his watch. "Time for us to leave." The number of troops in the beer hall was growing. "It's gonna be difficult leaving Rjukan with two garrisons on the streets."

"I took this from the barracks at Vemork," said Johanssen, revealing the wooden handle of a stick grenade within his jacket. "There's an anti-aircraft gun at the bottom of the street, and beyond it a checkpoint. Beyond that lies Vemork. Let me create a diversion, then you can get your men out unnoticed."

Hellstrøm nodded, and Jack realized that for all his bluster, the Norwegian admired the bravery of the little gray man from Vemork.

"Thank you," Jack said.

"For what?" asked Johanssen.

"Choosing a side."

...

Leaving by the beer hall's back door, Jack and Hellstrøm saw a figure slumped still in the snow. At first glance it looked like a drunk who'd passed out and collapsed against a wall, but as they drew closer Jack saw it was Hellstrøm's man, Larssen.

Crouching beside him, Hellstrøm lifted the man's head gently. His throat had been slashed, his collar torn, and some buttons were missing from his tunic; there had evidently been a struggle. That was also evident in the confusion of footprints, now half-covered with fresh snow.

"We must be cautious," Hellstrøm said. "Both of the enemy, and each other."

"Cam said our chutes were sabotaged before we jumped," Jack said. "It had to be one of mine."

"Possibly. But if there's an SS agent in Milorg as Johanssen suggested, it could well be one of mine. Come, and play dumb when we see the others."

They found the team huddled in the wood shed.

"Where's Larssen?" Hellstrøm asked.

"We ran into a patrol," Cammy said. "We had to split up. He was supposed to meet us here."

"Everything okay?" Billy asked.

Jack nodded. "We can't wait for him. Let's go."

...

As they moved toward the eastern edge of the town, they passed the anti-aircraft gun Johanssen had told Jack about, surrounded by sandbags with a pile of ammunition boxes stacked nearby. A sentry circled it casually, his machine-gun shouldered. The checkpoint was another hundred yards down the street, manned by six guards, all armed, two of them struggling with leashed German shepherds that snarled and barked as the group approached. Beyond the checkpoint was the sanctity of the Rjukan valley, which opened out into the safety of darkness.

Darting a glance to his right, Jack saw Lancaster and the Tommies shadowing their advance, using the buildings as cover. While he knew the machines could squash the checkpoint in a heartbeat, they couldn't risk the factory being alerted of the group's approach. If that happened, the Germans would lock down Vemork and turn the place into a fortress—one that even the Tommies couldn't break into.

Jack looked around at the group crunching through the snow. One of them was a traitor... a *killer*. He refused to believe it could be Billy. And Cammy? Well, while Jack had yet to determine the true nature of their relationship, she was an extremely unlikely suspect. Could it have been Hellstrøm? Jack had lost sight of him at the bar in the beer hall; he'd certainly had time to get outside and do the job. And then there were Haakon and Seim. While Jack didn't know the men, he'd witnessed their loyalty to Hellstrøm back in Gøystavatnet.

For now, he'd just have to watch his back and trust his friends to do the same.

"What's wrong?" Cammy said, falling in beside him.

Jack glanced at her. "Larssen's dead," he whispered.

Cammy's eyes widened.

"Say nothing, and trust no one."

There was a commotion behind them. Turning, Jack saw Johanssen talking to the guard by the anti-aircraft gun. The guard pushed Johanssen back with his machine-gun, then started shouting.

"Jack," Cammy said quietly.

Ahead of them, two checkpoint guards approached. "Papiere!" shouted one of the guards, looking past Jack's group at the disturbance by the anti-aircraft gun.

In the gloom between the buildings, Jack noticed the glow of the Tommies' lenses intensify.

"Wait for it," Jack said.

"Papiere!" shouted the checkpoint guard again.

Jack glanced back at Johanssen. The anti-aircraft guard had his machine gun leveled. Johanssen looked up the street at Jack and nodded— then he pulled the stick grenade from his pocket, yanked its detonation wire, and leapt onto the ammunition boxes.

Stifling a cry, the soldier squeezed his trigger, but it was too late. The boxes erupted in a blistering ball of orange flame that engulfed both him and Johanssen. Shells screamed wildly through the air, crippling the anti-aircraft gun, which collapsed as debris slapped onto the snow around it.

The German in front of Jack took off down the street with three other guards, leaving only two men at the checkpoint. Jack couldn't believe their luck.

One of the two remaining sentries approached Jack and Cammy. "Papiere!" he demanded.

Jack looked back over his shoulder. Soldiers were pouring from beer halls and brothels, scurrying about to put out the flames. A fire engine rattled up the street, the shrill ring of its bell cracking the night.

"*Papiere jetzt!*" the sentry repeated, losing patience.

He moved to raise his machine gun, but Jack cuffed him unconscious. At the same instant, Lancaster appeared behind the second soldier and brought his fist down so hard the man's helmet crunched into his skull.

The party fled into the night, leaving the chaos behind them.

...

Hellstrøm led them southward into the base of the valley, where they followed the meandering river. The trek was challenging, even for the Tommies, who struggled through deep snowdrifts, sometimes sinking to their waists. At one-point Hurricane had to carry Cammy on his shoulder to stop her from disappearing altogether.

On the river's banks, the ground was just as treacherous. The thaw had turned ice to slush, and the invisible undercurrent threatened to drag them beneath the surface if they slipped.

Jack squinted into the gale as clouds swept low overhead. The wind had increased by at least twenty miles an hour since they'd entered the valley, and they were buffeted by snow swept up off the ice dunes like picnic litter.

A storm was the one thing they didn't need now.

"We ski from here on," Hellstrøm said, setting his jaw.

Haakon and Seim unfastened skis and poles from their packs and distributed them to the human members of the group. The Tommies extended skis from the fronts and backs of their treads and took reinforced poles from their packs. Once everyone was kitted out, the group glided after Hellstrøm toward Vemork.

The first few miles along the valley were steep and straight, and everyone followed the Norwegian at a good pace in his tracks. Then the woodland thickened, and the group was forced to carry their equipment and clamber down through brush, where the snow was deep and loose, and the surface of it moved with the wind around their legs. The Tommies rammed their way through thickets of shrub and lopped-off branches of spruce trees to aid the party's advance. The technique of sliding and wading downward was exhausting, and though they tried to stay in formation it was tough, sometimes impossible in such harsh terrain, let alone at night in a blizzard. Hidden branches beneath the snow and unexpected rides into the darkness were a constant and exhausting hazard.

"How much farther is this bleedin' place?" Billy moaned, struggling with his fifty-pound rucksack.

"We're nearly there," Jack replied, watching Hellstrøm. He had to admit, the Norwegian had stamina and a boundless supply of energy. The man hadn't slowed his pace once since they'd entered the valley.

Jack glanced back at Billy and Cammy who were skiing beside Spitfire. The other Tommies skied to their rear, followed by Haakon and Seim.

Hellstrøm paused ahead of them and raised his right arm. The group hunkered down behind him. The Norwegian beckoned Jack forward.

"There is *föhn* on down-slopes," Hellstrøm said.

"What's that?"

"Bad luck. Is dry cool wind in lee of mountains. Slopes warm now, ice melts—ice on Måna."

Jack sighed. If Hellstrøm was right, then the ice on the river would thaw and the water level rise with snow water. The three feet of dry snow they were now trudging through would turn to slush. Not only that, Jack realized, but their escape across the gorge from the factory back to the Hardanger Plateau could also become seriously compromised.

Hellstrøm continued forward warily, and Jack heard the chronic throb of the plant as the raiding party neared their destination.

The group descended into the valley through a cluster of trees where there was more cover. Now and again the wind came in gusts so strong that it practically blew them onto their backs, but as Hellstrøm stated, the conditions couldn't have been better, for who else would be out on such a night?

Crouching in the tree line at the base of the gorge they finally saw the factory on the mountain above them.

"*Jesus Christ…*"

It was Billy, and he spoke for them all.

Clouds parted, and moonlight revealed the huge seven-story electrolysis building which loomed in front of the powerhouse on a ledge of rock between the mountain peak and the river in the valley below. Rising nine-hundred feet above the snow-covered roofs of these two buildings were twelve huge penstocks. Jack heard the whirl and whir of dynamos, and the complaint of gyrating machinery, as water plunged through the pipes.

The cacophony felt almost in tune with the tumult in Jack's heart, and as it closed in on him in a brief moment of sheer bloody panic, so too did the significance of what he was about to attempt.

Above them, Jack saw the silhouette of the suspension bridge come into focus through the falling snow. Two hundred feet up, it spanned the two-hundred-and-fifty-foot-wide gap of the valley, and just as Johanssen had said, two guards paced back and forth across it, keeping watch.

"We cross river here," Hellstrøm said quietly. The group followed him to the river's edge where the effects of his *föhn* were evident. Snow had turned to slush, and Jack heard it squelch beneath his boots. He looked out across the river and saw that the ice covering it resembled the deck of a sinking ship. Covered in flowing water in places, the ice looked fractured, precarious and uneven.

"We go one at a time," Hellstrøm said, then he turned and stepped onto the frozen river. The ice creaked beneath his boots as three inches of water rose up over them, the ice shifting beneath his weight. Jack held his breath as he watched Hellstrøm cross, surprisingly nimble, putting one foot here, another there, like a man playing hopscotch, until he reached the opposite bank. Then he turned and beckoned them across.

Jack summoned Billy forward.

"Why me?"

Jack glared at him. Billy reluctantly stepped forward.

"*Flyin'—parachutin'*—a minute from now, I'll be bleedin' *drownin'!*"

"Just shut up and crack on!" Jack hissed.

Billy muttered complaint, but started across the frozen river, following the same path over the ice bridge that Hellstrøm had taken. A minute later, he was stood beside the Norwegian.

Jack took Cammy's hand and helped her onto the ice. He felt her fear.

"Twenty seconds of bravery," he said softly, "an' you'll be stood next to Billy."

Cammy nodded, and started cautiously across the ice. She paused mid-way as it creaked threateningly beneath her boots. Jack held his breath, preparing to run out and help her, but she finally moved forward and reached the opposite bank.

Haakon and Seim were next, followed by Spitfire, who barely made it across, then Mosquito and Hurricane; both taking their time as the ice shifted beneath their weight.

"Okay Lanc, you're up," Jack said.

"I must be mad," Lancaster grumbled. He placed a tread on the ice which sank a few inches as water flooded over it. Moving as carefully as he could, the old machine trekked slowly across the frozen river.

Jack checked his watch—time was running out. He started across the river after Lancaster, who paused abruptly as ice fractured angrily beneath his treads.

"Easy," Jack said quietly, "slow and steady, eh?" Losing Lancaster in the river would cost valuable time to retrieve him. Lancaster cautiously started forward again and reached the opposite bank, followed shortly after by Jack.

The group gazed up at the side of the gorge before them. It was far steeper than the one they'd just left, and flowing down it like a wall of cascading glass, was the final obstacle between the raiding party and the factory—the frozen Rjuken waterfall. The crystalline beauty of the spectacle was surpassed only by the complexity of how to actually scale it. The cliffs on either side were shear, and at the waterfall's base were sharp fallen rocks. One mistake here could mean death, or worse, broken bones and interrogation at the hands of the Gestapo.

*Out of the frying pan*, Jack thought, *and into the fire…*

# 29

---

# RAT TRAP

**L**ANCASTER RAISED HIS LEFT ARM and spread his fingers wide. "*Anchors aweigh*," he muttered, then shot his grapple hook up onto the waterfall. The cable spiraled out of his arm, and he reeled it taut. The other Tommies repeated the action, removing climbing picks from their backpacks and kicking climbing spikes, which Cammy had fitted them with, from the fronts of their treads.

Jack and Billy tethered themselves to Lancaster, Cammy and Hellstrøm to Hurricane, Mosquito took Haakon and Seim, leaving Spitfire to focus on himself. One by one the Tommies reeled in their cables and, using their picks, quietly climbed up the slick glass of the waterfall toward the factory. The ice was unforgiving, and the Tommies' gears groaned as they fought to ascend in the gale.

Cammy held fast to Hurricane's arm as he moved, knowing that one slip could seal their fate. Lancaster was up above with Jack and Billy, and beneath her were Mosquito and Spitfire.

At long last the Tommies reached the top, a narrow rock shelf on which the train track ran. They regrouped and ducked for cover as a searchlight scanned the mountainside above them.

Jack noticed footprints in the snow. *Jerries*. It reminded him that in spite of their good fortune so far, one mistake could spell disaster.

He led the raiding party along the tracks. As they rounded a corner, their target finally came into view. *Vemork*.

The enormous concrete monolith loomed ominously from a plateau midway up the mountainside. Its main structure dwarfed a number of smaller outbuildings, including the barracks, where Jack could see soldiers coming and going. The ominous hum of turbines drifted on the wind around them, lending the plant a sinister air.

Jack checked his watch: six minutes to midnight. They were less than half a mile from the plant and right on time. "Let's go take a closer look," Jack said, starting forward.

Hellstrøm grabbed his arm. "Stay between tracks," he said, pointing to the earth on either side of the train track. "Mines and trip-wires."

"Talk about a warm welcome," Billy muttered.

The group followed Jack along the track as far as they could go without being seen by the watch towers. About six hundred feet shy of the main gate, he led them down an embankment to a snow-covered shed housing a small transformer station. While not big enough to house them all, it was sufficient cover to shelter the group from the enemy's searchlights.

Jack pulled a map from his tunic pocket and used a pencil torch to illuminate it.

"We do this by the numbers," he said. "Once we're inside the main gate, Billy, get your boys into covering positions around the bridge 'n' barracks as quick as you can."

Billy nodded.

"I'll take care of the second gate," Jack said, "then lead the demo team down into the basement where the high-concentration room's situated. Soon as we've planted the charges, I'll signal we're on our way out."

Jack looked around at the group. "Good luck, everyone."

The raiders took up their positions and waited.

At a minute to midnight, two German soldiers left the barracks in the plant's compound and started toward the suspension bridge to relieve the sentries there. A couple of minutes later, the relieved guards headed across the compound to the barracks, their march weary.

*A good sign*, Jack thought. He checked his watch again, looked at Cammy and nodded.

"Break out Bug," she said to Spitfire.

Spitfire opened a panel on his chest plate, and the little drone's lens glowed from a compartment within, accompanied by a whir and the click of its cogs. The machine crawled timidly out onto Spitfire's finger, and Cammy checked the drone's shell.

Hellstrøm, Haakon and Seim let out a gasp, fascinated.

"We good?" Jack asked.

Cammy nodded, tense.

Spitfire flicked his finger and the little drone took to the air. It hovered above them for a second, its miniature propellers spinning in their wing housing to compensate in the wind.

Spitfire looked down at the open compartment in his chest plate where a small black and white screen displayed the view from Bug's lens. Placing his thumbs and forefingers on dials either side of the screen, he turned them gently.

Bug spun around and drifted slowly toward the factory with a motorized buzz which was thankfully lost in the gale. Bobbing and weaving in the wind, it floated over the compound's chain link fence and headed toward the barracks.

Jack checked Spitfire's screen, watching as the drone drew level with the barracks windows. Through the static he watched the two relieved sentries flopping onto their bunks. Several others played cards at a table and another made coffee at a stove.

"Six in the barracks," Jack said, glancing at Billy.

"I think we can 'andle that, don't you?" said Billy smugly.

"Okay Spitfire, bring him home." Jack checked his watch again. It was a quarter after midnight. Almost time.

Bug descended onto Spitfire's finger and the little Tommy popped him back into his chest cavity, closing the panel.

As the final minutes passed by, the group fell under the hypnotic spell of the plant's production machinery which pounded rhythmically. Finally, at exactly twelve thirty, Jack gave the signal and the raiding party followed him up the embankment and along the remaining track to a storage shed about one hundred yards from the compound's gate. Jack pulled a pair of wire-cutting shears from Billy's pack, then looked at each member of the raiding party.

"This is it then," he said. "Ready?"

They nodded solemnly.

After all the team's training, all their hard work and the losses they'd endured, after their exhausting cross-country trek to get to Vemork with the enemy at their heels, their mission to prevent Nazi Germany from creating the first atomic bomb was about to enter its final phase. The course of history now depended upon Jack's team succeeding, for if they failed, Great Britain, the free world for that matter, would fall into a new dark age.

*No pressure then*, Jack thought, and then he sprinted for the gate.

Skidding beneath a searchlight that swung in his direction, he raised the shears and snipped open the thick chain securing the gate. It parted and fell loose with a rattle. He then gestured for the covering party to come forward and join him.

They slipped quietly through the gate into the compound and took up new covering positions. As soon as Jack saw Billy's signal that the covering team was established, Jack beckoned his demolition team forward, all too aware that their movements might attract the attention of some eagle-eyed Boy Scout from the barracks, but no alarm was raised. So far, so good.

As the demo team entered the compound, Jack raced for the second gate, where he once again cut the chain. As he was about to disappear, he saw Billy watching him. Jack nodded, and Billy hunkered down into his covering position, the barracks in his sights.

Jack and the demo team—Cammy, Hellstrøm, Lancaster, and Mosquito—slipped in through an unlocked door that led to a stairwell. Whether Johanssen had arranged for it to be open, Jack didn't know, still he was grateful. They descended at least thirty feet before reaching the basement level door and beyond it, the high-concentration area. Jack took out Johanssen's key and turned it in the lock. He heard a reassuring click and looked back at the group, smiling. Drawing his Enfield revolver, Jack nudged the door slowly open and peered around the frame. The corridor beyond was deserted. Things were going *too* well.

Jack pocketed the key and pulled out Johanssen's map. His revolver was cocked and ready as he led the team on through the labyrinthine halls of the plant's basement.

Footsteps approached.

Withdrawing quickly, the team hid under a stairwell. Four German guards appeared, but passed right by them, oblivious.

Jack looked at Cammy, who exhaled.

"That was a little *too* close," Mosquito said quietly.

"We're running out of time," Hellstrøm said, returning his knife to its sheath."

They continued on through the basement toward the room housing the heavy water cells.

...

In the compound outside, the covering team shrank into the snow as several German guards appeared at the barracks door smoking cigarettes.

Billy shot a glance at Hurricane, who already had them in his sights. Across the compound, Spitfire, Haakon, and Seim were all alert and ready for action, and while Spitfire was in pretty bad shape, he could still pack a bigger punch than the Norwegians if the Jerries kicked off. As the German soldiers laughed and joked, Billy checked his watch and said a silent prayer that they were all going to escape Norway alive.

...

Jack stopped at a door and double-checked his map. "This is it," he said, carefully turning the handle. The door was locked.

"Dammit," said Hellstrøm. He prepared to barge the door.

"Wait," Jack said, "someone'll hear."

He looked around for another way in, and spotted a gap in the brickwork above their heads through which a mass of wires and pipework fed. "What's that?"

"Looks like some kinda cable shaft," Cammy said.

"Too big for us," said Mosquito, glancing at Lancaster.

"But not for me." Jack shouldered off his rucksack. Lancaster gave him a boost, and Jack crawled inside.

He pushed his rucksack forward on his hands and knees over a tangle of cables and pipework, and heard an electrical drone ahead mixed with what sounded like... *polka music?* It appeared the room beneath him was occupied. Jack's blood raced, and he fought to calm his beating heart. Every muscle in his body was tense, for one false move, one slight noise, might spell disaster for his mission.

About halfway along the shaft, Jack reached a series of water pipelines passing through the roof of the tunnel and through a hole in its concrete floor. Jack crawled to the edge of the hole and peered into the room below.

His spirits were buoyed at the sight of his target: two parallel lines of glass water cells, eighteen in total, situated in the high-concentration area of Vemork's heavy water room. At a desk nearby sat a lone German guard, his back to Jack, reading a magazine and listening to a wireless blasting the polka music. The guard's rifle was slung over his shoulder, and Jack saw that an alarm switch was worryingly within the man's reach on a nearby wall.

If Jack drew his attention, even for a second...

Jack moved to unsheathe his commando knife, but as he did so his revolver slipped from his shoulder holster, and clattered against a water pipe. He ducked out of sight just as the guard turned and looked up. Jack fought desperately to calm his frenzied breathing, and remained perfectly still. He heard the guard's chair scrape on the floor. Was the man going for the alarm?

Then Jack heard footsteps—the guard was directly beneath him!

...

"What the 'ell's takin' 'im so long?" Lancaster muttered.

Mosquito peered around a corner, cocking his oversized sten gun as footsteps approached.

Cammy and Hellstrøm stiffened and drew their revolvers, hugging the wall behind him, but the footsteps slowly receded and they relaxed, sighing a collective gasp of relief.

...

Jack shimmied down a pipe behind the German, the blackened blade of his commando knife clenched between his teeth. While the guard's suspicions had been aroused at the sound of Jack's Enfield hitting the pipe, in a location where one's daily routine was performed to the deafening noise of machinery, the guard had quickly dismissed the clatter and returned to the desk and his magazine.

When Jack reached the ground, he took the knife in his right hand and moved stealthily forward, the polka music masking his advance.

And then Jack's luck ran out.

At that moment, the soldier casually leaned over, switched off the wireless, stood, and turned. His eyes went wide at the sight of Jack, standing a mere ten feet away. He spun to hit the alarm.

Jack quickly hurled his knife which thudded into the soldier's back, then Jack sprinted forward. The soldier cried out and fought wildly to reach the alarm, but Jack wrenched his blade free, wrestled the man to the ground and silenced the soldier forever.

...

"Clock is ticking, little woman," Hellstrøm said, glancing at Cammy.

"No alarm's been triggered," Cammy said. "We gotta give him more time."

"He shoulda been out by now," said Mosquito. "We 'ave to assume he's been compromised."

"Right, that's it," Lancaster said. "Stand back." He prepared to shoulder the door but with a click, the door opened, and Jack appeared. He ushered them inside with a silent gesture.

They moved quickly, for every second now was crucial to the mission's success. Mosquito opened his chest plate and pulled out several long, cylindrical charges. He passed them to the others, who started attaching them to the electrolysis chambers. Mosquito followed along behind them, rigging a two-minute fuse to each charge.

...

Billy shuddered, shaking snow from his shoulders as he waited for Jack and the others to emerge. The soldiers from the barracks had gone back inside to play cards and bask in the warmth of their stove—the lucky gits!

He was just thinking about how good a warm fire would be when a squad of Germans silently entered the main gate and crossed the compound. On the unspoken order of their commander, they set up three MG-42 machine guns on tripods. More soldiers appeared behind them and trained their guns on the inner gate.

Billy's wrist-wireless crackled. "*What the 'ell's goin' on?*" Hurricane whispered.

"I dunno, but it looks like they're gettin' ready to—" A horrible realization suddenly dawned on Billy. "How do they know to set this lot up if they don't know that we're—*Jesus!*"

He raised his wrist-wireless. "Jack? Lancaster? D'you read me? Get out of there now, you hear me? *It's a trap!*"

...

As Lancaster laid charges against the water cells, his wireless crackled. He tapped it and heard Billy's voice, but it cut out in a burst of static before he could make out any words.

"What's up?" Mosquito asked, unreeling fuse wire nearby.

"Sounded like William," Lancaster said, "I couldn't make him out."

"It'll be the walls in 'ere. Signals don't travel too good."

Lancaster's wireless crackled again, and this time Billy's words, though fighting through a storm of white noise, were loud and clear. "*I said it's a trap!*"

"What? William, can you 'ear me?" Lancaster turned to Mosquito. "Go 'n' get—"

Mosquito brought a thick iron bar down squarely on his head.

Rounding a corner, Jack saw Mosquito looming menacingly over Lancaster who lay motionless on the ground.

"Moz? What the 'ell are you doing?"

Jack drew his revolver, but Mosquito was upon him and batted it from his hand. He grabbed Jack's tunic, heaving him into the air. Jack crashed down on the other side of the water cells.

With a shout and a short burst of gun fire, German troops flooded into the room.

...

Hellstrøm and Cammy drew their guns but they were surrounded.

Hellstrøm pulled her behind him and backed into a corner, aiming his gun. But there were too many German soldiers; he knew he didn't stand a chance.

The soldiers closed in around them. One knocked the gun from Hellstrøm's hands and smashed him in the face with his rifle butt.

⋯

"*Hello? Anyone?*" Billy tapped his wrist-wireless frantically. "*Can anyone —*"

Hearing a noise behind him, Billy turned—and found himself looking down the barrel of a German machine-gun. The jig was up!

He gritted his teeth and slowly raised his hands in the air.

The soldier pulled him from his hiding place, clubbed him with the gun, and pushed him roughly into the courtyard. The other members of the covering party were rounded up without a single shot fired, and they were dragged down the steps into the building's basement.

⋯

Jack staggered to his feet. Crouched behind a water cell, he observed the scene. German troops had practically filled the room. Cammy was crouched in a corner beside Hellstrøm, whose broken nose was bleeding. And Mosquito was dragging Lancaster by the handles of his helmet hatch into the center of a circle of Nazis.

"Mosquito?" Cammy gasped. "I don't understand."

The sound of clapping filled the room. "*Bravissimo!*" shouted a voice.

The German troops parted, and Mörder stepped forward. He turned to Mosquito. "You've done well."

Mosquito nodded, dropping Lancaster face down onto the tiled floor with a resounding crack.

"No!" Cammy said, leaping to her feet. "*No!*" She lunged at Mosquito, but a soldier punched her in the stomach, and she dropped to her knees, coughing and gasping for air.

Jack moved instinctively, flying at the soldier who had struck Cammy. But there were too many. Two soldiers grabbed him and slammed him back against a wall, pinning him.

"Easy now," Mörder said. "I don't want the captain damaged. Not *yet*, anyway."

Footsteps heralded the arrival of more troops, and to Jack's dismay, they were leading Billy, Hurricane, and Hellstrøm's men. All captured.

But Spitfire was nowhere to be seen. Jack glanced at Cammy, it was clear she'd noticed his absence too. Had the little machine avoided capture, or had he met a worse fate?

"Only three machines?" Mörder mused. He looked at Jack.

"The other was destroyed in the crash," Jack said.

"Ah," Mörder said. "Well now, together at last. How nice."

With a groan, Lancaster climbed shakily to his feet. "What the 'ell's goin'—" His blue eyes widened at the sight of so many German guns trained on him. "Oh…"

"Mosquito's a traitor," Jack said. "He was with 'em all along."

"What?" Hurricane gasped.

"Moz?" Cammy said. "It's not true, is it?" Tears streamed down her cheeks.

Mosquito refused to meet her gaze.

"You bleedin' turncoat!" Hurricane yelled. "I always knew you were a bad 'un. Well you've picked the wrong side, mate, and you'll get yours. That's a promise! *You'll get yours!*" The soldiers fought to restrain Hurricane.

"*Enough!*" Mörder leveled his Luger at Cammy's temple, and Hurricane ceased his resistance. "You're right in part, Captain," Mörder said. "We had this machine's assistance; however, Johanssen was no martyr. He naturally wished to protect his daughter, and he did so by taking the only option I offered him: betraying the Milorg, and taking his own life, in order to bring you here."

"*Bastard!*" Hellstrøm growled.

"I've been called far worse by better," Mörder said casually. "Did his actions not *assure* you of his loyalty to the Resistance? Of course they did, or you wouldn't be here before me now. You see, it was *I* who allowed the key to fall into your hands, *I* who allowed Johanssen to give you the factory's plans. Everything that took place this evening did so because I constructed it. Johanssen's daughter is safe, our heavy water shipment is almost ready to be transported, and soon, very soon, *you* shall all be dead. Ordinarily I'd have you shot, but, call me old-fashioned, I like to play with my food before eating it."

He turned to the soldiers. "Lock the girl and the others up. Have the captain and the sergeant taken to the dark room."

Mörder leaned into Jack, his lidless eyes frenzied behind the mask. "You don't remember me, do you?"

"I can smell your stink, *Nazi*. That's enough," Jack said, feigning indifference. "Scrape yourself off my boot on the way out, would you?"

Mörder's eyes narrowed. "I'm your worst nightmare, *Jack*."

"How do you know my—"

Jack felt a sharp thud against his forehead, and slipped into a sea of unconsciousness.

# 30

## NEMESIS

**J**ACK AWOKE in a cold, dank and windowless room. He got the sense that the chamber was large, but the only light was provided by a single flickering candle, and its glow extended only a short distance before being swallowed by darkness.

*I'm underground*, Jack thought, trying desperately to ignore the ringing in his ears so he could focus.

He twisted and was relieved to see Lancaster chained to a concrete pillar beside him.

"Lanc?"

The old sergeant remained motionless.

Jack tried to reach out, but realized his wrists were manacled above his head to the skeleton of a metal mattress frame.

"Lancaster!"

The machine remained still, then with a click, his blue irises flickered on and he clattered to life.

"Cap-t-t-t-ain-n?" Lancaster stuttered, his voice weak.

"Atta boy," Jack whispered, exhaling a sigh of relief.

The sergeant's blue eyes smoldered to full brilliance.

"Where the 'ell are we?" Lancaster said, looking about.

"I dunno," Jack replied, "but wherever it is, it *ain't* good."

"I take no pleasure in killing…" hissed an ethereal voice.

Jack recognized it instantly as that of the German from the heavy water room. It echoed around the dungeon, but Jack couldn't find its source. It was as if the sinister voice were everywhere. "I took no pleasure in killing your comrades," said the ghost in the darkness. "I took no pleasure in killing my dear wife, but I must confess…"

Emerging from the shadows beside Jack, the mask blazed terrible fury. "I'm going to *savor* killing *you*."

…

Spitfire emerged from the shadows into the passageway.

Despite a worrying clank from his partially exposed skeleton, the whirring of his gears had so far been undetected by the guards he'd eluded during his journey through the plant.

"Quiet down, bug!" he whispered, as the little mech buzzed irritably within his chest cavity. "I told you already, we're *commandos*—we 'ave to be *stealthy* now!"

Footsteps approached.

Spitfire looked around and hurriedly opened a door to what was thankfully a dark storeroom. He stole quietly inside, drew his Webley, and peered out through the gap into the corridor.

Two German soldiers, a private and an officer, rounded a corner nearby.

"Der General will den lästigen, Hurrikan, demontiert," said the officer.

While Spitfire's German was rustier than Lancaster's backside, he recognized two words: *troublesome* and *Hurricane. Obvious really*, thought Spitfire, given the two went hand in hand. But while *demontiert* sounded familiar, its meaning eluded him.

"Hol die Vorschlaghämmer," ordered the officer.

The private nodded obediently and shouldered his machine-gun. He opened the store room door and flicked the light switch but the room remained shrouded in darkness. Squinting into the gloom, the private looked about nervously. He was a young man, and despite the reassurance given by his Schmeisser he glanced about fearfully. The general might have captured the Commandos but barrack room gossip of possible Milorg reprisals had got him spooked, and where better for them to start, than with the rescue of their now captive comrades.

"*Schnell!*" shouted his officer from the corridor.

The private sighed and adjusted his slung machine-gun. He tried to remain calm. Getting jittery here would only earn him a reputation and impact his chances of promotion.

He spied a row of sledgehammers stowed in a corner and moved toward them.

In the corridor, the officer checked his watch. Hearing a crash, he looked up and rolled his eyes. "*Schnell!*" he called again irritably. "*Lass uns gehen!*"

Silence.

The officer sighed and pushed open the door, flinching as he came face to muzzle with Spitfire's Webley. The little Tommy had finally remembered what *demontiert* meant.

Dismantled.

"Hurrikan," Spitfire growled, snatching a swatch of the officer's tunic. "*Schnell!*"

...

Candlelight flickered across the mask's crimson tarnish. The frenzied eyes behind it blazed wildly.

"You look confused, my dear boy, so let me refresh your memory." The mask leaned in close, so close in fact that Jack felt the heat of the man's breath through its mouth grille. "I'm the fellow you *destroyed* at Dunkirk."

Jack's eyes grew wide with realization. "*Mörder?*"

"I see you've been promoted since we last met," the general said. "Too bad it will be short-lived. I must say, however, that it's a pleasure to meet you face to face once again."

"Wish I could say the same," Jack said, squirming in vain to free his hands from the manacles.

Mörder observed him for a moment, then: "How do you like my torture chamber?" He waved an arm in the air with the flourish of a showman. "A little primitive I concede, but perfectly sufficient for my requirements."

Jack saw the outline of the boy in his mind's eye. He was stood behind Mörder in the shadows.

*No, not here*, Jack thought, *not now...*

He squeezed his eyes shut and tried to quell the panic rising within him.

"Jack Stone," he blurted suddenly, following his training. "Twenty-second of April 1918, Rhesus D Negative, Christian." He opened his eyes and saw Mörder studying him intently.

"I see *darkness* in you, Jack," said the general, ignoring his statement. "Some people *fear* darkness, whereas I... well, I *am* the darkness."

"You're a stinkin' Nazi animal!" Lancaster growled, "who ain't worth the steam off my oil!"

"Lanc," Jack warned.

"Ah yes, your sergeant," Mörder said, regarding Lancaster. "What a fascinating machine you are. So *spirited*. I'm very much going to enjoy disassembling you to see what makes you tick." He turned to Jack. "And you can rest assured, Captain, that I'll take equal pleasure in doing the same to you." Mörder laughed, a sickly disquieting noise. "Did you think we wouldn't discover your little scheme here?"

He waved a hand and two brutes emerged from the shadows. They lumbered over, pushing covered carts. Both wore brown butcher's aprons and gas masks.

"But I'm getting ahead of myself," Mörder said. He reached under the cloth covering the nearest cart and pulled out a bucket. He held it in front of Jack's face. "My men caught a fugitive out on the Hardangervidda earlier today," he said, "and she sang to me like a nightingale."

*No*, Jack thought. *Don't*—

Mörder tilted the bucket so Jack could see.

Jack gagged at the sight of Vanja Hellstrøm's head, staring up at him wide-eyed.

"You bloody animal!" Lancaster shouted. He strained impotently against his chains.

"Yes, that's the spirit!" said Mörder. "Wonderful! One-sided interrogations can be *so* tedious; your participation is greatly appreciated."

He pulled the cloths off of the two carts. One held Lancaster's Webleys, hammers, a crowbar and chisels. The other held Jack's revolver, a weathered leather pouch, and a selection of rusty butcher's knives beside a loaded syringe.

"Now before we begin, I want you to know Captain that I don't blame you for your actions at Dunkirk. War *is* war, after all. But now that I have you in my hands, I feel I owe you a little something for my new face."

Mörder rolled out the pouch, revealing a long line of tarnished silver surgical tools. "Where to begin?" he mused.

The general selected a scalpel, checked its weight across his forefinger, then turned to Jack. "You see, I need to thank you, Jack. Yes, you destroyed my life and all that I hold dear—but you also gave me my *rebirth*. And because of that, I am free from the shackles of humanity that weaken lesser men, and *one* with my sacred Fatherland. You in turn, appear to have prospered in the wake of Dunkirk, promoted from simple soldier to the leader of these... *automatons*, and charged with your now failed mission."

"I'm *nothing* like you!" Jack spat.

"Oh, but you *are*," Mörder hissed, raising the blade toward Jack's face. "Together in the darkness, we can choose to embrace what we are, our *true* natures, or rage impotently against them. But while my damage is external, I sense yours is locked deep within; a raw nerve, if you will, just waiting to be exposed." The scalpel hovered in front of Jack's eyeballs, its blade glinting in the candlelight. "I promise I'll do my best."

"Whatever you do," Lancaster said, "it won't change nothin'!"

"If by that you mean that you still intend to destroy this installation, then I'm afraid you are sadly mistaken. Your comrades have been imprisoned, and as I speak, the last barrels of heavy water are being loaded aboard a train bound for the port. Your mission here has failed."

Mörder raised a finger. "Oh—I almost forgot." He put down the scalpel and picked up the syringe. "I have a little cocktail for you, Jack. Something to keep you conscious throughout your interrogation. So, unlike myself and the sergeant there, you'll be able to feel every *excruciating* moment of it."

Mörder inserted the syringe into Jack's forearm, and his brutes took their hammers to Lancaster.

...

"Hurricane? Hurricane, wake up!"

It was Spitfire, his voice distant.

"*Please*, Hurricane…"

As Hurricane's world came back into focus, he heard the clank of chains unraveling.

"Kid?" Hurricane muttered, his lenses blinking awake. "What's goin' on?" He noticed a German officer slumped over Spitfire's treads.

"He's the reason I found you," said Spitfire. "We don't have much time, they're already loading the—"

"How did you escape?"

"There's a tactical advantage in being the smallest," Spitfire said as Hurricane helped him unravel the last of his chains.

"Are the others alright?"

"The officer said they're locked in a store room near here. I figured I'd come get you, then we'd go rescue the others and spring Jack 'n' the sarge."

"They're with a general? Did you see him?"

"Bastard in a Halloween mask," Hurricane muttered. "You can't miss 'im." He looked at Spitfire soberly. "Look kid, Mosquito, he…"

"What?"

"Well, he ain't playin' for our team no more."

Spitfire stared at him blankly.

"Lancaster's got the dents to prove it. Moz is a traitor, kid, always was, just like Hastings. Must've got to 'im at Achnacarry."

Spitfire handed him a Webley and Hurricane moved toward the door, then turned.

"Well, what're you waitin' for? Come on!"

Spitfire shook his head. "I—I'm afraid, H…"

Hurricane came back and put a hand on Spitfire's shoulder. "I know. But what is it Jack says? *Twenty seconds of bravery*, that's all it takes to change the world. You 'n' me? We can do this."

Spitfire nodded slowly.

Hurricane balled his fists.

"Now let's go rescue our mates!"

…

Jack screamed as Mörder inserted a small serrated spike into his shoulder and wound it clockwise.

"You know Jack, the concept of predation *fascinates* me."

Mörder withdrew the spike and Jack slumped, gasping.

"That is," Mörder continued, "the process by which a predator devours its prey. For instance, did you know that both predator and prey evolve together? Or that over time, prey animals adapt to their predators, enabling them to avoid being eaten. In turn, the predators develop more complex strategies, making them more effective at catching prey, and so the cycle continues."

Mörder turned to the cart and deliberated over a new instrument of pain.

"But an *invasive* species," he continued, "*that* is the one to watch out for. Invasive predators have the capacity to disrupt entire populations you see, dominating all native life. This in turn causes *trophic cascade*—a domino effect, if you will, whereby native species at all levels of a food chain are consumed by the invading force."

"Thanks for that," Jack wheezed. "A lovely bedtime story… gonna tuck me in too?"

"You see an *invasive* predator," Mörder continued, "has the power to alter the composition of entire populations, for it eliminates the *weaker* species unable to compete with, or evade, a new alpha predator—a new *superior* intellect."

"Is this going anywhere?" Jack gasped, spitting blood, "'cos I got a factory to blow up."

"Admirable British *stiff upper lip*," Mörder scorned, "even in the face of defeat."

Sparks flew from Lancaster's chest plate as one of Mörder's brutes smashed it with a hammer. The other, wielding a crowbar, strained to lever it open.

"*No!*" Jack cried. Bloody and bruised, he raged futilely against his manacles, then sagged, exhausted.

"I feel like a child on Christmas morning," Mörder said gleefully as the hammering intensified, "waiting to see what's inside." He turned to Jack. "But I'm neglecting you. I was so engrossed with the sergeant's interrogation there, that I quite forgot about your own. I'll leave my associates to open him up, and you and I, as your pretty American doctor might say, can *freewheel*."

Mörder produced a truck battery and a set of electrical leads from beneath the cart and placed them on the floor beside Jack.

"Electro-shock therapy has always been something of a hobby of mine." Mörder expertly attached the leads to the battery, then clipped the opposing ends to Jack's manacles. "Indeed, it was during my medical incarceration in Berlin, that I had a great deal of time to reflect on precisely how I could burn you the way you burned me."

"*Please!*" Lancaster pleaded. "Please don't—"

Mörder ignored him. "It's a delicious twist of irony, don't you think, that the power that breathes life into the sergeant there, may soon be the thief of your own?"

Jack tensed as Mörder's hand hovered over the battery switch. "Brace yourself, Captain," said Mörder quietly, "this is *really* going to hurt."

# 31

---

# BREAK OUT

"**C**AMMY?"

The voice came from the other side of the door. Cammy and the others—Billy, Hellstrøm, Haakon, and Seim—exchanged a look.

"Sounds like Spitfire!" Billy said.

"Get back!" hissed the voice.

Cammy's eyes went wide, then she yelled "Down!" She grabbed Hellstrøm and pushed him to the floor.

The door bucked on its hinges and fell inward with a clang. Spitfire stood in the doorway, leaning on the frame he stooped forward, nursing his crushed side.

Cammy ran to him. "I knew you wouldn't let me down, baby!"

"What about me?" Hurricane grumbled behind Spitfire. He let go of the two unconscious sentries he was holding.

"You too, you big lug!"

"Not bad for a bit of a kid though," Hurricane sniffed, nudging Spitfire.

"We know where they've taken Jack 'n' the sarge," Spitfire said.

"Then what are we waiting for?" Cammy moved toward the door but Hellstrøm grabbed her arm.

"The mission takes priority."

"You're shittin' me, right?" Cammy gasped.

"I want to help them too," Hellstrøm said, "but if charges are still in place, then there's a chance we can still destroy factory."

"And we will," Cammy urged. "But our odds of success go way up with Jack and Lancaster. And besides," she crossed her arms stubbornly, "I'm ain't leavin' here without 'em."

Hellstrøm pursed his lips.

Cammy looked at him, as the rest of the group fell in behind her.

"Okay, little woman." Hellstrøm nodded, resigned.

Cammy smiled. "So let's go kick ass, blow this dump and get the hell outta here!"

...

Mörder hit the switch on the battery again, sending hundreds of volts of electricity coursing through Jack's body. Rigid with pain, his eyes bulged, and his fingers contorted as he clenched his teeth in agony.

"No!" Lancaster yelled, as the brutes tore into him.

Mörder hit the switch and Jack slumped like a puppet with its strings cut. "Christ," Jack gasped, his chest heaving for air.

"Oh, he can't help you here," Mörder said. "Would *Christ* allow you to feel the pain you're experiencing? With every jolt I want you to remember, Jack, that you've really done this to yourself."

Mörder flicked the switch again.

Jack stiffened, foaming at the mouth as electricity surged rampant through every muscle within him. Mörder flicked the switch and then almost instantly flicked the switch again. Jack cried out and tensed. The veins in his face and neck swelled like balloons about to burst.

"*Bastards!*" Lancaster spat, as the brutes hammered at him.

Jack's veins burned. Then somewhere in the back of his mind he heard McNulty's words from his training. *Be strong, Jack. I can make you strong on the outside, but not in here*, the old man had said, tapping Jack's forehead. *In here, the time will come when you need to show mental fortitude—and it's then laddie, that you'll need to dig deep…*

Mörder switched off the pain, and Jack slumped once more. In a semi-conscious haze, he realized that in the frantic spasms of his torture, his right hand had slid partly out of his manacles.

"You know, you've made quite a stir in Berlin," Mörder said. "The Führer has issued an order stating that all Allied saboteurs or enemy agents encountered by German forces are henceforth to be executed immediately without trial."

"*Oi, Kraut,*" Lancaster slurred, the brutes still working at his chest plate. "Why don't you come over 'ere, pick on someone your own size, you bloody coward!"

"Lanc," Jack cautioned, looking up. But as Mörder turned his attention to the machine, Jack seized the opportunity to ease his right hand down slowly through the manacles.

*If only it'd been this easy at Dunkirk…*

"You feel *empathy* for it, Jack, is that it?" Mörder circled Lancaster like a shark circling prey. "Fascinating," he said, glancing into the darkness, "don't *you* think?"

Two blue irises winked on in the shadows, expanding to brilliant discs. "Yes, sir." Mosquito stepped forward.

"Moz?" Jack said. "Why?"

"Turncoat!" Lancaster muttered, straining at his restraints. "Betrayin' your own kind!"

Mörder took a crowbar from one of the brutes and handed it to Mosquito. The men stepped aside to let Mosquito approach.

"Moz, what you doin'?" Jack said. "Moz?"

"Hastings helped me see the light," Mosquito said. "The Nazis are disciplined, Sarge, organized. They have flair, panache. The Führer offers pride, *hope* to his people. What was it Churchill said? That he'd nothing to left to offer the country but blood, toil 'n' tears? And me? When this war ends, I wanna be on the *winning* side." He glanced over at Jack. "I'm sorry, Captain, but they lied to you from the beginning. You were part of a war you could never 'ope to win. This time next year, Churchill will be dead, the king'll be locked in the tower 'n' Great Britain a part of the Reich."

Mosquito raised the crowbar and approached Lancaster.

"Moz," Jack urged, "don't do this."

Mörder knocked on Mosquito's chest plate twice. "He speaks rather well, don't you think? Considering he's nothing more than a glorified panzer with a voice."

"Stand down soldier," commanded Lancaster as Mosquito loomed over him. "I said—"

Mosquito batted Lancaster's face plate with a single swipe, then plunged the crowbar into the sergeant's shoulder. With a flash of sparks and an ear-splitting grind of gears, Lancaster slumped and fell silent, the light in his blue eyes fizzling out.

Jack could only look on in shock.

*No. Not Lancaster.*

"What 'ave you done?" Jack said, tears welling in his eyes.

Mosquito stared at Lancaster, unmoving.

Mörder checked his watch. "Well, sadly I have a prior engagement, Jack, so I leave you in the capable hands of my associates here. They have orders to ensure that your passing from this world to the next is to be made as painful as humanly possible. And while the sergeant's remains will be returned to Berlin for examination, your body will be strung up beside

Hellstrøm as a warning of what it is to oppose the Reich. Nothing, in my experience, quells disorder like the stench of a freshly hung insurrectionist. Auf Wiedersehen, Jack."

Mörder turned to the brutes and nodded, then strode from the room with Mosquito, who closed the door behind them.

The two brutes stepped forward once more. Although their faces were hidden behind their gas masks, Jack could feel their perverse glee.

But Jack was ready. As the first brute approached, he slid his right hand free of the manacles and smashed the man's filter full on with the palm of his hand. The brute reeled in pain and wrenched his mask aside. But Jack wasn't done. Gripping the man with his legs, Jack slid the suicide pill from the collar of his tunic and jammed it into the brute's bloody mouth.

The German gagged and spat froth, dropping to his knees as the second brute grabbed a cleaver from the cart. Jack yanked at his left hand furiously but the manacles remained steadfast. *Déjà bloody vu*, he thought.

The second brute attacked.

Once again, Jack was ready.

Letting all his weight hang from his left hand, he swung his body, sweeping the brute's legs out from under him. The giant of a man fell to the floor with a thud. Jack quickly pulled free the jump leads from his manacles and clipped them to the brute's mask before the man could recover.

Then Jack kicked the switch on the battery.

The brute screamed and shook violently, his gas mask emitting a shower of sparks as the lenses exploded. When Jack kicked the battery off, the man didn't move. Unconscious—or otherwise, none of it mattered now. Lancaster was gone. The rest of the team were god knows where, and the Nazis had the upper hand. Mörder would deliver his shipment, and the Reich would have their bomb.

Game over.

The door burst open, and Cammy and the team rushed in. She ran to Jack's side with Hurricane who ripped open the manacles securing his left hand. Jack sagged into Billy's arms.

"Cammy!"

Cammy spun to see Spitfire beside Lancaster's smoking body.

"No." She looked at Jack. "Who did this?"

"Mosquito," Jack said. "Shoved the crowbar right through him. He just… shorted out."

"What can we do?" said Hurricane.

"Whatever it is, do it fast," Hellstrøm growled from the door where he stood watch with Haakon and Seim.

"We gotta try to jump-start him," Cammy said. She looked down at the battery, and at the leads attached to the brute. "This thing pack a charge?"

Jack nodded shakily. "I can testify to that."

Cammy attached the jump leads to the crowbar protruding from Lancaster's chest. "Okay, stand back," she said.

Saying a silent prayer, she flicked the switch.

Sparks flew from Lancaster's innards.

Cammy turned the power off and checked the sergeant for signs of life. "Nothing," she said quietly.

"Again," Jack said.

Cammy flicked the switch, and this time Lancaster smoked, hundreds of volts roaring through his shell.

Cammy turned off the power, examined him, and once again shook her head.

"C'mon, you stubborn old sod!" Jack said. "You've fought me this far! Don't quit on me now! *Fight!*" He looked at Cammy, "Again Cam!"

"Jack—"

"I said *again!*"

She flicked the switch and Lancaster bounced.

. . .

*The distant sounds of explosions, screams, rifle fire. A bomb landing nearby. Earth showering his face.*

*Lancaster opened his eyes.*

*A line of exhausted young men hugged a trench wall, knee deep in sludge. More waded by wearing gas bags, bearing stretchers containing barely recognizable boys; the mangled flesh of their faces dangled in the filth as the medics passed by.*

*Drawing his service revolver, Lancaster climbed a ladder. Gas canisters bounced down into the trench, and he blew a tin whistle to warn the others. The boys in the trench cried out and climbed ladders after him as the canisters spun, releasing curls of yellow death.*

*Gunfire and mortars erupted around them as the boys pulled on their gas bags and raced into the haze, their bayonets leveled.*

*A huge shell struck near Lancaster, and the explosion blew him into the air. He landed in No-Man's Land, amid the barbed wire and body parts. He clawed desperately through the mire and slid into a crater, where he found himself staring face-down into a puddle.*

*His reflection stared back at him. Though it was distorted by ripples from the tremors of explosions, it was clearly the face of a man.*

*"No," said the man in Lancaster's voice. "No!"*

...

Lancaster's blue eyes burned brightly, and he sat bolt upright.

"Lanc," Cammy exclaimed, tears rolled down her cheeks.

Jack crouched beside him. "Good to see you again, Sergeant. You okay?"

Lancaster reflected on his vision—or was it just a dream? Whatever it was, he had never experienced anything like it before. Would he ever do so again?

"I'm… *operational*?" was all the old machine could manage.

Cammy nodded, joining Billy and the others.

Lancaster clattered to his treads.

"Thought I'd lost you there, sergeant," Jack said quietly. "It's good to have you back."

"Yeah, well," Lancaster muttered, "can't leave you on your own to get my boys all shot up now, can I?"

Jack smiled.

"I misjudged you, Jack," Lancaster blurted suddenly, as if unburdening himself of a truth he'd known for too long. "And I'm sorry… that I *doubted* you, I mean."

"Well, you had good reason," Jack said. He grabbed his revolver from the cart, handing Lancaster his Webleys.

"Come on, pal." Jack holstered his revolver. "We've got a train to catch."

# 32

## SACRIFICE

"**T**AKE BILLY, HURRICANE AND SPITFIRE,**"** Jack said, striding along a corridor with Cammy. "Stick close to Hellstrøm and blow those cells."

"What about you?" Cammy asked, concerned.

"Lanc 'n' I will find the train, see if we can derail it."

"And just how d'you propose *we* do that?" Lancaster grumbled.

"Follow pipes," Hellstrøm said, pointing to the network of plumbing snaking above their heads. "Is how they transfer water from concentration room to loading bay."

"Jack, I don't like this," Billy said. "Let us come with you, eh?" Hurricane nodded in agreement. "Hellstrøm's boys can easily handle the —"

"I need you to stay with Cam," Jack said. He turned to Hurricane and Spitfire. "You too boys. With the number of guns milling about this place she's gonna need all the help she can get."

"Just watch your arse then, eh?" Billy said, realizing this might be the last time he saw his friend.

"Take care, boss," Spitfire said. "You too, Sarge."

"Just remember the plan," Lancaster said. "Set the charges, blow 'em, and we'll rendezvous back at the lodge."

"Good luck everyone," Jack said.

Hellstrøm nodded. The group followed him down the corridor but Cammy hung back.

Seeing her standing alone, Jack wanted to tell her how he felt, about how he'd felt ever since he'd first met her at Achnacarry.

Lancaster coughed awkwardly, shattering the moment.

Again.

Jack stared at him.

"Oh, for the love of—" Lancaster rolled his lenses. Annoyed, he turned and peered around a corner.

"Be careful," Cammy said. She wanted to say more, but now wasn't the time. They would see each other again—she was sure of it.

Maybe.

She turned to leave. "Cam?" She looked back at Jack.

"Tell me when we get home, huh?" Their eyes lingered for a second, then she ran after Hellstrøm and the others.

. . .

Constructed specifically for the hydro-electric plant, the Rjukan rail line was used primarily by technicians to shuttle between Vemork and its terminus, ten miles down the track at the ferry station in Mæl. This allowed the plant to move goods to the mouth of the Måna in Vestfjorddalen, where the river ran into Lake Tinnsjø.

Mörder emerged onto a platform overlooking the plant's loading bay. A nervous Rjukan Town Kommandant followed after him with his subordinates, Mosquito behind them.

Beneath them, a stationary smoking locomotive sat coupled to a coal car, a passenger carriage, two flatbeds, and a sandbagged machine-gun nest in a half-car to the rear. Nervous factory staff scurried about the bay facilitating the transfer of the heavy water barrels, which two forklifts transported on pallets to the train's flatbeds. German sentries moved among the bay staff, adding the requisite threat level to encourage a speedy transfer.

"This is an electric line," Mörder said, noting the cables overhead. "Why are you using a steam train?"

"Our electric locomotives were damaged in the sabotage attempt last year, sir," explained the Kommandant.

"Double the guard on the train."

The Kommandant saluted and returned to his men. He spoke quietly to a sentry who had just arrived, breathless.

Mosquito appeared at Mörder's side.

"I want you on board when it leaves," Mörder said.

"Of course."

Gazing out through a tunnel at the far end of the bay, Mörder saw a dark mountain range beyond.

"There's a quality to the solitude of night," he said, distant. "A melancholy."

"I don't understand."

"No. I don't suppose you do."

"General Mörder?" The Kommandant was nervous.

Klaxons suddenly blared around them.

"*Stone!*" Mörder said, clenching his fists.

...

The group followed Cammy up a corridor toward the high-concentration room. She rounded a corner and gunned down two sentries guarding the door. Klaxons blared around them.

"Bloody great this, innit?" Billy yelled above the gunfire. "What 'appened to Commandos bein' stealthy?"

"I *ain't* a damn Commando!" Cammy yelled.

More machine-guns opened up behind them, and Haakon spun as he was cut down.

"We got company!" Hurricane yelled from the group's rear. "Comin' in from the compound!"

"We need to think of something—fast!" yelled Spitfire.

Hellstrøm charged the cell room door with a roar. As it smashed open, two guards inside raised their guns. They dropped as Seim and Hellstrøm sprayed them with gun fire.

Cammy, Billy, and the Tommies entered the room behind them. They were relieved to see the charges still rigged to the water cells.

"Me 'n' the boys'll barricade the door," Billy said, breathless. "You sort those charges!"

As Hellstrøm, Cammy and Seim moved toward the cells, Cammy saw Hellstrøm stagger and clutch his stomach.

"You okay?" She took his hand and saw blood on his fingers.

"Is nothing," Hellstrøm growled. "Go on."

"Don't s'pose you've thought about how we get out of here?" Billy shouted, barricading the door with Hurricane and Spitfire.

Cammy looked about and spied a wireless on the desk. "Spitfire, can you rig up that radio, get a signal out?"

"I can try!"

"Do it, honey," she urged.

Spitfire grabbed the wireless and pulled the back off it. He extended his digi-tools and started unscrewing components.

Seim was checking the explosives. "They've taken the timer sticks!" he yelled.

"Dammit," Cammy said. "Then we'll just have to blow it old school."

"Hang on," Billy said. "That means…" But he knew what that meant, as did everyone else in the room—someone was going to have to stay back to blow the charges.

Boot steps and German shouting sounded in the corridor outside, and sledgehammers battered against the door.

· · ·

Jack and Lancaster crawled out onto a gantry above the loading bay, which was a hive of activity beneath them.

"Sounds like they've found Camilla," Lancaster said, hearing the klaxons. "I 'ope she's okay."

"She can handle herself."

Jack watched a forklift deposit a pallet of barrels onto a loaded flatbed.

"This ain't gonna be easy," Lancaster said.

"Is it ever?" And then in the midst of it all, Jack saw him. "Mörder," he whispered.

"An' his new pet snake," Lancaster growled, spying Mosquito following the general.

"We need to blow that train before it leaves."

"An' just where d'you suggest we get explosives?"

Jack peered around the bay. "There," he said, pointing to the half-car at the rear of the train.

Lancaster extended his eyes and scanned the half-car. A number of ammunition and grenade boxes were stacked beside a tripod-mounted machine-gun.

"Right," he said, looking at Jack with a glint in his lens. "Let's go play with some Nazis."

· · ·

The battering at the door continued as Cammy unraveled fuse wire between the water cells.

"Okay," she said, looking around the cylinder room to make sure she hadn't missed anything. "That's it."

A sledgehammer splintered the door. Hurricane sprayed gunfire through the hole into the corridor beyond, scattering the soldiers.

"At least they won't chuck grenades in," Billy said. "Too afraid they'll do the damage for us."

"How're you doing, baby?" Cammy asked.

"Almost there," Spitfire said, furiously screwing the wireless back together.

Cammy looked around. Everything was in place. There was just one thing to decide. Who would be the one to—

"*Come here… little woman*," Hellstrøm gasped.

He had slid down the wall onto the floor, leaving a bloody smear. His face was pale and his breathing labored. "Give me wires," he said, unsheathing his knife.

"Hellstrøm—" Cammy said, tears welling.

"*Humour an… ill-tempered old man*," Hellstrøm said, his voice weak. "*Let him die… with honor.*"

Cammy reluctantly nodded. She took his knife and scraped the plastic covering from the ends of the wires.

More machine-gun fire.

"They're coming through!" Billy yelled.

"*Tell Jack, I'm sorry… sorry I didn't get… to shake his hand.*"

"I don't understand," said Cammy.

"*But he will*," Hellstrøm said, smiling.

Seim joined them. "We'll hold them off for as long as we can."

Cammy was confused. "You aren't coming?"

"We've known each other many years, he and I," said Seim. "If he stays, I stay. We'll buy you some time to get out. We can destroy these cells. But Jack *must* destroy that shipment."

"*This is V for victory—repeat—V for victory, over?*" It was Remmy, crackling through the wireless.

"Cammy!" Spitfire looked up in disbelief.

"They're comin' through!" yelled Hurricane, his back against the crumbling barricade.

"Remmy's out there somewhere," Billy said, looking around for an escape route. He spied an air vent in the wall. "Spitfire—kick that out, would ya?"

Spitfire ran to the wall and promptly smashed his fist into the plaster, wrenching out the vent. He poked his head into the hole and peered up. A vertical access shaft with rungs built into the wall extended upwards. "I see light," he said. "Looks like a straight shot to the compound."

"*Go now, little woman*," Hellstrøm gasped. "*My time in this fight is over. Your time… now… to shine!*"

"Cam!" Hurricane yelled. He and Billy were straining to keep the door shut, but the forces on the other side were heaving it open, pushing the barricade back. "If we're goin', love, it needs to be now!"

Cammy kissed Hellstrøm's forehead. Then she, Spitfire, Billy, and

Hurricane climbed through the hole in the wall.

"*See you in Valhalla, little woman,*" Hellstrøm gasped.

Seim aimed his machine-gun at the door as it splintered inward, and opened fire.

...

Jack and Lancaster sat hunched behind a crate, watching the train. While they had made their way into the loading bay unnoticed, judging by the number of German troops milling about, Jack wouldn't have bet on their chances of getting any further.

The engineer had just climbed up into the train's cab, and after checking the engine's crankshaft and steam pipes, the fireman climbed up after him.

"Looks like they're ready to go," Lancaster said. "You sure about this?"

"We blow it here," Jack said, steel-jawed, "or we get on board and we've got ten miles to derail the thing. Either way, we can't let it reach that ferry."

"Was afraid you were gonna say that," Lancaster muttered. His gaze shifted. "Look!"

Mörder strode up the track leading a unit of troops. Breaking away from the line, several men climbed into the half-car and manned the machine-gun. Others climbed up onto the flatbeds containing the heavy water barrels, and settled in with their guns ready. Mörder reached the passenger carriage and climbed aboard with Mosquito and the remaining guards.

Hissing steam, the locomotive's engine rumbled and its chimney puffed smoke. The engineer poked his head out of the cab and looked down the train cars. He raised his whistle.

"We must be mad," Jack muttered.

"If I wasn't, what would I be doing 'ere with you?" Lancaster replied. "Outgunned, outnumbered, 'n' outta time. Just another day for us, innit?"

...

Troops stormed into the cell room.

"For Norway!" Seim yelled, opening fire, then spinning as he was cut down in a hail of German shells.

"Fan out!" yelled a Kommandant entering the room. "Find the saboteurs!"

As the men stepped cautiously between the cylinders, one soldier noticed a blood trail on the floor. He followed it cautiously—and rounding a corner saw Hellstrøm, panting for air in the shadows.

"*For Norway,*" Hellstrøm said, closing his eyes. He pictured himself with Vanja, running across the sun-drenched valleys of their youth.

The soldier raised his machine-gun.

Hellstrøm opened his eyes and smiled. "*For freedom…*"

He held up the wires.

The soldier's mouth gaped open.

"*Ka-Boom!*" Hellstrøm gasped, touching the tips of the wires together.

# 33

―――

# ALL OR NOTHING

**W**ITH AN APOCALYPTIC BOOM, a ball of orange flame blew out the walls of the basement.

In the compound, Cammy was thrown to the ground, covering her head as shattered glass and masonry rained down around her in a boiling blast of air. She squeezed her eyes shut and prayed she was in a safe spot.

...

The loading bay shook. The engineer panicked, blew his whistle, and released the train's brake lever. The locomotive ground forward with a shudder, drawing slowly out of the factory and into the tunnel.

"They did it!" Jack said.

"That's half the job," Lancaster replied. "Let's finish it!"

They leapt over the crates and raced for the train's half-car. For the first time ever, it felt like they were finally a team, a unit, and as they ran for the train, Jack realized they were doing exactly what they'd been trained to do. This was their time now, and nothing was going to stop them.

The machine-gun mounted on the train's half-car suddenly spun and opened fire, spattering the ground around them with lead. Lancaster returned fire and pushed on, providing cover for Jack who fell in behind him. Lancaster reached the half-car and threw himself inside.

At the same moment Jack heard more explosions, and the tunnel roof began to fracture.

Lancaster swatted the machine-gun crew out of the half-car, then extended an arm toward Jack, who was chasing the train at full speed, but barely gaining. "*C'mon, Jack!*"

Jack ran, the tunnel cracking wide above him. Not only did he have to catch up with the moving train, he now had to dodge the huge pieces of roof stone that crashed down onto the track.

"Hurry!" Lancaster shouted. He leaned out from the car as far as he could and gripped its rail so tightly with one hand that it bent the metal.

"Jack!"

"I know!"

"Come on—now!"

Jack leapt—and caught Lancaster's hand.

The train exited the tunnel and turned a bend, and for a moment Jack's legs flew out over a ravine—but then Lancaster dragged him aboard.

Jack looked back. The tunnel collapsed behind them, taking the factory's east wall with it in a deafening crash that echoed across the valley.

"I hope to God they weren't in there when it blew!" Lancaster said. A bullet pinged off his armor. He spun toward the soldiers in the heavy water car ahead of them, raised his guns, and opened fire.

...

Cammy grabbed a dazed soldier's machine-gun and knocked him unconscious with its butt.

"Cammy!" It was Spitfire. Thrown by the explosion, he was shaken, and having trouble getting to his treads. Oil was leaking from bullet holes in his armor.

Cammy helped him up, then searched for Billy and Hurricane. She spotted them on the far side of the compound, but there was no way she and Spitfire could reach them. Machine-guns stuttered and a line of fire raked the earth at their feet. They broke for cover and returned fire. Still more soldiers crowded into the compound, hemming them in.

Even as he fired, Spitfire noticed the train's lights on the mountainside. He extended his eyes and saw Jack and Lancaster under fire. "Oh no."

"What is it?" Cammy yelled, reloading. Following Spitfire's gaze, she saw the train. "Jack..."

The tilt of Spitfire's head was all the reaction she needed. "We gotta get after them!"

"With what?"

Cammy looked around the compound. An Opel truck sat off to one side—close enough to reach with a short sprint. "We're taking that truck! *C'mon!*"

Spraying covering fire, they ran to the truck. Cammy climbed into the cab, and Spitfire hurled himself into its rear and hauled up the tailgate.

As shells struck sparks off the hood and fractured the windshield, Cammy yanked out the ignition and hotwired it.

...

"What the hell is she doing?" Billy yelled.

"Buy her some time, Bill," Hurricane yelled back. "She's gonna come get us!"

The truck ground into gear and sped toward the main gate, crashing right through the Germans.

"Uh, where the 'ell's she going?"

"Oi, Cammy!" Hurricane yelled. "Come back!"

The truck sped out the gate and up the road in a flurry of snow. A half-track full of Germans took off after her.

"Bloody typical," Billy said. "What the hell are we s'posed to do now?"

Shells whizzed around them.

"Try to stay alive," Hurricane offered, returning fire.

. . .

"*C'mon, you Nazi bugger*," Jack croaked at the German throttling him from behind. "*Do your worst!*"

Jack cursed his loud-mouthed bravado when the German applied more pressure. "A little help?" he gasped.

Lancaster was in a brawl by his side. "Can't you see I'm busy?" He grabbed one of his assailants and flung him out of the flatbed. Two more soldiers wrestled him to the floor between the heavy water barrels as the train trundled onward at speed.

"Sod this," Jack grunted. He aimed his gun at Lancaster's chest.

"What the 'ell—"

Jack squeezed off a round. It hit Lancaster's armor, ricocheted off, and rebounded into the temple of the German throttling Jack. The man fell back, and Jack leapt on the two soldiers attacking Lancaster.

"We didn't start this," he yelled, punching one of the Germans, "but we're damn well—gonna—*finish it!*"

As he threw the dazed German aside, he noticed an Opel truck falling in beside the train. His eyes went wide at the sight of its driver.

. . .

"*Jack!*" Cammy yelled, as gun fire from the half-track pursuing her clattered along the truck's chassis and set the billowing tarpaulin alight.

. . .

Mosquito emerged from the door of the train's passenger carriage and climbed up onto its roof. He bounded down the train, preparing to leap onto Cammy's truck. But she swerved aside just in time and accelerated, and Mosquito opted for leaping onto the half-track chasing after her. Urging its driver on, he hung from the vehicles' cab as it too accelerated, shunting the truck's rear end.

. . .

"*Cammy!*" yelled Spitfire from the rear of the truck. They were dangerously close to the edge of the ravine and the track's mountain shelf was narrowing fast.

Spitfire glanced back at the half-track and saw the blue eyes of his friend Mosquito. No, not a friend. Spitfire knew now that they burned with a different fury.

Mosquito was gone.

"Just hold on!" Cammy screamed, veering wildly as the gun fire from the half-track intensified.

Spitfire raised his Webley's but they clicked emptily. Holstering them, he started breaking open crates inside the truck, searching desperately for something, anything, he could use as a weapon.

. . .

In the compound, Billy and Hurricane fought back to back as the enemy closed in around them but they were fighting a losing battle.

"Guess this is it, pal," Billy said, discarding his empty machine-gun.

"It's been a privilege, Bill."

A wall of German soldiers swarmed toward them, and Hurricane braced himself to protect Billy for as long as he possibly could. "Yea, though I walk through the valley o' the shadow of death, I will fear no evil…" he muttered.

Foreseeing their end, Billy joined him in the prayer, firing wildly. "For thou art with me, thy rod 'n' thy—"

A deafening roar split the air, and with a whoosh of snow the *Valiant*, still badly damaged, descended through the compound's inferno, her double roto-copter wings fanning the flames, forcing the Germans back. The fortress hovered above Billy and Hurricane, and her bay door dropped with a clang.

"*You guys comin' or what?*" Remmy yelled through the *Valiant's* loudhailer.

"You beautiful bloody Yank!" Hurricane shouted, and he grabbed Billy and clambered on board the fortress.

. . .

The half-track accelerated and drew alongside Cammy's truck. Mosquito leapt onto her cab roof and extended his commando blade, stabbing it down through the metal.

Cammy screamed as the blade thrust through the roof in front of her face. She swerved sharply, trying to shake Mosquito off.

Mosquito prized open the roof like he was opening a tin of beans. He peeled back the metal revealing Cammy, terrified, at the wheel.

She raised her pistol but Mosquito batted it from her hand.

"Moz!" Cammy pleaded, "please don't!"

"*Auf Wiedersehen*, Cammy!" Mosquito raised his blade.

Then he paused, his lenses widening in astonishment as he noticed Bug crawling nimbly down his forearm. He tried to shake the little automata off, but it clung desperately to the blade, then took to the air, fluttering wildly in front of Mosquito's lenses.

With a swipe, Mosquito batted the little machine into the cab beside Cammy, its lens shattered.

Cammy shrank back as Mosquito raised his blade once again.

"*Oi, traitor!*"

Mosquito spun to see Spitfire burst through the canvas behind him, holding a bazooka.

"*Eat this!*"

Spitfire pulled the trigger.

The blast propelled Mosquito off the truck, over the half-track which fell back, and onto the train's engine. He clung to the puffing chimney, nursing a smoking dent in his side.

The half-track rammed the truck from behind again in an attempt to force Cammy from the road, and its troops continued their fire.

"Er, Cammy?" Spitfire yelled from the roof.

"Kinda busy here, honey!"

"*Up ahead!*"

Cammy squinted into the night.

They were about to run out of road.

. . .

"Cam's in trouble," Jack said, ducking behind barrels as the troops in the next flatbed opened fire.

He and Lancaster were trapped and outgunned.

"What the hell do we do now?" Lancaster yelled, shells zinging off his armor and the heavy water barrels surrounding them.

"We can't get rid of this lot without getting hit," Jack said, jerking a thumb at the barrels.

"Then we need to stop the train."

"So we get to the engine."

"And after that?"

"Do what we always do," Jack said, reloading. "Get stuck in 'n' raise hell!"

...

Mörder emerged from the rear of the passenger carriage, leaned over its guardrail, and peered back down the train.

Mosquito leaped from the engine and landed on the carriage roof above him. The soldiers from Mörder's car climbed up to join him. "Well, what are you waiting for?" the general shouted. "Finish them!"

# 34

## UP 'N' AT 'EM

**B**ILLY SLID INTO THE CO-PILOT'S SEAT beside Remmy. "Never thought I'd be pleased to see *you*."

"Gee, thanks." Remmy gunned the *Valiant* forward.

"How'd you find us?"

"Are you kidding," Remmy heaved on his stick. "They heard that factory blast in London!"

The train's lights were visible up ahead, as was the glitter of gunfire. Remmy matched the train's speed, soaring above it. Billy could see Jack and Lancaster below, under fire on the flatbed, as well as Cammy's truck hurtling along beside the train, with the half-track in hot pursuit.

"So what's our play?" Remmy said.

"We need to take out that train," Billy said.

Remmy strained to see. "Hey, is that Mosquito down there? Hey man, he— he's firing on 'em?"

As Remmy watched, Mosquito looked up and pointed his guns at the *Valiant*.

"No," Billy said, "he's firing at *us!*"

Remmy wrenched his wheel in an attempt to avoid the gunfire.

The *Valiant* soared over the train and Remmy brought them round for another pass. He looked at Billy in shock.

"Long story," Billy yelled, holding on as the fortress yawned about. "He's one o'theirs now."

"Ain't that a peach," Remmy sighed. "Just when I think I got a bead on you crazy limeys!"

Billy heard a crash from the cargo bay. "How you doin' down there?"

Thrown around by the *Valiant's* erratic maneuvers, Hurricane clung desperately to his cage. "I've been better!"

Equipment was breaking loose all around him and rattling across the deck. He ducked as the crawlers ripped away from their restraints and bounced past him, out of the bay door into the night.

"Just 'ang on!" Billy shouted.

. . .

Cammy watched the end of the road speed rapidly toward her. Time was running out.

"Cammy?"

She looked up through the hole in the cab roof and saw Spitfire gazing down at her.

"We aren't getting out of this, baby, close your eyes." It was useless reassurance, but they were the only words she could muster, given their chances.

*Goodbye Jack…*

Cammy prepared to meet her maker.

Spitfire's hand shot down, grabbed her jacket, and yanked her out of the cab.

Their truck smashed through a barrier and careened out into the gorge.

Cammy screamed, clinging to Spitfire for her life as the little Tommy leapt from the cab roof into the void.

Freezing wind whipped Cammy's face and hair. She realized with a start that she was floating, seemingly flying. Even more surprising, that she wasn't dead.

She looked up and saw Spitfire clinging to a long strap of webbing fluttering from the *Valiant's* open cargo bay. Hurricane gazed down at them.

"It's like H always says," Spitfire yelled above the gale, "sometimes you just got to have faith!"

Below them, Cammy saw the half-track's lights dip as it followed the truck into the gorge, it's passengers crying out. There was a pause, then both vehicles hit the valley floor and exploded; two bright yellow-orange fireballs turning night into day as the *Valiant* came about and hurtled toward the train.

. . .

Cammy joined Billy on the flight deck and peered through the cockpit window.

"How'd you get hold of the *Valiant*?" she asked.

"After you guys cut loose we came down in Switzerland," Remmy said, chomping a stogie. "The kid was pretty beat up, sends his regards by the way. We liberated an ol' clunker and limped back to Hawkinge. They said this girl wasn't ready for action yet, but, what else you got that's big enough to get your boys home? 'Sides, I ain't never been one for followin' orders."

Cammy patted Remmy's shoulder. For all his faults—and Sal had many—he was a rule breaker, just like the rest of them, which made him a part of the team.

"We got company," Billy said.

Checking his wing, Remmy saw three Heinkels screaming down the valley toward them.

"How're the guns?" Cammy asked.

"Locked 'n' loaded."

Tracer fire cut across the *Valiant's* nose.

Cammy was already climbing down into the cargo bay.

Hurricane stood beside Spitfire who held Bug's motionless shell. Cammy had grabbed the little drone when Spitfire had snatched her from the truck, but the automata was in bad shape, its leg ticking involuntarily as exposed wires sparked.

"Can you fix him?" Spitfire asked.

"I dunno," Cammy said. "Maybe."

"But—"

"When we get home, baby, I promise."

"What is it?" Hurricane said.

"Go man the top gun," said Cammy. "Spitfire, jump in the belly. We got bandits tailing our ass."

The Tommies glanced at each other.

"*Now* guys!"

The machines ran to their stations as Billy climbed into the cargo bay.

"They're in trouble down there," Billy said. "If we can't stop that train, then—"

"You got any ideas?" Cammy said, as gun fire punctured the fuselage.

Billy looked about and, recalling Jack's stunt on the U-boat, pointed at something stashed across the loading bay. "What about that thing?"

. . .

Lancaster blasted his Webleys as he pushed on up the train. Jack followed, shielding himself behind the Sergeants' bulk as the mighty Tommy swatted Germans from the flatbed.

"Looks like we might 'ave a problem," Lancaster said, pausing.

Peering around him, Jack saw soldiers on the roof of Mörders' carriage constructing a second tripod-gun.

"If we try to uncouple the flatbed we'll be sitting ducks. We gotta get to that engine!" Jack yelled, balling his fist and cuffing a soldier over the side. "Are you with me?"

"Doesn't look like I 'ave much of a choice!" Lancaster replied. But despite the sarcasm, Lancaster felt invigorated, energized. He hadn't felt such power since the old days back in France with his lads, and for the first time since he and Jack had met, the old sergeant felt that they were finally working together—one unstoppable machine.

Jack picked up a German machine-gun and moving ahead of Lancaster, sprayed the gun crew with fire. Lancaster joined him, advancing, and hurling Germans into the air.

They fought their way forward along the flatbed, slowly gaining ground, and made for Mörder's carriage.

. . .

Remmy flicked on the com. "Okay boys, you ready?"

"I'm in!" Hurricane crackled from the turret on the *Valiant's* back.

"Me too," yelled Spitfire, from the belly gun.

"Stay frosty, boys, 'cos it's gonna get hot real quick!"

A Heinkel screamed out of the night, raking gunfire along the *Valiant's* fuselage.

"See?" Remmy yelled. "Eyes up!"

. . .

"Come on you bloody…"

Hurricane squeezed off a round, chasing the Heinkel with his gun sights, but it dropped out of sight beneath the *Valiant*.

"*Spitfire, three-o-clock!*"

. . .

"*I'm on him!*"

The Heinkel roared beneath Spitfire, who spun in his seat to target the fighter. Squeezing his triggers, Spitfire blew the Heinkel's tail off, and it spiraled into the mountainside with a boom.

"Not bad!" Remmy crackled through the com. "Maybe you boys're special after all!"

. . .

"*Remmy?*" Cammy crackling on the com this time. "*Take us in over the train!*"

"Are you insane? They got more guns down there than up here!"

"*Don't make me come up there, Sal!*" Cammy admonished.

Remmy winced.

"Savin' you guys was a bad idea!" Remmy chomped down on his stogie, cursed the day he ever learned to fly, and swooped in low over the train.

# 35

---

# WALTZING MATILDA

**L**ANCASTER HURLED the last German soldier from the flatbed, then: "It's over, Jack!"

Jack and Lancaster looked up and saw Mörder stood on the carriage roof above them, flanked by a row of German troops. Mosquito loomed behind them. The rogue machine nodded toward the *Valiant* as it soared up the tracks toward the half-car at the rear of the train.

"They can't 'elp you now."

"I wouldn't be so sure about that!" Lancaster said, noticing the *Valiant's* bay door opening.

The fortress hovered into position over the half-car, and with a groan something massive screeched out of its cargo bay.

The Mk I Matilda!

All eight tons of the outdated British infantry tank crashed onto the half-car, the impact nearly tearing it from the train.

Mörder's men instantly opened fire.

"*Cammy!*" Jack gasped, taking cover with Lancaster.

The Matilda's turret swiveled to target Mörder's carriage. Its machine gun rattled into action, and it lurched forward—

Mörder and his troops scattered, everyone except Mosquito.

Then wheezing, the tank juddered to a stop.

. . .

Inside the cramped confines of the turret, Billy winced as a hail of German gunfire clattered off the tank's rusted armor.

"What do you mean you've stalled it?" Cammy yelled from the machine gun, checking its now empty magazine. "I thought you said you could drive this thing?"

"I'm a squaddie, sweet'art, *you're* the engineer!" Billy winced as he ground the tank's gears. But the tank stubbornly refused to move. "What the 'ell're you doing back there anyway? You're s'posed to be loadin' a shell!"

"Well I don't *have* a goddamn shell! All I got is a lousy grenade I found when I first started cleanin' her up." She waved what looked like a rusty pineapple in front of Billy's face.

Annoyed, Billy batted her hand aside. "It's a tank, you dizzy mare, 'n' you ain't got no shells?"

"I was fixing the damn thing up—not prepping it for Armageddon!"

With a painful shriek, the tank finally locked into gear. Billy floored the accelerator.

"What's the plan?" Cammy yelled.

"No plan, love. We're wingin' it!"

Billy powered the Matilda forward up the train.

"*Stone' style!*"

Billy grinned as the tank crushed everything in their path.

…

"Stay 'ere." Lancaster muttered, moving to break cover as the tank rumbled toward them.

"Where you going?" Jack said, reloading furiously.

"I've got a score to settle!"

"Lancaster! *Get back 'ere!*"

Lancaster clambered up onto Mörder's carriage and launched himself at Mosquito.

"We're a *team!*" Jack yelled, but it was too late.

"*Let's finish this!*" cried Lancaster. Hurling men out of his way, Lancaster tackled the rogue Tommy from the carriage roof into the coal car.

Jack took advantage of the distraction to climb the ladder, but as his head rose above the carriage roof, Mörder's boot came out of nowhere, smashing him in the face and throwing him back onto the flatbed.

"Yes," Mörder said, drawing his Luger. "Lets."

…

Grappling in the coal car, Lancaster and Mosquito struggled violently with each other to get the upper hand. Mosquito pumped his Webley into the old sergeant's workings, striking sparks; and the coals beneath them began to smolder. Lancaster balled a fist and chinned Mosquito, propelling him back in a cloud of soot, then leapt on top of him and smashed his head repeatedly against the rusty rim of the coal car.

Watching the carnage from the train cab, the engineer and the fireman furiously stoked the furnace, spurring the train on into the night, desperate to reach the ferry port where they could finally escape the nightmare now playing out on board.

...

"You really think your *Tommies* can defeat Germany?" Mörder shouted, leaping onto Jack's flatbed. "As I speak, the secret of their creation is being deciphered in Berlin, and an army of scientists constructing a legion of iron troops. Once our bomb hits Churchill's London, the capital will be obliterated, and Europe's governments will fall over themselves to capitulate. The Reich shall expand to rule a new world order, with my Führer its rightful imperator!"

Jack scrabbled back across the flatbed as Mörder started toward him.

"It's inevitable, Jack. The wheels of destiny are in motion. *Nothing* can stop it now, but you, you shall not live to see it." Mörder slowly took aim. "*You've finally run out of luck!*"

...

"Bloody traitor!" Lancaster cried. He smashed a fist into Mosquito's shoulder which crunched inward, but Mosquito spun, grabbing Lancaster's arm and carrying them over the edge of the now flaming coal car.

The two machines landed hard on the coupling between the coal car and the engine, still struggling with one another as the track raced by beneath them.

"You're *finished!*" Mosquito yelled. "Your whole bleedin' country's *finished!* There's still time, Lancaster—you can *join* us!"

"And be a *Nazi?* I'd rather be scrap!"

"'appy to oblige!"

"Call yourself a Commando?"

"Not anymore!"

Lancaster forced Mosquito's head down toward the tracks, striking sparks from the metal brim of his helmet as it repeatedly smashed into the wooden ties speeding by beneath them.

"I called you my comrade—my *friend!*" Lancaster said, forcing Mosquito's head down.

"Then you were a *fool!*"

Mosquito flipped Lancaster over into the engine's cab.

As the two machines fought on, the engineer and fireman leapt from the cab onto the sidings, where they watched from safety as the train rocketed by, screeching as it careened around a curve in the mountainside.

...

Billy heaved on the tank's controls to keep it aboard the train as they rolled onto the second flatbed, crushing barrels beneath their tracks.

"We gotta get to Jack!" Cammy cried.

"I know!"

"We gotta help!!"

"*I know!*"

...

Mörder lost his balance. He staggered back, almost toppling off the flatbed as the train picked up speed downhill.

Jack seized the opportunity. He grabbed a rifle nearby and fired a round at Mörder, hitting him in the shoulder.

Mörder didn't flinch.

"You can't hurt me, Jack. I am *immortal!*"

...

"You see it?" Hurricane heard Remmy yell over the radio.

"I don't see nothin'," replied Hurricane.

"I'm on him!" Spitfire shouted, opening fire but missing. "H, he's right on top of you!"

The second Heinkel dropped out of cloud behind the *Valiant*.

Hurricane spun his turret ninety degrees and punched his triggers, shattering the fighter's canopy. The Heinkel stuttered, then screaming, it spiraled toward the mountainside.

"Think I'm gettin' the hang o' this," Hurricane said. A third Heinkel shot overhead. "Two down, boys, one to go!"

He settled in behind his sights, and then let his guns sing.

# 36

## ALL GUNS BLAZING

**J**ACK SENSED THE IMPACT a second before it happened, a lone Heinkel, peeling away from the *Valiant's* tail in flames as the fortress roared overhead, spiraled into the mountainside above the train and exploded on impact.

A deafening crack echoed across the Rjukan valley.

Jack and Mörder looked up, as all along the mountainside, the whisper of death shifted fresh snow atop the ice—and gave it life. It slid slowly down the mountainside, gathering momentum and increasing its mass in a cascading fury of white. Heading directly toward the track to the rear of the train, it sheared away black crags of rock, consuming everything in its path.

Jack seized the moment, raised his rifle and fired at Mörder again, but sensing the train's fate, the general retreated to the ladder of his carriage. He returned fire and climbed up onto its roof.

Jack threw aside his rifle, flinching as Mörder's shots zinged off the heavy water barrels around him.

And all the while, the steadily rising roar of the avalanche as it gained on the rear of the train.

...

"What's that noise?" Billy asked, peering out at the remaining soldiers on the flatbed ahead of the tank. Some were retreating back up to the engine, others leapt onto the sidings.

Cammy threw open the hatch above them and poked her head up. Her eyes grew wide at the sight of the vast white monster devouring the track to their rear.

"Billy?"

"What?"

"Make this thing go faster!"

The avalanche smashed into the half-car, sloughed up over it and, tearing it from its coupling, swept it into the valley in a powerful wave of destruction. A wave that now surged up the train toward them.

"*Do it!*" Cammy screamed.

...

Mosquito opened the furnace door in the train's cab and thrust Lancaster's head toward it.

"I *believed* in you!" Lancaster strained to resist.

"Oh, spare me the sermon. There's a new world coming—an' you ain't gonna stop it!"

"Maybe not," Lancaster threw an elbow, knocking Mosquito to his knees, "but I'll give it a bloody good go!" He grabbed Mosquito's armor, tossed him back onto the flaming coal car, then grabbed the fireman's shovel and leapt up after him.

Mosquito's commando knife thrust from his wrist and he charged Lancaster across the coals. Lancaster deflected his blows with the shovel, then smashed Mosquito in the face.

Mosquito spat oil, his shattered left eye spitting sparks. "You're gonna be sorry you did that, *old chum.*"

He leapt. The machines fought on in a swirling tornado of embers and flame, oblivious to the white death advancing upon them as the train rattled at breakneck speed along the tracks.

...

Jack climbed up the ladder onto the roof of Mörder's carriage, he led the way with his machine-gun. He wouldn't be surprised by a boot again. But as he gained his feet atop the roof, the train took a lurching bounce as the avalanche swallowed the rear-most flatbed, and the gun was thrown from his hand.

Mörder stood at the far end of the carriage, smiling coldly beneath his mask, his Luger at his side.

Jack darted a glance behind him. The old Matilda was grinding across the last flatbed toward them, the avalanche pursuing it, and the Valiant soared in its wake.

Mosquito leapt from the flaming coal car to land beside Mörder. He threw down Lancaster's dented helmet hatch. "It's over," Mosquito said. "He's gone."

"No!" Jack's stomach rolled.

A shovel came scything through the flames and struck Mosquito on the back of the head.

"*I may be down...*" said a familiar voice. Battered and beaten,

Lancaster staggered through the flames. "*But I ain't out!*"

Mörder took a step back as Mosquito dodged a second swipe.

Lancaster was exhausted, his body no match for his bravado. As the carriage rattled again he fell to his knees and looked up at Jack, oil dripping from his mouth grille. "*Sergeant Lancaster…*" he slurred, "*reporting for duty… sir.*" He clattered forward onto his face plate, smoke belching from the exposed cogs and gears in the back of his head—the mechanisms that made Lancaster who he was, now ruined. "*C'mon, J-Jack… Let's f-finish this… sss.*"

Mosquito picked up the shovel as Lancaster's blue eyes faded.

The carriage bounced and Jack lost his footing as the engine screeched sparks around a bend. He landed on his back, scrabbling desperately for something to grab on to.

Mörder had no such difficulty. He stepped forward to tower over Jack. "You've done an exemplary job," he said, "but your mission was always in vain. The heavy water cells you worked so tirelessly to destroy have already been replicated in Berlin, and are en route to a second installation."

Jack noticed Lancaster's eyes flicker back on and pulse.

"In a matter of months, we will not only have the ten thousand pounds of heavy water stowed aboard this train, but fifteen thousand pounds, with more in production."

"This train ain't going nowhere," Jack yelled. "An' you and I will soon be dead!"

"Maybe so," Mörder said with grim finality. "Great Britain may win this battle, but Germany will win the war."

Mörder pointed his Luger at Jack's chest. "Time to die."

# 37

———

# GUTS 'N' BOLTS

**S**UMMONING THE LAST of his strength, Lancaster pushed himself up, grabbed the hem of Mörder's trench coat with his right arm and yanked. Mörder's shot went wide, striking off the roof of the car.

Seeing the avalanche was almost upon them, Mörder took a last look at it, then retreated to the far end of the roof and slid down the ladder to escape into the carriage.

"Lanc?" Jack gasped, clinging on for dear life.

Lancaster pushed himself onto his hands and knees.

Mosquito raised the shovel.

. . .

"Billy!" Cammy yelled.

"I know…"

"We need to—"

"*I know!*"

Cammy braced herself for the impact as she heard the train groan from the tracks.

. . .

Mosquito brought the shovel down into Lancaster's right arm, slicing between its armor plating and severing wires and cables. He swung the shovel around and slammed it onto Lancaster's back, sending him crashing face down onto the carriage. The shovel's handle snapped in two, and Mosquito plunged its jagged metal end through Lancaster's back, pinning him to the roof.

"No!" Jack cried.

"*Jack…*" Lancaster croaked. He reached out to his friend, his blue flickering.

Mosquito raised his foot above Lancaster's head.

. . .

Cammy screamed as the avalanche smashed into the Matilda, propelling the tank forward. Billy put his arm around her and held on for dear life as the old tank hit the carriage.

...

Mosquito was thrown from the roof by the force of the impact.

Jack grabbed Lancaster's arm as an explosion of snow roared up over the remaining cars. With a groan, the engine was torn from the track as it was side swiped by the full force of the avalanche. It roared downhill, dragging the coal car, carriage and flatbed.

...

Clinging to webbing at the *Valiant*'s bay door, Hurricane and Spitfire watched the scene play out in horror as the engine and the cars behind it picked up speed toward the gaping mouth of an ice chasm.

"What can we do?" Spitfire said.

Hurricane had no words.

This was the end.

...

Jack rolled toward Lancaster as shots blasted up through the roof. It seemed Mörder was still alive.

"We almost made it, didn't we?" Lancaster said, gripping Jack's arm. "You need to jump. Save yourself."

Jack took Lancaster's hand. "If there's one thing I've learned from you, it's how to be bloody stubborn," he said, echoing the old sergeant's words. He cast a glance up at the *Valiant*. "Hold on!"

The engine continued to drag its cars down the slope toward disaster. As it careened toward the precipice, the carriage broke away from its couplings, separating from the flatbed. Pulled along by the engine and coal car, it plummeted into the icy abyss below.

With the other cars no longer connected, the flatbed holding the Matilda was swept further down the slope toward a cliff. It smashed into a ridge and as if by a miracle, groaned to a stop as the full force of the avalanche crashed over it into the valley below, leaving the flatbed teetering back and forth precariously on the edge of the ravine.

...

Jack clung to Lancaster as the carriage crashed into the void. The engine spun wildly in the darkness beneath them like a child's toy; the blazing coal car descending behind it, scattering burning coals that ricocheted around them.

As the gorge narrowed, the carriage bounced between the walls of ice, fighting for space to descend, until they were practically scraping both sides at once. Then the engine beneath them wedged fast, and with a crash the coal car and carriage slammed down on top of it, fusing together with the force of the impact. The mass of twisted metal creaked and groaned as shattered ice rained down. Burning coals illuminated the gloom with a smoldering orange half-light that shimmered off the ancient ice walls like flares in the darkness.

Battered and bloody, Jack slowly opened his eyes. He was sprawled over a now motionless Lancaster. The sergeant's huge hands secured him in place, and had presumably held him on the carriage during its descent, before the impact had stolen what little lifeforce he'd had left.

Jack suddenly felt nauseous, and his vision blurred. He saw the boy in his mind's eye, watching him through the flames.

This chasm was a lair of the dead, and death crouched in waiting nearby.

…

Cammy opened the tank's top hatch and cautiously emerged. She instantly froze, feeling the flatbed beneath the tank rock back and forth, and saw the abyss rising and falling beneath them.

"Cam?" Billy said from within the tank.

"Don't move—"

"*Cam?*"

"I said—" Cammy realized it wasn't Billy's voice this time.

A hand suddenly thrust through the darkness and grabbed at her jacket, its owner rising up over the turret.

Mosquito—impaled on the tank's cannon. Hanging helpless above the valley he looked up at her plaintively as the Matilda rocked back and forth.

"Help me… *please.*"

# 38

---

# TO THE LAST

**"D**ON'T BE AFRAID."

The voice was faint, *familiar*, but distant.

Jack's vision focused. Beside him, on the wreck, lay the boy. He stared at Jack, calm now, at peace.

As Jack's world went to hell all around him, he gazed into the eyes of his brother. Jack felt serenity and sadness. Love. He felt that if he were to just let himself slip into the darkness, they could finally be together—that if he allowed himself to forget the war, forget the whole damn world for that matter, that he could be with the one-person life had denied him. *Danny*, just as Jack remembered him from their youth.

But then what of Cammy, of Billy and the Tommies? So much now depended on their cause. What of *their* future, or the war and the lives *they* might save?

"*Live*, Jack…"

Jack heard the words in his head as clear as a summer sky. They were a call to action. His eyes flooded with tears, and he squeezed them shut.

When Jack reopened them, the vision had vanished.

He was utterly alone in the darkness.

"*Jack?*"

No… not alone.

*Lancaster!*

The sergeant's broken blue eyes flickered in the gloom.

As his world came back into focus, Jack remembered where he was. By some miracle, the train's engine had wedged itself in place and now held the carriage's weight across its broken back. But the mass of metal was slipping, losing purchase against the slick ice walls on either side.

"Hold on," Jack said. He looked up beyond the chasm at the night sky, and as the stars disappeared briefly, Jack thought he heard the *Valiant* soar overhead. "Just hold on. It's gonna be—"

Jack heard glass shatter.

A black gloved hand thrust up over the side of the carriage, slamming down onto the roof. As it flailed around and found purchase, a second appeared beside it.

"*Yes*," hissed Mörder, as he rose up onto the roof. "*Immortal*."

...

Cammy shook her head in disbelief.

"Cammy?" Mosquito pleaded, reaching out to her. "Please, I'm sorry, I — I'm *so* sorry…"

Cammy heard a roar and looked up to see Hurricane and Spitfire rappelling toward the tank from the Valiant.

"Don't listen to 'im!" Billy growled, rising from the turret behind Cammy.

"C'mon, Cam, gimme your 'and!" Hurricane dangled above Cammy from his cable, his arm outstretched.

"You too, Billy," Spitfire said, joining him. Mosquito grasped the canon and struggled to heave himself up toward the turret.

The tank groaned threateningly toward the gorge.

"Please, Cam," pleaded Mosquito. "I never meant for things to end like this, *I swear!*"

"*Liar!*" Hurricane spat. "I *always* knew you were a bad 'un."

Billy put a hand on Cammy's shoulder. "Hey, you aren't seriously thinkin'—"

"C'mon, Bill!" urged Spitfire. "The tank's gonna—" He grabbed Billy's hand and hauled him up.

"*Cammy*," Mosquito begged, clawing at the cannon as he started to slide away from her.

"I feel *responsible* somehow," Cammy said as if in a daze. She looked guiltily from Mosquito to Hurricane. "I mean, we have a chance to set things right here, complete the team." Cammy tentatively reached out her hand to Mosquito.

"*No!*" Hurricane yelled.

"*Yes!*" Mosquito said, his eyes burning bright. He reached out to her, his eager fingers outstretched.

Cammy smiled, and dropped something into the palm of his hand. "*Auf Wiedersehen*, Moz." She jumped up and grabbed Hurricane's hand.

Confused, Mosquito looked down at the object in his palm: a pineapple grenade, its pin removed.

"*Strike three, sapper!*" Hurricane muttered. He slid an arm around

Cammy's waist to secure her, and ascended toward the *Valiant* as it rose above the tank with a whine.

"Sullivan, *you bitch!*" Mosquito screamed.

The grenade erupted with a boom, and what was left of Mark One Serviceman Mosquito was blown from the cliff face with the tank, crashing into the valley below.

…

"Do your worst," Lancaster growled as Mörder approached.

Mörder examined Lancaster's damage, the exposed mechanisms whirring inside his skull. "I don't know, what do you think, Jack? Is there *really* a soul in there?

Jack staggered to his feet.

"Let's find out." Mörder pointed his Luger at Lancaster.

The train lurched as chunks of ice smashed onto it from above. Fighting to steady himself, Mörder dropped the Luger. It slid across the car.

"I'm going to kill you now," Jack said, advancing.

"This *hatred* you have for me, Jack…" Mörder was keeping a healthy distance. "Where does it come from?"

"You killed my brother!"

Mörder appeared to reflect on this. "Yes. Now I understand."

"In Mortsel," Jack said. "You tore 'im apart like he was *nothing!*"

"Ah, yes I remember, the young boy I quartered in Belgium. I recall him now. He made a fine example. It was a pity your unit chose to remain in the building, they might have saved him. *You* might have saved him."

Jack lunged across the carriage roof. Mörder sidestepped him with ease and brought his fist down hard on Jack's neck sending him reeling.

"Foolish," Mörder kicked Jack casually in the stomach. "His death, your death, *all* inconsequential. What matters is that the Führer's glorious Fatherland lives eternal."

"You're a madman," Lancaster gasped, struggling furiously to free himself from the spike which pinned him to the roof.

Jack lurched to his feet and lunged at Mörder again, fists raised, but the general gut-punched him with brutal efficiency, and Jack fell to his knees, coughing.

"Now," Mörder said, removing his black leather gloves, revealing skeletal fingers beneath. "We end this."

# 39

——

# A FAREWELL TO ARMS

"**M**URDERER!"

"Murder's a point of view, Jack," Mörder said. "Kill one man they send you to prison; kill a thousand—they give you a medal!"

"That what passes for honor in the Wehrmacht these days, is it?" Lancaster growled. "Bit o' tin on your chest."

"You killed my brother," Jack spat blood, hungry for retribution. "You're gonna pay!"

"Yes. Your hatred of me fuels your actions, doesn't it? Gives you purpose? Well, that makes two of us. As I said, we created each other you and I—two sides of the same coin."

"An' I told you already, I ain't nothin' like you!"

"Oh, but you are, Jack. A fighter, like your brother. Do you hear him in the cold lonely dark of the night, I wonder—crying out for deliverance, for a brother that never came?"

"*Bastard!*"

"Jack, don't listen to 'im," urged Lancaster. "He's tryin' to rile you, get you on the back foot."

Jack looked at Lancaster, tears welling in his eyes.

"Oh, you do!" Mörder exclaimed with glee. "How wonderful. He screamed for you at the end, did you know that? And where were you— *bruder!*"

With a cry of rage, Jack charged Mörder.

The general stepped deftly aside, tripping him.

As Jack climbed to his feet, Mörder drew his dagger. He expertly scythed the air with its blade, slicing into the arm of Jack's tunic. Jack threw himself onto Mörder, punching the mask repeatedly.

"That's the spirit!" cried Mörder, his mask shattering beneath its hook nose.

Jack's eyes widened, and his fist hovered, at the sight of the blackened incendiary damage across Mörder's skinless jaw. Charred muscle and sinew slid like wet flesh pulleys across saliva-drenched bone.

"Take a good long look," Mörder hissed. "You created this. Just as I created you! Made you the man you are today!"

He flung Jack onto his back and leapt on top of him. "Enough of this." Mörder raised the dagger but Jack grabbed his wrist, struggling as Mörder forced the blade down.

Jack grabbed a shard of ice from the carriage roof and plunged it into Mörder's shoulder. Mörder looked down at it with mild curiosity. Then he leaned in close to Jack's face, spittle dripping from between his teeth like a hungry angel of death.

"What the hell are you?" Jack cried.

"You," Mörder said, forcing the blade toward Jack's chest. "It's just you and me now, Jack. It was always just you and me."

"You're sick," Jack said, "an' twisted, an' you might've killed my brother, you might kill me 'n' the sergeant. But there's one thing your kind'll never kill—an' that's the spirit to resist!"

"I'm sure you're right." Mörder leaned forward, putting his full body weight behind the dagger, pressing it into Jack's sternum.

But instead of penetrating his chest, the blade's tip broke off and flew across the roof into the darkness.

Mörder gasped. Jack was equally surprised—until he recalled the dog tag Cammy had given him: *Danny's* dog tag.

*Now he can always be with you*, she'd told him, *keep you safe, close to your heart…*

"How can this be?" Mörder hissed, his lidless eyes wide with surprise. He raised the broken dagger again, but Jack seized the advantage and kicked him onto his back.

"The gun!" Lancaster cried.

Jack scrabbled across the roof toward it, but Mörder grabbed his leg. Heaving himself onto Jack, he reached for the Luger.

"I am the Führer's iron will!" he bellowed.

Twisting around, Jack scrabbled onto Mörder's back. "You ain't nothin' but a goose steppin'—Nazi—goon!" He wrapped his arms around Mörder's chest. "An' if I am gonna die on this train, then I can't risk the chance that you'll live!"

Lancaster's blue irises widened with realization. "Jack! What you doin'?" he yelled.

"Look after Cam 'n' the boys," Jack said, as he struggled to restrain

Mörder.

"No—" Mörder cried, trying desperately to free himself. "No!"

"Jack, what the 'ell are you—"

"Two sides of the same coin, eh?" Jack said through gritted teeth.

"What are you doing?" Mörder screamed. "What—"

Jack suddenly recalled Churchill's words from their meeting.

*Standing upon the brink, we stare into the abyss.*

"End o' the line, general!" Jack muttered, then he rolled backward, and kicked himself off the carriage roof dragging Mörder with him.

...

"No!" Lancaster yelled as Jack plummeted into the crevasse. Fighting to move his right arm, he spread his fingers wide and took aim. "Anchors aweigh!" he muttered with grim determination, then following the line of Jack's descent, he shot the grappling hook from his palm.

Jack cried out as the claw smashed through the flesh of his shoulder, expanded on exit, and locked him onto the cable. As his descent came to an abrupt stop, Jack slammed into an ice wall and Mörder was jerked from his grasp. The general flailed, screaming as he spiraled to his doom in the icy abyss below.

...

"Why're things never easy 'round you?" Lancaster sighed. He reeled Jack, now unconscious, back up to the carriage and dragged him onto the roof, sliding his arm around his young captain's waist to secure him.

Jack's eyes flickered open. "Couldn't bear to see me go, eh?" he gasped, wincing at the pain in his shoulder, pain all over for that matter.

"You were right, you know," Lancaster said. "We were always stronger together. I see that now."

"Together we prevailed." Jack smiled as he repeated McNulty's credo, then passed out again, slumping against Lancaster's armor.

Lancaster carefully removed his grapple hook from Jack's shoulder, then regarded the boy with admiration. "Together then," he said quietly.

A whistle cut short the moment.

Looking up, Lancaster saw Hurricane and Spitfire rappelling down the ice walls toward him, the Valiant hovering overhead. He returned his attention to Jack. "Come on then, son." Lancaster patted Jack's arm gently. "Let's go 'ome."

# 40

―――

# UNDERNEATH THE ARCHES

**I**T WAS LATE when Jack and Billy staggered back to Hawkinge Air Base. It had been several days since the team's return from Norway, and The Crooked House had been a welcome distraction.

Buoyed by his recent victory, Jack had had one too many.

"This is a *bad* idea!" he slurred.

"C'mon, Romeo." Billy grinned. "It's time you sorted this out!" He grabbed Jack's arm and dragged him along beside him.

At the staff block, Lancaster, Hurricane, and Spitfire were lurking suspiciously. While still not fully repaired, they'd insisted on joining Billy. "You're gonna treat her right, aren't you, boss?" Spitfire said. "No funny business?"

"What?" Jack flashed anger at Billy. "You told 'em?"

"'Course I told 'em. We need the boys' 'elp." Billy peered around the corner. "Okay, that's it," he said, pointing up to a window. "Second floor, third window from the left."

"What the hell am I s'posed to do?" Jack asked.

"You know," Lancaster said. "Woo 'er!"

"*Woo her?*" Billy laughed. "What the 'ell does that mean?" He shook his head.

Turning to Jack, he said, "Go on, then. Chuck somethin' up!"

"What? At her window?"

"I can always go smash her door down," Billy offered.

"What is it you always say, boss?" Spitfire said. "Twenty seconds of bravery?"

"The boy's right," said Lancaster.

Jack sighed, resigned. What had initially seemed like a great plan over a pint, had become twenty seconds of bloody stupidity.

He picked up a pebble in the darkness, stepped out from the wall, and lobbed it at Cammy's window. It missed its mark and bounced off the barrack block wall.

Sniggering drunkenly, Billy gestured for him to throw another.

Jack shook his head. Talking to Cammy—really *talking* about his feelings for her—had seemed like a great idea when Billy had bolstered his confidence back at the mess, but the chill night air was sobering him up, and the prospect of a conversation with Cammy was now more terrifying a confrontation than anything he'd experienced in Norway.

"Go on," Billy hissed. "Chuck another!"

Jack picked up another stone and tossed it up.

Another miss.

"Ah, we're getting no-where," Billy whispered. "He'll be sober by the time he gets it right." He picked up a rock by his boot and hurled it.

It smashed right through Cammy's window.

Jack spun and glared at him.

"*What?*" said Billy sheepishly. "You're an awful shot!"

"It got her attention," Spitfire said, with child-like excitement.

Jack looked up at Cammy's window. A light had flickered on in the room.

Jack glanced about helplessly, then, resigned to his fate, braced himself.

Cammy drew open her curtains, slid up the remains of her window, and peered into the night. "*Jack?* What the hell? You know it's the middle of the night, right?"

"Er, that was Billy!" Jack slurred.

"Great, that makes this so much better!" Cammy stepped back from her window and moved to close it.

Jack darted a glance at Billy, who turned to the Tommies. "He's dyin' out there, boys. Think of something!"

"My mind's gone blank," said Hurricane. "She scares the 'ell outta me when she's ticked off."

"Come on," Billy urged. "*Anything!*"

"Look, Cam, just—just give me a minute, okay?" Jack pleaded.

"You're loaded, Captain. Go sleep it off."

"C'mon, Cam, wait. Look... anything could happen tomorrow. We might not get another chance to—"

"*G'night, Jack.*"

A horrible rendition of a popular romantic song drifted across the parade ground. Cammy paused, startled.

Jack's mouth dropped open as Billy and the Tommies sauntered out from behind the wall, crooning badly, their hands on each other's shoulders. They stood behind Jack in a poor excuse for a line, swaying unevenly like backing vocalists.

They sounded truly awful.

Jack looked back up at the window. It was empty.

"Impressive."

Cammy now stood across the parade ground with a shawl around her shoulders.

"You make a habit of sneaking up on defenseless soldiers, Doctor?" Jack said.

"Oh, I think you're the kinda guy who can take care of himself." Cammy sauntered toward him. "I hear they call you *Union Jack* in Whitehall now?"

"Got a nice ring to it, don't you think? And—and—"

*C'mon, c'mon, twenty seconds of bravery…*

"Speaking of rings, Cam, I've been thinkin'—"

Cammy put a finger on his lips. "One way or another, all of the guys I've ever known have left me…" She trailed off, the right words evading her.

"What is it?" Jack asked gently.

"I'm sorry. I just can't stand the thought of losing—" She took a deep breath. "Sometimes it's better to be alone, you know? That way you can't get hurt."

"Cam, there's a war on," Jack said tenderly. "We're all gonna die someday, but it's how we *live* that's important in the end. You 'n' me? We're *good* together." He looked into her eyes. "I wouldn't let you down."

Jack took Cammy's hand and slid an arm around her waist.

"Slick move, Captain. McNulty teach you that?"

"Comes under *sneak attack*," Jack said, grinning. "So what d'you reckon? Beautiful girl like you, dashing fella like me?"

"Careful, Jack." Cammy smiled warily. "I honed my *resistance* skills in Norway." She draped her arms around his neck and looked into his eyes. "There are easier ways to get my attention than smashing my window, y'know."

"Wouldn't be as much fun though, would it?"

Cammy rolled her eyes.

"About that ring…"

Cammy put a finger on his lips. "Why don't we just start with that dance you owe me, huh? See where the rest o' the war takes us."

Jack was hypnotized. Being with Cammy intoxicated him. It was as if she canceled out every bad thing he'd ever done, had ever experienced. She'd made him whole again.

Billy and the Tommies finished their first terrible tune and moved on to murder a second. As their mangled notes drifted across the parade ground, the Tommies clicked their fingers, mostly out of time with the music.

Jack and Cammy giggled, dancing close and slow as the Tommies' eyes flickered waves of light that shimmered around them like dance hall glitter balls.

Tripping the light fantastic, the young couple waltzed on into the night beneath the stars, as if they didn't have a care in the world.

...

Hitler stared at Mörder's damaged mask as he listened intently to a wireless in his study at the Reich Chancellery.

"*We're playing by new rules now,*" Churchill crackled, "*and Great Britain will not sue for a peace deal!*"

Von Ribbentrop bit his lip as his master fumed.

"*Yes, we're playing by new rules,*" Churchill continued, "*and we are coming for you, Herr Hitler. It is your turn to live in fear, your turn to run and hide, to cower in the wake of bloody destruction! We are coming for you, and Great Britain will prevail!*"

Von Ribbentrop cowered as Hitler rose slowly from his chair. Seething, the Führer swept everything from his desk and screamed obscenities at Von Ribbentrop. He ripped the wireless from the wall, spun, and flung it through his window in utter fury.

As glass rained down, Adolf Hitler vowed to destroy Great Britain, to destroy Churchill and his damnable Tommies, yes, he would wipe them from the face of the earth if it was the last thing he ever did.

...

Jack and Cammy gazed across the English Channel from the white cliffs of Dover, watching the sun set.

"Winter's coming." Cammy shivered and linked Jack's arm, leaning against his shoulder. "What now?"

"*Now?*" Jack had never dared envisage a life beyond their first mission —yet here they were. Gulls cawed and swooped overhead, and the sea breeze whipped his hair. Beneath them, waves crashed unmercifully against the rocks.

Jack realized that he and Cammy, and the others who fought for Great Britain, were an extension of that rock: stolid, unyielding, guardians and defenders to those within. And no invaders were going to get in. *Not on our watch*, Jack vowed silently. The epiphany electrified him, inflamed his sense of purpose. It reinvigorated him for the battle yet to come.

"Now we *fight*," he said resolutely.

"All of us," said a familiar voice behind them.

Turning, they saw Billy leaning against Hurricane, Lancaster and Spitfire beside them. Now fully repaired, the Tommies gleamed in the twilight.

With a fluttering whir, Bug rose behind Spitfire and landed on his shoulder. It shook its lens and ticked. Spitfire opened his chest cavity and the little drone crawled inside. Spitfire gently patted the hatch shut.

As Jack looked at each member of his team, he felt an overwhelming sense of pride.

A familiar whine drew his gaze skyward, to where Parker soared above the ocean with 2 Squadron. "There's them up there," he said, "and there's us down here. France may've fallen, but it's fighting on, and that's just what we're gonna do. The old man wants to set Europe ablaze—so who're Commando One to disappoint him?"

"Up 'n' at 'em," Lancaster said, crossing the battlements. He offered Jack his hand.

"Yeah," Jack said, shaking it. "Up 'n' at 'em."

"We're with you, boss!" Spitfire said. "Where you go, we follow."

"Too bloody right," said Hurricane. "Billy still owes me a tenner from poker the other night—I ain't lettin' him outta my sight!"

"I woulda won too if you hadn't cheated." Billy said, then quietly to Jack he added, "And it's more like a fiver!"

"Together we prevail," Jack said, holding out a clenched fist.

Forming a circle around him, the team held out their fists and repeated the credo.

"I don't know what the future holds, boys," Jack said, "but I promise you it don't matter. 'Cos what unites us beats what sets us apart, and as long as we face challenges like we always 'ave, with hearts that stay true to each other and with courage no matter how great our enemies, then I know we'll win this war. We're gonna fight back, boys, 'n' we're going in with our safeties off!"

"Yes!" Spitfire said.

"I won't let you down," Jack said.

"Well, this is all very macho." Cammy folded her arms, annoyed. "But what about me, huh? When do I get to join your boys' club?"

"Oh, I dunno, Cam," Jack said, rubbing his chin. "I mean, it's gonna be dangerous."

"If you think I'm just gonna sit in the workshop knitting while you guys are out having fun—"

"What d'you reckon, boys?" Jack said.

Billy and the Tommies glanced at each other and chuckled.

"Are you for real?" Cammy said indignantly. "If it wasn't for me, your asses would all be rusting back in—"

"Okay, okay," Jack said. "As long as you promise to love, honor, 'n' obey orders some day!" he added with a grin.

Cammy punched his arm.

"Let's just stay alive for now, huh?"

Jack looked into her eyes as the team dispersed. All the possibilities of his future whirled within them.

"Er, got a minute, Captain?" Lancaster said.

Cammy kissed Jack's cheek tenderly, then left him and Lancaster to talk.

"What is it?" Jack asked.

Lancaster looked out to sea. He was quiet for a moment, then: "When I was out of it back in Norway in that bloody dungeon," he said, "I *saw* something. In 'ere." He tapped the side of his metal head with a finger. "Now, I don't know what it was, and perhaps I don't *want* to know, but I 'ave to understand what I saw. What I *am*, I mean. Where I—*we*—came from. What *we* are."

Jack nodded. "The documents Mörder took from Achnacarry. They're in Berlin now."

Lancaster looked at him, serious; the essence of determination. "Then that's where we 'ave to go."

"And we'll get there," Jack said. "That's a promise."

Lancaster studied Jack's face for a second, then nodded affirmation, his blue eyes burning brightly. "Come on, Captain," said the old sergeant with conviction. "Let's get to work."

# EPILOGUE

**TWELVE HUNDRED FEET** above the picturesque town of Berchtesgaden perched the Berghof. Christened "Haus Wachenfeld," the residence was built in 1916 by businessman Otto Winter atop the summit of the Kehlstein, high in the Bavarian Alps. Later nicknamed *Eagle's Nest* by a visiting French diplomat, the property was, like so many of Hitler's constructions, a grandiose homage to the triumph of German achievement.

Standing on the terrace, Hitler marveled at the breathtaking splendor of the Obersalzalberg. Its sweeping panorama exhilarated him as he stood high above the clouds. His journey to this peak from the obscure beginnings of the Nazi party had been arduous, but it had, he thought, been righteous. It was here that the Führer felt truly invigorated. At peace. He was a god among men, looking down at the world from Olympus.

Germany had awoken. *Destiny* was on his side.

While Mörder's failure in Norway had been unfortunate, it was, Hitler knew, not the end of his research into the power of atomic energy. Work had already commenced at several secret installations across Europe on the production of more heavy water. Norway was merely a setback, nothing more.

While Vemork had been largely destroyed, the delay in the project's success had afforded Hitler another opportunity: the chance to begin a long overdue restructure of his inner circle—and the chance to assess the future of a rising star within his ranks.

The young woman's ascension through Reichsführer Heinrich Himmler's school—the SS Academy at Wewelsburg in North Rhine-Westphalia—had been nothing short of astonishing. She was daughter to a prominent party member, and it had been observed that in her case, the apple had not fallen far from the tree. She had received leadership training, political and ideological indoctrination, and tactical instruction from some of the most accomplished military minds in the Reich, and was consistently top of her class. She was indeed her father's daughter, and while that fact filled many with unease, it imbued Hitler with a renewed sense of optimism. For with her support, he would smite the machines who had denied him his atom.

Yes, there was reason to be hopeful for the future—and her name was Ilsa Mörder. A proud Teutonic name, Ilsa meant *Noble Maid*, and no finer designation could have been given to the daughter of one the finest military minds Hitler had ever known. Ernst's loss had been a blow, but in Ilsa he lived again.

*Immortal.*

Ilsa's academy records confirmed that like her father, she was intelligent, ruthless and cunning. A true tactician. It had amused Hitler to learn that she had long been a thorn in Himmler's side, having far exceeded the Reichsführer in her capacity to outmaneuver him at every turn. This fact—combined with Ilsa's unswerving loyalty to the Reich—made her an ideal candidate to carry her father's torch in the destruction of the Tommies and ultimately replace Himmler, whom Hitler still regarded with suspicion and distrust, as head of the SS.

Himmler had been a devoted party member in the early days, and one of the best hired thugs in Berlin, but with the Reichsführer's ambitions now far exceeding his already inflated ego, Hitler feared a coup at best, an assassination at worst. And while Ilsa was entering her zenith, Himmler had reached his nadir. He had been locked away for weeks in Wewelsburg, a prisoner to his paranoia and obsession with the occult. His arrival at the Berghof with Ilsa would give Hitler a chance to study their dynamic. *Ignite the touch paper*, he thought, *let the two forces of nature clash—and to the victor the spoils.*

The SS needed new blood—*a woman's touch*, as his companion Eva Braun so frequently observed—and whoever possessed the loyalty of the SS, possessed Germany.

Yes, in Ilsa, the Fatherland's future was assured.

Gazing out across the heavens from the terrace, Hitler shivered. It was dark, and the sky threatened snow. He took a last long look at his empire, then retreated to the warmth of the Berghof's great hall.

. . .

"Check." Deftly sweeping a gilded ivory rook across a marble chessboard, Heinrich Himmler knocked his opponent's pawn aside. "It would appear I have you—how do the Americans put it? *On the ropes?*" Amused, he reclined in his high-backed burgundy leather chair with a controlled smile.

"Impressive, Reichsführer," said the young woman in the opposing seat. Young and intense, she studied her opponent with frost-blue eyes and barely concealed contempt. "But experience is no substitute for *ambition*." Her long slender fingers lingered momentarily over her chess pieces, carved ivory figures from Germanic myth, and selected a bishop, which countered Himmler's rook, blocking its path to her king.

Himmler studied the board. "Have a care, Hauptsturmführer. I am aware of your attempts to discredit me within the Reich," he said without looking up. "It would be *unwise* to underestimate my reach, should you press this fiasco in Norway."

"You credit me with too much, Reichsführer."

"It was *my* academy from which you graduated, Ilsa Mörder. I know your weaknesses, and your loyalties. I know what you are."

Ilsa studied him intently. Himmler looked away. He found her gaze unsettling, intense, as if one were staring into the eyes of Medusa and would turn to stone.

"And what am I?" Ilsa said quietly.

"You're a *monster*, like your father. Your poor mother always knew what he was."

"My mother was *weak*," Ilsa said, resolute, then she smiled graciously. "Was I not your *brightest* star?"

"Even the brightest stars collapse in time," Himmler said. "The Führer will tire of you eventually, just as he did poor Röhm."

Ilsa surveyed the board, envisaging Himmler's next moves.

"You said I was your greatest pupil," she said at last.

"Even my SS have limits."

Ilsa raised an eyebrow. "Times are changing, Reichsführer. In war, some limits should be exceeded."

"You may be the Führer's ward," Himmler hissed, leaning forward. "But I still have his ear."

"And these... *Tommies?*"

"The matter is in hand." Himmler sniffed, and efficiently swept his rook across the board, cornering her queen. "Check."

"Then Berlin will surely sleep soundly." Ilsa said. She countered with her knight, trapping Himmler's queen. "Check." She sat back with amused satisfaction.

Rattled, Himmler studied the board, searching for a chink in her defenses, or at least a willing sacrifice for his queen. At last, hesitantly, he moved a pawn forward.

"The attack which comes from within is that which is least expected," Ilsa said. "That these Tommies must be eliminated is not in question. Alas, like the Allies' High Command, the Reich's strategy is mired in the assumption of past victories—ergo *fresh* perspective is needed."

"Well said, my dear."

Hitler stood in the doorway, hunched, arms behind his back, hands clasped. Blondi, his loyal German shepherd trotted after him into the hall.

"My Führer," said Himmler. He stood obediently, saluted, and eagerly clicked his heels. Ilsa followed suit calmly as Hitler approached.

"This *fresh* perspective, my child; what is it you propose?"

Ilsa remained calm as she seized her moment. "These *Tommies* were designed to buoy British morale. Their destruction, therefore, will have the entirely opposite effect. By destroying the enemy from within, we conquer him through himself, and then we break the British spirit with surprise, terror—*assassination*." She glanced at Himmler. "*That* is the war of the future."

"My Führer—" Himmler stuttered.

Hitler silenced him with a gesture. "Go on."

"This matter requires subtlety," Ilsa said, crouching beside Blondi. She ran a finger along the dog's snout and looked up at Hitler, her rose red lips glistening in the firelight. "A *woman's* touch."

"Preposterous," Himmler blurted. "My Führer, I assure you—"

"Turned against each other, the Tommies will implode from within," Ilsa said confidently. "And the spirit of the Allies will die with them."

Hitler stood mesmerized by the nape of Ilsa's neck, the eloquent sweep of her jawbone, her perfect black uniform crowned by his glorious death's head insignia. So perfect, so Aryan... so *very* beautiful.

"Go on," he whispered tentatively.

"The machines' files obtained by my father are still at the Chancellery, are they not?"

"How do you know—" Himmler began.

Hitler nodded, crossing the room to a huge window and staring out across the Obersalzalberg.

"Then the means to destroy the Tommies lies in the palm of your hand." Turning to the chessboard, Ilsa swept her bishop across it and knocked aside Himmler's queen. "Checkmate, Reichsführer." She smiled coldly at Himmler. "What is it the Americans say? *Close*, but no cigar?"

"You presume *too* much," Himmler fumed, flushing red.

"I would say that on this occasion, *ambition* trumps experience, no?"

Himmler swiped his cap from the table and levelled a finger at Ilsa. "This *game* isn't over!"

"Leave us," Hitler said coolly.

Incensed, Himmler stormed from the room.

"You are a woman of *remarkable* ingenuity," Hitler said.

"My only desire is to succeed in my father's stead. To serve you as he did. To serve Germany."

Hitler approached Ilsa and caressed her cheek with the back of his hand. Ilsa noted it trembled faintly.

A woman's silhouette appeared in the doorway. Hitler nervously withdrew his hand. "Eva, my dear, I was just—"

Saying nothing, Eva withdrew down the corridor.

A pall descended over Hitler's expression. "What do you require?" he said, suddenly distant.

Ilsa stepped closer. "The files obtained by my father. I understand from the British news media that the American doctor is key to the machines' evolution. Persuaded to work for the Reich, she could be invaluable in the production of future assets.

"Then you have my mandate," Hitler said, stroking Blondi's head. He stared at the flames dancing in the great marble fireplace.

Great Britain would burn as they did.

"I will not fail you," Ilsa vowed. She pulled on her cap, saluted, and strode to the door, then paused without turning. "And the others?"

Hitler's expression turned vengeful.

"*Make them pay!*"

# THE END

## But...

Commando One returns in

# TIN CAN TOMMIES

# RETRIBUTION

*They won the battle in Norway but it was only the start of their war…*

October 1940. After a daring escape from Colditz, Jack Stone and the Tin Can Tommies return to an England blinded by optimism following their recent victories abroad. Now symbols of British defiance they're revered by the people—and feared by their enemies!

Joining the French Resistance the team go underground on a daring kidnap mission, but with a new yet familiar foe leading murderous machines of her own, the Tommies must work as one or implode from within as they're forced to confront not only their deadliest enemy, but a sinister truth locked deep within themselves, in their most perilous test of the war.

## Please enjoy the following taster…

# PROLOGUE

*France, Fall, 1940...*

THE REMOTE RURAL PROVINCE of Ardèche was, like many municipalities in central France, as quiet and charming a region as a traveler could hope to find south-west of the Alps. Nestled deep within the province's Rhône valley, the sleepy town of Vinezac, surrounded by forests and picturesque snowcapped plateaus, was a perfect location for the acres of vineyards and olive trees that thrived across its slopes.

It was here in this picturesque idyll—untouched by the bourgeois sophistication of the north for generations—that the region remained fiercely proud of its heritage, its traditions and its faith.

...

Church bells clanged from the belfry of a Romanesque tower. The chimes echoed across town, disturbing the serenity of a sleepy Sunday morning and rousing parishioners to worship.

Dating back to the Middle Ages, Vinezac's walls housed a labyrinth of narrow streets connecting rows of sandstone cottages, their facades hidden beneath interwoven layers of fragrant Lauriers roses, to a square where townsfolk played Pétanque in the cooling shade of mulberry trees.

An old man surveyed the calm from beneath the awning of his favorite café. He sipped coffee, smiling wistfully. He was seated at his regular table overlooking the square, and he glanced at the empty chair beside him. His wife, the old man's best friend for nearly fifty years had recently gone to glory, but it comforted him to maintain their old routine.

He watched children laugh as they played care-free in the dawn sun, their families strolling to give prayers of thanks that, for now at least, their paradise remained untouched by the corrosive influence of the Nazis northern occupation.

The old man closed his eyes, enjoying the music of life.

*Life...*

He'd felt his own had come to an end after the loss of his dear Vivienne. Tending his wife at her bedside, her frail hand had slipped from his and the old man's world had imploded, and for a time after her departure he'd considered following her.

"Monsieur?"

The old man opened his eyes to see Maria, his pretty young waitress. She had roused him from his darkness with a plate of bagels and cheese. He nodded gratitude as she left him to his thoughts. Yes, life had dealt him a blow but he had survived. He was lucky to see another day.

He would live it for his wife.

For Vivienne.

The old man picked up his newspaper, adjusting his spectacles to examine the headline.

Since capitulating to Germany, northern France had been controlled by the Nazis who had allowed Philippe Pétain, the nation's old war horse and newly appointed premier, to govern an unoccupied 'free zone' from the southern city of Vichy. In return for its independence, Pétain had paid a heavy price in the form of tributes to honor his overlords governing Paris. The Germans now controlled all capital media outlets which, as with other newly acquired territories, reeked with the stench of anti-Semitism, and while their hate fueled propaganda had not yet infected Vinezac, the old man sensed that it was only a matter of time before it permeated even the province's parochial tabloids.

Deep in thought, he lowered the newspaper. Pétain's pleas for people to remain calm in order to preserve a precarious peace conflicted bitterly with the rumors emerging from Paris.

Rumors of horrors.

Of defiance.

Resistance.

The old man was grateful to live in the south, far from the occupation and Hitler's political machinations. Here one might while away the war until De Gaulle, now an exile in England, returned with the British to expel France's brutal invaders. The old man had fought in the Great War, and while the Nazis wore new uniforms, their stink remained the same. But the Fatherland had been defeated once, he thought, it could be defeated again. All patriotic free French believed that.

*He* believed that.

The morning's calm was shattered by the roar of two Opel trucks which ground into the square. They were followed by a rumbling half-track carrying a number of armed German troops; their coal scuttle helmets bobbing in the sunlight as the carrier bounced across the cobbles. The vehicles yawned around in an arc, stopping at the foot of the church steps.

The townsfolk watched in shock as the driver of each truck jumped from their cab and saying nothing, ran to the half-track at their rear and clambered up into it.

The old man frowned. It was an ominous sight given Vinezac's location in the free zone. The stunned townsfolk glanced nervously at one another with the same unspoken question.

What was going on?

With a roar the half-track accelerated and swerving around the trucks, bounced out of the square.

Then silence.

All eyes turned to the old man. His seniority in the town had earned him the people's respect; indeed, he'd watched many of them grow into adults and have children of their own. While the good lord had never seen fit to bless the old man and his wife with a miracle, they had come to terms with their grief and quietly mourning a happiness that had never been, took pleasure from the children of others—children now looking to him for comfort.

Not knowing what to say, the old man took his cane and stepped from beneath the awning. He cautiously approached the nearest truck.

"*Fais attention!*"

The old man turned to see Jean Petit—Vinezac's mayor and a good man, recently a father himself. The old man raised a reassuring hand, and reached out to lift the canopy.

A child began to cry.

The old man paused, glancing nervously back at the townsfolk. The children were scared, hugging their parents for comfort.

Something clicked inside the truck.

The old man spun; eyes narrow. He leaned forward cautiously and took a handful of canvas. Raising it, he peered into the gloom—

Nothing.

He turned to the townsfolk to speak—

Then a motor roared from within the truck!

"*Sacré bleu!*" The old man staggered back.

The truck's canopy shredded outwards in a hail of machine-gun fire which sprayed wildly into the square. The canvas of the truck to its rear also dissolved in flames.

Villagers screamed, scattering as the silhouettes of four lithe figures—two in the rear of each truck—leaped from the vehicles' blazing carcasses onto the cobbles. Shimmering in flames, they levelled their weapons and advanced into the square.

The townsfolk ran for cover as their aggressors showered hails of white-hot death around them. The old man fell to his knees, losing his spectacles. Then he clawed across the cobbles on his belly as machine-gun fire seared the air around him. The dull pump of a mortar sounded nearby, and the old man clamped both hands over his ears as a chain of explosions showered him in masonry. Choking black smoke consumed him, and he felt the hot sandpaper sting of brick dust against his skin as shock-waves pounded around him.

The old man tried to crawl toward the café, but without his spectacles his eyes were useless guides. Then the ground erupted beneath him and he was hurled through the air, landing on the café's awning and crashing through it. A table broke his fall, collapsing beneath his weight and spilling him onto the floor. He saw his waitress Marie nearby, lying on her side. Her remaining eye blind to the atrocities unfolding around her.

Screams.

Men, women—the children, all crying out as they were violently slain and Vinezac razed to ashes, destroyed by this terrible, unknown horror.

The old man clambered to his feet, tears blurring his already poor vision. Of one thing he was certain—news of this atrocity would spread like ripples across a mill pond, fueling the rebellion growing within his country.

Resistance.

France would fight back and in doing so, *endure*.

All free French believed that. *He* believed that.

And then he saw her.

*Vivienne…*

The old man wiped dirt from his eyes in utter disbelief, but his vision had not deceived him—she looked as beautiful as the day they'd first met. The old man extended his arms as the vision glided through flames toward him, her shimmering silhouette iridescent.

"*Mon amour*," the old man whispered, reaching to caress her cheek.

The siren gazed down at him, tilting her head as if curious.

The old man's fingertips caressed her skin.

Cold, emotionless steel.

The old man gasped, then heard a click and a roar.

"Vivienne?"

...

With a boom the church tower sagged, collapsing in a billowing cloud of flame and smoke. Its bells clanged mournfully as they crashed into the inferno, silencing screams that echoed across the valley, leaving only the staccato chatter of machine-gun fire.

Ilsa Mörder allowed herself a glimmer of satisfaction.

Her test had been a success.

"Impressive."

Ilsa glanced at the man beside her on the ridge. Young, Japanese, he bowed at the neck respectfully as she handed him her binoculars. Clad in an ill-fitting black suit and bowler hat, he appeared an almost laughable parody of twenties fashion.

But Akita Chang was a genius.

"This was a trial," Ilsa observed. "Nothing more."

"The schematics obtained by your father drove the Valhalla program this far, Hauptsturmführer." Chang peered keenly through the binoculars. "My creations, supported by your patronage, will propel our achievements —"

"*Our* achievements?"

Chang hesitated, then returned Ilsa's binoculars. "*Your* achievements, of course, beyond even the Führer's wildest aspirations."

A senior professor and Chief Industrial Physicist in Japan's Imperial Nuclear Programme, Chang had been dispatched to Berlin in early 1940 by Emperor Hirohito as a gift. The Emperor, persuaded by his military advisors, had sent the young scientist in return for the promise of arms, tanks, and a possible pact with the Axis. Germany's nuclear programme had suffered a severe setback at the hands of the Tin Can Tommies— tenacious machines and the first of Churchill's newly formed British Commandos led by their maverick young leader, Jack Stone.

While Hitler had been close to producing enough Heavy Water in Norway to create Germany's first atom bomb, Stone's team had all but destroyed his manufacturing facility setting the Führer's machinations back months.

"I am not my father, Professor. This *is* our achievement."

Chang had subsequently learned that Ilsa held Stone accountable for the death of her father, General Ernst Mörder—the Jackal of Leipzig.

"Contrary to the Führer's beliefs," Ilsa continued, "blind obedience to the Reich will not win this war. My father's fate proved that."

Chang had heard the rumours. The General's body, lost to an icy crevasse in Rjuken at Stone's hands had not been recovered but it was clear, given the circumstances surrounding his death, that he would never return to Germany.

Chang winced as a final enormous explosion sent shockwaves across the valley. From what knowledge he'd gleaned on Ilsa, Chang suspected she possessed the same brilliant tactician's mind as her father, tempered with the ability to control what many in Hitler's inner circle considered to be the man's more *feral* attributes.

Traits it seemed, which had led to his downfall.

"They require refinements, of course," Ilsa said. "And must learn to operate independently of their unit's cohesion, but this is an encouraging first step." She turned, starting up the hill to her waiting staff car; its red and black swastika flags fluttering from the hood.

"With your permission," Chang said, following, "I'd like to—"

Ilsa focused on the battles yet to come. Initially championed by her tutor and former mentor, Heinrich Himmler, she had taken a dangerously ambitious risk humiliating him in front of the Führer at Berchtesgaden. It was a risk that had paid dividends however, as Hitler had endorsed her plan to destroy the Tin Can Tommies. But Himmler was as much of an enemy to her now as any Allied combatant, more so perhaps given the traitor's blade was the most silent.

She had to maintain focus.

The Tommies were her priority.

Stone, and from the intelligence she'd received the rabble he now commanded would let their guard down soon enough and when they did, Ilsa would be there to claim them.

*Retribution.*

Commando One's day was coming—it was just a matter of time.

"Hauptsturmführer?"

Ilsa looked up to see her driver approaching. Behind him stood a messenger astride a motorcycle.

The driver clicked his heels and saluted. "It's Stone sir, er, ma'am."

"What of him?"

"He's been captured, Hauptsturmführer."

Ilsa stopped dead in her tracks—she hadn't envisaged such luck this early in the game. *And where Stone goes*, she thought, *the Tommies will follow*. "Where is he now?"

"Imprisoned, Hauptsturmführer, at a POW facility in Saxony."

"Prepare my transport," Ilsa ordered. "Secure him until I arrive."

The officer nodded curtly and returned to the messenger.

"It would appear Stone's unworthy of his reputation," Chang mused.

"Don't underestimate the man who defeated my father," said Ilsa. "Stone and his degenerates may have snatched victory from the jaws of defeat in Norway, but he still has one disadvantage."

"And what is that?" Chang asked cautiously.

Ilsa smiled thinly—her frost blue eyes burning with righteous fury.

"He's yet to encounter *me*."

# COMING SOON

# One last thing…

Thank you for buying this book! Readers like you mean everything to independent authors like me. I hope you enjoyed the story and if so, please leave an honest review on *Darkest Hour's* Amazon page at **https://amzn.to/34F43gf**. I read all reviews personally to capture your feedback and make the Tommies' future adventures even better.

I hope to write these stories for as long as you care to read them, so if there's a particular historical character or situation that you'd like featured I'd love to hear from you.

Thanks for supporting my work.

*Now up 'n' at 'em!*

Mark

Facebook: @tincantommies